MASQ

The master ran his hand over the rounded swell of Annabel Manley's delectable buttocks. Already the scars had faded from yesterday's beating. That was the beauty of immortality. Flesh healed, wounds disappeared and soon it was possible to have all the pleasure of inflicting them all over again. He selected a malacca cane from the half-dozen or so he always kept in his office and gave it a practice swipe. Perfect. He could feel his cock swelling already . . .

Masque of Flesh

Valentina Cilescu

Delta

First published in 1995
by HEADLINE BOOK PUBLISHING

A HEADLINE DELTA paperback

10 9 8 7 6 5 4 3 2

ISBN 0 7472 4864 8

Typeset by CBS, Felixstowe, Suffolk

Printed and bound in Great Britain by
Mackays of Chatham plc, Chatham, Kent

HEADLINE BOOK PUBLISHING
A division of the Hodder Headline Group
338 Euston Road
London NW1 3BH

www.headline.co.uk
www.hodderheadline.com

Masque of Flesh

Introduction
The Story So Far

Vampire sorcerer the Master is determined to take over the world – and already he has succeeded in becoming leader of Her Majesty's Opposition, through a campaign of corruption, seduction and subliminal propaganda.

The Master and his undead followers survive by feeding on the sexual energies of their victims; from time to time initiating other beautiful and influential people as vampire sex-slaves.

Long imprisoned by white magicians in a block of crystal, the Master escaped by taking over the body of unwary journalist Andreas Hunt, whilst Hunt's lover Mara was forced to surrender her mortal flesh to the Master's evil queen, Sedet.

But unbeknown to the Master, his hated rivals Mara and Andreas have not been eliminated. Mara's spirit now lives on within the body of luscious vampire-slut Anastasia Dubois, whilst Andreas has taken on the identity of an insatiable MP, Nicholas Weatherall. They are determined to oppose the Master and bring down his evil empire of lust from within.

Psychic investigator Max Trevidian, enlisted by Andreas and Mara to help them in the struggle, has apparently been vaporised by the Master on the steps of his own country house. Or has he? Has he survived to return and exact his revenge?

Meanwhile, Britain has a new Prime Minister – the glamorous and talented but clean-living Harry Laurent

1

Baptiste. He has unwittingly become the custodian of a crystal ring in which resides the increasingly degenerate and malicious spirit of the Master's former whoremaster, Delgado. Delgado delights not only in destruction but in living out his own perverse sexual fantasies through whoever wears the ring.

Harry Baptiste is said by many to be the purest man in the whole of England. But is his spirit pure enough to withstand the corrupting power of the crystal ring?

And there are other questions which demand urgent answers. Is the world really about to end? And what chaotic, malevolent power is causing tidal waves, volcanic eruptions, civil strife and global turmoil on an unprecedented scale?

Because for once, it isn't the Master . . .

Prologue

PC Colin Wavell had never seen anything like it in his life – not even when he'd dropped that tab of LSD at art school.

There, slap-bang in the middle of the road, sat the back end of an old Routemaster bus. It was sticking up out of the tarmac like an elephant's arse, one back wheel still spinning and the other thirty feet away in a hedge. The legend 'Ed's Mystery Tours' spanned the back, in large yellow letters.

Colin got off his bike and walked towards the bus. Half the inhabitants of the leafy suburb were out gawping at it, some of them still in their pyjamas and that prick-tease Deirdre Goodmansterne flaunting her tits in a little pink baby-doll job that scarcely covered her jet-black muff. Colin had ached for her all through secondary school but Deirdre had never yielded once.

'What the hell happened here?' demanded Colin.

'Fuck me, I dunno,' replied a tattooed youth, spitting on the ground with a disrespectful pleasure. 'Ground just sort of opened up, didn't it?'

'Anyone hurt?'

'Nah. Ed parked the bus outside his house last night like he always does and he was just having his breakfast when . . .'

'When what?' Colin flipped open his notebook and took a couple of steps nearer the bus. It seemed to be nestling in the neatest of holes, like a boiled egg in an eggcup.

'I told you, *officer*, the ground just sort of opened up and it fell in.'

'It was an earthquake, that's what it was,' declared Deirdre Goodmansterne, shivering dramatically, in a way that made her large, firm breasts wobble like strawberry blancmange. Gawd, thought Colin, I could definitely give her one and the sleeping snake in his trousers uncoiled in ever-hopeful anticipation.

'Don't be daft,' sniggered Darren. 'You don't get earthquakes in Congleton.'

No sooner had he spoken than the earth began to shake, at first almost imperceptibly, then with a gentle insistence that grew to a roaring, juddering crescendo. Colin gaped in disbelief.

'What the . . . ?'

He stepped back from the brink of the hole as he saw cracks appearing in the tarmac, big grey lumps of it splintering off, the way toffee splinters under a hammer. As he watched, transfixed, the bus slipped a little further into the yawning maw of the chasm beneath it. He wanted to run away but it was like being in the Crazy House at Blackpool Pleasure Beach, where all the floors and walls move about and it feels like the world is trying to shake itself to bits.

'Colin!' squealed Deirdre. And Colin turned towards her. It was the first time in ten long years that Deirdre Goodmansterne had taken the trouble to notice him. The shaking earth was making her whole body quiver deliciously, her nipples stiff with fear and hard as nuts underneath her flimsy nightie. But Colin wasn't looking at her nipples any more. He was looking at her face, contorted in terror as the earth rippled, cracked and opened up yards from her feet, its hunger predatory and obscene.

'Colin – do something!'

He tried, he really tried. But every time he moved he stumbled on the bucking earth. He took one more step and feel to his knees. He felt sick, scared – no he didn't, he felt bloody terrified. The whole earth seemed to be tilting sideways and now he was fighting to stay alive, his fingers scrabbling for a hold on the cracked road surface. Out of the corner of his eye he saw his brand-new police-issue bicycle slide away and disappear into the earth. Ah well, now they'd have to give him a Panda car.

And suddenly he was holding on with all his might. Holding on for grim death.

1: A Dark Dawning

CONGLETON EARTHQUAKE. PC IN DEATH-PLUNGE HORROR

Daily Comet, 29 May.

'Well, I'll be . . .'

'Hmm?' Mara Fleming snuggled closer to her lover in the deep, warm hotel bed and slipped her arm round his waist. To her disappointment, Andreas did not respond immediately but went on reading from the paper.

'There's been another earthquake. Five point five on the Richter Scale and three dead. In *Congleton*.'

'So?' Her fingers traced the smoothness of Hunt's belly, easing nearer, millimetre by millimetre, to the apex of his pleasure.

'So it's not exactly the San Andreas Fault, is it? I tell you, there are some weird things going on right now.' Mara's fingertips just grazed the fringed purse of his balls and he moaned his profound satisfaction.

'You're a witch, Mara Fleming.'

'Are you complaining?'

'Not so's you'd notice.' His eyes were bright with freshly aroused interest. Mara Fleming was quite some woman. She could make you fuck her all night long and you'd be as hard as iron for her in the morning.

Still celebrating his escape from the crystal, still exploring the newness of his borrowed body, Andreas was like a small boy in a sweetshop. He really couldn't make up his

7

mind which he preferred – Mara in her original body, or Mara in this new body, the one that had once belonged to Anastasia Dubois. It was the spirit inside that made Mara everything she was – a playful, seductive, irresistible temptress; truly a witch of a woman. The beginnings of a Cheshire Cat grin spread over his handsome face. Hunt, you're a jammy bastard, he told himself. Accident-prone maybe, but definitely jammy.

'I'm glad you've no complaints. We don't want you going off me now, do we?' Mara snuggled into the crook of Andreas's arm and let her fingers dance wantonly over his bare belly. He gave a long, luxurious groan of satisfaction as his penis jumped to instant attention. 'Whatever would the Master say?'

Andreas's smile dimmed momentarily. He didn't enjoy being reminded of the Master, nor the role that he was being forced to play just to survive. As far as the Master was concerned, Andreas Hunt was dead and gone; and the dark-haired man who served him so assiduously as his PPS was Nationalist MP Nicholas Weatherall. If it wasn't for the magical protection of the crystal bracelet Andreas wore, it wouldn't take five minutes for the Master to work out that Weatherall was really Hunt. And it would take Andreas more than fast talking to get him out of that one . . .

'Do you suppose the Master's behind all this?' Andreas turned to page three of the morning paper. 'Earthquakes in Congleton, floods in Australia, giant lizards in Sweden, it's all a bit bloody peculiar if you ask me.'

He scanned the news report again. Of course, if he'd been writing it he'd have played up the apocalyptic angle a bit, but it was still a good bit of sensationalised tabloid journalism. Why, there was even a picture of a sobbing girl in a see-through nightie, so it couldn't be bad.

'All the Master's interested in is getting himself elected Prime Minister,' replied Mara. Slowly she began manipulating Andreas's prick into aching hardness. It felt so good between her fingers, that smooth, hard flesh that promised the taste of cream on her thirsty tongue. 'I can't see why he'd want to be bothered with giant lizards.'

'No. No, I suppose not.' Abandoning any attempt at rational thought, Andreas gave in to the sexual impulses that were coursing through his body. If he and Mara were supposed to be sex-vampires, they might as well behave as if they were. He threw down the newspaper and it landed in a crumpled heap on the floor. 'Come here and suck me off, you shameless hussy.'

Mara laughed and rolled away from him, leaving him stiff and swollen and hungry for her.

'Come and make me.'

'Is that a challenge?'

'Uh-huh.'

He straddled her, flinging aside the duvet so that he could drink in the full beauty of her smooth, creamy flanks and heavy breasts. Her skin was deliciously cool and silky between his thighs; her large, firm breasts jiggled slightly as he pinned her to the bed by her arms.

Mara's wide green eyes looked up into his, daring him, and he bent to take her right nipple into his mouth, teasing and biting it into rubbery hardness. Slowly he insinuated his leg between her bare thighs, working the hardness of bone and muscle against the forested mound of her pubis. Her sex lips parted and the first gush of her wetness smeared itself over his thigh, slippery and fragrant and exhilarating.

Mara gasped.

'Oh, Andreas. Make me come again.' She ground against his thigh, using it to masturbate herself; and that too excited him beyond belief. He had never wanted a woman the way he wanted Mara Fleming. And every day he woke up wanting her more. 'Make me, make me . . .'

He released her nipple and bent to kiss her full on the lips. As his tongue thrust its way into her sex-scented mouth, the curving rod of his penis touched her belly, leaving a little trace of sex juice.

'Only if you suck my cock again.'

Her red lips curved into a wicked smile. She loved to tease just as much as he did.

'And why would I want to suck your cock?'

He let go of her left arm and with his free hand pinched her nipple.

'Because if you do I'll lick you out.'

Without waiting for Mara's reply, Andreas turned round so that he was facing her feet, his thighs on either side of her head and the wet tip of his cock dripping moisture onto her upturned face. She put out her tongue and licked a drop of salty cock-juice from his glans. It tasted richly seasoned, a distillation of his juices and hers; a nectar of semen and cunt juice that made her thirsty for more.

As she opened her mouth and engulfed the hot, throbbing shaft of his cock, Andreas felt his whole body shake with need for her. Quickly he seized hold of her, the flesh firm and strong under his fingers as he prised her thighs apart and nuzzled deep into the fragrant glade of her sex.

The auburn curls which decorated her mound of Venus were crisp with semen, the longer hairs fringing her plump sex-lips dewy-moist and appetising, inviting bolder and deeper caresses. Andreas ran his tongue along the deep-pink frill of flesh which pouted between her outer cunt-lips, lapping from the fathomless well of her sex, tasting the honeydew of her desire mixed with the leavings of his own passion. He thought of all the other men who had spurted their come into that warm and welcoming haven and the very thought fired him both with jealousy and irresistible excitement.

Mara's lips were closing tighter and tighter around the swollen shaft of his prick, her tongue wetting and stroking him as she sucked him, drawing the hunger out of him, making him madder than ever for her. He let his own tongue-tip dart into the depths of Mara's sex and felt her whole body shudder. The tight, wet tunnel of her vagina welcomed his fingers and he began frigging her – at first with just one finger and then with three, stretching and teasing the elastic walls as they moved in and out of her.

His tongue moved swiftly to the tiny stalk of her swollen clitoris. At the first touch of tongue-tip on love-bud Mara gave a stifled sob of pleasure, her body trembling and writhing as he licked and sucked with merciless precision.

He knew it could not last long for either of them, for the need was too urgent and too strong. Later, when their passion had been blunted a little, they would fuck long and slowly, for the simple pleasure of feeling their two naked bodies pressed together, the sweat trickling over their skin, coursing, mingling, drying in the sun.

But now the need was for quick and brutal satisfaction. Andreas closed his lips over Mara's clitoris and let the very points of his teeth graze the engorged flesh. Mara responded by squeezing his balls, running her sharp nails over the hairy purse of his scrotum, pressing the tip of her tongue into the gaping eye of his penis.

Mara came first, a fraction of a second before Andreas, her vaginal muscles suddenly tensing, then beginning the long, ecstatic series of peristaltic waves which seemed to suck Andreas's fingers into the river-wet depths of Mara's sex. His mouth brim-full of Mara's juices, Andreas felt his own body respond to the excitement of his lover's orgasm; and suddenly it felt as though his entire being was spurting out of him in flood upon flood of creamy-white jism which Mara swallowed down joyfully.

As they sprawled across the sex-moistened sheets, letting the warm May sunshine dry the sweat from their bodies, Andreas stroked Mara's breasts and flanks with reverential delight. Even now, whenever he touched her, he felt the thrill of discovering her body, the way he had discovered it that very first time in Whitby, so long ago, in another life. A life which the Master had not only fucked up – he'd as good as hijacked it, along with Andreas's body.

Andreas Hunt wasn't a vengeful man. No, really, he

wasn't. He didn't normally bear grudges – well, only against newspaper editors. But that bastard LeMaître was going to pay for what he'd done to Andreas and Mara.

Andreas glanced down at the crumpled newspaper on the floor by the bed. Earthquakes, tidal waves, Swedish lizards . . . was Mara right, or was the Master really behind all this apocalyptic nonsense?

Mara's feather-soft kisses on his reawakened prick made him shiver with delicious anticipation.

No. Mara was right. That sort of thing just wasn't the Master's style.

'Master?'

'What is it now, Cheviot?'

The Rt Hon Anthony LeMaître, Nationalist MP and leader of Her Majesty's opposition, was not in the best of moods.

Sir Anthony Cheviot came into the Master's Westminster office, closing and relocking the door carefully behind him. It really wouldn't do to be disturbed.

'I wondered if I might have a quiet word, Master.'

The Master's eyes flashed irritation. Bent back over his large mahogany desk, his private secretary Annabel Manley lay with her skirt up around her waist, her suspendered thighs creamy and inviting and the fringed casket of her cunt glistening with the slippery wetness of her desire.

Her brown eyes appealed to him to free her from the torment of her need, but the Master was not particularly interested in his vampire slut's pleasure, though her moans and groans of frustrated desire gave him a certain satisfaction. His only concern was for himself. With a swift sword-thrust he pierced her, lodging the fat baton of his cock deep inside her sex.

'Very well, Cheviot.' The Master fucked his secretary with long, hard, almost brutal strokes which made the girl's whole body shake, her small but perfect breasts dancing beneath the semi-diaphanous fabric of her white chiffon blouse.

'It is Baptiste, Master.'

The Master's eyes narrowed slightly at the mention of Harry Baptiste, Britain's new Prime Minister. When he had so effectively discredited the governing Republican Party the previous year, the Master had been confident of provoking a General Election within months. And once an election had been called, his elevation to Number 10 would be assured. Not even the brain-dead British electorate would return a government made up of perverts, crooks and the certifiably insane.

But he had not reckoned with Harry Laurent Baptiste: handsome, razor-witted, charming, squeaky-clean Baptiste, who had inexplicably succeeded in making the nation take him to their hearts and rejuvenated the Republicans into the bargain. Yes, Baptiste constituted an obstacle which – incredibly – the Master had not foreseen. Sooner rather than later, Baptiste was going to have to be destroyed.

'What of him?' demanded the Master between clenched teeth. 'Have our agents obtained the necessary material to discredit him?'

'N-no, Master.'

The Master's eyes blazed fire but when he spoke again his voice was icy calm.

'You dare come here simply to tell me that?' He made another thrust into Annabel's belly, a sharp stabbing movement which made her cry out – whether in ecstasy or pain he did not know and frankly did not care. 'Be silent, slut,' he commanded her, and thrust into her a second time, physically strengthened and yet strangely unsatisfied by her young and highly desirable body.

'No, Master. It seems that Baptiste is planning a personal visit to the North of England, to visit the victims of the recent earthquake. In public relations terms . . .'

'Send Kruger', snapped the Master. 'Make sure he gets there before Baptiste and steals his thunder. Have Takimoto disrupt any television coverage of Baptiste.'

'Yes, Master.'

'Better still, ensure that Baptiste does not get there at all.' This satisfying thought so pleased the Master that he came to a sudden climax, his sperm jetting out of him in hot, thick spurts.

'I will do as you instruct, Master.' Cheviot hesitated for a moment. 'Master . . .'

The Master withdrew from Annabel Manley's cunt. A white ooze of spunk was trickling out of her onto the tooled-leather desktop, leaving a sticky pool.

'Lick it up at once,' the Master commanded her, and the girl obligingly rolled onto her belly, lapping at the pool of cooling semen with her little pink tongue. Her skirt was still up round her waist, and the twin globes of her buttocks invited fresh attentions. 'Every drop, or you will be punished severely.' The girl would be punished anyway, thought the Master to himself; but he liked to instil hope only to dash it down again. And fear was so sexually stimulating. He turned back to Cheviot, irritated and very slightly apprehensive. The news had been bad recently. Things had not been going to plan.

'Master,' continued Cheviot. 'The earthquakes. The floods. There has been much speculation . . .'

'It is not your place to speculate.'

'No, Master.'

'It is your place to serve.' The Master's voice fell to a low and menacing whisper. 'Only those who are worthy will share the everlasting empire of lust with me.'

'Forgive me, Master.'

'Shut up, Cheviot. You are irritating me.'

The Master turned away in anger, hiding his confusion. He was certainly not about to admit to one of his minions that he, the all-powerful, all-seeing Master, was as confused as they were about the wave of bizarre phenomena that had been sweeping the globe. Nor that his astral sight was failing him and his well-laid plans for ultimate power had begun to go alarmingly wrong.

He ran his hand down over the rounded swell of Annabel Manley's delectable buttocks. Already the scars had faded from yesterday's beating. That was the beauty of immortality. Flesh healed, wounds disappeared, and soon it was possible to have all the pleasure of inflicting them all over again. He selected a malacca cane from the half-dozen or so he always kept in his office and gave it a practice swipe. Perfect. He could feel his cock swelling already.

'You need to learn humility, Cheviot.'

'Yes, Master.'

'Undress.'

Cheviot's eyes widened.

'I . . . Master?'

'Close the blinds and undress.' The Master gripped the cane with a connoisseur's relish. 'First I shall render your flesh more receptive and then I shall bugger you. I am sure you will enjoy the experience, Cheviot. I know I shall.'

It was dark. Darker than all the blackness of eternity.

Wetness dripped from the ancient stone walls of the subterranean chamber, the irregular plink, plink of the water-drops cutting through the heavy silence.

And there were other sounds in this nightmare world, too: the husky rasp of breath drawn from the foetid air; the shuffle of feet on the bare floor; the chink of a thick iron chain against stone.

The young woman was naked in the darkness. Her hands and feet held fast in rusting iron manacles, attached by chains to the huge stone altar so that she was spreadeagled upon it in utter helplessness. The darkness was of no consequence to her, for she was blindfolded and gagged, lost in her own world of blackness and silence, unable to cry out, unable to resist.

She tried to struggle in her chains, but she was held quite fast, her body a gift to the darkness, her every secret place opened up and offered to it.

He was coming for her. She knew he was there, though she could not see him. She could hear his breathing, the rustle of fabric as he took off his gown and let it fall to the ground, the sound his feet made as he came towards her.

Unseen in the blackness, he smiled. The Master was going to pay for what he had done.

In fact the whole world was going to pay.

Queen Sedet lay on a sumptuous day-bed of carved sandalwood, gilded with pure gold and set with an inlay of carnelian and lapis lazuli. Her long, tanned limbs shimmered a deep gold through the gossamer-thin, white pleated muslin of her Egyptian robe. Drawn tight across her large breasts, the robe had the effect of pushing them together, creating a deep cleavage in which sparkled the crystal amulet which she always wore on a chain around her neck.

Her slender, brown arms were encased from wrist to elbow in golden bangles, and her finger and toenails were capped with little sheaths of purest beaten gold. Her long, jet-black hair was plaited with beads and ornaments and shone with scented oils.

The Egyptian Room at Winterbourne was one of Sedet's favourite places. She found it most conducive to her psychic energies and stimulating to her sexual needs.

Lying back on the couch, she parted her thighs and ruched up the skirt of her light summer robe. Four thousand years ago, when she was a humble temple slut, she had worn robes like these on the banks of the Nile. Four thousand years ago, when the Master had found her and chosen her.

Now she was his immortal queen. Immortal, insatiable, gloriously invincible. She parted her thighs and let her gold-capped fingertips dance on the bare mound of her shaven pubis. She often enjoyed tormenting her slaves by allowing them to perform intimate services upon her body – shaving, grooming, oiling, massaging – then depriving them of the sexual release for which they begged.

How it amused and excited her to see their cocks arch
and strain, the grovelling wretches, the tears coursing
down their pretty faces as they begged her to let them wank
themselves to orgasm. Sometimes, when she was feeling
soft-hearted, she would allow them to masturbate over her
naked body. And then, when they had massaged every
drop of their creamy sperm into her skin and were stone-
hard for her again, she would punish them for having
lustful thoughts. How sweet it was to see their pain, to
taste their blood . . .

Eyes closed, she stroked her bare pubis, pushing her
fingers a little further so that smooth metal met the slippery
wetness of her inner labia. She pinched and stroked her
nipple whilst her right hand rubbed and caressed between
her thighs. The little gold finger-sheaths felt hard and alien
on her soft flesh. It was almost like being wanked by some
godlike machine that knew her every weakness, her every
source of pleasure.

Even the discomfort of rough metal edges gave Sedet
pleasure; for well she understood the subtle links between
pleasure and pain. Had she not endured the agonies of
having her inner labia pierced, knowing instinctively that
in the greatest pain lay the most exquisite pleasure?

'And so I find you waiting for me, my queen.'

Sedet's violet eyes flicked open.

'My lord!'

From the doorway to the Egyptian Room the Master
had been watching his queen, drinking in the sexual energy
as she began to masturbate, rubbing and pinching and
teasing with her skilful fingers.

Her self-pleasure had not angered but excited him and
his hand strayed to the front of his trousers, rubbing
himself through the fabric, enjoying its tightness, stretched
taut across his swelling prick. He wanted her and he would
have her. Now.

'You are pleasingly attired,' he observed coolly. Sedet's
painted nipples glowed scarlet through the flimsy muslin

17

of her robe, fiery and juicy as cherries. Her shaven pubis, too, demanded to be kissed and bitten and enjoyed.

She lowered her long, sweeping eyelashes.

'I dress to honour you, my Master.'

'That is as it should be.'

'Come to me, my lord,' she purred, reaching out her arms to beckon him towards her.

She reached up and unzipped his flies, reaching inside for the curving bow of his hungry prick. Her fingers were cool as marble on his flesh, so subtle and yet so firm that he almost spurted onto her face. He tilted his pelvis back and forth, working his shaft in and out of her grasp, intensifying the burning need, the pressure of the boiling seed in his balls.

When greed and impatience overwhelmed him he took her, pushing her onto her belly on the couch and entering her from behind, his cock sliding into her well-greased sheath with a single rapier-thrust as he held her firm, tanned arse-cheeks apart.

As ever, she was a good and stimulating fuck. But as he rode her and their energies met and mingled, the Master became aware – not for the first time – of a psychic barrier thrown up between them, subtle but strong.

And then the Master knew for sure and rage filled him like a poisonous, choking gas.

That afternoon in the Egyptian Room Sedet had indeed been waiting for someone. But that someone was not the Master.

2: Omens

'KOREANS CLAIM EARTH ON COLLISION COURSE
WITH VENUS. NASA "UNIMPRESSED".'
(*New Jersey Daily Recorder*, 30 May

Black, beautiful and arguably the best Prime Minister
Britain had ever had: that was Harry Baptiste.

As he stepped up to the despatch box for Prime Minister's
Question Time, Baptiste oozed confidence and control.
He wasn't one of your old-fashioned, tub-thumping
socialists, any more than he was a lentils-and-garlic liberal
or an oily tory. Oh no. Harry Baptiste had his finger on the
people's pulse and he knew it.

Ambrose Cosworth, Shadow Employment Secretary,
got to his feet. The Master watched from the front bench
with a mixture of anticipation and unease.

'Would the Prime Minister care to explain how this
country can possibly afford to squander almost a billion
pounds on so-called equal opportunities programmes when
there are over three million unemployed?'

The smile never left Baptiste's face.

'This government does not believe that money spent on
equal opportunities policies is anything other than an
investment in the future', he replied. 'We are investing in a
more able, more flexible, better-qualified workforce and
confidently expect to reduce unemployment by
approximately one million over the next five years.' He
took off his glasses and popped them in his top pocket.

'Which is more than the Nationalists ever managed in fifteen years of government.'

The Master glared back into Baptiste's open, honest, intelligent face and felt the whole force of his psychic anger rush out of him like the backdraught from an inferno. Under normal circumstances the sheer force of that psychic energy would have caused turmoil, but circumstances were not normal. Lately, the Master had been feeling drained and encumbered, as though some external source were tapping into his power and interfering with his astral sight.

The Master got to his feet.

'May I remind the Right Honourable Member for Humberside East that unemployment has risen by over two hundred and fifty thousand since the Republicans came to power?'

'Indeed it has. As a direct consequence of policies implemented by the last Nationalist government,' snapped back Baptiste, perfectly unruffled by this line of attack.

'At least the Nationalist Party upholds traditional moral values,' thundered the Master. 'Everyone knows that the Republican Party is no better than a hotbed of scandal and moral degeneration.'

Baptiste regarded him with an infuriatingly cool air of amused detachment.

'We are all human beings, subject to human weaknesses and failings,' he replied. 'And personally, I find it impossible to trust *any* man who is quite as perfect as you would have us believe, Mr LeMaître.'

I shall destroy you, the Master promised himself as he resumed his seat. I shall crush and destroy and obliterate you like the insignificant insect you are, Mr Harry Baptiste.

Cheviot touched his arm and the Master resisted the impulse to swat him like a bluebottle. Here in the House, a certain decorum must be maintained if the Nationalists were to build on their shaky reputation as 'the party of clean government'.

'Master. We shall soon wipe that smile off his face.'

'You had better be right, Cheviot.' The Master threw Cheviot a stony-faced look. 'Because if you are not, you will face the consequences of my displeasure.'

He glanced around the other front bench spokesmen and women. At least Weatherall was putting forward some semblance of an argument – that was one young man who had exceeded his expectations over the last few months.

'I have been investigating possible ways of discrediting Baptiste, Master,' hazarded Cheviot.

The Master barely reacted. His voice was a quiet, venomous hiss of irritation.

'Indeed.'

'The brides, Master. Why not let them set a trap to catch him? Joanna and Sonja – they have never failed you.'

Purse-lipped, the Master gave a curt nod.

'Very well. See to it.'

His eyes were narrowed to slits, his knuckles bone-white from the tension in his hands. He was staring at Baptiste, but he was no longer listening to what the Prime Minister had to say. He was looking at the long, slender fingers of Baptiste's right hand.

Watching the way the sunlight glinted off that ornate crystal ring.

Andreas didn't care for circuses and funfairs. Mostly they gave him the creeps – especially the clowns. He remembered being taken to Blackpool Tower Circus as a little kid and being so terrified when Coco came on that he'd wet himself. On the whole, not an occasion he tended to brag about.

But tonight, Andreas and Mara were going to the funfair whether they liked it or not. The Master's instructions had been quite specific: get your arse up to that constituency of yours, Weatherall, and start pressing flesh. And take the Dubois woman with you – it'll cost us votes if they start thinking you're gay.

They parked the car and walked through wooded parkland down to the River Dee, where a million coloured bulbs lit up the garish red and yellow striped canopies of the sideshows, and the big wheel spun round and round like a fiery catherine-wheel against the dark, dusky-blue of the evening sky.

Mara linked her arm through his and he felt the electricity of her touch through the arm of his thin summer jacket. It was a sultry evening, heavy and rather too hot for late May; and the air was stuffy and unbreathable, with hardly a breath of a breeze coming in off the river. Something peculiar and not altogether pleasant was happening to the weather. Andreas was no psychic, but even he could feel the menace of thunder in the air. Perhaps that Korean religious sect was right after all and the earth really was about to collide with Venus.

'Looking forward to this?' teased Mara.

'I hope that's a joke.'

'If you're good I'll give you a lick of my candyfloss.'

'And if I'm bad?'

'If you're *really* bad, I'll let you eat me all up.'

Andreas felt slightly uneasy in his laughter. Pretending to be Nationalist bigot Nicholas Weatherall was a strain at the best of times and here, in-Weatherall's own Chester constituency, it was like being put under a microscope, waiting for somebody to catch him out. Still, he'd got this far without being rumbled, so there was no reason to think that he couldn't continue to carry it off for a while at least, especially with Mara and the crystal ID bracelet to protect him.

He consoled himself by giving Mara's arse a thorough grope. It was as plump and soft as a feather pillow, yet firm and shapely as sculptured stone. She was wearing no panties and the white sheath-dress clung to her curves like a second skin, giving tantalising hints at the shadowy cleft between her twin bum-cheeks. Andreas thought longingly of the pleasures that sublime arse had given him, of the

22

sheer joy of ruching up that dress, baring one peach-pink bum cheek and running his greedy tongue over and over the moist flesh.

Hunger made his cock stiffen and he adjusted himself surreptitiously, hoping that no-one would notice his inconveniently large erection. But Mara had noticed, and her hand strayed shamelessly to the front of his pants, gently squeezing and stroking.

In the relative seclusion of a copse of trees he stopped, allowing himself a little groan of torment.

'Mara . . . what the hell are you trying to do to me?'

'I want you, Andreas.'

'We're in the middle of Chester!'

'That's never stopped us before.' Mara smiled. 'Remember that time in the Cathedral cloisters?' She felt for his glans and rubbed the flat of her hand over it, hard enough to make him wince with pleasurable discomfort. It wouldn't take much of that to make him spurt and she damn well knew it, thought Andreas.

'I'm supposed to be promoting "traditional moral values" – what if we get caught?'

'It'll do wonders for your reputation.'

Mara pressed her firm young body against him and he let her push him back against the thick, rough trunk of an ancient sycamore tree. He was only resisting for form's sake and she knew it. They were like rutting beasts, the pair of them, doing it anywhere and everywhere, just for the sheer, dizzying pleasure of being *able* to do it.

'Oh yes?' It was Andreas's turn to tease. 'And what about *your* reputation, eh?'

Mara giggled.

'Oh don't worry about me, I'm just a shameless hussy.'

A family of six passed by, only yards away, on their way to the fair – but here in the shade of the trees Andreas and Mara were at least sheltered from the casual gaze. Andreas's eyes opened in surprise and delight as Mara calmly pulled down first one shoulder strap and then the other.

That dress had been tormenting him all the way up from Winterbourne. She'd chosen it specially because it was Andreas's favourite, the one that always gave him a hard-on like a steel bar. On the hanger the dress was nothing special – just a simple sheath of white stretchy jersey, cut tight in all the right places, with narrow straps and a scoop neckline: sexy but smart.

But on Mara it was an erotic time-bomb; the subtle wrapping that turned Mara's undeniably exciting body into an irresistible fantasy land that no red-blooded man could resist. Andreas certainly couldn't. The first time he'd seen her wearing it, he'd almost shot his load just looking at her sway her hips. And the sight of her large, firm, unfettered breasts moving, fluid and stiff-nippled, beneath that tight white fabric had him in a turmoil every time.

With her back to the distant road, she slipped off the shoulder straps, then took hold of the scoop neckline and pulled it down at the front, baring the gloriously juicy fruits of her breasts.

'I want you to screw me, Andreas.'

'Here?' Wonderingly he cupped her breasts, flicking the flats of his thumbs over the engorged nipples. She gave an appreciative sigh.

'Here. Up against the tree. If we're quiet, no-one will even notice we're here.'

Andreas wasn't so sure, but what the heck? He was only human. And Mara's fingers felt heaven-soft on his dick as she unzipped his flies and felt for his hardness. Her touch was cool but it made him blaze hotter than a furnace for her and he clawed at the tight skirt of her dress, sliding it upwards over her bare thighs.

Auburn curls adorned her pubis and he savoured the feeling of their silky moistness on his fingers as he worked his hand between her thighs. Mara slid her feet a little further apart to let him in and, as she did so, her bare breasts jiggled delightfully, demanding his kisses.

He slid his hands under her backside and, bracing his back against the rough bark of the sycamore, he hoisted her up and she clasped his waist with her thighs. Then, with the suddenness of maddened hunger, he brought her whole body down to meet the waiting hardness of his eager prick, holding apart her arse cheeks so that he slid into her in a single, smooth movement.

'Give it to me,' gasped Mara.

'You're a tease, Mara Fleming,' groaned Andreas as he worked her up and down on his shaft. 'You've been teasing me all day.'

'Only to make you want me more. You *do* want me, don't you?'

He silenced her with a passionate kiss on the lips, their tongues meeting and joisting in the warm, wet pleasure-palace of her mouth. And as if in answer her cunt began oozing its own sweet wetness around his prick, lubricating the stone-hard shaft as they fucked in the curious half-dusk of the glade, broken only by the flashes of multicolored light from the nearby funfair.

Andreas felt he had been at exploding point almost forever, yet Mara held him there, making him wait, making him want her more and more. His balls ached, swollen and loaded with creamy-white spunk that longed to jet inside her. His heart was thumping and rivulets of sweat were coursing down Mara's bare breasts, the salty fluid dampening the front of his once-crisp white shirt.

'Fuck me, fuck me, fuck me,' whispered Mara, repeating this simple mantra over and over again.

He felt his balls tense in response and the rush of jism seemed to come from the depths of his belly, as if he were fucking her not just with his body but with his soul.

He felt her cunt spasming, welcoming him in, heard her little shuddering cry as she clasped his neck and kissed his face, murmuring his name.

'Andreas, Andreas. Oh . . . Andreas . . .'

He wanted to do it all over again – they both did – but it

was getting late and Andreas knew he ought to make sure he showed his face before everyone was too tanked up on beer and burgers to notice he was there. He sighed inwardly as he watched Mara wriggle her dress back into some semblance of respectability, longing to lay her down on the soft green grass, press his face to the fragrant wet triangle between her thighs and lap at the oozing well-spring of her sex.

Mara planted a kiss on his hungry lips, then patted the creases out of his jacket.

'Ready?'

'As ready as I'll ever be. Do you think anyone . . . ?'

'Do you care?'

He laughed.

'I suppose not. As long as it wasn't some tosser from the *Comet* with a Leica and a long lens.'

They walked together towards the crescendo of sound coming from the fairground. It was situated on a piece of waste ground usually used as a car park which was commandeered once a year by the travelling fair which visited the city to capitalise on the extra trade during race week.

An archway lit with red and yellow lights proclaimed: 'Busby's Funfair – Welcome.' They walked through it and to Andreas it was like walking into one of the outer circles of hell. Screams and laughter pierced the night air, backed by thunderous recorded music from the waltzers, the big wheel, the ghost train and dozens of tacky sideshows.

'Well, now, if it ain't Mr Weatherall himself!' A candy-floss seller beckoned Andreas over to shake his hand. 'And his very lovely lady too.'

'Pleased to meet you,' hazarded Andreas, his hand half-crushed by the old woman's grip.

'I'm a good judge of character,' volunteered the old woman. 'And I always vote Nationalist. It's that nice Mr LeMaître – he's got such lovely honest eyes.'

Suppressing a smile, Andreas bought a stick of candy

floss and handed it to Mara with a wink.

'You did promise,' he reminded her.

'Depends on how bad you're going to be, remember?'

'Believe me, I'm working on it right now.'

'Try your luck sir, miss?' A hopeful-looking youth waved an air rifle at them as they walked past his shooting range.

'Go on.' Mara nudged him forward. 'It's good PR.'

'I couldn't hit a barn door with a cricket bat,' Andreas protested.

'Even better PR.'

He stepped forward, wishing to goodness he didn't look so damned conspicuous in his stuffy grey suit. Everyone else seemed to be in jeans and T-shirts. He paid his money and picked up the air rifle, watched by a crowd of curious onlookers.

'All the cans for a teddy, sir. Three for a special prize.'

'Yeah, yeah, right.' Andreas didn't pay much attention. He knew this scam from his days as a reporter on one of the local rags. If the cans weren't actually glued to the shelf (and they usually were), they'd be stacked up so carefully that Annie Oakley herself couldn't shift them with three shots.

One hideous plastic key-ring later, Andreas and Mara escaped from the small crowd that had gathered. Andreas took off his tie and stuffed it into his pocket. He was beginning to feel like a sideshow himself. And to make matters worse it was hotter than ever now; the air felt like treacle as he fought to draw it into his lungs.

'God, these places give me a headache.' He switched on a smile to greet two teenage girls in microskirts which almost – but not quite – concealed the colour of their knickers. 'Hello, ladies.' He was greeted by a barrage of girlish giggles.

'Go on, Mandy, ask him.'

'I can't!'

'I dare you.'

'I told you, I can't. Look, you're making me go all red.'

The taller of the two girls, a brunette with thin legs and highlights, pushed the chunky blonde forward.

'Mandy wants to ask you for a kiss,' she announced. 'She really fancies you.' She then promptly exploded into giggles.

Beetroot-red, Mandy turned on her companion.

'You mean *you* do!' she countered. 'Sorry, Mr Weatherall,' she stuttered, hardly able to speak in the presence of her idol. 'It's just Caz, she's so . . . immature!'

At that both girls fell about giggling.

'Don't!' squeaked Caz. 'I'll piss myself!'

'Well, I'm charmed to meet you both,' lied Andreas, honouring both with a peck on the cheek which turned the giggles to sudden, reverential silence. As he and Mara went on their way they could hear the two girls talking behind them.

'My dad says the Nationalists are a bunch of upper-class wankers.'

'I don't care what your dad says. He's a fat slob.'

'And he says it's the Nationalists causing all these earthquakes and fires and tidal waves and things.'

'Don't talk bloody daft.'

'It's what he says, that's all.'

'Yeah, well, stuff that. Next election I'm voting for Weatherall. He's so *horny*.'

The air was so thick and heavy that it was like breathing in a woollen blanket. Even with the top two buttons of his shirt undone, Andreas felt as though there were fingers around his throat, trying to choke the life out of him. Sweat had dampened Mara's skin, making her white dress cling to her even more alluringly, her nipples hard and prominent beneath the moist fabric and the small of her back wet with perspiration.

'Had enough?' asked Andreas casually.

He was thinking of the big, deep corner bath in their suite at the four-star Grosvenor Hotel, of the fun they could have with the whirlpool sending swirling jets of cool water all over their overheated bodies. And then there were the crisp white sheets on the king-size bed. They could fuck slowly and languidly all night long and, when dawn came up, they could start all over again.

Reading his mind, as she always did, Mara smiled wickedly.

'Oh no, darling. I haven't had nearly enough.' She kissed him, her lips moist and soft and ardent against his, and her tongue darting into his mouth like a miniature penis.

Andreas and Mara might have headed straight back to the hotel there and then, if it hadn't been for the weather turning distinctly nasty. A flash of bright blue light announced the beginning of a massive storm. For a split second it lit up the whole funfair as brightly as if it were day, creating an eerie snapshot of upturned faces, frozen in surprise, or fear, or laughter, or relief; the features picked out in a ghastly, almost fluorescent pallor, like ultraviolet strobes in a psychedelic disco.

'The storm's very close.' Andreas eyed up the possibilities for shelter as a deafening roar of thunder drowned out the tinny music from the dodgems.

'Almost overhead.' Unafraid and rather exhilarated by the build-up of cosmic energy all around her, Mara threw back her head and let the electricity flow and crackle through her. For the first time she had begun to comprehend the true meaning of invulnerability, the incorruptibility of this immortal flesh with which the Master had cursed her. 'The rain will come soon.' Her voice was low. 'Do you know what I'd like to do, Andreas?'

He held her close, his hand resting on the perfect curve of her arse.

'Tell me.'

'I'd like to fuck you right in the middle of this storm, that's what I'd like to do.' She laughed, and her laughter was an explosion of sexual energy that made Andreas's prick strain with need. 'I'd like to fuck you right at the very top of the big wheel.'

A second flash of lightning, and then a third, and suddenly one of the overhead lighting gantries was hit, blowing out dozens of bulbs with an immense sparking and sizzling and exploding of glass fragments. People were alarmed now, scattering as quickly as they could, heading away in any direction they could. It was as though they already realised, through some deep-rooted instinct, that this was no ordinary storm.

The big wheel stopped with a jerk; a chorus of shrieks and moans accompanying the sudden jolt as the power was cut and the passengers were plunged into darkness.

And then the rain came. Rain that burned as it fell, for it was as hot as bathwater, and steamed and fizzed as it touched the overheated ground. A woman ran past, her hair in rats'-tails and her sodden frock plastered to her wiry body. Others sheltered under the awnings of the sideshows, huddled together as though a thin sheet of red-and-yellow-striped plastic would protect them from the anger of the elements raging around them.

'Hell of a storm. *Hell* of a storm,' murmured Andreas as the wind began to stir, blowing discarded burger-boxes and old paper bags along the aisles between the stalls like tumbleweed in some Hollywood western. Was this the Master up to his old tricks again? He knew that was what Mara must be thinking.

And he couldn't help remembering that very first time he'd come to Chester, looking for Mara; that time when the Master had tried to fry him with a thunderbolt from the sky. He held Mara very tightly to him, completely forgetting that it was she who was invulnerable and he – the mere mortal – who was at the mercy of the storm. He might be a hard-bitten journo but Andreas got stupid like that sometimes.

Sudden, piercing screams rent the air, and a fraction of a second later Mara and Andreas understood why.

Something was raining down from the sky – and it wasn't raindrops. No, not something. Some*things*.

One of them fell with surprising force onto Andreas's shoulder. It was cold and hard and yet curiously soft, and it slithered off him, then bounced onto the ground. As lightning flashed overhead he saw it glistening on the ground at his feet, its eyes like glass marbles in its little green head. There were others. Lots and lots of others, falling and tumbling from the sky, wriggling and running and leaping.

Frogs. *Frogs?*

He picked one up and it was very real, very alive. My God, thought Andreas, it really is raining frogs. And to think I always took the mickey out of the *Fortean Times*.

At that moment Mara voiced his darkest thoughts.

'Could this be the Master . . . ?'

'But why, Mara? Why would he want to make it rain frogs? I don't understand.'

'He's evil, Andreas. Really evil. I'm not sure I want to understand.'

'But he'd tell us if he was going to pull a stunt like this.' Andreas watched the frogs, hundreds and thousands of them, hopping away across the waterlogged ground. 'Surely he would. Wouldn't he . . . ?'

'The Master is my lord. Queen Sedet is my mistress.'

'When the Master is away, I am your lord. I am the Lord of Winterbourne.'

Liz Exley was taking her punishment in the conservatory at Winterbourne. She resented every blow of the whip upon her lithe, smooth back, not because of the pain – which she had been taught to enjoy – but because it was being inflicted by arrogant, self-satisfied Joachim Heimdal.

Since the demise of the Master's former whoremaster, Delgado, Heimdal had come into his own. Being initiated into the Master's empire of the undead had been the best career move Heimdal had ever made. He revelled in the status and privileges which the Master's favour had conferred upon him and, as self-styled Lord of Winterbourne, he enjoyed almost unlimited power during the Master's long absences on parliamentary business.

Of course there were a few – like this troublesome slut – who were slow to accept Heimdal's *de facto* authority. But Heimdal rather enjoyed imposing his will upon Winterbourne's more 'difficult' converts. The more spirited a slut was, the more fun he could have in breaking that spirit.

He brought the tip of the bullwhip stinging down between Liz's shoulder-blades, but she did not flinch. The insolent slut had learned to tolerate – and savour – the most extreme pain. It was difficult to find new ways of disciplining her.

'You must learn obedience,' he told her.

'I shall never obey you,' she snapped back.

This time he brought the whip down with less force but greater ingenuity, directing its tip between the pretty arse-cheeks which he had so long admired. He was rewarded with a moan of distress as the wasp-keen sting of the whip tormented her delicate membranes.

'Oh but you will,' he assured her. But not yet awhile perhaps, he told himself with a certain satisfaction. The longer she resists, the more pleasurable it will be for me when at last I break her resistance. 'You will do exactly as I tell you.'

He nodded to the Ethiopian slave Ibrahim, his magnificent body oiled and scented and his ten-inch cock pierced with three rings of purest gold. There was certainly never any difficulty in ensuring Ibrahim's complete obedience. The Ethiopian was one of Winterbourne's most eager initiates and he had given enthusiastic service to Heimdal on many memorable occasions.

Ibrahim tied Liz more securely to the heavy wrought-iron garden seat, so that she was spreadeagled across it, bent sharply forward with her hands above her head and her ankles tied to the legs of the bench, forcing apart her thighs. Heimdal licked his lips. The Exley slut had such a lean, fit body, her athletic physique the result of hard training – and hard sex. Heimdal was confident that he could supply plenty of the latter.

Liz was ready for the sting of the whip, but not for the intense thrill of pleasure which it sent vibrating through her. Without being able to see it, she knew the Heimdal was using his special cat-o'-nine-tails on her – the one with the long, supple leather thongs, each one tipped with a little ball of lead shot. It was such a sensual weapon, its carved ivory handle a work of art in itself and the pain it produced – in skilled hands – a magnificent tapestry of sensations.

'You. Will. Obey. Me.'

Heimdal punctuated each word with a fresh swipe of the cat and, in spite of her dislike of him, Liz felt her body responding.

'Obey me.'

Liz let out a shuddering hiss of breath as one of the lead-tipped thongs snaked round the side of her body and stung the sensitive flesh of her nipple.

'Obey me, slut.'

'I . . . obey.'

From between her pouting cunt-lips trickled the thin, clear ooze of her arousal, and Heimdal laughed delightedly to see the beauty of her humiliation. That Liz's capitulation was carefully stage-managed he was too full of himself to notice, she knew that. He could not see the mocking laughter on her hidden face as she spoke the words his ego longed to hear.

'I obey. I obey you in all things.'

'That is better.' She could hear the excitement in Heimdal's voice, and pictured the hard curve of his massively erect prick, the jade serpent-ring passing so neatly through the glans. 'I am your master and your lord, Liz, do you hear me?'

Anger rose inside her but her voice was a purr of humility.

'I hear you.'

'I hear you, *my lord.*'

She swallowed down the bile of her resentment.

'My lord.'

Heimdal pushed into her, sealing his victory with a bayonet thrust of his impressively thick penis. Liz gasped with an appropriate degree of pleasure and, as if to symbolise the completeness of her submission, she raised her head and parted her red lips to receive Ibrahim's ebony shaft.

'Good. Good *girl.*' Heimdal was praising her like a pet dog, a little mongrel bitch on heat with her backside in the air, begging for dick. Liz longed to tell him how pathetic he was, how inadequate by comparison with her beloved Master. But the pleasure she felt was genuine enough; and the heat spreading out from her clitoris in delicious waves an energising force she welcomed and savoured like a sweet wine.

Yet even as she submitted to the force of her own desire, rebellious thoughts were going round and round in Liz's head. She was cleverer than Heimdal thought. She had seen him whispering in corners with Queen Sedet when the Master was not around. Perhaps if she listened more carefully to what they were saying, she would learn something which she could use against them.

Something that she could use to gain greater favour with her one true Master.

In the library at Winterbourne, the Master was alone with his thoughts.

They were not welcome thoughts – quite the reverse. Only a few months ago, his continuing progress towards ultimate power had seemed almost a formality. Everything had been planned out and was working perfectly – the sex-smear campaign against the Republicans, the subliminal TV and video messages, the mind-altering fast food. All he had to do was arrange for a General Election, get Weatherall to manage his campaign, and the rest would take care of itself.

Not so. Things had started to go wrong – and the Master wanted to know the reason why.

First there had been the blurring of his astral sight, as though someone or something was deliberately confusing him, throwing him off the scent. Then the strange phenomena had begun: tidal waves, extinct volcanoes coming to life, two-headed dogs and insects the size of rats. Of course, that had led to an outbreak of end-of-the-world-itis, an attack of pre-Millennium fever with the usual brisk trade in weird cults and deathbed conversions. And as if that wasn't enough, the Republicans had acquired themselves a pristine new PM with a disturbing taste in jewellery.

It was almost funny really. But the Master wasn't laughing.

He gathered together all his strength and sent it out into the darkness of the night. Somewhere out there, darker than all the surrounding blackness, was a force almost equal to his own in treachery and lust and cunning. If only he could see it, catch and ensnare it. Drain it of its strength and then strangle the life from it.

An ancient, leather-bound book lay on the library table. The Master flicked through the thick leaves of vellum, until at last he found what he was looking for.

One thing and one thing alone could give him back the power of infinite sight.

The Eye of Baloch.

Deep in the heart of Soho, it was business as usual. The cinema club on the corner was showing *Nympho Cowgirls* and in the peep-show opposite a steady stream of punters were forking out crisp tenners to watch two girls simulating sex.

The sandwich-man trudged wearily up Ventura Street

handing out leaflets to anyone who would take them. He wasn't having much luck, but then he never did. The heavy board was making his shoulders ache, but you couldn't let a little thing like that get you down, could you?

At that moment a tremendous commotion brought the rhythm of Soho street-life to a complete halt. The door of the Doritas Massage Studio burst open and a collection of screaming girls rushed out, some in short white 'uniforms', others naked except for g-strings. Several were spattered with a thick, bright red liquid, one naked girl drenched in it from head to foot, her once-blonde locks plastered to her head. Pushing past them came three ashen-faced men, one pulling on his trousers, another naked except for a pair of baggy white underpants, liberally splashed with red.

'Taxi. Taxi! For God's sake, take me away from this place.'

'What's going on?' demanded the proprietor of the Swedish bookshop next door.

'Blood! It's blood!' screeched the naked girl, making an ineffectual attempt to cover her naked breasts with her red-soaked hands. 'It's coming out of the taps, the showers . . . all of a sudden they just started running red!'

'Fuckin' Ada,' whistled the bookshop proprietor, taking a step backwards. Red, coppery-smelling liquid dripped from the girl's erect nipples to the pavement, forming lurid polka-dots on the paving-stones.

Calmly and slowly, the sandwich-man turned and walked back down Ventura Street, stuffing a handful of leaflets into the bookshop-owner's hand as he disappeared into the distance; the legend on his sandwich-board starkly black and white:

THE END OF THE WORLD IS NIGH.

3: The Eye of Baloch

'PLAGUE OF LOCUSTS HITS BALMORAL. PRINCE OF WALES PREDICTS END OF WORLD.'

(*International Enquirer*, 1 June)

Drip, drip, drip.

Almost filling one wall of the huge arched room, the water clock marked the seconds to eternity.

The man looked out through the stone-mullioned windows as the weather closed in. Hardly a scrap of blue remained now, only the tumultuous grey and pink of stormclouds gathering in an iron-grey sky. He smiled.

Before him knelt the girl. Her cascade of glossy black hair had been tied back into a waist-length rope; he liked to see her face when she was sucking him off. It provoked an agreeable sensation to see those soft, pink, virginal lips closing about the tip of his prick.

His prick was so stiff for her today. As her tongue wound its way along his shaft it felt as if he was screwing the whole world and, in a way, he was.

The girl lapped at his oozing glans with a kitten's eagerness and he thrust into her, slowly and rhythmically. There was luxury in the pleasure he was taking from her, in the exhilaration as his power flowed and the elements gathered to obey him.

'Harder.'

She too obeyed him with an automatic grace which delighted him. Her mouth closed about him and she

37

sucked hard, so that he felt as though she were sucking the very marrow out of his bones. Her teeth teased his shaft, her tongue moistening and caressing as her cool fingers cradled his balls.

Power and pleasure, pleasure and power. The two were inextricably mingled within him. He could feel the power building up, gaining momentum as his climax grew nearer. The seed was boiling in his balls, a tidal wave waiting to break the banks of his self-control.

He mastered the pleasure, savoured and controlled it. Outside the windows the sky was growing darker, lowering and ominous as a furrowed brow. A hot wind bent the trees into curious, stunted shapes like cowering bodies.

'Now.'

She ran her nails lightly over the heavy seed-sacs between his thighs and he summoned up the full force of his pleasure. It began as a heavy ache in his belly, a tingling in his balls, a spreading warmth that made his whole body tense in anticipation.

It came like lava from a volcano, spilling and gushing out of him into her welcoming mouth; overflowing her greedy lips and trickling down her chin as he thrust into her up to the hilt, half-choking her with the force of his orgasm.

Lightning forked across the sky once, twice, and then the rain came, in great wind-blown torrents. He flung open the windows and bared his nakedness to the storm, revelling in the cosmic energies he alone had summoned up.

And then he threw back his head and laughed till tears of mirth joined the raindrops coursing down his face.

'You summoned me, Master?'

Liz Exley stood in the doorway of the Master's study. She knew she looked good. The rubber catsuit was so skintight that every small feature of her athletic body was thrown into relief – the gentle undulations of her ribs and breasts, the coffee-bean hardness of her nipples. The suit was open at the crotch, revealing a tangle of bushy brown curls that contrasted sharply with the peroxide crop of her hair; and two circular openings gaped at the back, revealing two perfect white moons of buttock-flesh. She had prepared herself particularly carefully for her Master this evening.

The Master beckoned her in with a distracted snap of the fingers. He was sitting in his favourite leather armchair, legs apart, tailored flannels open at the fly and his cock and balls exposed. Between his thighs knelt one of Winterbourne's slave-boys, a handsome teenager Igushi Takimoto had picked up in a video arcade. Easy prey and tender as spring chicken. Takimoto had developed quite an eye for young meat.

As Liz entered the room the Master pushed the slave-boy away.

'Enough, Pietro.'

'But, Master . . .'

'I said enough. Disobey me and you will be punished again.'

Pushed to the ground, the young man crawled away on hands and knees, a look of pained resentment on his face. A studded dog-collar was fastened about his slender neck and he trailed behind him a long leather leash. He watched from the corner as Liz approached.

The Master looked Liz up and down. Things might not be going entirely to plan but some things remained as good as ever. Liz Exley's body was one of those things.

'Master?'

'Pietro has been slow to obey me,' the Master informed her, settling back in his chair to enjoy the spectacle. 'He requires disciplining.'

This information was music to Liz's ears. She had learned much of the art of discipline from her mistress, Sedet, and long nights of torment and ecstasy in the Hall of Darkness. She turned her eyes on Pietro. He had scuttled into the corner of the room and was crouching there, but Liz seized hold of his leash hauled him out, half-strangling him as she dragged him back into the centre of the room.

'Please, please, no!' he gasped.

'Be quiet,' she snapped. She noticed how his eyes followed each movement of her graceful body and how they kept returning to the glossy brown bush that grew so prettily over the secret triangle of her sex. She raised her ringed hand and struck him on the side of his face. 'And take your filthy eyes off me, slave!'

He whined like a kicked spaniel, his brown eyes imploring mercy. She struck him again. Her heart was beating with the excitement of it, and she could see how much Pietro was enjoying the game – beneath his tight, ripped jeans his cock was a long truncheon of swollen flesh. She cast a swift sidelong glance at the Master and, to her satisfaction, saw that he was slowly wanking, his eyes fixed on the spectacle of mistress and servant.

'Kiss my boots.' Liz kicked Pietro in the lower belly, not too hard, carefully avoiding his testicles. She only wanted to make him suffer a little, not put him out of action. From what she had heard, Pietro was a tireless performer.

Pietro doubled up for a few seconds, wheezing and clasping his belly. That gave Liz a golden opportunity to punish him a little more.

'I said, kiss my boots. Do you dare to disobey me?'

Still struggling for breath, Pietro shook his head vigorously.

'Answer me. Do you dare disobey me?'

'N-no.'

This time the sole of her boot collided with the side of Pietro's face and he slumped to the ground, a red mark on his cheek.

'No, *mistress*.'

'No, mistress. Forgive me, mistress.'

'Kiss my boots.'

Pietro obeyed, planting a small kiss on the toe of Liz's right boot.

'Now the other.'

No sooner had he done this that Liz jerked the dog-leash, making him choke and claw at the collar.

'You have dirtied my boots, slave. You have left marks on them with your filthy lips. You must be punished for this.'

'I am sorry, mistress.'

'Undress.'

'Mistress?'

'You heard me – undress. Take off your jeans and your pants.'

Pietro struggled out of shirt, jeans and underpants, revealing the most appetisingly golden body that Liz had seen in a long while. As she had anticipated, his cock was hard as only a young man's cock can be, an arrogant arc of hunger at the base of his belly.

'You dare desire me, slave?'

'Y-yes, mistress.'

She slid her legs a little further apart to intensify Pietro's agony. From where he half-knelt, half-crouched, she knew he had an unrivalled view of her fur-trimmed muff and the gash of deep pink where her inner labia peeped out from between her plump outer sex-lips. It must be torment for him. The very thought stimulated her own desire and she almost orgasmed at the very sight of her pretty slave.

'Now kiss my boots. I want them spotlessly clean.'

'Yes, mistress.'

Pietro got to his knees and bent to lick the glossy toe of Liz's right boot. His tongue was long, very pink, very muscular – and Liz couldn't help wondering what it would feel like on her skin. As he licked, he left a shiny trail of saliva on the patent leather toe-cap.

To prolong Pietro's agony, Liz opened up her sex lips with the fingers of her left hand and felt for the hard stalk of her clitoris. It was huge and hypersensitive with excitement.

'I am masturbating, Pietro. I'm touching my own clitoris.'

She felt him shudder but he kept on licking her boots.

'I bet you'd like to do that to me, wouldn't you, Pietro? You'd like to have my clitoris on your fingers. Or maybe your tongue . . .'

He did not reply but kept on licking her boots, afraid to stop. In mock anger, Liz kicked him away.

'Answer me, slave!'

He looked up at her, round-eyed and panting. Little threads of clear sex-fluid anointed his cock tip, and the velvety purse of his scrotum was tight and tense over his spunk-filled balls.

'Yes, Mistress.'

'Tell me what you would like to do to me, slave.'

Liz went on masturbating, spreading her cunt lips wide apart, letting Pietro feast his hungry eyes on the glistening bounty within. The pink pearl of her clitoris rolled deliciously under her fingertips, well-lubricated with the slippery juices of her own desire.

'I . . . I would like to lick your juices, mistress.' Once the first words were spoken, the rest came tumbling out. 'I would like to take your clitoris between my teeth. I would like to run my tongue along the wonderful pink furrow between your cunt and your arse . . . Oh mistress, if you would only permit me . . .'

But Liz only laughed and rubbed her clitoris a little harder.

'Do you really think I would let you touch me with your lips, filthy slave? Look, watch me. See how my cunt opens and closes like a little flower.' She turned to the Master, gazing straight into his eyes. 'It longs only for the touch of the one true Master,' she purred.

'Come here, slut.' The Master beckoned her to him and stood up. Liz felt her heart skip with excitement.

'Master?'

'You have pleased me, slut, with your little pantomime. You shall have your reward.' He cast a bored glance at Pietro. 'You have much to learn. Get out.'

'But, Master!' Pietro's dejection was obvious and extreme.

'Get out. Cheviot awaits you in the Hall of Mirrors. No doubt he will devise some special punishment for you.'

The slave left and at last Liz was alone with the Master. She seldom had him to herself. So often she had to share him with Queen Sedet and Winterbourne's many other vampire sluts when, in her heart of hearts, she knew that she was the only one worthy of him. The only one worthy of being his consort.

She purred contentedly as he pushed her onto her hands and knees and scythed into her cunt, his fingernails tearing roughly at the exposed white flesh of her moon-perfect buttocks. If only she might spend the whole of her immortality worshipping the Master and his beautiful manhood. His dick was her paradise, her only joy. Why should she share it with anyone else?

She knew how she would begin. She would bide her time, pleasure him, drink in the power from their fucking. And then, when he had praised her for her skill, she would innocently mention the last time she had seen Sedet and Heimdal together . . .

Igushi Takimoto sat in front of the bank of television monitors. The same period drama was playing out on a dozen or more screens, the frames interspersed at regular intervals by subliminal messages too brief to be perceived by the naked eye:

BAPTISTE. TRAITOR. BAPTISTE. TRAITOR.

LEMAITRE. MASTER. LEMAITRE. MASTER.

FUCK. FUCK FOR YOUR MASTER.

He put down the computer print-out and stared at it in silence for some time. He was doing everything right, he knew he was, but it wasn't working any more. It didn't make sense. When it had first been launched, Empire TV had taken the country by storm, its subtle subliminals whipping up adulation for the Master as Takimoto had known they would.

And then it had all started going awry.

Takimoto rubbed the back of his hand across his brow. He was sweating. Well, anybody would break out in a cold sweat at the prospect of facing the Master's fury.

He hardly noticed the geisha's fingers on his cock as he went through the figures yet again. Why wasn't sex-TV working any more? How could people just stop responding? It went against all the laws of science.

And more to the point: precisely how had Harry Baptiste risen above the secret, silent propaganda war to become the most popular man in Britain?

'I thought I'd find you here.'

'Mara!'

Andreas gave up on the Nautilus machine and flopped back onto the exercise bench. He was sure all this working out in the House of Commons gym was going to succeed where the Master had failed and kill him off, but that was the trouble with taking over somebody else's body – you had to act the part. Nick Weatherall enjoyed punishing workouts three times a week. Andreas Hunt did not.

Mara perched herself on the edge of the exercise bench, bent over him and licked the sweat from his face.

'How's Mr Atlas today then?'

'Piss off.' Andreas reached up a weary hand to cup one of Mara's soft, round breasts and felt suddenly rejuvenated. God but she looked good in a leotard.

'Not very popular this place, is it?' observed Mara, running questing fingers down Andreas's belly and under the waistband of his shorts. It was an understatement: the gym complex was like the Marie Celeste.

'That's because all the other MPs have got a grain of

sense,' grunted Andreas, flexing a thigh and wishing he hadn't. 'There won't be another soul in this damn place till the Sports Minister turns up at five o'clock. They'll all be up in the dining room with their noses in a bucket of claret. Lucky sods.'

'Not enjoying your fitness programme then?'

'Let's just say I'm glad Nick Weatherall isn't into running marathons.' He paused. 'He isn't, is he?'

Mara laughed.

'Relax. The only marathons he ever went in for were all-night sessions between the sheets.' Her fingers brushed the tip of Andreas's swelling penis and he shivered with pleasure.

'Hmm. Maybe Weatherall *is* my kind of guy after all.'

To Andreas's disappointment, Mara left off exploring the inside of his shorts and got up from the exercise bench. He sat up and towelled the sweat from his torso as he watched her climb onto one of the exercise bikes. That was an erotic experience in itself, watching those long, long legs stretch and part as she mounted the saddle. And when she started pedalling, the way her breasts sort of jiggled inside the leotard, inadequately fettered by the stretchy green material . . . well, it was just too much to bear.

'You're a prick-tease,' he observed, easing down the front of his shorts. 'Just look what you've done to me!'

Mara said nothing but pedalled a little faster, so that her breasts jumped and wobbled inside their Lycra prison.

'You know what you deserve, don't you?'

'What's that?'

'A thorough fucking.'

She smiled.

'Oh yeah?'

'Oh yeah.'

Mara moved down into a lower gear so that she had to push harder to make the pedals go round and leant over the handlebars so that her breasts hung down. Andreas was treated to a wonderful view of the cleavage revealed by her low-cut neckline. As Andreas watched he saw that she was grinding her pubis against the apex of the saddle, exciting herself, dampening the gusset of her leotard.

'You'd better come and get me then.'

Andreas needed no second bidding. Suddenly he didn't feel the least bit tired any more. He pulled her off the exercise bike and she made no attempt to resist him, sliding seductively into his embrace as she had done so many times before. How was it that, no matter how many times they fucked, Mara could never get enough of Andreas Hunt?

'There are other ways of getting exercise, you know,' murmured Andreas, nuzzling into Mara's neck and nibbling at the sweat-seasoned flesh. It tasted salty-sweet and he wanted more. A lot more. 'Like taking all your clothes off and having your wicked way with me.'

'Now, would I take advantage of a helpless, sex-crazed MP?' demanded Mara.

'I hope so.'

He growled with pleasure as her butterfly-gentle fingers slid down his shorts, exposing the knotty root of his penis, the sap-filled stem that longed to blossom at her touch.

In sweet retaliation, he slid his fingers down Mara's belly and between her thighs. The gusset of her leotard was wet through and as he rubbed hard he felt an inundation of warm love-juice soaking through the fabric. She obliged by spreading her thighs wider for him and he succeeded in slipping a finger under the edge of the leotard.

Her labia were swollen and slippery, the long tunnel of her sex already gaping wide, inviting him to penetrate her. She gasped.

'Oh, Andreas. Andreas, I want you.'

Pushing aside the gusset and bunching up his fingers, he pushed them into her and she helped him by grinding down on his hand, almost sucking him up inside her.

'Oh yes, yes, do it to me! Yes . . .'

With his fingers buried in her cunt, he flicked his thumb

over the hard nubbin of her clitoris and she writhed and gripped his prick, her fingers jerking him up and down with a seductive violence that drove him into a frenzy of need.

Eyes closed, Mara felt the power that joined them, the empathy that had brought them together and given them the strength to go on, even when the Master's strength seemed unassailable. The energies of their joining crackled and fizzed through their bodies like electricity, and Mara began moaning softly as Andreas frigged her.

'Please, please, oh yes.'

'I love it when you're wet for me,' murmured Andreas, excited beyond belief by the feel of Mara's abundant juices dripping down over his fingers, their strong, musky scent filling his head and making him dizzy with desire for her. And he was wet for her too, the tip of his poor lonely dick glistening with a sheen of slippery juice.

'Want you, want you,' moaned Mara, her hips moving rhythmically back and forth as she wanked herself on Andreas's fingers.

He pushed his hand a little further into her and stretched and teased the elastic walls of her vagina. She gave a little sob as his fingertips found the spongy, hypersensitive g-spot and sent great shivers of pleasure running through her body, shaking her like a rag doll. He pressed harder and she all but collapsed in his arms, her cunt opening and closing about his fingers like the mouth of some greedy sea-creature.

'I'm coming Andreas. I'm going to . . .'

She never finished the sentence, for at that moment she reached the summit of her pleasure and her sex muscles clenched in ecstasy. A great rush of honeydew gushed out of her, a river of sweet nectar which Andreas would have loved to lap from its source.

But his cock was at bursting point and he could wait no longer. Picking her up in his arms he carried her across to the exercise bench and laid her down. Lying on her back, with her thighs spread wide and her feet on the floor on either side of the narrow bench, Mara made the perfect temptress. The gusset of her leotard was hardly more than a bedraggled string, forced to one side exposing the plump pink bounty of her auburn-fringed cunt-lips.

'Come to me, Andreas. Put your cock in me! Make me come again!'

He put his right hand to his face and breathed in deeply. Mara's fragrance was sweet, exotic, irresistible. He ran his fingers along her deep furrow and a trickle of juice escaped her parted lips, leaving a small wet stain on the leather-covered bench.

She thrust up her hips to meet his invading cock and he entered her with a shuddering sigh of the deepest satisfaction. He would have liked just to lie there for a few moments, savouring the feel of flesh on flesh, the coolness of her as she wrapped herself around his burning cock. But instinct was too strong and, as she placed her hands on his hips, he began to thrust.

At first he moved in and out of her gently and smoothly. But the pleasure urged him on, the burning in his cock making him want her with such violence that he began fucking her with increasing abandon.

'Fuck me, Andreas. Fuck me harder,' she urged and he obeyed her with a wild pleasure which made him want to laugh out loud for the sheer joy of being able to fuck. He had been too long a prisoner in the crystal not to rejoice in the freedom of this borrowed body.

The orgasm began slowly, as a languid warmth deep in his belly, then spread through his whole body like a warm and shimmering liquid, molten gold and silver mingling, dazzling him, soothing and exciting. Suddenly he felt Mara come, her cunt tightening in that most intimate of kisses, and the sensation was so delicious that he climaxed with her, his semen spurting into her with a force that left him drained yet unbelievably exhilarated.

He kissed her as they lay together, their sensual energies

mingling like precious metals, strengthening the bond between them. And the magical bracelet on Andreas's wrist glittered as the dragon's crystal eye caught the sun, defying the Master's evil power.

That afternoon, in the House, Andreas surprised himself with his own brilliance. Not that he hadn't always known he was brilliant (despite his Editor's repeated attempts to sack him) but politics had never really been his forte – added to which, Nick Weatherall did have a tendency to spout unintelligible fascist rubbish.

The Master looked on from the Opposition front bench, mildly impressed by Weatherall's latest *tour de force*. Initiation had certainly changed Weatherall for the better, he concluded – and he was running rings round the Minister for Transport. An idea was forming itself in his head.

He turned to the Shadow Heritage Secretary, by his side.

'Cheviot.'

'Master?'

'Send Weatherall to my office after the division.'

'Yes, Master.'

'And make sure he brings the Dubois slut with him. I have something important for them to do.'

Annabel Manley gazed out of the Master's office window into the royal-blue dusk of a London evening. No casual passer-by would have guessed that her tight skirt was up round her waist and she was enjoying the erotic attentions of the Master's press officer – but then the Master trained all his minions to be discreet.

The Master looked on with approval as his press officer, kneeling on the floor behind Annabel, pulled apart the young woman's firm white buttocks and thrust the point of his tongue into her arsehole. Annabel gave no sign of emotion, save the smallest sigh of pleasure at this welcome

49

invasion, and this pleased the Master. If the Manley slut continued to behave with such control and obedience, he would consider rewarding her by piercing her clitoris – a mark of favour accorded only to his favourite whores. She was sure to enjoy the pain almost as much as he would.

He took hold of his Indian servant's turbanned head and pushed it harder onto his turgid prick. He was glad he'd brought Sanjay back with him from New Delhi – the young initiate's Tantric skills gave unrivalled stimulation and a welcome respite from the cares of high office. Perhaps he ought to introduce Sanjay to Harry Baptiste . . .

A knock on the door interrupted his sexual reverie.

'Who is it?'

'Weatherall.'

The Master nodded to Cheviot, who unlocked the door.

'Enter.'

Andreas and Mara passed into the Master's office and Cheviot locked the door behind them. No matter how often he walked into the middle of one of the Master's sexual 'entertainments', it was always a struggle for Andreas not to react. The sight of that Manley girl's creamy-white buttocks, dimpled and trembling as the press officer pressed his face between them, set the blood pumping twice as fast and twice as hard round Andreas's over-stressed veins. Suddenly very hot, he eased his shirt collar away from his constricted neck with a fingertip.

'You summoned us, Master?'

The Master ejaculated, cleanly and efficiently, into Sanjay's mouth, watched him swallow the last drop, then pushed the Indian servant away. His dick was still marble-hard and he stroked it reflectively with his right hand. He cast Mara a long, searching gaze which made her tremble with apprehension.

'How many cocks have you sucked today, slut?'

'Three, Master,' replied Mara.

'Insufficient. You will suck mine.'

Andreas fairly boiled with indignation to see Mara – *his* Mara – forced to kneel at the Master's feet and take his cock into her mouth. But there was nothing he could do about it – not until he and Mara found some way of destroying the Master and all he stood for. He watched, transfixed, half furious and half turned-on by the sight of Mara's ruby lips closing around the Master's swollen shaft.

Enjoying the caresses of Mara's skilful fingers and tongue, the Master relaxed a little. It was an agreeable tableau: Annabel Manley and the press officer putting on a little show for him whilst the Dubois slut sucked the pleasure from his dick.

'I have a job for you to do,' the Master announced.

'Another job for me?' repeated Andreas stupidly. He wasn't at all sure what to make of this new development – he was only just getting used to not being Andreas Hunt.

'For you and the Dubois slut.' The Master let out a small grunt of enjoyment as Mara twisted her long and flexible tongue around his shaft. Yes, if anyone could succeed in this it was the resourceful Anastasia Dubois. He snapped his fingers and Cheviot approached.

'Master?'

'Bring me the book.'

Cheviot returned a moment later with a heavy, ancient book, each leaf a thick sheet of yellowed vellum. He placed the book on the Master's desk.

'Open it.'

Cheviot obeyed, opening the book at a page of illuminated script, headed by a curious hand-painted illustration.

'Look at that picture, Weatherall. Look at it very carefully. You and the slut are going to find that object for me.'

Andreas crossed the room and looked down at the page. The illustration meant nothing to him. It was just an old picture like any other old picture, all wobbly lines and no sense of perspective.

'What is it, Master?'

The Master let out a sigh of impatience. Perhaps Weatherall had not changed that much, after all.

'It is an eye, Weatherall.'

'Yes, Master, but . . .'

'It is the Eye of Baloch.'

Mara prayed that the Master did not sense the frisson of fear run through her as he spoke those words. The Eye of Baloch! As a white witch she had heard of it, though she had never seen it – no-one had, not for years, centuries even, for it seemed to have disappeared off the face of the earth. But Mara had heard of its power and she feared and respected it for its great magical purity.

'The Eye of Baloch, Weatherall, is an ancient object of great magical power. With it, I shall have the power to see through all deceptions, uncover all mysteries, read every secret of the universe. No-one and nothing will be able to oppose me undetected.'

Oh shit, thought Andreas. That's all we need.

'And you,' continued the Master, 'you and the slut are going to track it down and bring it back to me. *Aren't you?*' His eyes seemed to penetrate Andreas's like laser-beams, as though the Master had already guessed that Nick Weatherall was not all he seemed and was just torturing him for his own amusement.

'I . . . er, yes, Master,' replied Andreas. And he wondered how he was going to wriggle out of this one.

Later that night, alone in the darkness of his Westminster office, the Master stood by the open window, staring up at the moonless sky. Its darkness seemed to mock him, defying all his attempts to elevate his spirit to the astral plane.

Someone or something, something powerful, was challenging him to try his strength. He had tried, many times, to probe and explore it with his psyche but each time it had resisted him with disturbing ease, its black intensity like a thick, impenetrable blanket of evil he both despised and admired.

He must have the Eye of Baloch. With it, the power of all sight would be his. Success and power would be assured.

So why did he feel the first stirrings of fear? Why, whenever he closed his eyes, could he hear the distant echoes of mocking laughter?

4: The Way

'MONSTER 4-INCH MOSQUITOS DRAIN TOURIST DRY'

(*Buenos Aires Herald*, 2 June)

The Range-Rover headed on through the sleeping city, Andreas peering out of the side window into the eerie, shifting shadows of a London night.

'Weird,' he observed.

Mara took her eyes off the road for a moment and glanced at the multicoloured panorama of the night sky. Andreas was right. It shouldn't look like that, daubed with splashes of red and purple and yellow.

'Perhaps there'll be another storm,' she suggested. But it didn't take a psychic sixth sense to know there was more to it than that. The whole city looked ghostly and unreal, the jagged shapes of the buildings painted on to the apocalyptic sky. Tension was building up in the heavy air, every hypersensitive nerve in her body jangling for release.

'Something bad's going to happen.'

'Not if we can help it,' replied Mara with grim resolution. They moved on through the night, past garishly lit shops and neon signs that stabbed the eyes with an unnatural brilliance. As they drove on into the suburbs, the roads became gradually busier, a silent convoy of cars and vans moving along together as though they shared some common purpose. And each and every one of them heading west.

'That bastard's really dropped us in it this time.' Andreas

55

wriggled uncomfortably in his seat. He was hot, irritable and worried. Who wouldn't be? 'It's a real Catch-22. If we don't find this Eye of Baloch thing he'll know we're up to something and if we do . . .' He drew his finger across his throat in a graphic illustration.

'If we do, we'll just have to make sure the Master doesn't get his hands on it. Maybe we can find some way of using its power against him. But the first thing we have to do is get there.'

'Get where? You still haven't told me where we're going.'

'Stonehenge.'

'*Stonehenge?*'

'Stonehenge is where most of the really important ley-lines meet. Certain powerful Celtic objects have a distorting effect on the energy fields produced by those ley-lines, and the Eye of Baloch is a *very* powerful Celtic object. When we get there we'll need to perform a finding ritual.'

'Will it work?'

'I wish I knew.'

Andreas squinted up at the moon, its single bloodshot eye peering insolently back at him from behind a bank of reddish-orange clouds. Its light filtered down on the slow-moving column of traffic, still flowing west with a steady determination.

'Ever had the feeling you're being followed? Looks like every nut in the land is going to Stonehenge.'

He leaned back in his seat and rubbed his neck, trying to break the cycle of tension. The muscles in his neck and shoulders were rock-hard and knotted like lengths of steel cable.

'There's a lot of work ahead of us. You really should try to relax.' Mara slid her hand onto Andreas's knee and teased the flesh of his inner thigh through his thin summer trousers.

Andreas groaned in mock agony as his entire body tensed in glorious expectancy.

'You really think that makes me feel *relaxed*?'

Mara let her fingers walk a little higher up his thigh, so that her fingertips were a hair's-breath away from the plump roundness of his testicles. Instinctively Andreas held his breath, waiting and longing for the intensity of that first touch.

'No, but maybe this will help take your mind off things.'

Eyes on the road, right hand on the wheel, Mara felt for the tag of Andreas's zipper. He didn't put up much of a fight, in fact he helped things along by unzipping his flies. Her fingers slid inside his pants with an angel's softness and a devil's skill, finding the swelling baton of his penis and stroking it through his boxer shorts, already damp with the secretions of his eager desire.

His aching neck and shoulders forgotten, Andreas sank back into the passenger seat and entered a world of pure sensation. Did it help? You bet it did.

She threaded her fingers through the front vent of his shorts and took out his prick – more accurately it sprang into her hand. Why play hard to get? Mara knew a thousand different ways to give pleasure and he wanted to experience every one of them a thousand times – and then begin again.

Mara's thumb flicked over his glans with practised skill, spreading the lubricating fluid evenly over the swollen purple head, producing the most exquisite sensations. His shaft she held quite loosely between her fingers, sliding it up and down just firmly enough to drive him wild but not so hard or so fast that she risked bringing him to a premature climax.

Andreas's mouth was dry with excitement, his heart racing. A van slid smoothly past them, running level with them for a few seconds before overtaking. Its two occupants were wide-eyed with interest at the scene in the Range-Rover, but Andreas didn't give a damn. He reached out and touched Mara's thigh and she shivered at his touch, inviting more daring caresses.

The skirt of her dress was filmy and thin and she was

wearing no petticoat. It was a delicious torment to see her bronzed thighs beneath the veiling fabric, the tiny white scrap of the panties she so hated to wear. Quickly he ruched up her skirt, baring inch after inch of bare, smooth thigh. How he longed to run his tongue over that golden flesh, tasting it with a gourmet's delight, inching his way towards the epicentre of her pleasure.

Her touch on him was irresistible in its power.

'Pull over,' he gasped. 'I want you.'

She laughed.

'What do you want to do that we can't do here?'

Taking her left hand from Andreas's cock, she pulled up her skirt so that it was draped across the tops of her thighs, exposing the white lace triangle that just – but only just – covered her auburn curls.

His breath was coming with difficulty, it was so hard to control the excitement pulsing and flooding through him.

'You . . . want me to . . .'

'I want you to frig me, Andreas. Right here, right now.' As if in illustration, she gave her pubis a little rub through the lace panties, and Andreas caught a hint of her delicious smell.

She began masturbating him again, sliding his foreskin across his glans so beautifully that she kept him almost on the very brink of orgasm. It was exhausting yet exhilarating. Andreas reached out and placed his hand on Mara's thigh. The vibrations from the Range-Rover's engine were making her firm, tanned flesh tremble and when he touched it the answering vibrations of her excitement communicated themselves to his own body.

'Oh yes, touch me, Andreas.'

Eyes fixed on the road, Mara kept driving, pointing the Range-Rover's nose west towards Salisbury Plain. But her left hand was stroking Andreas's penis, and her thighs were parting, urging him to give her as much pleasure as she was giving him.

He slipped his index finger under the elastic of Mara's

panties and into the silky pleasure-garden of her maidenhair. She wriggled her arse appreciatively and a damp stain of cunt-juice spread over the gusset of her panties, making the lacy material almost translucent. Could he manage to get her panties off without sending the car careering off the road? He hadn't forgotten the time when that vampire slut Katja had landed him in hospital, trying to seduce him in the front seat of his car and causing an almighty pile-up.

But this was different. This was Mara. He tugged at the panties and Mara obligingly lifted her backside clear of the leather seat. The Range-Rover swerved for just a second then Mara was in control again – and the white lace panties were round her ankles. She reached down, kicked them off and put them on the dashboard. Andreas picked them up, pressed them to his face and breathed in deeply. He only had to breathe in the smallest hint of Mara's scent and it always gave him the most phenomenal hard-on. The crisp handful of damp lace almost made him ejaculate on the spot.

He scrunched the panties up in his hand and a wicked smile spread across his face.

'You wouldn't,' said Mara, casting him a sidelong glance.

'Oh yes I would.' Andreas wound down the window, held the panties in the slipstream for a moment then let go of them. They landed some distance away, on the bonnet of a Ford Cortina.

Mara retaliated by squeezing his prick very hard, at once making him want to spurt all over her hand and making it impossible for him to do so.

'Swine,' she said with a grin. But she spread her legs wider to let him in.

It wasn't until he started wanking her that Andreas realised just how aroused Mara was. Her cunt was like a warm river, the slippery ooze of her juices running all over his fingers.

As soon as he parted her cunt lips they released a tide of honeydew which inundated his hand and dampened both

Mara's thighs and the expensive leather upholstery under her backside. She was wearing a clitty-ring today – the gold ring set with a many-faceted crystal whose heaviness distended the stalk of her clitoris and intensified her sexual pleasure to a point which few would have been able to bear. He felt for the ring and twisted it gently, listening for the change in her breathing which would tell him that his caresses pleased her.

She took her breaths in quick, hoarse gasps, and her words were framed with the greatest difficulty. It was taking all her concentration to keep the car on the road and not to be overwhelmed by the great neap-tide of sensations Andreas had stirred up in her belly.

'Andreas. Yes. Yes. More . . .'

Not for the first time, Andreas wished he had several cocks and an extra pair of hands. In the wild, telepathic dreams which he and Mara sometimes shared, he often imagined that he could fuck her in cunt and arse and mouth all at once, and yet still slide his cock between her ample breasts whilst fingering her clitty and the juicy betel-nuts of her nipples.

But reality was even better than he had remembered it. That was the way with Mara – sex with her was always better than you had imagined it would be, because each time she found something new, some secret spice to drive you crazy and make you want to keep on screwing her until the end of time.

He contented himself with rubbing Mara's pierced clitty, manipulating it so that the golden ring was always under his fingertip, using it to give her greater and greater sensation as the little fleshy hood of her clitoris was pushed back and forth.

Lost deep in the exhilaration of their shared pleasure, Mara slid her fingers down Andreas's shaft; squeezing and stroking him as, with each downward stroke, she pressed down on the sap-filled sacs of his testicles. She felt the powerful energies of their passion, strengthening them for what lay ahead, and yearned for the moment to last forever. If only they could escape together to a world where only their desire existed and the Master was nothing but a half-forgotten nightmare.

Orgasm came soon, too soon, like a great white light that arched between them, joining mind and body and spirit. Andreas felt the pleasure crashing in on him a split-second before Mara: his balls tingling, aching, tensing, shooting a great cascade of semen that bubbled and spurted over Mara's long, slender fingers. And his own fingers were wet with pleasure – the slippery-smooth pleasure that oozed and dripped from Mara's womanhood as her sex muscles contracted in the first of many long, exhilarating spasms.

Andreas lay, panting, in the front passenger seat, his cock still semi-erect and his heart pounding like a steam-hammer. Slowly he felt a familiar delicious drowsiness stealing over him. At last he began to let go and relax.

Eyes half-closed, he listened to the regular drone of the engine as the Range-Rover sped on towards Wiltshire.

'Stonehenge?' he repeated drowsily, almost wondering if he'd got himself caught in some bizarre dream.

'Stonehenge.'

'Another magic ritual?'

''Fraid so.'

'I can take it,' said Andreas and promptly fell asleep.

'My dear Ethilda, may I introduce you to the Prime Minister?'

The Rt Hon Harry Laurent Baptiste QC MP extended an elegant hand to Mrs Ethilda Wright-Fawley, President of the North Anglia Disaster Relief Fund.

'I am so pleased to meet you, Mrs Wright-Fawley,' he beamed. His voice was as smooth as cream liqueur.

Madame President blushed prettily. At thirty-six she was still a damned fine-looking woman and she cherished secret hopes of making a deep impression on Harry Baptiste.

Every Prime Minister needed a mistress.

'Please, Prime Minister, call me Ethilda.'

'Then you must call me Harry,' he replied with the same disarming friendliness which had half the female population of Britain – and not a small percentage of the men – wetting their pants for him. 'Everyone does, you know.'

Harry Baptiste was flying the flag at a fund-raising dinner for victims of the freak fires which had caused such dreadful devastation in the North Anglian region over the last few months. No-one was quite sure what was causing them. The Fire Service said it might be electrical, the electricity people said it was the freak storms, and you couldn't get any sense at all out of the Met Office. A man in Leighton Buzzard said it was the Second Coming but then he swore he had Martians living in his garden shed.

Baptiste moved round the invited guests with tireless ease, never forgetting a name, always making people feel special. That was how he'd transformed the Republican government from an electoral disaster-in-waiting to The People's Choice. Nothing, it seemed, could prevent him from leading the Republican government into the next millennium – not even the charismatic Anthony LeMaitre.

Tonight, of all nights, Sonja Kerensky and Joanna Konigsberg were dressed to kill.

Sonja's tousled blonde hair tumbled over bare shoulders, the crystal-studded collar about her neck setting off the hungry glint in her baby-blue eyes. Her lips pouted scarlet, wet and glossy from the constant flicking of her moist tongue-tip, and her juicy breasts bobbed like rosy apples, her nipples scarcely covered by the low-cut bodice of her black leather camisole, laced tight to the waist. Her evening attire was finished off with a pair of elbow length leather gloves, knee boots and a matching skirt slashed to the thigh, revealing a crimson garter.

Joanna was the perfect ice-maiden to Sonja's vamp. Her smooth, white-blonde hair hung in a single loose braid that swished lazily across her bare back, like a cat's tail. Her dress was an ice-green satin sheath, boned in the bodice so that her small, ivory-white breasts were sculpted into a perfect, marble-cool cleavage. The sheath-dress was ankle-length and clung to her slender, lithe body, with a fish-tail skirt and a slit at the front that bared her long, slim thighs when she walked.

They did not speak, but watched and waited. There was no need to rush things – after all, no-one could see them.

No-one but Harry Baptiste.

Baptiste moved among the diners, shaking hands, obtaining promises of money, votes, patronage. He was doing himself nothing but good. Joanna let out a little low hiss of anger, revealing a double row of perfect, diamond-sharp teeth. But Sonja laughed, secure in the power of her own immortal charms.

'Come, sister. The Master has work for us to do.'

Baptiste was dancing now, waltzing adeptly across the dance floor with the rather heavily built general manager of the local leisure centre. Sonja and Joanna moved quickly and lightly towards them, their insubstantial forms slipping as easily and imperceptibly as a summer breeze between the closely packed dancers.

'Harry.'

'Harry, *darling*.'

Sonja put up her scarlet-taloned fingers and ran them over Baptiste's face. She knew he could see her, feel her too, but he never moved a muscle – not even when she scratched her nails down the side of his smoothly shaven cheek.

Standing behind him, Joanna smoothed her hands over his black, wavy hair, wound a lock of it around her finger, nuzzled her face into the nape of his neck, kissing and nibbling. Surely no man could resist such seductive power. But Harry Baptiste could. He just went on dancing as though nothing at all was happening.

'You dance divinely, Mr Baptiste,' commented the

leisure-centre manager as the dance ended. 'It's such a tremendous honour to have you here as our guest . . .'

Baptiste led her back to her seat and kissed her hand.

'Believe me, madam, the honour is all mine.'

'You will stay on to draw the raffle?'

'But of course. I am entirely at your service.'

He left her with a glittering smile, casually readjusting his bow-tie as he strolled off towards the bar. Furious at Baptiste's rejection, the vampire sluts withdrew to the shadows, watching and waiting, planning their next move.

'Can he not see us?' demanded Sonja.

'He sees us.' Joanna's face was white with anger. No man resisted her. *No man.*

'Then perhaps he does not desire us.'

Joanna turned on her sister vamp with a cool fury.

'Little fool. He will desire *me.*'

With a click of her long white fingers, she banished the ice-green dress, the white gloves, the trappings of the cool ice-maiden. Now she was naked and unfettered, an ivory-skinned fury spitting cold fire. Her long hair floated free in a silver-white swirl, now concealing now revealing the beauties of her perfect body as she stalked her prey.

Baptiste was standing alone at the bar, taking sips from a glass of non-alcoholic fruit punch as he ostensibly watched the dancers. Joanna knew he was really watching her. She would make him notice her, make him bow to her will. And then, at last, she would be the Master's most favoured whore – not Liz Exley, not Queen Sedet, not Anastasia Dubois and certainly not Sonja Kerensky. Herself. Joanna Königsberg.

'Darling.'

Once again, Baptiste did not react. Joanna flicked her long curtain of hair over her shoulder, displaying her round white breasts more alluringly for his delectation. The nipples were as succulent and pink as little mounds of strawberry ice-cream.

'Darling, I *know* you want me.'

Baptiste lifted his glass to his lips and took a long, slow draught of fruit punch, as though drinking a toast to her. Furious, Joanna raised her arm and tried to dash the glass from his hand, but to her astonishment he anticipated and parried the blow, staring right through her. A half-smile played about his lips.

Refusing to be deterred, Joanna ran her hands over her own body, showing him the delights of her flesh, the pleasures that could be his if only he would abandon himself to her.

'Don't deny yourself,' she whispered, pressing herself close against him, thrusting her thigh between his, grinding her pelvis against the root of his prick.

But Baptiste turned away, summoning the barman with a snap of his fingers.

'Excellent punch, Grahame,' he said, pushing his glass across the bar.

'Thank you, sir.'

'Top her up, will you?'

And as Baptiste raised the brimming glass to his lips and drank deeply, his smile never wavered, even for an instant.

Queen Sedet, Mistress of Winterbourne, was tired of being left to her own devices.

It was about time the Master sat up and took notice of her again. It was too bad, going off and leaving her for days on end. She was bored and resentful. Bored, bored, bored.

But this little game was providing an interesting diversion. At the foot of Winterbourne's great staircase, Sedet paused and sniffed the scented air. Heimdal was at her side in an instant.

'Mistress?'

Sedet ran her fingers down Heimdal's muscular body. She liked to see him like this, naked to the waist with nothing but that ridiculously tiny leather apron to veil his impressive manhood. She could trace its outline through the thin leather, a dozing python waiting only for her touch to spring once again into vibrant life. Heimdal made such an attentive and obedient servant. And better than that: with his well-developed psychic abilities, Heimdal understood her needs perfectly.

Sedet flared her aristocratic nostrils.

'The Master's trail is very strong here. I can sense the excitement in his sexual energy. We shall follow the trail and see where it leads.'

'As you wish, Mistress.'

Heimdal, too, was enjoying himself. He wasn't the naturally subservient type – quite the reverse – but he knew exactly how to please his mistress, and they understood each other well. Besides, he was prepared to do just about anything if it got him what he wanted: more power.

He followed Sedet along the corridor which divided the ground-floor of the great house. Whatever faults Delgado might have had (and Heimdal was profoundly glad that Winterbourne's former whoremaster was dead), the man had certainly known all there was to know about the design of a first-rate bordello.

The corridor was lined with identical brown doors, each bearing an inscribed name-plate: Wild West, Queen of Nile, Orient Express, Imperial Russia, Outer Space . . . the list seemed endless. Potentially it was endless, because whenever a need was identified Winterbourne adapted to meet it. If a potential initiate displayed a sexual preference for deep-sea divers or traffic wardens, Winterbourne would provide them.

They walked down the corridor, Heimdal keeping a small but respectful distance behind his queen. At this stage, it would not do to appear too familiar. At the corner, Sedet paused, her whole body rigid with attentiveness and excitement.

'This way. Can you not feel it? The Master's energy is all around us . . .'

Without waiting for an answer, Sedet pushed through the door and began climbing the private staircase which

led up to the great library. Heimdal strode behind, admiring
the sinuous curves of the body that had once been Mara
Fleming's. Sedet's spirit did it far more justice, of course:
hers was a noble spirit, whereas Mara had never been
anything but an opportunistic slut who had dared suggest
that her psychic powers were greater than those of Lord
Heimdal. Mara, Hunt, Delgado: Heimdal's life was infinitely
better without the lot of them.

At the top of the stairs Sedet turned right and walked
toward the library door.

'Yes. In here.'

They entered, Sedet sweeping into the room like an
empress. She knew exactly what effect her every movement
had on Heimdal. She could feel the waves of sexual need
pulsing out of him with every step she took, every breath
she drew into her lungs, and his adoration was like meat
and drink to her.

The trail was not an easy one to follow. The book was
just one in a million ancient volumes, lining the walls of the
splendid, high-ceilinged chamber, but the Master's energies
were strong and led Sedet to her quarry.

She raised her right hand and summoned the book to
her. High on the topmost shelf of the bookcase, the heavy
leather-bound volume stirred and shook, then slid smoothly
out of position and floated down, landing gently on the
Master's library-table.

'Get on your hands and knees.'

'Mistress?'

Sedet loved to play the strict mistress with her new toy.

'Hands and knees. Quickly now – or have you ceased to
fear my displeasure?'

'No, Mistress. Forgive me.'

Heimdal crouched on hands and knees on the polished
parquet of the library floor. This game of mistress and
servant was still new enough to hold a certain novelty-
value for him. He was unaccustomed to humiliation,
generally preferring to inflict it rather than be on the

receiving end. But Mistress Sedet had a voice of velvet cruelty and he felt his massive cock twitching into aching life at her command.

Sedet snapped her fingers and the book hovered above the table, floated a short distance and came to land on Heimdal's glistening bare back. Sedet licked her lips in anticipation of the games they would play together, she and her devoted slave. She pointed at the book.

'Open.'

At her command, the vellum leaves fanned as though blown by a powerful wind; finally falling open at a picture. The curious picture of an eye.

Now that *was* interesting.

'Yes, yes, that has possibilities,' she murmured.

'Mistress?'

'Be silent,' snapped Sedet. But already her body was readying itself for a delicious invasion by Heimdal's hard, thick cock. How she loved to let her tongue toy with the jade cock-ring, loved to taste his creamy tribute in her mouth. Or would she, as a mark of her special favour, perhaps allow him to explore the delights of her arse with his own long and muscular tongue?

She deciphered the text, appraised the illustration with considerable and growing interest. The Eye of Baloch, well, well. An ultimate, all-seeing power. Now that might be worth acquiring . . .

'Mistress?'

'I did not give you permission to speak.'

'No, Mistress. Please forgive me.'

'Perhaps.' Sedet smiled to herself. 'But only if you please me first.'

'I ask only to serve.'

'Good. That is very good.' Sedet loosed the bronze shoulder-clasps of her robe and it fell to the ground in a whisper of raw silk. She stood in front of Heimdal, her thighs wide and her shaven pubis inviting and fragrant. Seizing hold of Heimdal's face she pressed it against her cunt lips. 'Lick me out, slave, and make sure you do it well.'

'Yes, Mistress,' whispered Heimdal and he wondered how much better life could get.

Engrossed in their passion, neither Heimdal nor the Queen noticed Sedet's golden serpent-bangle awakening to sinuous life. Its garnet-red eyes glowing, it slipped from her arm onto the page of the book, watched them for a moment then slunk silently away into the shadows.

'Sorry mate, nobody comes through here. Oh sorry, Mr Weatherall sir, I didn't recognise you and your lady-friend.'

Andreas adjusted his tie and put on his best mind-who-you're-speaking-to voice.

'Yes, well, officer, if you'd just let us through.'

'I'd love to, Mr Weatherall, sir, only the Chief Constable's given us strict instructions not to let anyone through to the stones until further notice.'

'And why would he do that?' demanded Mara. 'It's not even the summer solstice yet.'

'It's all these civil disturbances we've been having, madam. Every nutter in the country's heading for Stonehenge. If you ask me, sir, the bloody thing's more trouble than it's worth. They ought to bulldoze it into the ground – now that'd be one in the eye for them New Age yobs . . .'

'Nobody asked you for your opinion, constable,' replied Andreas acidly. 'But I'm now asking you to let me through this road block.'

Constable McGraw tipped his helmet back on his head and drew in a long intake of breath.

'Trouble is, sir, I need an official authorisation.'

Andreas could feel his blood pressure reaching dangerous levels. There were the standing stones, not more than a couple of hundred yards away and PC Plod here was pulling rank on him. Back in his days with the Fleet Street rat-pack things would have been easier. He'd have bunged the plod fifty quid to turn a blind eye or simply legged it round the back and sneaked in over the fence. But you had to play things more carefully when you were supposed to be a pillar of the soon-to-be-establishment. He took a deep breath and counted to ten.

'I don't need an official authorisation – I *am* an official authorisation, constable. I am a Member of Parliament – and may I remind you that I sit on the Cross-Parliamentary Police Committee?'

This seemed to produce a perceptible shift in Constable McGraw's attitude.

'Ah well, sir, now if you're here on what we might term official business . . .' He handed back Andreas's driving licence.

'So we can go up to the stones?' Mara leaned forward to talk to Constable McGraw – just far enough forward so that he could see down the front of her dress. As she had anticipated, McGraw's eyes were drawn to her impressive cleavage as though by a powerful magnet. 'Is that right, constable?'

McGraw coughed, surreptitiously readjusted his crotch and scratched his ear.

'I suppose it'll be all right, sir, miss,' he conceded. He wished he could think of a good reason to take the red-haired woman into protective custody.

Reluctantly he waved them on and the Range-Rover slid through the road block and on up the road towards the stone circle.

'It doesn't seem right,' sighed Mara.

'What doesn't?'

'Us being allowed into the circle while all those pagan worshippers can't get within a mile of the stones.'

'It's just as well they can't,' pointed out Andreas. 'Don't want them joining in our ritual, do we?'

They parked the car just beyond the perimeter fence which encircled the standing stones.

'Better leave the headlights switched on,' Andreas observed as he jumped down and almost twisted his ankle.

The perimeter fence had been erected a couple of years previously as a faintly pathetic attempt to deter New Age travellers from setting up camp for a free festival. It was a pig-ugly mess of orange plastic netting that made majestic Stonehenge look for all the world like lumpy shopping in a string bag. Andreas's long legs strode easily over the fence, then he turned round and lifted Mara over it bodily, his hand cradling her bare rump as his head filled with eager, lustful notions.

'How sad,' said Mara, running her fingers over the age-smoothened stones. 'This place was never meant to be alone. There should be people here, to worship, like there were in the old days.'

She pressed her face against the stone and let its coolness flow into her like a fast-moving stream. Not just its coolness, but the long and sinuous river of its memories, trapped within the stone and forever replayed to anyone with the power to understand. She could see and feel and live every second of the stone's history – pain and exhilaration and fear and excitement pulsing into her through her hyper-sensitive fingertips.

Andreas watched her in the gleam from the Land-Rover's headlamps. She was beautiful, his Mara. Something special. The glare from the headlights made her look like a living statue, a marble sculpture of light and shade; her smooth, muscular thighs and rounded breasts eminently kissable beneath her flimsy, filmy dress. She was breathing slowly and deeply, each breath making her breasts rise and fall under the insubstantial fabric.

He wanted her like crazy and in a funny way this unearthly place seemed to intensify the wanting. It was like standing in the middle of a forcefield of pure, undiluted sex. In this circle of light, surrounded by bleak darkness, Nicholas Weatherall and Anastasia Dubois had no place.

Here, only two people existed: Andreas Hunt and Mara Fleming.

Her eyes closed, Mara let her fingers move lightly over the surface of the stone, like a blind girl reading braille.

'I can feel it, Andreas. I can *see* it.'

'The Eye of Baloch?'

'No, not that. The whole history of this place.'

He moved closer, into the circle of light, letting it bathe him and her together, uniting them with its cold kiss. He reached out, burning to touch her, but his fingertips stopped short of brushing against her skin. He dared not break the spell which bound her.

'What can you see, Mara?'

'I can see dancers. Naked dancers, holding hands in a ring. Men and women, stroking each other's bodies. Painted bodies. Stroking, kissing . . .'

This time, he touched her, but very very gently. She let out a tiny yelp, but did not open her eyes. He felt her whole body quiver at his touch and suddenly he too could see it – the circle of dancers, wild-eyed and tangle-haired, their naked bodies glistening with sweat and the rivulets of a daubed, bluish-purple dye.

In his mind's eye he saw their dance grow wilder, the men's cocks growing stiff and menacing and the women's nipples peeping hard and brownish-pink from beneath necklaces made from row upon row of threaded shells.

Andreas was among them in his trance. His hands were exploring the firm, willing body of a red-haired woman with eyes like green fire. And that woman was Mara, drawing his face down to hers to make him kiss her as she sank to the ground, her thighs gaping wide and her scent enveloping him like a perfumed cloud.

'Now, Andreas. Now. Take me now.'

He was aware of her voice, a distant echo in his brain; and her fingers, caressing his body, awakening a deeper and more ravenous hunger within him.

And when he opened his eyes again he saw that the

dancers were gone. Only he and Mara remained, their bodies locked in a passionate embrace.

'Take me now,' repeated Mara, her voice a breathless gasp. He saw that rivulets of sweat were coursing over her bare arms, her throat, running down into the deep valley between her succulent breasts. 'The power is here, within us. We must fuck now before we lose the chance forever . . .'

They sank to the ground, Andreas fumbling with the buttons that ran down the front of Mara's floaty summer dress. There seemed to be dozens and dozens of them; tiny little discs that defied his clumsy fingers as he struggled to bare the golden flesh he hungered to possess. By contrast, Mara's fingers felt butterfly-soft and skilful as they unbuttoned his shirt then unfastened the buckle of his trouser belt.

His cock felt at bursting-point, though as yet she had not even touched him, not there. A warm ooze of wetness was soaking into the front of his boxer-shorts, making the wet silk stick to his overheated flesh, and he was afraid he might come in his pants before she had even exposed his cock to her silky caresses.

Mara's buttons were yielding more easily now, the two sides of her dress peeling apart to bare the soft hillocks of her pink-nippled breasts, leading down to a deep valley and the gently-undulating plain of her firm, golden belly.

He smoothed the flat of his hand over her breasts, enjoying the feel of her hard nipples nuzzling into his palm.

'Yes, yes,' moaned Mara. And her fingers worked at his zip, tugging it down, releasing a little of the agonising pressure on his swollen prick as she pulled down his trousers. Andreas slipped his thumb under the waistband of his boxer shorts and slid them down. His prick sprang free, its tip searching blindly for the ecstatic haven of Mara's tight, wet cunt.

Her fingers curled about his shaft and he cried out, his voice carried away on the soft June air. As she began wanking him, he slipped up her skirt and pressed his leg between her thighs. The wet ooze of her longing moistened his bare flesh as he pushed against her, parting her plump cunt-lips.

The grass was crisp and dry beneath their bodies as they writhed in a passionate embrace, Mara's fingers tight-closed about Andreas's prick and his thigh sliding up and down, pushing hard again Mara's mound of Venus.

At last, when he could bear the torment no longer, Andreas slid his prick from Mara's hand and pressed its tip between her thighs, nudging into the soft, wet pleasure-glade between her auburn pubic curls.

'Yes, yes, aah . . .' Her back arched and she raised her pelvis to take the full thrust of his penis as it entered her. He had meant to fuck her slowly and gently, but the tightness of her beautiful wet cunt drove him wild for her and with each thrust he felt his hunger for her growing wilder and more intense.

Mara's eyes were closed but her lips were moving. Andreas knew that she was speaking the words of an incantation – the ritual of finding that would perhaps show them where the Eye of Baloch could be found.

The thought chilled Andreas's soul for a moment as the craziness of the situation filtered through into his consciousness. Here they were, putting all their energies into searching for the very thing that might prove to be their undoing. It enraged Andreas to feel that he and Mara had so easily fallen victim, once again, to the Master's instinct for the most perfect cruelty.

But the thought left him as quickly as it had come, overtaken by the power of their mutual passion. He ground his pelvis against hers, the root of his penis rubbing hard against the stiff stalk of Mara's clitoris, pushing its fleshy hood back and forth. Mara writhed in an agony of pleasure, the images in her mind swirling and unfocussed as she neared the crescendo of her orgasm.

Sensing that his own crisis was near, Andreas slipped a

finger between Mara's sex lips, teasing the tip of her clitty with a juice-soaked fingertip and skated across its head, glass-smooth and slippery.

The result was almost instantaneous. Andreas felt Mara's pelvis buck and thrust as her hands clawed at him, pulling him more deeply into her, thirsty to drink every drop of his creamy tribute. And the first tremulous caress of her vagina brought the spunk rushing from his balls, gushing up his shaft, flooding the deep well of her sex.

The feelings were so intense that Andreas and Mara lost all track of time and space, aware only of the pleasure that filled their consciousness, making every nerve-fibre within their bodies sing.

To Mara, it was as if extreme pleasure had opened a gateway in her mind, breaking down one of the last remaining barriers and letting the psychic power within her flood out, summoning up images of the past and present and distant future of this sacred place.

And then all was very silent, very still. Opening their eyes, Mara and Andreas looked up at the night sky. Gone was the glare from the Range-Rover's headlights, that had tinged the velvet-black sky yellow, leaching out the power of moon and stars. And as they looked up at the sky they saw the moon and stars themselves swirl and dance, as though sucked out of the sky by some unseen force that suddenly tore them out of the air and sent them tumbling in a glittering shower to earth.

'Mara. Mara, what the hell's happening?'

'Hush.' Mara's calming hand soothed him, smoothing the fear from Andreas's body. 'Wait.'

The glittering rain of stars was at an end, all light stolen from earth and sky so that Mara and Andreas were together in the middle of an impenetrably black void. Andreas swallowed, his throat dry, his limbs suddenly like lead.

'What happened – where are we?'

'Nowhere . . . somewhere. The beginning.'

'You've lost me.'

'Stand up.'

Andreas obeyed awkwardly, cursing the zipper on his pants that refused to do what it was told. It was too bad, getting flung into the black depths of eternity with his pants round his ankles.

He felt for Mara's hand, and their fingers entwined. Almost instantaneously a great surge of power made every muscle in their bodies tense, locking them together in a searing orgasm of fear, at once more horrible and more wonderful than anything Andreas had ever felt before.

'Now,' whispered Mara.

Andreas blinked in the sudden light. The dark silhouettes of the stones had disappeared – in fact every damn thing seemed to have disappeared, except for the light. Light that formed five separate pathways; strips of brilliant whiteness like little rivers of quicksilver, radiating out of the circle in five different directions like the spokes of a wheel, extending as far as the eye could see.

'Pathways,' Mara explained. 'We're being shown the way.'

'But *which* way? Why five pathways?'

Mara was no surer than he was. But one path seemed just a little brighter than the rest.

'That way.'

'Are you sure?'

'No.'

'That's all right then. I wouldn't like to think we knew what we were doing.'

Together, not without fear, Andreas and Mara took their first step into the light.

5: Pendeil

'BOLT OF LIGHTNING TURNS WOMAN INTO MAN'

(*Mombasa Gazette*, 5 June)

'OK, folks, we've arrived. Collect your bags from the driver on your way into the hotel . . .'

The light was so astonishingly bright that it was a long time before Andreas could see anything. He blinked, opened his eyes, closed them again. Behind his lowered eyelids everything glared angry red, like it did when you'd squinted into the sun.

When things finally did resolve themselves into recognisable pictures, they didn't make the slightest bit of sense. For a start, it wasn't night any more, it was broad daylight. And how could he be at Stonehenge one minute and sitting on the back seat of a long-distance motor-coach the next?

He glanced sideways. Mara was sitting next to him, still wearing that selfsame semi-diaphanous dress, modestly doing up the last of the buttons. She whispered:

'Are you OK? You look as white as a sheet.'

'I'm dreaming, Mara.'

Mara shook her head.

'No. Not dreaming. We took the path – don't you remember?'

'I remember all right. I'm just having trouble believing it.'

Andreas surveyed the scene around him. All things considered, it was a good job they'd landed on the back seat of the coach and not smack in the middle, on somebody's lap. The coach was fairly ancient and battered, not what you'd call a luxury vehicle, and the front two-thirds were almost full of what looked like students. Right now, a guy with a goatee beard and a clipboard was chivvying them about as they got off the coach and collected their belongings from the luggage compartment. By some amazing stroke of luck no-one was paying them a blind bit of notice. He peered out of the side window of the coach.

'Where do you suppose we are?'

Mara followed his gaze. The coach had stopped outside an olde-worlde hotel in the middle of a largish village. She couldn't suppress a grin as her eyes travelled over the young, firm, athletic bodies of half a dozen hunky male students. She'd had quite a bit of fun with students in the past, one way or another.

When she'd been a Traveller with Gareth and Kai she'd met hordes of them at festivals – and taught some of them a thing or two, as well. In particular she remembered that time at Glastonbury, when a girl called Lynette had come up to them and offered herself to Jason and Clem. But Mara's twin lovers had had other ideas and the day had ended with Mara screwing not only Lynette, but Lynette's boyfriend Joe and Joe's younger brother, Tom. As Mara recalled, her other lover, Gareth, had been on hand to take a video film of the whole delicious romp. She wondered what had happened to it. But that was in the past, in quite another life. Who could say where destiny might take her and Andreas this time?

'I'm sure we'll find out where we are and why we're here,' she assured Andreas, sliding off her seat. 'Let's go into the hotel and see why all these people are here.'

The material of her summer dress really was very thin, mused Andreas, vaguely turned-on by the prospect of all those hormone-packed young bucks catching glimpses of

Mara's imperfectly veiled body.

They got off the coach and mingled – as far as it was possible for a man in a suit and a woman in a see-through summer dress to mingle – with a crowd of grunge-clad students. Mara felt all eyes on her, not just the eyes of the young men either – the girls were eyeing her up and down too, some clearly jealous, others mentally undressing her, wondering how it might be to go to bed with the gorgeous, big-bosomed beauty.

It was exciting to feel their desire. Since her spirit had made its home in the body of the vampire slut Anastasia Dubois, Mara had found her psychic awareness heightened, and at times she found she could see into the minds of those around her – not just the Master's more empty-headed followers but the living too. She needed their desire to survive, for sexual energy had been Anastasia's sustenance and now it must be hers.

That girl over there – the blonde one with the small breasts and the rosebud mouth. You wouldn't think butter would melt in that mouth but Mara's whole body was tingling with the sexual energies given off by the girl's desire. She had only to concentrate for a moment and she was reading the girl's thoughts, feeling the strength of her need. Virgins like that were always the worst – little fireballs of pent-up sexuality, longing for a chance to explode.

Andreas and Mara followed the straggling crowd into the hotel, an old country inn. Being students, they made straight for the bar – and that was fine by Andreas. Perching himself on a stool he summoned the bartender.

'Chilled white wine for me,' Mara slipped onto the stool next to Andreas. It was all he could do not to put his hand up her skirt again, press his face to her cunt and lick out the warm leavings of their coupling. She made him hotter than a Sahara noon.

'Pint of best.' Andreas pushed a note across the bar. At least his wallet hadn't dematerialised – now that *would* have been inconvenient. Picking up his change, he noticed the map of Wales over the bar. Wales eh? Nice to know it wasn't Katmandu.

Mara listened as she sipped her wine, letting snippets of conversation wash over her.

'Look, Tristan, just because I sleep with you doesn't mean you own me.'

'I never said it did.'

'So you admit it's my right to have other lovers?'

'Y-yeah. Sure.'

'But?'

'But . . . but I just didn't think they'd be women, that's all.'

'So I like to suck pussy. Do you have problem with that? Or is it just that you want to come to bed with us and watch? You men are all the same . . .'

Other voices floated over from the other side of the bar.

'I never wanted to come here in the first place. The only thing that's ever happened to this God-awful hole is that half of it fell into the sea in the fourteenth century. This is a waste of perfectly good revision time if you ask me.'

'Don't be such a pain, Janey. We're going to have fun. And anyhow it'll be good experience, visiting the site.'

'I'm training to be an Egyptologist, Simon, not a bloody deep-sea diver. Underwater villages aren't my scene . . .'

'But Dr Nikephoros is, isn't he?'

'What do you mean?'

'I've seen the way you look at him. Don't come the innocent with me, Janey Simpson. You've been leading him on ever since we went on that field trip to see the *Mary Rose* . . .'

Raised voices now.

'Oh, don't talk bollocks, Simon . . .'

'If it's bollocks, how come you're getting so worked up?'

'You think you're God's gift to women, don't you, Simon Barrymore?'

Mara and Andreas exchanged glances.

'Ah, what it is to be young and over-sexed,' observed

Andreas nostalgically, draining his glass in a single gulp.

'Darling,' smiled Mara. 'You should know.'

'This Dr Nikephoros – do you suppose he's important?'

'Who knows? We'll need to talk to him later.'

'And what do we do now?'

'You go and exercise your charms on the receptionist and see if she can give us a room for the night.' Mara raised a hand to flick her hair back over her shoulder and her right breast jiggled irresistibly. Her eyes twinkled with mischief. 'You know, I'm worn out. I'll just go and freshen up a bit and then afterwards . . . I don't suppose you fancy going to bed?'

Mara pushed open the door of the Ladies and went inside. Astral travel always made her hot and sticky, and she yearned for a long, cool, luxurious shower; for now she'd have to make do with what her granny had always called 'a lick and a promise'.

She walked over to the line of washbasins, directly opposite the four toilet cubicles. A few stifled giggles could be heard coming from one of the locked cubicles but Mara didn't pay much attention. Kids in general – and students in particular – got up to the most bizarre things when they were let off the leash.

She bent over one of the washbasins, filled it with tepid water and splashed her face liberally, dabbing off the excess with a couple of paper towels. As she straightened up, she caught sight of her face in the mirror . . . only it wasn't just *her* image she saw there, it was the reflection of a rather stimulating tableau.

As she stared into the mirror, she heard the bolt slide back and the cubicle door opened, revealing two figures inside. Mara recognised them immediately as two of the girls she'd heard chatting in the bar. One was the dark-haired, dark-eyed Janey Simpson; the other was an innocently sensual powder-puff of a girl, all swan's-down and blonde curls, with long, long legs and skin like porcelain.

81

She must have been nineteen or twenty but she looked all of twelve.

Mara drew in breath sharply, her green eyes widening in surprise as she watched Janey unbutton the blonde girl's blouse very, very deliberately, little by little exposing the rosy buds of her small, juicy breasts.

She found herself looking right into Janey's dark eyes, reflected in the mirror. Janey blew her a kiss, then smiled. It was a smile of the purest, most lascivious pleasure.

'Glad to see you could join us,' said Janey, pulling back the sides of the blonde's blouse to display the pubescent beauty of her breasts.

Mara turned round quite slowly, until she was facing the two girls. She amused herself by reading their thoughts. It wasn't difficult and they weren't very sophisticated. Basically, they were fed up with guys and they just wanted to fuck girls for a while.

'Pleased to meet you I'm sure,' said Mara quite coolly.

She noticed that her dress had slipped down on one shoulder and the two girls were getting a nice view of her ample cleavage, not to mention the dark triangle of her pubic hair, dimly visible through her semi-diaphanous dress. Mara could feel the vibrations of their juvenile lust as strongly as if they were earthquake tremors. It was lucky for them that the Master wasn't here, she thought to herself. He'd be bound to spot that these two would make perfect additions to his stable of vampire whores.

'Want to party?' enquired Janey. As Mara watched, she unfastened the blonde girl's baby-blue satin miniskirt and it fell to the ground with a soft swish, revealing pink lace panties with a matching satin suspender belt and pale, almost white stockings. 'Billie and I do, don't we, Billie?'

Billie's full, candy-pink lips blossomed into a pout of welcome.

'Oh yes,' she breathed. 'Oh *yes*.'

Janey's hands roamed over Billie's breasts and the small pink circles of her nipples swelled into hard, puckered cones of dusky-pink flesh. Mara felt a surge of interest.

'Maybe,' she smiled. And she started undressing, unzipping her filmy frock so that it floated away from her skin, revealing the voluptuous curves beneath the inconsequential fabric. 'But you'll have to persuade me.'

The atmosphere crackled with the electricity of desire as Janey and Billie walked towards her. She felt their hands on her body, their kisses darting lightly all over her bare flesh.

'She's beautiful,' whispered Billie.

'I want her,' said Janey, her fingers toying with the heavy fullness of Mara's breasts. I want her. My cunt's aching . . .'

'I want to lick her out,' murmured Billie, sliding to her knees and planting passionate kisses on Mara's thighs. 'I want to taste her. I want to feel her clit on my tongue.'

'I wish I was a man,' growled Janey, her voice dark and husky with sensual hunger. 'I wish I had a huge, hard dick to fuck her with.'

Mara was experiencing the most curious feeling of liberation, leaning back against the washbasins as Janey and Billie explored the fertile beauty of her body. Why should she take the initiative? Why not just lie back and let them discover for themselves how good it felt to taste a woman's come.

She stroked Billie's blonde head and the round blue eyes flicked up to gaze with a lewd innocence into her own; pleading, silently beseeching, half-afraid to take what she craved.

'If you want to suck my pussy, Billie,' she said, 'Go right ahead.' And parting her legs, she pressed the blonde girl's face to the fragrant triangle between her thighs. She felt Billie tremble with excitement in those first few, hesitant seconds as her tongue-tip darted between Mara's plump labia and discovered the sweet, hot, river of her sex.

'Mmm,' sighed Mara as the warm waves of pleasure washed over her. 'That feels *good*, you're learning fast.

Lick up all my juices, that's a good girl, feel how you're making my clit swell . . .'

From underneath her half-closed eyelids, Mara could see Janey's expression of tormented hunger; the resentful excitement on her face as she watched her sweet, submissive lover drinking down a stranger's pussy-juice. Jealousy was a wonderful thing.

Not that Janey had any need to be jealous. Even as Billie was licking her towards a climax, Mara's mind was devising new lessons in lust; new and ingenious sex-games which all three of them could play . . .

Later that afternoon, Mara and Andreas lay curled up together in bed. Andreas felt quite smug. At first, the landlady had insisted the inn was fully booked, but he'd spun her a line about being on honeymoon and hey presto! she'd come up with this small but cosy attic room, almost filled by its enormous, downy-soft feather bed.

Naked but for her crystal pendant and a silky bathrobe borrowed from the landlady of the inn, Mara slipped out of bed and walked across to the tiny mullioned window. To the right rose a line of greenish-brown hills, to the left, the sparkling expanse of a greenish-blue sea, stretching from the margin of the small, half-forgotten town of Pendeilo to the distant pencil-smudge of the horizon.

'Come back to bed,' murmured Andreas, warm and relaxed after their coupling. He was very pleasantly drunk and had quite forgotten how disgruntled he'd been to discover the sexy secret of why Mara had spent so long in the ladies.

'I will,' promised Mara. She knelt on the window-seat and gazed out at the view, thinking, wondering. In the event it was Andreas who voiced her thoughts.

'So why are we here? In mid-Wales, with a bunch of sex-crazed archaeology students?'

'Because the Eye of Baloch is here. It must be. I just wish I knew where.'

She stared into the middle distance, not really seeing anything, just wondering the same thing over and over again – where could the Eye of Baloch possibly be in a place like Pendeilo?

Mara had never even heard of Pendeilo before – that's how famous it was. According to what she'd been told by Janey and Billie, its only claim to fame was that half of it had fallen into the sea in 1348, taking fifty-two of the inhabitants with it. There were some who said the town had been cursed by a witch, others that the disaster had been God's vengeance for sinful excesses; but the archaeologists preferred to blame unstable cliffs, freak storms and severe tidal erosion.

All of which was interesting enough; but what did it have to do with the Eye of Baloch?

Mara turned to face Andreas, letting go of the silky robe so that it floated down off her shoulders, landing in a little candy-pink cloud around her ankles. Andreas felt suddenly wide awake.

'Fancy a shower?' she suggested, just the hint of a sexy pout in those ruby lips of hers.

Andreas rolled over onto his belly.

'That depends.'

'On what?'

'On whether I get to soap your back.'

Mara laughed and threw him the cake of soap from the wash basin. He caught it one-handed, with an animal growl of approval.

They had been lucky, in the circumstances, very lucky in fact. The Blue Boar was booked solid for a fortnight with students, sharing four to a room. But the landlord and landlady had taken quite a shine to the ultra-respectable MP and his glamorous lady-friend, with the result that they had given up their own bedroom, complete with en-suite bathroom.

Mara turned on the water while Andreas, ever the hedonist, began pouring another glass of chilled wine from the bottle beside the bed. On second thoughts he brought the entire bottle into the bathroom and set it down on the sink.

'You're such a sophisticate,' laughed Mara, and she embraced him, the taste of her own cunt juice still spicy on his lips.

'Piss-artist is the word,' replied Andreas and, picking up the wine bottle, he poured a stream of the cold fluid first into Mara's mouth then into his. Then, on a whim, he raised the bottle and emptied its remaining content over Mara's naked body, drenching shoulders and neck and breasts and belly and curly auburn muff.

'Beast!' squealed Mara, shaking not so much with the sudden chill as with uncontrollable laughter.

'Heck but you're gorgeous,' replied Andreas, perfectly unperturbed, his eager thumbs flicking back and forth over Mara's gloriously hard pink nipples. 'Come here and fuck me.'

'Not until you've licked it all off,' countered Mara. 'Every last drop of it.'

The mere thought of licking chilled white wine from Mara's naked body made Andreas harder for her than he could have believed possible. Her flesh glistened with the tangy-fresh liquid, rivulets of it running down her thighs and calves and dripping onto the tiled bathroom floor. Behind her the water thundered into the shower-cabinet like a foaming, steaming waterfall.

'And what if I miss a drop?'

'I'll make you start all over again.'

She braced her back against the wall. This had the effect of throwing her breasts forward, emphasising their firm, rounded globes and defying Andreas not to find their juicy-hard stalks irresistible.

He parted his lips and stuck out his tongue. Stooping, he began beneath the overhang of her breast, running his tongue-tip up its underside until he reached the nipple and then sucking off the droplets of wine that had collected there. Her own irresistible taste mingled with the tangy sweetness of the wine, making him thirst for more.

As he licked and sucked her delicious flesh, his hand slid down over the smooth, firm curve of her flank, revelling in the orgy of sensations. Playfully he let his fingers wind a slow, wet trail round from her hip to the base of her belly, where her dripping forest of auburn hair invited more intimate caresses. He slipped a finger in among the wine-drenched curls, but Mara caught his hand, preventing him from going further.

He looked up at her in surprise. She gave the sexiest of sulky pouts.

'I said *lick* it off!'

'I was just going to stroke . . .'

'Lick me, Andreas. Please. I want you to caress me with your tongue.'

Never one to refuse a lady, Andreas got down on his knees on the bathroom floor. Behind Mara the shower was still thundering, stray drops of water bouncing off her skin like warm sea-spray. He pressed his face against her cunt. In his fantasy she was a beautiful mermaid and she was going to drown him in the hot gush of her come.

Mara slid her bare feet further apart as Andreas wound her wine-wet curls about his tongue. Mara was right of course. Nothing tasted as good as Mara's wet cunt, and the mingling of her sex juice and the spilt wine had produced a heady cocktail.

He drank deeply, his fingers stroking Mara's inner thighs as she caressed his hair, her own head thrown back and her eyes closed in mute ecstasy. She was rubbing herself against him now, slowly moving her hips back and forth so that Andreas's tongue slid in and out of her like a small, muscular penis. She flooded his mouth, her juices flowing so freely and so fast that he could scarcely swallow them all down. Little trickles escaped his tongue and dripped from his parted lips, running in sticky trails down his chin.

No man had a right to feel this good. The nectar flowing from between Mara's scented love-lips had him drunk with excitement, his head reeling and the blood pumping round his eager veins. His cock was swollen and ached for Mara's touch but he had learnt a little about self-control, at least enough to know that sometimes a tantalising wait could make the ultimate pleasure all the more intoxicating.

He moved his hands from Mara's thighs and slid them over her backside, savouring the ripe firmness of her flesh. Then he seized hold of her buttocks and pulled them apart. He knew how much Mara loved to have her arse teased and stroked. His fingertips ran down through the deep amber furrow that began at the small of her back and ended at the juice-dripping entrance to her cunt. The wetness from her cunt formed the perfect lubricant and, as his well-greased fingertip slid over her puckered hole, he felt it respond, dilating and contracting like the hungry mouth of a sea anemone.

Mara's hands stroked his hair, his face, the back of his neck, pushed his face just a little deeper into the soft wet cleft between her gaping sex lips. She did not speak, but Andreas knew that she was almost there, at the glittering summit of her pleasure.

Gently yet firmly, he tested the resistance of her most secret gateway. It yielded to him as a flower bud yields to the sun, blossoming at his touch. His fingertip disappeared inside her and he felt the moist warmth of her arse engulf him, inviting him deeper inside her. Still sucking and licking her inner labia, Andreas began sliding his index finger in and out of Mara's arsehole. He used small, winding, circular movements that gently stretched the anal flesh and made her give little cries of helpless pleasure.

When her orgasm came, she clasped him very tightly, making him keep his promise to drink down every last, honeysweet drop. In fact, when she bent to kiss him, he was almost reluctant to leave the warm, sweet haven he knew so well. Its spicy taste filled his mouth, the very elixir of sex.

But Mara's fingers were stroking his balls, making his cock strain and throb, and it was all he could do not to come into her hand. She held him firmly, yet with such skilful gentleness that Andreas knew she could hold him on the very edge of ecstasy for as long as either of them wanted.

'Come here and let me fuck you, you shameless little hussy.'

'Come and get me.'

Mara let go of his cock and stepped under the shower, turning the water up hot and high so that it steamed and splashed about her bare golden flesh. She threw back her head and let the water cascade over her hair and face, trickling and bouncing over her shoulders, breasts and belly.

Picking up the bar of soap, Andreas stepped into the shower cabinet beside her. It was quite a tight squeeze – obviously the landlord and his wife didn't go in for bathtime frolics.

Laughing, Mara wriggled and squirmed under the thundering water as Andreas ran the bar of soap over her erect nipples, then smoothed it round and round in a widening spiral. Creamy lather dripped from her nipples, coursed down her flanks like warm, wet spunk and collected in the auburn forest of her pubic hair.

Andreas slid the soap bar between Mara's legs and she sighed with pleasure, so wet that the soap slipped right up inside her, emerging fragrant and slippery with her own cunt juice.

Their laughter turned to lust; pure, untainted, burning lust that demanded to be satisfied. Suddenly famished with the need for her, Andreas seized Mara by the hips and hoisted her up, wrapping her legs around his waist.

'Tiger,' she giggled.

Andreas growled and caught her in a hungry embrace.

'Mmm. *My* tiger. Let me feel your claws.'

Her sex lips were swollen and gaping, and it was a simple task to impale her on the spike of his prick, ramming her down onto the swollen flesh so hard that he felt his cock-tip nudging impatiently against the neck of her womb.

Andreas was in paradise. Mara was divinely tight, and her breasts bobbed like ripe apples as she moved on his prick in an irresistible dance of desire. She was running her fingernails up and down his back and he loved every minute of it, revelling in her gentle, playful cruelty.

The hot and steaming water coursed over their bodies as they moved together in the throes of their passion. Nothing existed beyond their coupling, and the ecstasy they would soon share. Yet as Mara closed her eyes and opened her whole being to the pleasure, the strangest images floated into her mind.

There was water everywhere about her. Not the hot water of the shower, but cold, green water that chilled the body and the spirit. All was silence. She tried to make out what surrounded her, but everything seemed blurred and distant, as though she were looking at it through obscured glass.

Dark shapes. Jagged shapes, alien yet half-recognised. She tried to reach out and touch them but her arms were heavy as lead and her legs refused to move. It was cold, so cold. Only the crystal pendant glowing between her naked breasts felt hot, almost too hot to bear.

Andreas. Andreas . . .

She tried to open her mouth to call to him, but the words were lost on the cold tide even before they were spoken. She was alone.

Gone. Gone. Gone.

The mournful sound seemed to echo through her very soul, and she tried to turn her head to see where it was coming from. Tangles of green weed wound about her like dead men's hair but she fought to push them aside.

And then, for a split second only, she saw it. The waters

cleared and she saw a belltower, cracked and lopsided but with the bell still within it, tolling like the cry of a lost soul.

Mara. Mara. Mara.

She fought for breath as the icy sea-water swirled about her, trying to force its way into her lungs. She lost her footing and the next thing she knew, she was tumbling and falling, her body tossed like matchwood in the stormy waters.

'Mara!'

Coughing and spluttering, she opened her eyes. Andreas was kneeling over her and she was lying on her back on the tiled bathroom floor, her lungs full of the hot shower-water. She sat up, shaky and shivery, and Andreas breathed a sigh of relief.

'What on earth happened, Mara? One minute we were fucking, the next you were screaming and breathing in water . . .'

'Screaming?'

'Like something out of a B-movie.' He sat down on the floor beside her, putting his arm round her shoulders. 'What's going on, Mara?'

'I don't know.' Mara dried her hair with a soft fluffy towel. She noticed that the crystal pendant had cooled a little but was still hot, and glowing a faint pink. 'It may be one of the Master's tricks. But I just may have an idea where to find the Eye of Baloch.'

'Charmed to meet you I'm sure, Miss . . .?'

Mara held out her hand.

'Dubois. Anastasia Dubois. And this is my . . . friend and colleague, Nick Weatherall. Do you mind if we join you?'

'Not at all. I'd be delighted.'

Internationally renowned archaeologist Dr Patros Nikephoros got up from his seat at the breakfast table, shook hands then sat down again to butter his toast. Andreas had noticed the way Nikephoros looked at Mara –

the way he looked at all beautiful women, or so it seemed – but right now Andreas's attentions were distracted by the archaeologist's blonde assistant, Helena Duxbury.

Now, Andreas Hunt had never been what you might call over-sophisticated in his sexual tastes. Never say no – that had been his motto in the old days. And these days, what with having to keep on the right side of the Master, screwing beautiful women was on the way to becoming not so much a dream as an occupational hazard. But that didn't stop his hormones going crazy whenever he saw a tasty wench like Helena Duxbury. The way she licked raspberry yoghurt off that teaspoon, he couldn't help wondering what it would feel like to have her licking it off his prick.

Mara wasn't paying much attention to the girl with the cropped blonde hair and the skimpy T-shirt. She was looking at Patros Nikephoros, with his olive skin and glossy black hair and those dark piercing eyes that seemed to have a magnetic power all of their own.

Nevertheless it was Helena who spoke first, her voice cool and smooth as melted ice-cream.

'Are you here on holiday, Mr Weatherall?'

Andreas felt his blood pressure rise several points. That sleeveless white T-shirt she was wearing really was amazingly tight across her nipples, and what with the armholes being cut so low you could see the sides of her not-insubstantial breasts. She wasn't wearing a bra of course. Girls like her never did, they liked to flaunt it. Andreas's mouth was dry as dust and he had to take a swig of orange juice before he replied.

'Er yes, sort of. Business and pleasure mixed.'

Helena looked at him from underneath her long sweep of mascara-laden lashes.

'Personally, I've never understood people who said you shouldn't mix business with pleasure,' she said. 'I do it all the time.'

'I understand you're leading the archaeological team

here, Dr Nikephoras,' began Mara, taking a sip from her coffee cup.

Nikephoros smiled, a dark smile with a hint of mystery behind the rugged good looks.

'Indeed, Miss Dubois.' Nikephoros held a sugar lump on the surface of his coffee and watched it change colour as the liquid was drawn up it. When it had turned from white to creamy-beige he let it fall into the coffee with a soft splash. 'We are diving on the site of the sunken village.'

'Why?' enquired Andreas.

Nikephoros shrugged.

'Why not? I am a marine archaeologist, Mr Weatherall. It is my job.'

'Are you looking for anything in particular?'

Andreas thought he caught a slight darkening of the Greek's expression but perhaps he was just paranoid.

'No, Mr Weatherall.' Nikephoros looked him straight in the eye. 'Should I be?'

Mara kicked Andreas under the table.

'We were wondering, Mr Nikephoros . . .'

The archaeologist smiled, exuding charm, and patted the back of Mara's slender hand.

'Patros, my dear. You must call me Patros. All my close friends do . . . and I so hope that we shall be *close* friends.'

Mara returned his gaze with all the casual coolness that she could muster, though in reality those dark, mysterious eyes were burning her up. Could he see into her heart? Could he sense what he was doing to her, making the blood pound in her veins and that familiar moistness soak into the gusset of her tiny cotton panties?

'We were wondering,' she continued, 'if it might be possible for us to have a look at the archaeological site – maybe even dive down to it. We're both fascinated by archaeology, aren't we, Nick?'

A meaningful glance and a second kick on the shins had Andreas nodding and assuring Dr Nikephoros that there was nothing he liked better than poking about an old ruin.

Whereas the truth was that he much preferred poking a shameless slut with bright red lipstick and her tits hanging out . . .

'Well . . . I don't know.' Nikephoros looked doubtful. 'There might be dangers, insurance complications . . .'

'What about the students?' pointed out Andreas. 'They seem to be swarming all over the place.'

'They have come only to observe our methodology,' replied Nikephoros. 'And to assist us with the conservation of some small artifacts.'

'We are both excellent swimmers,' pleaded Mara. She couldn't let this chance pass them by, no matter what it meant, no matter what she might have to do to get what she wanted.

'With diving experience?'

'Not exactly, but . . .'

Nikephoros smiled. He took another sip of scalding black coffee, his eyes never leaving Mara's face for a second. His gaze was like a brutal caress, the caress of a man who would accept nothing less than a total surrender.

'I shall think about you and your . . . interesting proposition, Miss Dubois,' he assured her. 'Believe me, I shall think about it very carefully indeed.'

Sir Anthony Cheviot was angry and frustrated.

It wasn't the sex, he got plenty of that and there were always new variations to divert and delight him. The Master took care to provide a banquet of sensual delights for his faithful minions.

But Cheviot wanted to serve. Things had not been going well for the Master lately, he knew that, and he wanted to put things right. But everything he did seemed to go awry. Thus far his every attempt to discredit Harry Baptiste had ended in ignominious failure – even luscious Sonya and sensual Joanna had been spurned, and now the Master was furious and vengeful. Just what kind of man was Baptiste – a man of stone?

'Would you like to have me now, Sir Anthony? I have a very tight arse.'

Cheviot glanced down at the girl. Seventeen, maybe eighteen years old, she was naked except for an animal pelt slung over her back, leaving most of her nubile nakedness exposed. She was on hands and knees, her full breasts hanging down like udders and her bare white bottom criss-crossed with angry red stripes. Around her neck was a thick choke-chain, the end of which was held by a man dressed in a zoo-keeper's uniform.

He waved her away.

'Not now. Later perhaps.'

Normally he would have been more than ready to take her up on her offer. This was a perfectly good party, after all. It had been arranged by one of Sir Robert Hackman's deviant friends, a society crimper who had two ruling passions: sixteen year-old boys and snakes. The former he collected with priapic enthusiasm, the latter in a sort of Freudian frenzy which probably had a lot to do with the diminutive size of his penis.

The trouble was, Cheviot just wasn't in the mood.

He stood in front of the vivarium with a glass of champagne in one hand and a large rock in the other. He hated snakes. But he did like to see things writhe.

Yes, watch them writhe. Watch them writhe just a little bit longer.

And then kill them.

'Well! If it isn't Mr Weatherall.'

'Nick, please.'

Andreas was walking past the front door of the Blue Boar when he almost collided with Helena Duxbury. He couldn't have organised it better if he'd planned it – and he had, a thousand times, in his head.

'Get friendly,' Mara had urged him. 'You fancy her, don't you?'

He could hardly deny it, could he? He only had to look

at the Duxbury girl and his dick sprang to painful attention. It was one of those purely physical things, and you couldn't argue with your hormones, could you?

'Go for it,' that's what Mara had said. 'We need to get permission to go on a dive. The Duxbury girl is close to Nikephoros. Maybe if you're screwing her, she'll put in a good word . . .'

They'd thought it through quite carefully, he and Mara. But now that he was face to face with Helena he forgot all about plans and objectives and Baloch and his infuriating eye. He felt like a horny teenager, trying to think of a politically correct way of saying, 'Spread 'em, darling, I want to get inside your pants.' Fortunately Helena saved him from his own inarticulacy.

'Fancy a walk?'

'What? Oh, yes, why not?'

A walk wasn't what he really fancied, of course, but what better excuse to observe the girl at close quarters? And there was a lot of her on view, what with that teeny-weeny crop-top and the acid-green Lycra cycling shorts that hugged her hard little bum so tightly you could almost count her goose-bumps.

With a towel slung over her shoulder, Helena led the way through the village towards the seashore. It was early evening and there was no-one about – not even the students, who had all gone off in the coach to Cardiff, for a piss-up.

'I thought I'd go for a swim,' said Helena. 'Want to join me?'

'I . . . er . . . I haven't got any gear with me.'

Helena laughed – a sexy, throaty chuckle that made him hugely erect in his loose-fitting trousers. Enthusiastic wasn't the word.

'You don't need any. Not embarrassed are you? There's nobody but me to see you . . .'

They reached the beach, its jumble of rocks and shingle and soft sand the legacy left when half the town had fallen into the sea, all those years ago. Helena was right, thought

Andreas. The place was deserted and there was plenty of cover. Nobody would notice one guy without his pants on. If only his erection would go down . . .

Helena ran her fingers through her cropped blonde hair, and Andreas caught sight of the undyed roots. For all her college education, there was something irresistibly tarty about Helena Duxbury. When she bent down to take off her trainers, the sight of her Lycra-clad backside made him want to take out his cock and wank all over her.

'I like you,' said Helena, straightening up.

'I like you too.'

'There's no need to be scared you know.'

'What are you talking about?'

'You, Nick. You look like a startled rabbit. Lighten up – I'm not going to *bite* you.'

At Helena's words he almost did a double-take, for one horrible second imagining that the Master had sent her to torment him, to tell him that the game was up and no-one had every really believed that he was Nick Weatherall anyway. But he looked back at Helena and she was laughing like a carefree kid. Andreas decided to enter into the spirit of the game.

'Not going to bite me, huh?'

'That's right.'

'But what if I wanted to bite *you*?'

He pulled a face and made to grab her and suddenly he was chasing her up the beach, her breasts bouncing inside her top and the muscles of her thighs and buttocks rippling like the fetlocks of some thoroughbred mare.

It was just as well Weatherall was a keep-fit fanatic. Time was when Andreas Hunt wouldn't have got halfway up the beach without having to stop to get his breath. In fact it was Helena who stopped, suddenly wheeling round to face him, her face full of laughter.

He stopped dead in his tracks, just a yard or two away from catching her. As he watched, she took hold of the bottom edge of her cropped T-shirt and jerked it upward.

Her big round breasts popped out like corks from a bottle, their nipples standing proud as Helena pulled the T-shirt off over her head and let it fall to the sand.

Neither of them said a word. Andreas just stood and stared as Helena slipped her thumbs under the waistband of her cycling shorts, easing them down over her hips millimetre by millimetre with perfect unselfconsciousness.

Underneath she was wearing nothing – not even the tiniest g-string. She followed his gaze and grinned.

'Panties spoil the line of my cycling shorts,' she told him, teasingly running her fingers over her hips and the dyed blonde fuzz of her pubic hair. 'I spend hours and hours exercising. I'm very particular about the way I look.'

'I can see that,' observed Andreas, swallowing what seemed like pints of saliva.

Helena approached him, her skin white and creamy against the reddish-gold of the sun.

'Do *you* like the way I look?'

He answered her by grabbing her and pulling her towards him, his hands roaming all over her shameless nakedness. Instinct had taken over completely by now. He pressed his lips against hers, forcing his tongue between her lips and, as he seized a juicy handful of firm buttock-flesh, he instinctively pressed the hardened shaft of his penis against her lower belly.

'Mmm,' murmured Helena as he released her, panting, from his kiss. 'And there I was thinking you were just a shy boy . . .'

And there I was thinking you were a red-hot, shameless seductress, thought Andreas. And I was right.

He slid off his tie one-handed and unbuttoned his shirt with over-eager-fingers, botching the job until Helena obligingly bit off the last two buttons and tore off his shirt.

'Nice,' she observed, running her tongue over Andreas's well-honed physique. 'So you like to keep in shape too. I like that in a man.' Her fingers worked their way down to his trouser-belt but he got there first, unbuckling it and unzipping his pants.

Her hands were hot and moist with desire, matching the furnace-heat of his prick. But she did not hold and stroke him for long, as though she sensed that if she did, she would bring him off in her hand.

Suddenly they were rolling naked in the sand. It was damp and gritty underneath him, but Andreas's mind was on higher things – like the things Helena Duxbury was doing to him. She rolled onto her back, her white skin dusted with a sugar-frosting of sand grains that shimmered in the reddish evening sunlight.

Kneeling astride her, he thought she wanted him to thrust into her cunt, but then she took hold of his cock and stroked it so beautifully that he moved further up her body, so that its tip was within reach of her questing tongue.

Squeezing her breasts together, Helena pressed their flesh around the shaft of Andreas's prick. Instinctively he thrust forward, and the resistance of the firm breast-flesh pushed back his foreskin, sliding his lubricating fluid all over his glans. The sensations were everything he had hoped they would be. He was a starving man and she was a feast, not just a necessity – a delight.

His balls ached and tingled with the need to shoot their load and, when Helena opened her mouth and began licking the tip of his penis, he knew he could not last out for very long. She had a long, pink tongue, athletic like the rest of her body, and she was inventive with it. Its pointed tip darted into the weeping eye of his glans, then flicked back and forth across his glans, lingering only long enough to drive him into a complete frenzy of desire.

At last he felt it coming – the slow, delicious build-up of pressure in his balls and then the tingling excitement as the whole world seemed to hold its breath.

His seed spurted out of him suddenly, violently, its thick white flood falling in hot, creamy gobbets on Helena's face and throat and chest. It was so abundant that rivulets of it ran down from her neck and shoulders to form opalescent pools on the damp sand beneath her.

Utterly spent, Andreas rolled off onto the sand. He noticed that the tide was coming in, the water's edge only perhaps eight or ten feet away, lapping like a cold tongue around the soggy mass of his discarded shirt. But he was too drowsy and pleased with himself to care much. He gave Helena's flank an idle caress.

'So what *are* you doing here?'

'Who?'

'You and Nikephoros.'

'What sort of question is that? I've told you, we're here to study the sunken village.'

'Yes, but – why?'

'How should I know?'

Puzzled, Andreas propped himself up on one elbow.

'You work with the guy, you must know.'

Helena shrugged.

'No, you're mistaken. I'm just his assistant – someone the University hired to help him when he came over to England to do his excavations. I'm not even an archaeologist, more of an administrator.'

'Then why . . .?'

She kissed the tip of his nose then rolled over onto her belly.

'Full of questions today, aren't we?'

'Sorry.' Andreas thought of Mara's warnings about acting suspiciously and gave himself a mental slap on the wrist. He was acting too free and easy, forgetting about the danger, forgetting that this wasn't chequebook journalism any more. Forgetting the dangers he might be placing Mara in, too. 'Didn't mean to be nosey.'

Helena gave a sign which turned into a low chuckle.

'Well, it's no secret really is it? He pays me well to type up his notes and I get to sleep with him.'

'And that's all there is to it?'

'It's enough for me, honeypie. He's got a dick like a steel

bar and he can get it on all night long. Believe me, I'm not complaining.'

Helena got to her feet, brushing the sand off her belly and backside. In the reddish glow of the setting sun, she looked slightly unreal, like one of those too-perfect, super-athletic figures off the side of a Grecian urn. She glanced out towards the ocean, with a half-smile curling up the corners of her mouth.

'Ever done it there?'

'Where?'

'In the sea.'

Andreas got to his feet, his interest already twitching back into life.

'Nope,' he replied with a Cheshire Cat grin. 'But they do say there's a first time for everything.'

6: The Deep

'KILLER CROCODILE SHOT IN FOSSVOG CEMETERY'

(*Reykyavik Monthly*, June issue)

It was no good denying it. Mara was jealous – jealous as hell.

She sat in the seafront bar with an untouched gin and tonic, her mind helplessly tuned in to the sexual electricity crackling between Andreas and Helena Duxbury.

Oh, there was nothing between Andreas and the girl – or at least, nothing but red-hot sex. And, let's face it, both Mara and Andreas had had sex with countless other people in their unwilling service of the Master. But there was something about the Duxbury girl that made Mara's hackles rise. That smug expression, that pouting smile, those too-tight tee-shirts and shorts and the way she wiggled her snaky-smooth arse when she walked. Well, Helena Duxbury would smirk on the other side of her face (both of them) if Mistress Sedet ever lured her into the Hall of Darkness.

Mara shook herself free of the brooding jealousy. She knew she was being unreasonable and she trusted Andreas completely. It was just that she was hungry . . .

Her floaty skirt spread out around her, she shifted a little on the bar stool, and the rough moquette seat-covering rasped across the bare skin of her buttocks. That felt good, very good. If she spread her thighs just a *little*

103

wider, her pussy lips would part and the scratchy moquette would tease the moist, unbelievably sensitive folds of her inner labia. Mmm yes, so good, so hungry. If only Andreas were here to tease her with fingers and tongue and cock.

Mara turned her head towards the windows of the bar and watched the last of the sunlight sink into the sea in an orgy of scarlet and crimson, like a blood sacrifice smeared across the horizon. At this time of day, the bar was almost empty apart from that couple of stray students sitting together by the window.

Lipstick lesbians like Janey and Billie, thought Mara, her green eyes casually roaming over their tanned bodies, loosely entwined in an affectionate embrace. Pendeilo was no place for leather dykes. The taller of the two girls, a brunette with long curly hair swept up at the back and held in place with tortoiseshell combs, was stroking her partner's arm, her fingers easing ever-so-slowly up towards the small, firm swelling of her breast, round and firm beneath the thin muslin blouse.

But she wasn't looking at her lover, she was looking at Mara, her brown eyes gazing almost insolently into Mara's green ones. Asking the question: well, do you want me? Do you *dare* want me?

Mara turned back to her drink, snapping out of the spell of the girl's caressing gaze. Dare? If only the girl knew how much Mara Fleming had dared since the day the Master first lured her to Winterbourne.

She was vaguely aware of a dark shape at her side and then someone slid onto the bar stool next to her.

'Miss Dubois?'

She knew who it was before she looked round. She had known it was him even before he entered the bar, sensing the power of his presence.

'Dr Nikephoros . . . Patros.'

'All alone? I don't know how that colleague of yours can bear not to be with you every moment of every day.'

'It's very flattering of you to say so . . .'

Nikephoros caught her hand and put it to his lips, their hot, dry warmth flooding into her marble-cool flesh.

'Not at all. You are a very beautiful woman, Anastasia. And I am a connoisseur of beautiful women.'

'So I believe.' Mara's mouth twitched in faint amusement. Nikephoros had hardly been in Pendeilo five minutes, but already tales of his sexual prowess were doing the rounds of the village. It wasn't a very big village. If he stayed here much longer there wouldn't be any virgins left for him to seduce.

'Have you any plans for this evening? I thought I might perhaps persuade you to have dinner with me.' He paused for a moment, waiting to see her reaction, then added, 'In my hotel room . . .'

Mara looked deep into Nikephoros's dark eyes. There was something there, behind the velvet-soft voice and the darkly handsome face, something that scared her half to death. But she had only to look at him to recall the burning hunger she had felt the very first time she had set eyes on him. He frightened her, it was true, though she knew not why; but he also excited her and right now her hunger was far too strong to be denied.

She returned his smile, her gaze steady but her fingers trembling around the stem of the glass.

'You might. If you're *very* persuasive.'

Nikephoros drained his glass.

'I hope you're hungry, Anastasia.'

Mara stood up, smoothing back the long, amber curtain of her glossy hair.

'Oh, I have quite an appetite already, Dr Nikephoros.'

The sauna was oven-hot and so steamy you could hardly see your hand in front of your face.

'Harder, bitch! Or do you wish me to punish you again?'

Lying face-down on the slatted wooden bench, the Master savoured the touch of the Japanese girl's fingers on his bare back. Naked to the waist, she made an enthusiastic but not always efficient masseuse, and he was teaching her greater discipline. The angry red stripes criss-crossing her back and breasts testified to her slowness at learning even the simplest of lessons. But then again, there was a certain pleasure to be derived from the exercise of strict discipline . . .

'Forgive me, Master. Forgive me.'

The girl worked her small but strong hands up from the small of his back towards his shoulder-blades, working out the tension. Not that there would be any tension to soothe away if Cheviot and Takimoto did their jobs properly. And if he could only find out who or what was doing its damnedest to destroy his power.

Angry and frustrated, he pushed the slut roughly away from him. She fell heavily against one of the other benches and a bare arm emerged from the swirling steam, hooking itself about her waist, pulling her towards an unseen figure. Sir Robert Hackman was feeling particularly randy today. He had already debauched his way through all the girls Heimdal had initiated on his last visit to a Thai sex-club and now Hackman was in need of the Japanese slut's peculiarly reviving caresses.

But the Master was indifferent to Hackman's needs. What mattered was his own satisfaction. He snapped his fingers.

'Ibrahim.'

A dark figure emerged from the mist of steam, black skin glossy and running with sweat.

'Master?'

'Fellate me.'

'You honour me, Master.'

The benches in the steam-room had been cleverly constructed, on Delgado's instructions, so that they were raised well off the ground, with wide gaps between the wooden slats. Gaps easily wide enough for a swollen penis and ripe, juicy balls to hang down, heavy and inviting.

Ibrahim got down on his knees underneath the Master's

bench and opened his mouth to engulf the swollen stalk of the Master's throbbing penis. He had done this many times before but each time the experience filled him with a greater sense of pride. The Master had chosen *him* to suck his cock, to swallow down the sacred gift of his beautiful, heavy balls. The Ethiopian yearned for the day when the Master would accept the humble gift of his ten-inch cock, thrust into the tight haven of his backside. For Ibrahim lived only for his Master's pleasure.

The Master relaxed slightly at the agreeable feeling of Ibrahim's lips and tongue on his turgid prick. The Japanese girl might be a half-trained incompetent, but Ibrahim never failed to pleasure him. Perhaps later, if the Ethiopian performed particularly well, he would allow him to bugger the young American rock-singer Sonja Kerensky had seduced the previous evening, and brought home to Winterbourne.

As Ibrahim worked away at his dick with his tongue, the Master gazed at the large metal pail of cold water on the floor beside the bench. He reached down and let his fingers skim the surface, hoping to call up pictures which would reassure him of the ultimate success which he knew must be his.

The depths of the water seemed to churn and ripple, the clear water becoming as murky as Indian ink and then suddenly clearing to a crystal sharpness. A procession of images swam across the liquid screen, recalling past triumphs and hinting at others still to come.

Look – there was a man standing with a crystal dagger sticking out of his heart and an expression of terrified astonishment on his face – how that made the Master laugh. Andreas Hunt's body had served him well, far better than it had ever served that prize fool, Hunt. And look: that was so-called psychic investigator Max Trevidian, blasted to a microscopic mist by the sheer force of the Master's will as behind him, Felsham Manor went up like a Roman candle.

He ejaculated with a grunt of pleasure into Ibrahim's mouth as he feasted on narcissistic images of his own beauty, his own cleverness, his own seductive power.

Beautiful sluts, women who had fallen at his feet – and men too, politicians and princes forced to kiss the Master's dick and surrender their black hearts to the greater blackness of his evil empire. Minds clouded, bodies and souls stolen away to serve him in a great, universal masque of flesh where the reddest, most kissable lips concealed the whitest, sharpest teeth.

As he passed his hands across the water a second time, demanding the assurance of his great and glorious future, the Master saw the surface cloud again. And this time there were other images, far more disturbing than anything that had gone before. Images of chaos, turmoil, destruction – and none of it of the Master's making.

No, not that! Damn it. Damn this insidious force, that dared resist his power.

The Eye. The Eye of Baloch. He *must* have it, must have it soon.

Distracted and angry, he pushed over the pail and the water spread over the floor of the sauna, filling the room with even denser clouds of steam. He rolled onto his back.

'Slut!'

'Master?'

Four pretty faces appeared before him, angels' faces that seemed to float in the clouds of steam. They at least obeyed him without question. And right now he felt the need to reassert his absolute authority.

He reached out and seized the first of them, pulling her towards him by the golden chain which passed through her pierced tongue.

She would do. For a start.

Patros Nikephoros reached out and dipped his spoon into the dish of double cream. When he raised it and let the blob of cream fall onto Mara's bare shoulder, she felt a thrill of excitement ripple through her body. There was something forbidden about this; something she ought not to be doing.

Why was she refusing to listen to the psychic sixth-sense that screamed *no, no, no*? Why hadn't she politely refused his dinner invitation and found some other way of persuading him to let her explore the sunken village of Pendeilo?

Why? Because all she wanted to do right now was lie on Nikephoros's bed and let him lick whipped cream from her naked body.

A second, cold trickle of cream landed on her bare flesh, this time falling on her breast and spreading down over the flattened dome of flesh into the golden valley of her cleavage.

'Beautiful,' murmured Nikephoros.

Stooping, he picked up the cream jug and this time emptied the entire contents over her, the thick cream falling in an irregular stream over breasts and belly and thighs and the amber-gold forest of her pubic curls, already moistened with the honeydew of desire.

She watched through half-closed eyelids as Nikephoros unbuttoned his shirt, slowly, methodically. The flesh beneath was tanned – the deep, old-gold colour that tells of a life spent in the open air, doing hard, physical labour. His arms and torso were well-muscled with a thick sprinkling of black hair, his belly flat with not so much as a hint of spare flesh.

Mara's body was crying out for him to take her. All through the meal it had been sheer torment, pretending to eat, but hungering only for the touch that would awaken and then satiate the raging volcano of desire within her. She had not felt so overwhelmingly randy for some time. Perhaps she had been neglecting the sexual sustenance which her immortal body craved? Or perhaps the quest on which she and Andreas had embarked required a special type of sustenance? Either way, she was willing to suspend every doubt, every fear if only she could have Nikephoros's dick inside her.

In an agony of excitement she watched him unbuckle his trouser belt, unfasten the top button of his pants and slide them down, with unbearable slowness, over his hips. Underneath he was wearing white designer briefs that clung to him like a second skin and left her in no doubt that all the village gossip about him was true.

His erect dick lay like a massive rod of flesh beneath the white cotton, a slanting baton so large that its moist pink tip had pushed its way out from beneath the waistband and was clearly visible. Mara yearned to lick the heavy dewdrop of sex fluid from it, to take that fat pink cock between her greedy lips.

Nikephoros pulled down his briefs and stepped out of them, and his tool danced in the joy of its liberation, its shaft so hard and thick that Mara doubted very much that she could encircle it with the fingers of one hand.

'You like my body?' he enquired, his studied coolness driving Mara to distraction.

'You have a beautiful cock,' replied Mara, squirming with sexual frustration on Nikephoros's freshly laundered white sheets. 'I want you. I want you now.'

He smiled and she wondered why his eyes did not smile with his lips.

'Patience, little one,' he whispered. 'All things will come. But first, I must make you ready.'

He knelt on the bed and bent to lick the first of the cream from Mara's body, his tongue lapping slowly at her throat then moving down to wind its way about her breasts. When he reached her swollen nipple, she cried out with the pain of her frustration.

'You taste delicious,' he purred. 'You have a scent and a taste of your very own. And this little alpine strawberry here . . .' He gave her nipple a playful nip. 'It is so juicy and ripe that I could suck and lick it for ever.'

He went on licking her until every drop of cream was

gone – every drop save for the sticky mass that matted her pubic curls. She knew that he had saved that for last simply to drive her wild. And when his tongue began lapping at her mound of Venus she wondered how much longer she could bear it before she wept and pleaded with him to lick the burning nubbin of her clitoris.

She writhed and twisted, her pelvis bucking and tilting instinctively at each new intimacy, each new unbearably intense situation. Her right knee was bent up, parting her love lips, and floods of her own clear, sweet nectar were gushing out of her. But it seemed forever before at last Nikephoros slid the tip of his index finger into her wet and gaping hole.

'Now, I think, you are ready for me at last,' he smiled.

'Take me. Oh, please . . . don't make me feel like this any longer, I can't bear it,' Mara half-sobbed.

'You want me to make love to you?'

'Yes! Oh yes . . .'

'Then tell me, Anastasia. Tell me what it is that you want me to do to you.'

'I . . . I want you to fuck me, Patros. I want you to take me, fuck me, screw me . . .'

Her words ended in a long, low cry of ecstasy as he slid his iron rod into her welcoming cunt. Ecstasy and yet fear, for as he fucked her and brought her ever-closer to the brink of dizzying pleasure, Mara looked into his eyes and saw a darkness, a madness, that threatened to engulf her.

'So what happened next?'

Andreas stepped out of the shower, towelling his wavy brown hair. He'd washed it twice and there was still sand in it.

'She had her wicked way with me.'

He exchanged looks with Mara and she burst out laughing.

'So she's some sort of man-eater, is she, Miss Helena Duxbury?'

Andreas sat down on the bed, wiping the water out of his ears.

'Well, actually . . .'

'Go on.'

'I got this really weird feeling that I wasn't in control of what was happening. I wanted to fuck her, you bet I did, but then it was as if she called all the shots.'

Mara sat down beside him, idly walking her fingers down Andreas's nicely honed body. Tall and strong and slim it was, but not muscle-bound. Let's face it, he was much more to her taste than the darkly dominant Patros Nikephoros.

'Funnily enough, I know just what you mean.'

'Nikephoros?'

She nodded. In the cold, clear light of day it all sounded a bit peculiar, but she was certain of what she had felt.

'I got this feeling that there was something . . . oh I don't know . . . something *dark* about him. I tried to read his thoughts, get inside his spirit, but there was a sort of brick wall there. I just couldn't get through.'

'Do you think there's something dangerous about him, then?'

Mara shrugged.

'I don't know. It's probably just me being paranoid. I mean, it's hard not to be when you've lived at Winterbourne. But all the time he was fucking me, I was thinking "This is wonderful, this is incredible, but I want it to stop." Does that make sense?'

'No. But then again, nothing much makes sense any more, does it?'

Andreas stretched out, naked, on the patchwork bedspread. Nice bed it was, good and bouncy and it didn't squeak like most hotel beds did. It would be a shame not to make thorough and enthusiastic use of it.

'So . . . did you . . . get anywhere with Patros?'

'What's that supposed to mean?' teased Mara. She knew how Andreas felt about her screwing Patros

Nikephoros. Pretty much the same way she felt about that bitch Helena Duxbury.

'Did you ask him about the sunken village?'

'He says we can go along with them on the next dive. We can dive down and get a look at the village.'

'Great!' Andreas sat up then flopped back onto the bed. 'Hang on a mo, I don't know the first thing about diving.'

'So? Neither do I. We'll improvise.'

'Yeah, I guess so.' Andreas brightened. 'Fancy a roll in the hay?'

'We haven't got any hay.'

He grinned.

'We'll improvise.'

The old converted trawler *Mary-Ann* bobbed on a light sea-swell, just off Pendeilo.

Clammy and uncomfortable in his wet suit, Andreas peered over the side.

'Are you sure this is going to be OK?'

'If you are not confident about diving, Mr Weatherall, you are welcome to remain on the boat with the support staff,' suggested Patros Nikephoros. 'Miss Dubois and I will dive down to the ruins alone.'

That just about made up Andreas's mind for him – he wasn't going to let that smarmy sod get the better of him and have Mara all to himself.

'I'll be fine.'

'Good, excellent. I am sure you will enjoy the experience.'

Andreas hated the way that whenever he looked at Nikephoros, he felt as if he had almost – but not quite – caught him laughing.

He perched himself on the edge of the boat as he had been instructed by Helena. It had only been one half-hour's instruction and, frankly, Helena had ensured that his mind was on other things.

'That's right, Mr Weatherall. Mouthpiece firmly between

the lips, a few good breaths then just let yourself fall
backwards.'

Mara went first, making it all look so easy. She even
looked good in that wetsuit, the curves of her trim and
supple body moulded exactly by the pink and black suit.
Taking three deep breaths of the oxygen mixture, Andreas
let himself topple backwards.

He hit the water with a loud splash but was totally
unaware of it because he was plummeting down through
the cold green water like a stone.

There was Mara, her long waves of red hair streaming
out behind her like rippling tendrils of seaweed. She
beckoned to him and he followed her down, everything
happening in slow motion now, the cold water resisting his
unco-ordinated body. It was like swimming through cold
treacle.

The deeper and the further they swam, the deeper
green the water became, not murky but a rich emerald, like
the glass of a wine bottle. Andreas didn't quite know what
to expect from the sunken village. He knew that some of
the stone buildings were supposed to be lying almost intact
in their watery grave, but he wasn't prepared for the sight
which met his eyes as he and Mara slid through the dark
green waters.

The rugged shapes of fishermen's cottages, missing
only their slate roofs, rose up before him like broken teeth
in a dead man's smile. Shoals of fish swam through the
doors and windows, emerging from the chimneys like
living smoke. Over the centuries, tufts and banks of weed
had attached themselves in multicoloured patches to the
exposed stone, and sand from the sea-bottom had drifted
in long, smooth waves that threatened to engulf the cottages
for good.

Mara swam slowly along what must once have been the
main street of the village. Here, most of the buildings had
gone, the wattle and timber rotted away or eaten by sea-
worm. But stone foundations remained, and the occasional

wall that stood defiantly against the depredations of time and tide. A forest of sea anemones covered the rubble-strewn sea-bed, their mouths opening and closing like some long-dead, silent choir.

This place gave Andreas the creeps. He looked at Mara and he saw that, behind the glass face-mask, her eyes were brimming with tears. How much more tragic must this dead place seem to be, with her telepathic power and psychic sensibilities? Could she hear the cries of the drowning, see their faces as the sea rose up and claimed them, never to give them up until Judgement Day?

Mara raised her arm and pointed, but he had already seen it. How could he miss the massive, hunched shape of the old chapel, its solid walls defiant and its belltower still pointing upwards like a squat, accusing finger?

The chapel lay slightly askew on the seabed, its slates scattered all around it like discarded teaplates, and a broken stone cross resting its three shattered fragments across what remained of the porch.

A grey, bone-numbing chill was seeping through Andreas's skin, and it had nothing to do with the temperature of the water. He caught Mara's arm and she turned to look at him, her green eyes wide with alarm. Could she feel it too? Of course she could. But Mara was not one to be deterred by her own fear.

She swam up, her body undulating like an eel's as she cut through the water, rising over the chapel roof until at last she was on a level with the open belltower. By some miracle the bell was still hanging there, a little drunkenly because of the angle, but apparently secure. So perhaps it was true what the locals said about stormy nights, that you could hear the bell tolling its mournful knell beneath the waves. Had her vision also been true?

Afraid, she touched the bell. It was encrusted with barnacles but in places she could still make out the gleam of tarnished brass. Could it really be here, the Eye of Baloch?

Her fingers explored the surface of the bell, her stomach in knots and her whole body shivering with apprehension. There was a darkness here, a bleakness that soaked into your soul and might make you lose your reason.

Inside, it must be inside.

Feverishly she felt up inside the bell, feeling for the clapper. But there was nothing there, nothing at all. The iron must have rusted away long centuries since.

Disappointment mingled with relief flooded into her as she stroked the bell reflectively. So she had been wrong. There had been nothing here all along, she had been imagining it. Just as the people of Pendeilo had been imagining this bell tolling underneath the waves. For how could a bell toll if it had no clapper to strike the brass?

As she laid her hand on the fat belly of the bell, she felt it move; at first almost imperceptibly and then with a sickening lurch.

Come here, Mara. Get away from it. Come here. Frustrated by his inability to call to her, Andreas waved his arms about and tried to telepath his fears into her mind. *Come here, something bad's going to happen, I can feel it . . .*

The bell slipped from its anchorage with devastating suddenness. Mara and Andreas watched in horrified silence as it seemed first to plummet and then to fall in slow motion towards the sea-bed.

As it landed in a cloud of swirling sand, they heard it toll. Once, twice, thrice.

Gone. Gone. Gone.

And then silence.

They sat together in the lounge of the Blue Boar for an hour and a half, sharing gloomily silent thoughts, before at last Andreas spoke.

'We've buggered it up, haven't we?'

'Looks that way,' admitted Mara.

'We can't go back without it. The Master would . . .'

'Yes. I know.' Mara stirred a spoonful of sugar into her

116

coffee. 'I don't even want to think about what the Master would do, thank you very much. What I don't understand is how I could possibly have had that vision of the belltower if the Eye wasn't there.'

'Perhaps someone's playing games with us,' suggested Andreas grimly. 'After all, someone's been playing games with the Master – why not us? Unless, of course, it *is* the Master.'

Mara shook her head.

'No, not the Master, I'm sure he's as confused as we are. I could read his thoughts . . . he suspected nothing . . .'

'Then what?' Andreas got up and started pacing up and down the room. 'I wouldn't care, but that thing just makes me feel worse – like rubbing salt into the wound.' He cast a malevolent glance at Patros Nikephoros's scale model of the sunken village, a meticulous reconstruction in a large glass tank, complete with water and sand. If there was one thing that made Andreas feel better, it was knowing that, since he and Mara had paid the village a visit, Nikephoros's scale model was now slightly less accurate than it had been . . .

'The model! Yes, why didn't I . . .?' Mara got to her feet. 'The feeling, it's so strong – I should have known.'

'Known what?'

'Reach into the tank, Andreas.'

'You think . . .?'

'Please, Andreas.'

Andreas rolled up his shirt sleeve and reached into the tank as Mara had asked him. He needed no further instructions – he knew where she meant him to look. His fingers felt for the top of the belltower, and the top of it came away in his hand.

Removing it, he turned it over in his hand, and the diamond-bright glint half-dazzled him.

Inside the model belltower was a four-sided crystal pyramid, pale green in colour. He held it in his hand and even he could feel the energy coming out of the thing, sending pins and needles running up his arm.

'It doesn't look much like an eye to me,' he observed, handing it to Mara.

'That's because it's only one part of it,' replied Mara.

'You mean there are other bits?'

'At least four others, to judge from the shape of this.' She stroked it, feeling its strength, and at her touch the crystal began to glow – red, green, yellow, a rainbow of bright colours.

'Mara – the door!'

She raised her hand and followed Andreas's gaze to the far side of the hotel lounge. The door to the dining room was glowing too, its colours matching the colours of the crystal pyramid.

'What do we do now?' demanded Andreas, though he already had his suspicions.

'Go through the door, of course.'

'I was afraid you were going to say that.'

It was a chip shop.

Of that, at least, there could be little doubt. Andreas and Mara stepped through the doorway into the fragrant cloud of steam from a stainless-steel frying range, behind which a woman with red arms was shovelling chips into a paper bag.

The queue – four men and a dog – turned around as one and stared at the new arrivals: a man in a suit and a red-haired woman with a floaty dress, dangly earrings and the most gorgeous tits this secluded seaside town had seen in a long, long time.

Mara turned to Andreas, but Andreas was staring open-mouthed out of the doorway. As she followed his gaze she could see why. It was the front door of the chip shop, any fool could see that, so why could she still see the lounge of the Blue Boar when she looked through it?

Through a sort of heat haze, she could still make out the model of the sunken village in its glass tank, the sofa where she and Andreas had fucked, and the doorway to the dining-room beyond. Yet, when she looked out of the front window of the chip shop, she could see hills and hotels and a curving promenade – a promenade which definitely didn't belong to the Welsh seaside village of Pendeilo.

They exchanged looks. Andreas gave a shrug, closed the door and opened it again, much to the bafflement of the assembled customers. This time, when Mara and Andreas looked out, all they could see was a seaside promenade and a tall hill with a scattering of blackened ruins atop it.

'Bloody hell,' whistled Andreas. 'Don't you recognise this place? It's *Whitby*. Look – there's the Abbey . . .'

A woman's abrasive tones made Andreas and Mara turn back to the counter.

'Did you want something or are you just going to stand there admiring the view?'

Andreas forced his face into a smile and felt in his pocket for a fiver.

'Cod and chips twice,' he said.

7: The Brotherhood

'CARDINAL CLAIMS POPE IS SEX-MAD ALIEN'
(*Church Chronicle*, 10 June)

Joachim Heimdal relished a challenge, particularly when it had been set for him by Mistress Sedet. For Mistress Sedet understood that, in order to be truly fulfilling, every challenge must include a large measure of sex.

Idly stroking his luxuriant blond beard, Heimdal watched the street names glide past. When Caledonian Street came into view he rapped on the dashboard.

'Park here. Somewhere inconspicuous.'

Geoffrey Potter swung the red BMW into a sharp left turn and the car slid to a halt in a narrow alleyway.

'Here all right?'

Heimdal grunted.

'I suppose it will have to suffice. Wait for me here. I may be some time . . .'

He got out and started walking back towards the main road. The Aylesbury Museum of Celtic History stood in a recently restored Georgian terrace near to the centre of the historic town. It was all quite picturesque, but the only architecture Heimdal was interested in was the architecture of the naked female form.

'Can I help you, sir?'

The girl on the reception desk was small and appetising, and he adored the way her dark eyes followed the line of his muscular torso down below the brass-buckled belt to the flies of his skintight leather trousers. From the way she licked her lips, it wasn't difficult to deduce that she was pretty desperate for him. All he had to do was click his fingers and she'd be on her knees before him, begging him to let her suck his cock. He liked having that sort of power over a woman.

Regrettably she would have to wait until later. Today he must attend to certain other priorities.

He laid a ringed hand on the girl's, loving the way she trembled at his touch. Knowing yet virginal, just the way he liked them.

'I *do* hope you can help me, my dear,' he replied, taking a business card from his shirt pocket and pushing it across the counter. 'Joachim Heimdal, Winterbourne Trust. I have an appointment to see Miss Candice Dorigo.'

The receptionist skimmed the list of names in the diary on her desk.

'Ah yes, Mr Heimdal. I'll just ring through to Miss Dorigo's office to see if she's free.'

Oh, she'll be free, thought Heimdal as he smiled inwardly. After our brief meeting last week, I'll warrant she'd cancel all her appointments for a week just for the chance to kiss my beautiful dick.

Sure enough, the receptionist handed him a plastic identity badge and beckoned to him to follow, leading him up a spiral staircase to the first floor. Her plump arse quivered very slightly as she walked, the line of her panties quite clearly delineated beneath her short, tight skirt. Heimdal had to fight to control the rush of hunger which had in no way been diminished by a night in the Imperial Russia room with Joanna Königsberg and Sonja Kerensky.

At the top of the stairs, they turned right and the receptionist stopped in front of a panelled door labelled 'Miss C Dorigo, Keeper of Celtic Artefacts'. The girl knocked.

'Come in.'

She put her head round the door.

'Mr Heimdal to see you, Miss Dorigo.'

'Send him in.'

Was that a breath of excitement in that cool, disinterested voice? Heimdal knew that it was. He entered the office and pushed the door quietly shut behind him.

Candice Dorigo was a woman of perhaps thirty-two, handsome in an unforgiving sort of way. There was steel in that blue-eyed gaze, those high, well-chiselled cheekbones. Short, light-brown hair framed an oval face. She wore little make-up, but then again she didn't need make-up. She had the good looks of a racehorse, aloof and highly strung. As she stood up to shake Heimdal's hand, he savoured the long, elegant lines of her body, hard and lithe beneath the cool beige linen dress.

'Mr Heimdal, so nice to see you again.'

He sat down, not on the chair she indicated, but on the edge of her desk.

'Believe me, *Candice*, the pleasure is all mine.'

'Can I get you anything . . . coffee, tea?'

For all her coolness, she was flustered, Heimdal noted with smug self-satisfaction. Oh, how his dick was straining for release. It was a good thing the slut was so eager for him and he wouldn't have to wait long for satisfaction. He laid his hand on her bare arm, holding the fingers still for a few seconds, then beginning to stroke the flesh very gently, very subtly.

'I have all I need here, Candice.'

She drew back, as though suddenly taking stock of the situation; cleared her throat, shuffled her papers. But Heimdal had seen the hard lines of her nipples, pushing insolently against the underside of the pale, plain linen. She couldn't fool him.

'You . . . you wanted to see me to ask me about Celtic artefacts, Mr Heimdal?'

'You are the acknowledged expert,' purred Heimdal. 'I myself have an exhaustive knowledge of the Viking period, but of the Celts I know relatively little.'

'Ask away, Mr Heimdal.'

'Joachim, please.'

'Ask anything you like . . .'

She was looking straight into his eyes as she spoke the words, and Heimdal knew exactly what she was really saying to him.

'Would you like me to fuck you?'

For a moment she stared back at him in shocked silence, her tongue moistening her dry lips with little nervous flicking movements. Heimdal ran his fingers up the inside of her arm and let his fingertips brush the swell of her breast.

'I . . .'

'There is no need for this little charade, Candice.' Heimdal unfastened the top button of her dress and slid his hand inside, smoothing it across the bare skin of neck and throat, moving ever-so-slowly downwards. 'I know what your answer will be. I know *you*.'

Her eyes registered surprise now, as she began to understand the truth of Heimdal's words.

'I know what you like, Candice. I know how you love men to use you.'

She shivered, a frisson of fear seasoning the excitement she felt at Heimdal's caresses.

'I know such a lot about you, Candice.' He smiled. It had been so, so easy to see into this young woman's head. That first time they had met, all he had had to do was shake her hand and all her desire had come tumbling out of her, into his mind. Such piquant desire they were too, for such a cool, elegant young woman.

She returned his gaze, not fighting his fingers as they released the second button on the front of her dress. Heimdal knew what a superhuman effort it must be taking her to keep her voice from shaking.

'And what else do you know about me, Mr Heimdal?'

'I know how you love the whip. I know how you love to be beaten.' With a certain regret he took his hand from her

124

cleavage and unbuckled the thick leather belt which encircled his waist. It slipped through the loops with a soft swish.

Her eyes half-closing, Candice Dorigo gave a long, low moan of pleasure at the sight of the heavy leather strap lying across Heimdal's palm.

'Good, good,' whispered Heimdal. He was going to enjoy this – possibly even more than Candice was, although, to judge from the way her nipples were poking through the fabric of her dress, she was hot as a vixen for him already. He worked at the next two buttons of her dress, exposing the wire and lace of her white uplift bra.

'The door,' gasped Candice. 'You must lock the door. If someone comes in . . .'

Heimdal laughed.

'No-one will come in.'

'But if they do . . .'

If they did, thought Heimdal, it would just add to the fun. And besides, he knew this sex-bitch's fears and desires. The fear of discovery would add to her pleasure.

'Take off your dress,' he snapped, suddenly no longer the urbane seducer. Now he must play the part of the bitch-master, the part he had always played to perfection.

'No, no, I can't.'

He ran the leather belt through his fingers, gripped it and brought it down hard across his palm with a satisfying smack of leather on flesh.

'Take off your dress. Quickly – or you will feel the weight of my anger.'

Which was, of course, exactly what Candice Dorigo wanted to feel. But you had to play the game, build up the excitement, get her good and hot and fearful.

She unfastened the last of the buttons and slipped the dress off over her shoulders. Underneath she was wearing just the white push-up bra and a pair of frilly white panties, from which not even the smallest wisp of pubic hair escaped. Her legs were bare and tanned a golden brown which no doubt came out of a bottle – not that that bothered Heimdal. Any woman was capable of turning him on, from the vilest, filthiest slut to the coolest ice-princess, as long as she had a tight wet cunt and a willing arse.

'Take off your bra.'

Candice reached behind her and released the catch of her bra. The back-straps sprang free and she bent slightly forward as she slipped off the shoulder-straps, making her small breasts dangle like ripe fruits.

'Now bend over the desk.'

She obeyed him – but not quickly enough. It was almost as though she wanted him to be angry with her, so that she could enjoy the sublime pleasure of punishment.

'Slut!'

Heimdal brought the leather belt swishing down on her bare back with a moderate degree of force. Candice's back arched at the sudden, stinging blow and she let out a startled gasp.

'Aah . . .!'

'Silence! I did not give you permission to speak.' He was really enjoying himself now. How many times had he acted out this most agreeable of scenes in Sedet's Hall of Darkness, mortifying the flesh of some new initiate until his own pleasure came pumping out of his loins, spattering over the girl's battered and bloodstained back?

'Oh. Oh, please . . .' She was leading him on, forcing him to punish her more severely. He obliged with another fierce swipe of the belt, this time so skilfully directed that its tip snaked round her torso and stung the softly jiggling flesh of her breast. 'No, please, no!'

'If I give you permission to speak you will address me as Master.'

'Oh. Oh yes, Master. No more . . .'

Which was the exact opposite of what she really wanted, mused Heimdal. And he hit her a little harder, just to show that he understood her even better than she realised, understood her *every* desire, no matter how base.

'I will decide upon the severity of your punishment. I alone will decide when it is to stop – or if it is to stop.'

Her back was reddening nicely, her breathing coming in great rasping gulps as she braced herself and fought to control the overwhelming impulses throbbing and burning through her body.

Excellent. A truly excellent subject. Mistress Sedet had been quite correct in her assessment of the Dorigo woman. A fine academic brain, but a body so sensually corrupt that she would sell her very soul to feel the lash biting into her skin. It would not be difficult to raise her sexual energies to a point at which his mind could probe hers and feed upon her knowledge of the new toy his mistress desired: the mystical Eye of Baloch.

He wrenched down her panties. They were white and frilly, like a little girl's panties. For that was all Miss Candice Dorigo was, for all her airs and graces: just a naughty schoolgirl who wanted to be taken into the headmaster's office and given the thrashing of her life. The thrashing and the fucking . . .

'Wicked slut.'

'Master?'

'You have soiled your panties with the filthy secretions of your desire. How dare you have sexual desires when I am punishing you.'

'I'm sorry.'

'Sorry, *Master*.' The belt hit home dead-centre between the tight white buttocks, entering the deep amber furrow and making Candice squirm.

'I'm sorry, Master.'

For all her pretended contrition, Candice Dorigo had the heart of a slut. That was plain to see, plainer still to feel. With her thighs spread wide and her panties down round her knees, her sex lips were pouting a welcome – a hot, wet, warm ooze of need. And every time he struck her with the belt he felt a sizzle of sexual energy leaving her body and enter his, lighting up a snapshot-image of wild, untamed sex in his hungry mind.

'Wider apart, slut. I am going to examine you.'

She shuffled her feet a little further apart and he ran his fingers all over her buttocks and up the deep, wet crack that ran from anus to pubis. She was shaven. Shaven like a little girl, her pubis and sex lips kept assiduously bare of even the downiest fuzz of hair. Candice Dorigo was the little girl who would never grow up.

He explored her hidden depths and she writhed appreciatively at the brutal entrance of his ringed finger into her vagina. Tight. Mmm, yes, very nearly virgin-tight, with strong muscles that clenched at his invading finger as though trying to suck him in deeper and never let him go.

In, out; in, out; he loved to feel her tightening about his finger, then losing grip as another torrent of clear sex-juice came spilling out of her, flooding his hand.

With his right index finger buried up to the knuckle in Candice's cunt, Heimdal let his thumb roam a little farther afield, searching out the secret place, the shameful place, where Candice had never been touched. He knew this, simply from the way her whole body tensed as his thumb skated lightly over the puckered flesh, and from the pictures of guilty, fearful longing which entered his mind.

'I think I shall bugger you, Candice Dorigo.'

For a few seconds her body went rigid with fear.

'No, Master, please, you can't!'

'I can do anything I please with you. You are my slave. You exist only as the instrument of my pleasure.'

Candice gave a low sob as Heimdal's thumbnail grazed the tight anal opening.

'Master, oh Master, please. I've never let any man touch me there. Not any man, ever.'

'You will submit to me.' He struck her forcefully with the belt and her cunt spilled more of its honeysweet juice. Heimdal's cock was already dancing its joy against the inside of his tight leather pants, longing to be released, to have its will.

'I'm afraid . . .'

'The pain will be brief, the pleasure unending.'

'Master!'

'You will obey me.'

He jabbed his thumb into her with a sudden, violent movement. Candice let out a thin, high cry but he paid her no attention. He could feel how the pain excited her, how much she wanted him to tear his will from her soft, sweet flesh.

In a swift movement he unzipped his flies. He was naked underneath, hating any garment which veiled the beauty of his wonderful pierced dick. He loved to go naked under his tight trousers, the outline of his jade cock-ring clearly visible through the leather. Loved to torment them, his would-be worshippers, perhaps once in a while offering one or two of them the benevolent gesture of his cock in their mouths. He was not, after all, a selfish man.

'I am going to bugger you, you delicious slut, and there is nothing you can do to stop me.' He was holding Candice firmly and her body was trembling in his hands. She was struggling but so ineffectually that he knew her heart was not in it. She wanted this, wanted it more than anything else in the whole, wide world.

'No!'

'Can you feel it? The tip of my beautiful dick pressing against the tightness of your hole? It's a very tight hole, perhaps I shall hurt you more than I had expected . . .'

Without warning, he drove into her. Unable to control herself any longer, she let out a scream of pain-mingled pleasure. Heimdal knew that cry, he knew the joy of ecstasy mixed with pain. Why, did he not recall that selfsame feeling from his own initiation at the delicious hands and lips of Anastasia Dubois?

The violence of his thrusts almost flattened her against the desk, but still he could feel her beginning to push back against his cock, at first convulsively, then rhythmically, the surest indication of her pleasure. Her bare, shaven pubis was rubbing against the blotter on the desk, her sex lips pouting open at each new thrust, and a clear trail of sex juice running out of her onto the pink blotting-paper.

It felt good, so very good. But the pleasure was not entirely physical, for Heimdal was exploring the world of Candice's thoughts. Her knowledge and her desires whirled in multicoloured images inside his brain as he buggered her, each new thrust intensifying the clarity of the pictures.

Scenes of the cruellest, most extraordinary pleasure mingled with scenes from history, the Celtic history which Candice Dorigo knew so well. Naked men and women with painted bodies and wild eyes danced and fucked around a glittering flame. And in the very midst of that flame something glittered.

Something that looked like an unwinking eye.

And now he could see it lying on the ground, sparks of blinding light arrowing out of it, filling the air with such intense forks of lightning that they seemed like arrows of purest pain.

But there was worse, much worse. Screams filling the air, sounds and sights and scents the like of which Heimdal had never encountered before, not even in the Master's evil realm of the undead. Suddenly the whole world seemed to be crumbling, sinking, burning, dying . . .

And in the midst of it all sat the baleful Eye of Baloch.

Heimdal wanted, needed to see more but he felt the girl climax and he came with her, his seed filling her like the great malign tidal wave of his vision, that had threatened to engulf the earth.

She was still trembling underneath him, her arse working itself up against his belly, urging him to do it again, do it again only harder.

'I like it, Master. I like it. Please . . .'

He hadn't meant to do it, had only meant to fuck her and use her and forget her. But there was such talent within her, such sexual energy which might be of use to him and Sedet. He stooped to nuzzle her neck and she gave the faintest of ecstatic sighs as his teeth pierced the soft flesh of her throat.

It might have been five minutes later, ten, half an hour. He had lost track of time. Candice lay sprawled on the desk before him, but her blood was still sweet on his tongue and he felt better, stronger, more potent than he had ever done.

The door opened with a sudden click and a brown-curled head peered in.

'Miss Dorigo? I wondered . . . oh God no!'

The receptionist's voice tailed off in a shrill squeak, her eyes round and her face white with shock. But Heimdal did not turn a hair. He fixed her with his cool blue eyes and beckoned her into the room.

'My dear child! I'm so very glad you decided to join us.'

Andreas strolled along the seafront at Whitby, watching the 'Esk' chugging wearily out to sea with its load of dredged-up silt. Some things, at least, never changed.

'Feeling better?' enquired Mara.

'Well . . . a bit.' Andreas glanced down at the not-quite-trendy shorts and T-shirt which were the best Whitby could offer. 'But I can't see me winning any fashion awards.'

Mara laughed.

'At least you get a chance to show off your sexy knees.'

In the rush to find less conspicuous clothes, she had fared rather better than Andreas, having remembered the tiny ethnic shop with its rows of beads and tie-dyed muslins. The Indian cotton dress, with its tight bodice and semi-diaphanous skirt, took her right back to that first time in Whitby.

Then, she had been working as a fortune-teller and Andreas had been sent up to the town by his editor, to follow up a lead implicating local MP Sir Anthony Cheviot in a series of bizarre sex-scandals. Neither of them could have guessed, not in their wildest dreams, what the truth would turn out to be.

Mara slipped her arm through Andreas's.

'What are you thinking?'

'If you really want to know, I was just thinking that I used to be Andreas Hunt. God, I was a clever dick.'

Mara gave an amused chuckle.

'And you're not now?'

'Bitch.'

'Bonehead.'

They walked on together towards the swing bridge which divided the two halves of the town.

'What the fuck's going on here? That's what I'd like to know.' Andreas scanned the crowds swarming around the quayside. For every plain grey Pacamac there was at least one shaven head and two or three multicoloured robes. Not to mention the bare torsos and the young girls with their right tits hanging out of their dresses. 'Don't tell me – the circus is in town.'

'I haven't a clue.' Mara's gaze followed a couple of strapping youths clad only in sandals and loin-cloths of saffron-coloured cotton. Golden rings joined by a chain pierced their nipples, with a second chain which began between the nipples and led downwards, to be hidden at last by the folds of the loin-cloth.

'New Age Travellers, do you suppose?'

'Good grief no. Some sort of weird pagans maybe. No sort that I know.'

As if in answer to their confusion, a girl with naked breasts and a shaven, tattooed head pushed through the crowd, handing out leaflets. Andreas grabbed one as she passed by and she treated him to a dazzling smile which gave him a clear view of the three jewelled studs set into her pierced tongue.

'What does it say?' Mara perched on the bench beside Andreas and craned her neck to read.

'"THE END OF THE WORLD IS AT HAND",' read Andreas. He groaned. Not *another* loony predicting that the world was going to end on December 31, 1999. '"But the blessed Brother Julius will deliver us from eternal torment by the power of sensual penance and sexual worship." Oh he will, will he? "Through mortification of the flesh and the offering up of sexuality, the Brotherhood will teach you how to attain salvation. Join with us at the ruined abbey on the hill, and experience the physical and spiritual joy of Brother Julius's message of deliverance."' Andreas screwed the leaflet up into a ball and took aim. It landed neatly in the rubbish bin. 'Bollocks,' he concluded.

'That's your considered opinion?'

'You bet it is. After working on the *Comet* I ought to know a pervert when I see one.'

'Well, I think we ought to go and check out this so-called Brother Julius. Maybe it's a sign. Maybe he'll lead us to the next piece of the Eye of Baloch.'

Andreas watched a half-naked girl sashay past him, a long, glossy plait of brown hair swishing across her bare back. She wasn't a patch on Mara, of course, but even a dead man would have twitched into life at the sight of that fine, firm arse, wiggling its way up the promenade towards the pier.

'Mmm. Maybe. But just supposing we do find all the bits of this Eye thing, what do we do then? Hand it over to the Master and wait for him to put two and two together? If he ends up with twenty-twenty astral vision I'm going to need more than this dragon's-eye bracelet to protect me.'

Mara laid a soothing hand on his arm.

'I told you, Andreas. We'll use it against him.'

'But how?'

'I don't know yet. We'll find a way.'

Andreas looked at his feet, wiggling his toes – the way he always did when he was remembering something he'd rather not.

'I bet Max would have thought of a way,' he observed

gloomily. His thoughts wandered back, unbidden, to Max Trevidian – the psychic investigator who had helped them, only to find himself persecuted and destroyed by the Master. Andreas couldn't help feeling it was all his fault. 'Stupid bastard – going and getting himself vapourised like that. He owed me ten quid, you know.'

Mara squeezed his arm. She felt guilty too. If she hadn't persuaded Max to help her rescue Andreas, who knows? Max might still be around today, with his battered cords and his Morris Traveller.

'I know.'

Andreas got to his feet. This was no time to wax sentimental – he had things to do. For a start off, Whitby was full of eminently shaggable girls and he really ought to get to know some of them at least a *bit* better. Call it in-depth research. And then there was the thorny matter of acting in character. What would Nicholas Weatherall MP do on a sunny day in picturesque Whitby? He'd get completely pissed, that's what.

'I could murder a pint. The Hope and Anchor's just across the bridge.'

'You go. I'll wait for you here.'

'Sure?'

'Positive.'

Andreas strolled off across the swing-bridge and Mara relaxed in the sunshine, kicking off the painted Indian sandals and drawing her bare feet up so that she was sitting cross-legged on the bench with her skirt floating about her in the light breeze.

Alone, she was better able to tune in to the atmosphere of this place. It had changed. The last time she had been in Whitby the psychic vibrations had also been strong, but nowhere near as strong as this. The intensity of them now was both sensual and slightly frightening.

She let the breeze caress her, listening with her entire soul, feeling with her whole being. She felt aroused, excited, afraid. There was a power all around her, a power that was closing in like the embers of demon lover.

'You are very beautiful.'

Her eyes snapped open and she was looking into the face of a thin young man with a spider's web tattoo covering one side of his face and neck. His head was almost completely shaven, save for a cluster of long, thin, multicoloured plaits that trailed down his bare back.

She looked at him in silence for a moment, the directness of his approach startling yet oddly satisfying.

'It's true. You *are* beautiful.'

The young man sat down on the bench beside her and she did not protest. There was a magnetic attraction in the young man's eyes, and the intensity of his smile. His long, tanned fingers reached out and touched her bare shoulder and she could not suppress a little sigh. She fought to regain her composure.

'Who are you?'

'Someone, no-one. My friends call me Jak.'

'And why . . .?'

'I am a follower of Brother Julius.' As though that were sufficient introduction and explanation, Jak pressed his lips against the cool flesh of Mara's bare shoulder, running his tongue over her skin, tracing a path which led down towards her fingers. To her own surprise, she felt no desire to push him away. What he was doing was so entirely pleasurable that she did not want it to stop. 'So beautiful. Your body is an act of worship in itself, Mara Fleming.'

She stared at him, stunned.

'My name is Anastasia. Anastasia Dubois.'

Jak seemed unconcerned – either at Mara's reaction or the curious glances of passers-by.

'As you choose. All flesh is but a mask for the divine sensuality within us.' He slid his hand over her cheek, her throat, down over the swelling curve of her breast, and she felt the nipple swell and harden at his touch.

'Please, Jak . . .'

'Have no fear, Mara. Worship with me and glorify in the

divine power of your sexuality.'

He pinched her nipple and she moaned, almost silently, afraid to betray the secret of her arousal. Jak's smile was gentle, beatific.

'My penis is hard as iron for you, Mara Fleming.' He took hold of Mara's hand and placed it on his crotch. She felt his heat throbbing and burning into her and wanted it, craved it, yearned for it to be inside her. 'Will you kiss the lance of your salvation? Will you come with me to Brother Julius and perform an act of sexual worship?'

Mara's head was reeling, her senses overwhelmed by need. What power was this? What power could override her every instinct of self-preservation and make her crave sex with a complete stranger – a stranger she would not normally have given a second look?

It required the summoning of all her powers but she pulled away, breaking the silver thread of desire which bound them together, leaving Jak the startled one. His eyes were eagle-bright with hunger and disappointment.

'I have to meet someone,' she told him. And rather than let him sap her strength again, she turned away and began walking very quickly over the swing-bridge towards the Hope and Anchor.

In the ruined Abbey church of St Hilda, high on a hill above the town, Brother Julius was preaching the end of the world.

It was a hot day – a good deal hotter than it ought to have been in Whitby in June, in fact hotter than it would normally have been in August. This part of the North Yorkshire coast was renowned for its 'bracing' climate and for impressive sales of thermal underwear. But this year it was like a furnace.

It was as if Brother Julius was right and God really was stoking up the flames of Hell, ready to destroy the world in a torrent of fiery destruction.

Andreas and Mara sat on a travelling rug on the parched

grass, somewhere in the middle of the seething crowd. Andreas glanced around. How many people were here – four thousand, five? That wouldn't have been a bad gate for a rock concert, but this wasn't your typical rock-groupie crowd.

Oh, there were young people here, and lots of them – notably the 'Disciples' in their saffron loin-cloths and not much else – but the crowd spanned the spectrum of age, gender and class. Kids, mums and dads, even the odd Darby and Joan: it seemed that Brother Julius's message of brimstone and bonking carried a pretty universal appeal.

Brother Julius himself was not much to look at – more your Rasputin than your Billy Graham. Wild-eyed and tousle-haired, he had that vaguely messianic appeal which starts wars and charms empresses into bed. He had the gift of the gab too – a rich, sonorous voice that rang out, bell-like, on the sultry air.

'The world will end, brothers and sisters. It will end, and we will be destroyed with it. But there is a way, a way in which we can turn away the Lord's righteous anger . . .'

Mara nudged Andreas's elbow.

'I'm sure this is the place.'

'You think there's another piece of the Eye here?'

'I can feel it. If only I knew where . . .'

Andreas could feel it too. Since his imprisonment in the crystal, his own meagre psychic abilities had begun to develop a little. And he could sense something indefinably scary in the air. Frankly, topless sex-kittens or no, he just wanted to get away.

'I don't like it. He gives me the creeps. They all give me the creeps – look at the way they're *smiling*. It's like they've all been brainwashed.'

'I know. But we have to stay, we have no choice.'

Brother Julius's words were those of a complete madman, yet here among the ancient stones of the Abbey, they attained a curious plausibility. You'd have had to have been a hermit not to have noticed the peculiar things that were happening in the world. In some ways, imminent Armageddon was easier to believe in than the mystical Eye of Baloch.

'Salvation, brothers and sisters!' cried Brother Julius. Andreas could make out the line of a large and swelling cock beneath the silky white monastic robes.

'Salvation!' chorused the crowd.

Brother Julius lowered his voice to a dramatic whisper which seemed to make the very stones of the ancient Abbey vibrate to the rhythm of his creed.

'Salvation through sexual worship. It is the only way, the truly holy way.'

A gasp, a murmur, a sigh of approval ran through the crowd, and Andreas felt a hand on his bare thigh. He turned and saw that the girl beside him was wearing nothing but a smile and a double string of love-beads that swung invitingly between her painted breasts.

'Salvation,' she whispered. And Andreas was almost convinced.

'Andreas – look, look!'

He snapped his eyes away from the seductively naked acolyte and followed Mara's gaze. On the makeshift wooden platform Brother Julius was raising his arms above his head, showing the crowd something. And the crowd were keening, weeping, laughing, chanting with excitement.

'What . . .?'

'Can't you *feel* it?'

Julius raised the object aloft and a buzz of energy seemed to zip through Andreas's body. Yet it was a very ordinary-looking thing, a rather ugly goblet carved from some sort of grey stone.

'The Grail,' cried Brother Julius. 'The Grail has been sent to us as a sign. If we are to be saved we must offer our full and absolute obedience . . .'

'That?' Andreas looked at Mara. 'That's the second piece of the Eye?'

'Not the stone chalice itself. I think the piece of crystal

must be inside it. But how are we going to get at it, that's the question . . .'

The crowd were going mad, already tearing off their clothes, dancing and singing.

'If we do not offer our obedience, then the world will burn and we will burn with it!' thundered Brother Julius. 'Will you obey?'

'Obey, obey, obey!' chorused the crowd. 'We will obey.'

'Then offer your bodies as a sign of your obedient worship,' he commanded. And, unknotting his rope-belt, he slipped off his robes, standing naked before the crowd. His cock, although of average length, was impressively thick and sprang from the dark-brown tangle of his pubic curls like some sap-filled bough. His scrotum was pierced in several places to take an elaborate scrotal harness of golden chains whose heaviness weighed down his already-full and heavy balls.

'Brother, Brother Julius!' screamed a girl in the crowd, and Julius beckoned to her to join him on the platform. 'Come, child. Come and offer the sweet, sacred worship of your tender young body.'

She ran towards the stage, scrambling over the bodies of others who envied her this greatest of honours and clutched at her body as though it were the body of Brother Julius himself.

Julius stood motionless as a statue as the girl dropped to her knees before him, the Grail-chalice still raised above his head and his eyes wide and wild with some inner ecstasy.

As her lips closed around the shaft of his dick he began moving back and forth, almost imperceptibly, intensifying the sensations which her skilful young mouth was imparting to his hungry shaft.

'Worship, my children! Worship the divine sexuality within you!'

The effect of his words was instantaneous. Andreas felt hands clutching, clawing, stroking, pulling him to the ground, tearing off his clothes. He looked for Mara but he could not see her. Everything seemed submerged in a seething, ravenous sea of coupling bodies.

A lithe young girl sat astride him, working his penis into hardness, ramming her wet cunt down onto the spike of his erection whilst another knelt astride his face, offering up the honeysweet gift of her shaven cunt to be sucked and licked. Someone took hold of his right hand and pressed it into a warm, wet haven, and he felt the hard nut of a swollen clitoris under his fingertips. If this was Heaven, it was better than he'd expected. If it was Hell, he'd try harder to be bad.

Suddenly alone in the crowd, Mara called out to Andreas but she had lost all sight of him. Only the stroking, grasping hands and the thirsty tongues existed now. She could feel her body, already moist with sweat, producing a waterfall of juice that dripped down from her open sex lips onto the flesh of her upper thighs.

Sex. Sex. Sex. She had to have it, yearned to have it, needed it as mortals need food and drink. And she could feel herself sinking beneath the dark neap-tide of lust, submitting to the insistent kisses and caresses rising up her body, stripping away the last vestiges of her clothing.

'Well, well. Anastasia, my darling slut.'

A familiar voice, unpleasantly syrupy and with just a hint of menace, made her look up.

Sir Anthony Cheviot, close confidant of Anthony LeMaître and Nationalist MP for Whitby, was standing over her, his naked dick as threatening as a curving sabre. He was smiling.

'Sir Anthony . . . I . . .'

Cheviot clicked his fingers and two of his minders pushed off the young women who were sucking and licking at Mara's body.

'Your body is far too . . . talented to waste on such mortal scum,' he told her, forcing her onto her belly on the rough grass. 'And it is too long since I had you.'

She prepared herself for the rapier thrust of his cock, and he entered her with a smug brutality, holding apart her buttocks to expose the tight brown O of her arse.

Mara moved with his thrusts, giving him as much pleasure as a woman could give a man, concealing the fear that nagged and gnawed inside her.

Was Cheviot here by chance – or by design? And was it possible that he knew something which might destroy both Mara Fleming and Andreas Hunt?

8: The Abbey

'BLIZZARDS IN AUSTRALIA: RUSSIANS BLAMED'
(*Sydney Daily Sun*, 14 June)

The young slave placed the silver tray on the table and backed out, making a low bow. His jewelled cock-rings sparkled in the light from the chandelier, sending out flashes of ruby-red light.

Cheviot watched him leave, well-satisfied with his new acquisition, then turned to his guests.

'What do you think of Tojo?'

'He is very handsome,' replied Mara, unsure what she was supposed to say.

Cheviot laughed.

'*All* my slaves are handsome, as are all my sluts. But Tojo is perhaps a favourite of mine. The Japanese make such amusing slaves. It is almost a pity to break their spirit.'

Andreas toyed with the stem of his cut-glass goblet. Meeting Cheviot up here had been bad enough; being summoned to his huge country house was somewhat worse. But the very worst thing of all had been getting here to discover that Cheviot's mistress, Viviane, was here too.

Andreas had uncomfortable memories of Viviane, the red-haired vampire-slut who had initiated Cheviot into the Master's empire of lust. Of course, Andreas hadn't known she was a vampire when he'd first tracked her down. He'd thought she was just some tart who liked screwing MPs.

143

Consequently she'd very nearly succeeded in sinking her teeth into his throat.

Viviane slid almost noiselessly into the room, her teeth sharp and white and her slinky body encased in a figure-hugging sheath of black, sequinned fabric. She draped herself over the chaise-longue to such good effect that Andreas had a breathtaking view of her cleavage and one long, creamy thigh.

'So, Mr Weatherall, what do you think of Anthony's little country retreat?'

He regarded her, goldfish-like, for a split second, convinced that as soon as he spoke she would see through his fleshly disguise to the unwary journalist beneath.

'It's . . . very impressive.'

Viviane threw back her head and laughed, her laughter crystal-bright, her firm breasts quivering with amusement.

'It is a palace, Mr Weatherall. Our palace, given to us by the Master.'

'The Master is most generous,' murmured Andreas, thinking murderous thoughts.

'I thought you would be in London,' hazarded Mara. 'With Parliament still sitting and Baptiste so . . . troublesome.'

Cheviot met her gaze. She noticed a slight tightening at the corners of his mouth and fervently hoped she had not overstepped the mark.

'Baptiste is a mere insect,' he replied with apparent coolness. 'His destruction is imminent.'

Really, thought Andreas. Is that why your hands are shaking, Cheviot?

'Besides,' continued Cheviot, 'there is other work which must be done on behalf of the Master. Work which only those whom he trusts utterly may be permitted to undertake.'

Mara felt her resolve withering under Cheviot's searching gaze, but she knew he was all bluster. There was little about Cheviot that was remarkable, save perhaps his ferocious loyalty to the Master. But his mind was irritatingly difficult to probe, clouded and elusive, and that made her uneasy.

'Indeed?' Mara sat down in one of Cheviot's rather fine Louis XV fauteuils, crossing her legs to show a nice bit of thigh. She knew how much Cheviot appreciated a good pair of thighs, though Viviane's eyes narrowed at the sight of the Dubois slut's flirtatiousness. Mara knew she would have to be careful – Viviane would make a dangerous opponent. 'You are here on the Master's business?'

Cheviot hesitated, as though undecided about how much he should say. But after all, however unworthy he might consider them to be, Weatherall and the Dubois slut were two of the Master's most valued servants.

'The Master and his Queen plan to honour us with a visit in the autumn,' he said. 'And I must ensure that all is worthy of them. I must find more and better sex-sluts . . .' He regarded Andreas through hooded eyes for a few moments. 'And what brings you to Whitby?'

Mara cut in.

'I . . . well, we . . . the Master ordered us . . .'

Andreas threw her a meaningful glance. Better not to tell Cheviot anything, better by far.

'The Master has sent us on a fact-finding mission. We are touring the North, looking for suitable initiates for Winterbourne. Anyone who might prove valuable to the cause.'

'Is that so? The Master has commanded me to observe Brother Julius . . .'

'Julius – so that was why you were up at the Abbey?' Andreas sat up and took notice.

'The Master is considering him as a possible candidate for initiation, though personally I consider him rather too . . . volatile.'

Mara smiled. She had thought of a way . . .

'Really? I find him . . . interesting. Very, very interesting.' She gave a sexy purr and thrust her tits out a little further.

She knew how interesting Cheviot found *them*. 'I had rather hoped to meet him . . .'

Cheviot nodded, the glint of reawakened lust in his eyes.

'Ah yes,' he agreed. 'The man is certainly full of sexual vigour. I can quite appreciate your interest in him – why, I would not be averse to enjoying the man's flesh myself. If you wish to meet him, I am sure it can be arranged . . .'

'You are so kind,' purred Mara, slipping down the straps of her evening gown so that her stiff-nippled breasts sprang out. 'Would you like to fuck me now?'

Cheviot needed no second bidding. Smoothing down his rather fine new snakeskin waistcoat, he unzipped his cock and dived into paradise.

As Mara climbed the two hundred steps which led from the town to the Abbey, she was transported back in time to her last visit to Whitby. Then she had simply been Mara Fleming, innocent of everything except the arts of white magic and the desire to make the most of the sensual body nature had given her. Now, innocence had given way to self-preservation, desire to an insatiable, burning hunger.

Strange how the thought of her assignation with Brother Julius both revolted and excited her. She had felt his aura, tasted the dark strength that oozed out of the man like spilt blood, and she knew he would make a formidable opponent.

It was getting dark, the old fishing town was bathed in the navy-blue haze of dusk. Lights twinkled around the harbour, a single boat was gliding out on the evening tide. Soon it would be dark. Darker than Mara cared to imagine.

At the entrance to the old Abbey church twin girls emerged from the shadows to greet her, their identical, perfect bodies only partially veiled by their brightly coloured wraps. The orange and yellow muslin was so fine that it was scarcely thicker than a spider's web, accentuating rather than concealing the scarlet-painted crests of their nipples and the jewels they wore in their navels. The right breast of each girl was bare, its nacreous flesh decorated with intricate stencilled patterns in henna dye about the rich red cherry of her nipple.

'Do you come in peace?' asked one of the young women.

'I come in peace.'

'What do you seek?'

Mara smiled inwardly at the irony of her own words.

'I seek enlightenment.'

'And how shall you seek it?'

'At the feet of the blessed Brother Julius.'

'You may enter our camp. But first you must disrobe and put on the garments of worship.'

The two young women led her into a small stone outbuilding, lit by lamps of hollowed-out stone, in which burned a sweetly scented oil. The vapours made Mara's head spin and she recognised the scent of essential oils which had been used by her coven on nights of high and sensual ritual.

Her blouse and skirt were stripped from her, neatly folded and laid on a chair. There was a measured, almost ritualistic quality to the disrobing, although nothing was said, no prayer or incantation spoken. Next came her sandals – it seemed that no-one must approach Brother Julius except barefoot.

One of the girls disappeared for a moment and re-emerged with drifts of fine, glittery, spangled material dyed in shades of yellow, orange and flame-red. Mara stood obediently as the two girls prepared her, oiling and braiding her hair with silver thread, then winding the long swathe of fabric about her body, leaving the right breast bare.

A soft-bristled paintbrush was dipped into a small jar of pigment and one of the girls painted tiny stars on Mara's exposed breast, finishing by colouring her nipple a bright and juicy scarlet.

'You are ready now,' the girl announced. 'Come with us.'

Mara was led out once again into the sultry night air. It

was much darker now, the royal blue of twilight giving way to the deeper blue of a night sky punctuated by stars and softened by the large round moon sailing above the old town.

She was used to going barefoot and the dry grass felt almost comforting beneath her feet, as though she was once again in touch with the earth-spirits who had once governed and blessed her life. But it made her a little afraid to be led into the darkness by two strangers. She chided herself – why be afraid? What could Brother Julius do to her that Mistress Sedet and the Master had not already done a thousand times? Yet still she felt fear: the apprehension of one who knows, who understands, who *feels* the danger as though it were a tangible presence.

This place was eerie. So quiet. She knew for a fact that hundreds of Brother Julius's disciples were encamped up here in the Abbey grounds, yet there seemed little evidence of their existence. They were utterly silent. Silent as the grave.

'Here.'

The girl's voice came out of the silent darkness so suddenly that Mara started.

'Take a step down. Feel with your foot.'

Tentatively, Mara put out her foot and felt the ground with her bare toes. The grass went on for a few inches, then petered out and was replaced by cold, smooth stone. She might have expected that, after a day of sticky, sultry heat, the sun-baked stones would long retain some of the sun's warmth. But this stone was cold with a bone-deep chill.

'Please. Take a step down. You will not fall.'

She blinked and peered into the darkness, just making out the indistinct outline of a flight of steps and the faintest glow of light beyond. The first step took her into an atmosphere so heavy with incense that she almost swooned, but she continued descending the staircase into the waiting unknown.

At the bottom of the steps she found herself in a narrow, low-roofed passageway cut out of the rock, the darkness softening to a rosy glow as she approached the chamber at its end.

It was a small room with rough stone walls, lit by the flicker from half a dozen rosy-red candles set in stone candlesticks. There was little else in the room save for a narrow wooden bed, a table and chair, and – hanging on the walls – a selection of whips, manacles and canes.

In the centre of the room, clad in a rough woollen shift, knelt Brother Julius. At first glance he seemed in a trance, his eyes closed and his arms raised, finger and forefinger of either hand forming a perfect O. He was silent, save for the slow, regular rhythm of his breathing.

The twin girls withdrew, leaving Mara alone with Brother Julius.

'Brother? Brother Julius?'

He did not reply, though his breathing halted for a brief second, then recommenced, even and slow.

'Brother, I have come to you seeking enlightenment and the salvation of the world.'

'And how may this be accomplished, Sister?'

'Through sexual worship.'

It seemed to Mara that the merest ghost of a smile flitted across Brother Julius's lips, but when he spoke his voice was sonorous and solemn.

'Are you worthy, child?'

Slightly nonplussed, Mara cast around for the answer Brother Julius would most like to hear.

'I hope so, Brother – with your help and teaching.'

Julius turned his head slowly towards her, his eyes opening. They were bright and searching, the pupils huge and black as though dilated by some narcotic drug.

'The way is long and hard, Sister.'

Mara knelt on the floor before Brother Julius and raised his right hand to her lips, kissing it and winding her tongue about his index finger as though it were a miniature penis.

'Lead me, Brother.'

Julius smoothed his hand over Mara's cheek, neck and the bare, shameless swell of her right breast, weighing the flesh, flicking his thumb over the stiff red crest. It felt good – better than Mara might have wished to admit.

'You have a certain . . . spirituality,' Julius concluded. 'And your humility is pleasing to me. You are willing to undergo ordeals that will cleanse and scour your very soul, making it receptive to the purest and most divine sexual pleasures?'

'I am willing.'

'So be it.' Julius's voice was not the sanctimonious drone of a priest, but a low growl of pleasure, so sensual that Mara felt shivers of recognition trembling through her.

He stood up and pulled Mara to him, crushing his lips against hers.

'Feel the power of divine sexuality, Sister.' His hand roamed once again over Mara's bare breast, then he stooped and took her nipple into his mouth, first sucking and then biting it, hard enough to cause a surprisingly agreeable mélange of pleasure and pain. 'It is the strongest and most divine power in the universe.'

'Yes, Brother. I seek only to know . . .'

To know something far beyond this bizarre ritual of sexual worship, thought Mara to herself. But in order to stand any chance of obtaining the next piece of the Eye of Baloch, she must first go along with whatever Brother Julius demanded of her.

'Disrobe, Sister.'

He took a step back, as though better to admire the spectacle of this most attractive of neophytes, peeling off the flimsy veils which floated about her firm, juicy body.

It was the work of seconds; and then Mara was standing before Brother Julius, her heart pounding so loudly that she was sure he must be able to hear it.

'I am ready to be cleansed, Brother.'

'Stand at the end of the bed.'

Mara obeyed.

'Bend over the bedstead.'

She did so, thrusting out her gloriously rounded backside, peachy and firm, and Brother Julius selected a cane from the half-dozen mounted on the walls of his spartan cell. It was a springy cane, about four feet long and half an inch in diameter, soaked in water to increase its flexibility and springiness. Varnished black, it was finished off with a plain silver hand-grip.

Mara braced herself for what would come next. The swish of the cane, the grunt of effort as it sliced down through the air to smack into the creamy-white flesh of her backside. But when it came, the discomfort was more severe than she had expected – for Brother Julius had an expert hand, schooled to perfection on the soft white backsides of his many young acolytes, both boys and girls.

'Do you confess your wickedness?'

'Yes, Brother.'

'Do you accept the divine purity of sexual desire and the supreme ecstasy of orgasm?'

'I accept.'

'Mortification of the flesh,' gasped Brother Julius as he wielded the cane a second and a third time, 'is the surest way to purge the soul of impurity, and open up our flesh to the acceptance of divine sexuality.'

Mara could not help noticing how his breath came in fits and starts, and how his voice was becoming more hoarse and husky. She knew the signs of a man's lust and knowing that Brother Julius desired her excited her own desires.

In time, as she knew it would, the pain began to reduce in its intensity, not because Brother Julius was using any less effort on her chastisement, but because something in the nature of the pain began to change. Instead of the intense, unbearable burning, the sensation began to mellow to a more sensual heat. The heat seemed to begin deep in her belly and spread out to her whole body – tits and cunt and arse and even to the very tips of her fingers and toes.

Brother Julius seemed to sense that her excitement mirrored his own for he began to urge her on in his husky voice, dripping with sex.

'Admit the power of your desire, Sister. Spread your thighs wide and let me see the joyful spendings of your cunt. Let your breasts hang down like swollen fruit, heavy with sweet juice. Open yourself to desire, Sister, open yourself to me . . .'

His words and his skill very nearly brought her to the point of orgasm, but as the moment when she felt she could take no more, Brother Julius ordered her to lie on her back on the bed.

The rough bed-cover abraded her torn back and bruised backside but Brother Julius's brand of spiritual zeal offered no respite, no concessions to weakness. Mara tried not to cry out as he lowered her onto the bed and told her to draw her knees up, parting her thighs and offering an unimpeded view of her blossoming sex.

'Lie still, Sister. The pain is good. The pain cleanses.'

Brother Julius was standing over her, one of the stone candlesticks in his hand and the pinkish-red glow from the candle illuminating his wild-eyed face. Mara sensed what he was going to do and both feared and desired this new torment.

The first drop of candle wax fell in a rosy-red splash between her breasts. It burned like a hornet sting and scorched a trail down her belly until it hardened into a wriggling red snake. She squirmed, trying not to show her pain, but when Brother Julius held the candlestick over her right breast, she cried out even before the wax dropped, slow and syrupy, from the candle.

Its burning kiss was not quite like anything she had experienced before, despite the ingenuities of Mistress Sedet's cruelty. Wide-eyed, she gazed up into Brother Julius's face and saw that it was filled with a fanatical zeal.

'Open yourself to the cleansing pain, Sister. And to the pleasure which will surely follow.'

He did not lie. For as the wax made patterns on her flesh, Mara felt once again that same subtle change from suffering to pleasure. She found herself anticipating the sensation of the hot wax on her skin, sending out her spirit to meet it and melting in the incandescence which surrounded her whole being like a fiery, caressing hand.

Her cunt was hot, wet, welcoming. She spread her thighs a little wider, though terror filled her heart as she saw the candle poised above her open cunt-lips.

The wax dripped over her pubis, hot red rivulets that ran down through the auburn forest of her maidenhair and entered the secret garden of her pleasure.

No. No. No. Her fear cried out in the silence of her heart, but her body was screaming *Yes, yes, yes.*

And then the burning turned to ecstasy and her sex muscles were opening and closing in orgasm as though they too longed to kiss this new and merciless instrument of delight.

'My *dear* Sister.' Brother Julius's voice was smooth as silk, warm with satisfaction. A wet stain of semen was clearly visible on the front of his robe. So that was how he liked to get his kicks.

'I have pleased you, Brother?'

'You may yet please me more, by one further act of worship.'

'Anything, Brother. Show me how to worship.'

Brother Julius turned away and walked across the dimly lit cell to a rough wooden chest. Turning the rusty iron key, he lifted the lid and took out an object wrapped in hessian. He unwrapped it lovingly, as a man might undress his lover, slowly and sensuously.

Mara knew it was the Grail-chalice even before she saw it. She held her breath. Was this truly where she would find the next piece of the Eye? Here, in the Abbey precincts, its presence was so strong. She could feel it all around her.

Brother Julius walked slowly back across the cell, holding the Grail-chalice before him. Stopping by the bed, he kissed it, then held it to Mara's lips. She pressed them against it, anticipating the rush of psychic energy that would tell her she had found what she was looking for. To her surprise, she felt nothing – only the sexual excitement of being here, of lying open-thighed on Brother Julius's bed, waiting for him to dream up the next exquisite torture.

'Open yourself, Sister. To pleasure . . .'

Julius whispered to her; a lover's whisper, soft, gentle, full of the most intense sensuality. But his hands were not so gentle. They were pressing the stem of the Grail-chalice between her thighs, forcing her to open wider and wider to accommodate the cold grey stone, slipping it inside her until she was stretched so tight she felt sure that he would tear her apart.

Yet the pleasure. Oh, the pleasure. The chalice felt like a man's curled fist in her cunt, turning round and round, pressing itself against her cunt walls and the neck of her womb. Pleasure so intense that she could have wept.

Pleasure – but not enlightenment. If what she sought was indeed in the Abbey precincts, it was certainly not in the Grail-chalice. Oh, the chalice might have its own source of power, but it was a poor sort of power compared to the all-seeing, all-consuming force of the Eye of Baloch.

Mara opened herself – body, soul and spirit – to the pleasure, and as she did so she felt her powers intensify, her psychic sight clarify, the seed of an answer implanting itself in her mind.

Perhaps the next piece of the Eye was not to be found in the chalice but she had a good idea where it might be.

Liz Exley had always enjoyed going to the theatre. These days, it wasn't the action on the stage she was interested in – it was the endless possibilities for sexual recreation.

The toilet cubicle at the Alhambra Theatre was a little

on the small side, but that simply added to Liz's enjoyment. It was so intimate, so wicked – and besides, she had long since passed the point of no return. Her hunger burned, making her salivate with lust for the young rock singer.

Brent Harley was a celebrity guest at the thousandth performance of *London Nights*, an all-British stage show backed by – among others – a certain Anthony LeMaître MP. The show had been a huge hit and was shortly to cross the Atlantic to Broadway, not to mention the big-budget Hollywood film . . . In short, anyone who was anyone wanted to be associated with the show, and that was how teen idol Brent Harley had found himself sitting in the front row of the circle, bored to tears and looking for some action.

Liz was looking for action too. She'd fixed on Harley the moment she saw him. He was perfect for the way she felt, with his ripped designer jeans showing tasty glimpses of tanned thigh, his Dior T-shirt and the shaggy mane of expensively permed blond hair. He liked to work out, she could see that. He was no muscle-bound hunk but his body was beautifully sculpted, the tanned flesh of his bare arms gently undulating as he raised his arm to sweep a hank of hair off his forehead.

It came as little surprise to either of them when he accepted Liz's invitation with such enthusiasm. He liked his chicks slim and sassy and small-breasted, and Liz's glossy red PVC minidress had set his taste-buds tingling and his pulse racing. After a couple of drinks in the theatre bar, Harley was easy meat.

Leaning her back against the partition wall, Liz put one foot on the toilet seat and, as her legs parted, the skintight PVC skirt of her minidress started rolling up her thighs as though it had a mind of its own.

Harley gave an appreciative whistle.

'Way to go, bitch-queen!'

He pushed a ringed hand into the steamy delta between

Liz's thighs and the row of rings piercing her shaven outer labia jingled together.

'I've had over a thousand women, you know,' bragged Harley, working Liz's juices between his fingers and savouring the silky-wet texture. 'None of them are quite like you, though.' He ran his fingertip all along the baby-soft, freshly shaven pussy-lips. 'Did I ever tell you I just *love* shaven pussy?'

'No, I don't think you did.'

But Liz knew anyway. Liz knew a surprising amount about Brent Harley.

'No, you're not like any of the other groupies I've had,' Harley told her, teasing the hard bud of her clitoris.

'That's because I'm not a groupie,' retorted Liz, running scarlet talons over Harley's neck and shoulders, and suddenly rending the stretchy cotton of his T-shirt, baring his chest. 'I'm a connoisseur.'

Excited by Liz's assertiveness (as she had known he would be), Brent Harley peeled off the remnants of his T-shirt and put his hand to the fly-buttons of his 501s.

'No, let me.'

Liz's fingers were so much more skilful than his – despite which, it was a whole lot more fun having a beautiful woman take your cock out of your pants for you. A bit like having your nursery-school teacher do it for you when you were a little kid . . . only about a million times more exciting.

Supple and athletic, Liz liked to have sex not just in interesting places, but in interesting positions. Bracing herself against the toilet wall, she raised her left leg with all the ease of a ballet dancer and rested her foot on Harley's shoulder. He really liked the feel of the red patent leather shoe pressing against his cheek, the spiky heel just a fraction from his jugular. And women who wore little gold chains round their ankles had always turned him on.

But it was the sight of Liz's wide-open pussy that made him give a tom-cat yowl of excitement.

'Shh! Someone will hear,' teased Liz, kissing her index finger and laying it on his lips.

'I don't give a fuck.'

Liz pouted in mock disappointment.

'And there I was, hoping you would . . .'

He answered her by pushing his dick very suddenly, and very ineptly, between her legs. For a man who had had a thousand women, Brent Harley was a surprisingly unskilled lover. Liz took hold of him and guided him with an expert hand to her wet and willing hole.

'Aah!' The breath exploded from him as he shuddered with pleasure at that first, exhilarating contact of cock and cunt.

'Fuck me,' Liz commanded him; and proceeded to fuck him, pumping her hips down onto his thick hard spike, practically sucking the pleasure from him like juice from a ripe fruit.

As for Brent Harley, he'd seldom known such pleasure – and it had certainly never lasted this long. The best fucks he'd had had all been high-class hookers or groupies with a list of conquests as long as Superman's dick: women of resourcefulness and talent, who could coax and command an over-enthusiastic young buck. None of them had been this good, though. Why, the sex was so good it was almost supernatural. Maybe he'd write a song about it . . .

Liz enjoyed feeding on Harley's sexual energies, although he was frankly rather hard work – so trigger-happy that she had to use all her sensual artistry to keep him from coming into her before she was good and ready.

She left him drained and unconscious, slumped on the toilet seat with his pants round his ankles. He'd be deeply embarrassed in the morning, when the tabloids published a photograph of him half-naked in a theatre toilet. Blind drunk, they'd say. Liz knew different. And Brent Harley would never know how close he'd come to being kissed by Liz Exley's very white, sharp teeth.

Feeling invigorated after her encounter with Harley, Liz

tidied herself up and shimmied sexily through to the theatre bar, downing a couple of recreational Bloody Marys before making her way back to the auditorium for the rest of the second half.

At the end of the show, she followed the crowd through the foyer to the front door of the Alhambra. It was a beautiful night, why bother with a taxi? Why not just walk through the darkness and let it caress your skin? Why not walk naked beneath the stars and delight in the power and perfection of immortality?

She turned right past Leicester Square tube station and spotted three figures she recognised, standing beside a gleaming limousine. Two were a young man and woman – the famous theatrical couple Kieran Baskerville and his wife Estelle. And they were chatting to someone Liz had wanted to meet for a long, long time.

A certain Harry Baptiste.

Liz gave a little growl at the back of her throat. Oh yes, she'd wanted to meet Mr Baptiste for simple ages. What a feather in her cap it would be if she – not Sonja or Joanna or even Sedet – could be the one to break through that ridiculous facade of spotless morality.

But how to break in to Mr Baptiste's intimate little discussion . . .?

In the event she did not need to use her wits, for Kieran and Estelle Baskerville said their goodnights, hailed a taxi and disappeared into the night. Harry Baptiste was just about to get into his limousine when a tall, slim blonde with short hair and an even shorter red PVC dress just happened to walk past.

She smiled at him. He returned her smile, his eyes following her as she walked slowly past him for a few yards, making sure that he had got a really good view of her backside and long, long legs.

'Miss . . .?'

She spun round.

'Yes?'

Harry Baptiste took a few steps nearer and held out his hand in affable greeting.

'Good evening. Don't I know you from somewhere?'

'I don't understand,' protested Andreas, following Mara up the last few steps to the Abbey. There was one good thing about climbing all these blasted steps, though – he had an opportunity to admire Mara's splendid backside, clad today in the tightest of tight denim shorts.

'I thought I explained.' Mara reached the top of the steps and turned to gaze out and over the blue-grey sea beyond the town. Yep, thought Andreas to himself. Not just a great arse – brilliant tits as well. Boy, have you got good taste, Hunt.

'Tell me again.'

Mara set off not for Brother Julius's camp at the Abbey, but towards the graveyard of the nearby parish church. The graveyard, funnily enough, where Dracula was supposed to have done quite a lot of his lurking and biting. Huh! thought Andreas – garlic and pointy sticks. If only the Master could be dealt with that easily.

'I was wrong about the Grail-chalice. The Eye isn't there, it has nothing to do with the chalice.'

'So why did we both get that really weird feeling?'

'It wasn't the chalice that did it, it was the atmosphere. You remember what it was like – all that hysteria, all that build-up of sexual energy. It must have activated the power of the Eye.'

'But that still doesn't tell us where the Eye is,' pointed out Andreas, following Mara through the gate into the graveyard. Thankfully at this time of the morning the place was deserted – he didn't fancy running into Brother Julius and his merry mob out for a morning stroll.

'Don't worry,' replied Mara with just a hint of smugness. 'I think I *know* where it is.'

'How?'

'I did what I should have done in the first place. I

stopped trying so hard and followed my psychic intuition. I knew the next piece of the Eye must be here somewhere.'

'Here? In this churchyard?'

'Shush. Let me think. No, let me *feel*.'

Mara closed her eyes and put her hands to her temples. The power was certainly here, very real, very close. It felt like electricity from a generator, pulsing into her brain from her fingertips. After what seemed like an age to Andreas, she opened her eyes.

'Come on.'

'You know where it is?'

'Come on!'

She half-walked, half-ran across the churchyard, past well-tended graves and crumbling old monuments.

'Here.'

She pointed to an old family mausoleum, a squat stone-built monstrosity with weeping angels and iron gates hanging open on a single hinge.

'Spooky,' commented Andreas.

'It's not the dead we should be afraid of, Andreas. It's the undead who want to destroy us.'

Mara felt sudden tears rising to her eyes and blinked them away. Until I find a way to escape from this prison of flesh, she thought to herself, I too am one of the undead.

She felt along the weather-smoothed walls of the family tomb, the inscriptions almost obliterated by years of wind and frost. In its design, it was a rather unusual mausoleum – instead of the usual blank stone walls, it had small, decorative windows along the sides, showing rural scenes depicted in stained and painted glass.

The power was almost too strong to bear. She could feel it shaking her body as she forced herself to follow the trail.

Pain. Exhilaration. Release.

The window showed shepherds tending their flocks on a sunny hillside. Above them, in a periwinkle-blue sky, hung a huge and golden radiating sun. The moment her fingers touched the sun she knew that she had found what she was looking for.

At her touch, she felt the roundel of stained glass loosen as the ancient lead seemed to soften and give way. Silently, the golden sun fell into the palm of her hand.

She held out her hand. Andreas peered at the glass sun. 'Is that it?'

'Look – look at the centre. It's a pure, flawless crystal.'

She touched it with her index finger and it was frosty-cold like ice, so cold that it was like touching the inside of a freezer. And the warmth from her dissolved it almost instantly, leaving a circular hole in the centre of the glass sun and a powdery, glittering frost on her palm.

Mara picked up the glass and held it up to the light.

'Don't you see?' she said. 'It's the iris and pupil of an eye.'

As she held it between finger and thumb, Andreas noticed that the sunlight was shining through it. Only it couldn't be the sun, because the real sun was shining into Mara's face but the light that was coming out of the glass sun seemed to be radiating from Mara's body.

A shaft of golden light emerged from the circular centre of the glass sun, falling onto a bare patch of ground in front of them. As it touched the ground, steam began to rise, at first just a few wisps, but then great clouds of it, hiding the earth. Andreas and Mara had to shield their faces from the heat.

When the clouds of steam at last cleared, things had changed. Topographically speaking, the impossible had happened – but then, Andreas was becoming accustomed to the impossible. He took one look at the flight of stone steps leading down into the earth and decided it was high time *he* took the first step into the unknown.

Better go grab Destiny by the balls before it had a chance to do the same to you.

9: Polmadoc

'ATOMIC CLOCKS GO MAD. SCIENTIST CLAIMS
TIME IS RUNNING BACKWARDS'
(Florida Science Gazette, 23 June)

The flight of jagged and crumbling stone steps descended
steeply, past walls of cut earth where red-eyed millipedes
scuttled suddenly out of the darkness and ghost-white
worms wriggled underfoot.

Leading Mara by the hand, Andreas took each step with
the uncomfortable feeling that it might be his last. A dark,
reddish fog swirled around him, making it impossible to
see more than a few inches in front of his face. Somewhere
in front of them a light blazed, making the red fog fluoresce
like dry ice at a rock concert. The nearer they got to it, the
more its brilliance intensified, until it was almost painful to
look into the light.

Stumbling half-blind down the last few steps, they
emerged into the mouth of a cave – and suddenly the fierce
red blaze was gone. In its place was a cool, green
luminescence. Blinking and rubbing their eyes, they stepped
forward.

They were standing in a secluded forest glade, the
greenish light coming from the sun's rays, filtering gently
down through the canopy of leaves. When Andreas turned
to look back, he saw that everything – the cave-mouth, the
reddish glare, the flight of steps – had disappeared. And
they were alone in the green twilight of the forest.

Or perhaps not quite alone . . .

'Which way now?' Mara surveyed the tall pillars of tree trunks, extending in long, irregular lines as far as the eye could see. For once, she could feel no force guiding her. She slipped the glass sun into the pocket of her shorts.

The sound of a woman's laughter, somewhere among the trees, made up Andreas's mind for him.

'That way.'

They started walking through the trees towards the source of the sound. But no matter how far they walked, it always seemed to be about the same distance away – a low, husky giggle and then a series of long sighs that began quite clearly, then faded into the sound of a summer wind, shaking the branches of the trees.

'It's a trap,' said Mara nervously. 'Someone's playing games with us.'

'Sounds like someone's playing games with *her*,' observed Andreas, and kept on walking. The sound of the woman's distant laughter was so irresistibly sensual that he could not think of turning back and, besides, the thought of crawling back to the Master empty-handed was enough to inspire anyone to acts of folly.

The trees began to thin out a little and then they saw it: a small, grassy clearing almost hidden in the heart of the forest. Within a circle of brightly coloured toadstools, a man of twenty-five or so was lying on his back on the grass, his wiry straw-blond hair spread out about his face. His naked torso was deeply tanned, his body muscular and hard like a labourer's.

He was reaching up to touch the heavy, pendulous breasts of a woman who was kneeling astride him. She had tumbling, bleached-blonde curls that fell over her shoulders and brushed her pouting scarlet lips. She was wearing a tight white cotton blouse, partially unbuttoned so that her large soft breasts spilled forward, almost falling out of her lacy black underwired bra. Her skirt was up around her backside, revealing tanned bare thighs as smooth as silk and as strong as iron.

She laughed again and the sound was like cool water, trickling over Andreas's skin. He looked at Mara, and saw that she was breathing quickly, excitedly, already aroused by the scene unfolding before them. He slid his hand across and felt for the firm curve of her bum cheek, stroking and kneading it until she responded and her fingers traced along the bulging line of his zipper.

Andreas gave the faintest murmur of approval at Mara's caress – not wanting to disturb the couple in the clearing who were unwittingly providing such a diverting entertainment. But he could have sung for joy as Mara slid down his fly-zipper, releasing the imprisoned serpent of his desire.

As he watched the young man undoing the last of his lover's buttons, Andreas unfastened Mara's shorts and she obligingly wriggled out of them, letting them fall to the ground around her feet. Kicking them away, she pulled up her tight black T-shirt and eased it over her head, dropping it on top of the shorts and shaking out her glossy auburn curls. Her tongue moistened the red ox-bow of her lips and Andreas shared her hunger.

He submitted joyfully to Mara's skilful hands, letting her take charge of his pleasure. And when they were naked they began to caress each other, teasing each other's bodies like the youth and his lover who were still acting out their sensual tableau.

The man's hands slipped round his lover's back and fumbled for the catch of her bra. She laughed and tightened her thighs about his hips, pushing herself down a little so that her pubic delta was rubbing up and down the bone-hard shaft of his dick.

'Hot little slut,' he breathed and, as the catch of her brassière yielded, he grabbed full handfuls of her breast flesh, squeezing and kneading and delighting in its doughy malleability. She too seemed to enjoy these rough caresses, for she reached down and put her hand between her thighs, feeling for her lover's cock.

'You're good and hard . . .'

'I'm always hard for you, Patsy. Don't matter where or when.'

'Here and now is always the best.'

Without further ado she raised herself by her strong thighs and thrust down hard, engulfing his hardness in her wet haven. Andreas, feeling for the soft wetness of Mara's cunt, at first regretted that he could not see the young woman's cunt lips tightly kissing the dick-shaft as she moved up and down on top of her lover.

But her skirt swirled and floated so prettily about her thighs that it was not so much what he could see, as what he could not see that turned Andreas on. For a split second the skirt would move up a fraction, revealing the perfect globe of a plump white buttock – and then that glimpse would be gone, replaced by some other tantalising and fleeting image.

He did not question what was happening. In this place it felt right to have a lover's hand on your dick and your fingers probing deep into the squelchy-wet paradise of her quim. So, so right.

Mara let her mind explore the pleasure which was overtaking her. No longer watching the two lovers before her, she closed her eyes and entered their bodies, feeling what they felt, adding their pleasure to her own. Could Andreas feel it too? She tightened her fingers about his cock and he gave a soft moan as it grew harder, closer still to the point of no return.

Orgasm, when it came, was an ocean of sensations – great tumbling breakers of pleasure. Not the pleasure of a single individual, or even of two individuals pleasuring each other. This was the shared ecstasy of four lovers, their minds and spirits joined for a few brief seconds before the last waves of orgasm died away.

Patsy and her lover seemed quite oblivious to the confusion their little diversion had caused. Seemingly unaware of the fact that Mara and Andreas were watching them, they got up, calmly put on their clothes and walked slowly and silently out of the clearing.

'Andreas!'

Mara was already struggling into her clothes. Andreas rolled over lazily, his body still warm and his mind drowsy from Mara's hand-fuck.

'Where's the fire?'

'It's them, Andreas. I didn't realise it, but I do now. We have to follow *them*.'

'But . . .'

'Get dressed – hurry up, or everything will go wrong!'

Reluctant but resigned, Andreas threw his clothes back on and followed Mara across the clearing and into the trees. He could just make out the disappearing forms of Patsy and her lover, her arm draped around his waist and his hand on her backside.

'There – over there.'

They set off in pursuit, stumbling over tree roots and stepping into rabbitholes in their haste to catch up with the two lovers. But, like Patsy's laughter, the two figures always seemed the same distance away. It didn't matter if you walked or ran or crawled, Patsy and her blond hunk would always be ahead of you, laughing, kissing, strolling through the trees.

But suddenly they weren't there any more. And neither were the trees. One minute Andreas and Mara were walking through a forest, the next, standing on an empty moor looking out over rocky cliffs and an endless, stormy grey ocean.

'What the . . .?'

This was more than disorientating, it was maddening. Mara had been right – someone *was* playing games with them and Andreas wasn't a bit impressed with their sense of humour.

A voice behind them, calm, dark, a little sardonic, cut through their thoughts and made Mara's blood run cold.

She had felt no approaching presence, sensed nothing but the loneliness of this wild place.

'I am Pendorran,' the voice announced. 'You will come with me.'

In the African Room at Winterbourne, two officials from the French Embassy were enjoying the Master's unique brand of hospitality.

Winterbourne remained the best-kept secret in England, its existence only revealed to those who could be of assistance in increasing the Master's power. An invitation to the exclusive pleasure-place was a coveted prize only ever awarded to the wealthy, the influential and the beautiful. And it was rightly coveted. For no matter how perverse your desires and how carefully you had hidden them under a veneer of morality, your every dream would be made flesh at Winterbourne.

The Master had no particular fondness for French neo-fascists, but he urgently needed a network of reliable initiates in Europe, followers who would obey him implicitly and prepare themselves for the extension of his power over all the world.

Once he had the Eye of Baloch and had eliminated the troublesome power which was seeking to thwart him, there would be nothing to stop him becoming Master of the whole world. And he'd stop at nothing to ensure that it happened. The Devil himself was not too evil to be the bedfellow of Anthony LeMaître.

He stood in the corridor outside the African Room, closed his eyes and feasted on the scene unrolling on the other side of the door. Messieurs Rémy and DeFarge were *pieds noirs*, old colonials who missed the days back in the Fifties when they had had a constant supply of toothsome young Algerians who knew a thousand tricks to tease a flaccid prick into life. They did not hold with all this independence nonsense – it conflicted far too violently with their sexual pleasures.

The Master had known instantly what would best please them. A return to the 'good old days' back in North Africa, that's what they wanted. And he had instructed Heimdal to prepare a welcome which Rémy and DeFarge would not forget for a very long time.

The room had been cunningly transformed to represent a cell in a North African *commissariat de police*, and the two Frenchmen were dressed in full police uniform – light khaki tunic, jodphurs and shiny brown knee-boots. A ceiling fan circled lazily beneath the ceiling but the atmosphere was hot and steamy.

Ibrahim and Kasim played the parts of penitent prisoners, kneeling on the floor of the cell with their hands tied behind their backs. They were stripped to the waist, their djabellahs already torn by their captors' enthusiastic hands and their back striped from the first strokes of the lash.

Rémy was staring at Ibrahim, drinking in the sheer magnificence of his perfect physique, the oiled skin smooth and glossy as polished haematite and the well-honed musculature rippling beneath the flesh at every tiny movement. He turned to his colleague. But DeFarge seemed more than occupied with his greedy contemplation of the Arab kneeling before him.

Kasim was the embodiment of DeFarge's every wet dream for the last ten years. Curly brown hair, dusky skin and full lips; with downswept eyelashes so silky and so long that they were more beautiful than a girl's. How could LeMaître possibly have guessed at his fetish for young, downy-cheeked Arabs with slender, girlish bodies and slim hands with painted nails? He had kept his predilection strictly under wraps ever since his return from North Africa and only allowed himself the smallest indulgences on his annual visit to the Turkish brothels. It would be disastrous if the Party got wind of his sexual preferences. He'd been almost fanatically careful. So how . . .?

The young Arab looked up at him and the sight of those

liquid-brown, innocent eyes almost made DeFarge come on the spot. He imagined how exciting it would be to wank himself and, when the spunk came, letting it splash over that pretty, upturned face, soiling it with the mark of his superiority and his possession.

'Please, Inspecteur DeFarge . . .'

Kasim was good at this little game. He had been well-schooled by Ibrahim, who had initiated a good many powerful men and women into the ways of Winterbourne. And Ibrahim adored his work – almost as much as he adored the Master. Beyond the door, the Master revelled in the strength of Ibrahim's devotion, making a mental note to reward him by letting him fuck Mistress Sedet while he looked on.

'You will not speak until you are spoken to.' DeFarge pushed the sole of his boot into Kasim's face and gave a hard shove, sending Kasim spinning to the ground. He turned back to Rémy, whose cock was clearly straining under his khaki trousers. 'How are the prisoners charged, Capitaine Rémy?'

Rémy's eyes glinted with delicious anticipation. This agreeable charade was just the thing he needed to get him hard and horny again after years of putting up with his tedious wife and mistress.

'They were found performing an indecent sexual act in the street, Inspecteur. They are filthy scum . . .'

'Indeed.' DeFarge swallowed down the saliva which was gathering in his mouth. He always salivated copiously in anticipation of a good dinner or a tight-arsed youth. Tonight, he had already enjoyed the former and the latter could only be short moments away. 'And what was the precise nature of this indecent act?'

'It does not say on the charge sheet,' replied Rémy innocently.

'Then perhaps we should require the prisoners to give us a demonstration?'

DeFarge's watery eyes gleamed as he gave the command.

'Show us exactly what you were doing when you were arrested.'

'But, Inspecteur . . .' protested Kasim.

'Do it.'

To their credit, thought the Master, Ibrahim and Kasim put up a creditable show of reluctance, struggling and protesting and demanding to be freed – until Rémy and DeFarge ripped off their remaining clothes and forced Ibrahim's dick into Kasim's mouth.

Rémy had seen a good many beautiful cocks in his time but none finer than Ibrahim's. The Ethiopian boxer had been chosen by the Master's late servant Delgado precisely because of his physical beauty. His cock had the smooth, hard beauty of sculpted black marble, rising up from shaven balls that were as heavy and as juicy-firm as ripe plums. And oh! the length and thickness of that pierced black shaft, sliding in and out of the wet haven of Kasim's mouth.

Ibrahim was kneeling up, Kasim almost prostrate before him, helpless to do anything but keep on sucking as Ibrahim thrust his dick slowly in and out of his mouth. The ten inches of firm black flesh were almost too much to take, half-choking him as the glans hit the back of his throat again and again, but Kasim enjoyed discomfort. And as a result he was one of the Master's favourite fucks.

DeFarge rubbed his hand over the front of his trousers. Watching was all very well, but if he didn't get some real action pretty soon he was going to find it impossible to control himself. That drink Madame LeCoeur had given him – some sort of herbal concoction mixed with wine – well, she'd said it would 'intensify and prolong his libidinous urges', but she hadn't said it would do it quite so effectively. He'd tried just about everything in his time – Spanish Fly, poppers, cocaine, hashish – but nothing had made him feel quite this randy. He felt as if he could come and then keep on coming all night long.

Which was exactly what the Master intended. After all,

he was a thoughtful and generous host. He liked his guests to enjoy themselves before subjecting them to the sharp and deadly kiss of initiation.

'I have seen enough.' DeFarge pushed Kasim away and clear threads of saliva and Ibrahim's pre-come trailed from the young Arab's mouth. He was so, so sweet, thought DeFarge. Sweet and tender as a spring chicken. 'You will go to prison for this outrage against public decency.'

'Non, non, Inspecteur, je vous en prie . . .'

Ibrahim's French wasn't perfect but it was improving. It was certainly good enough to play the part of the young and frightened Algerian, begging for mercy from the cruel and powerful French police inspector.

'Well . . .' DeFarge glanced at Rémy and a broad smile crept across Rémy's face. 'There might be another way. What do you think, Capitaine Rémy? Should we offer the prisoners a chance to redeem themselves?'

'I think, in this instance, that mercy might be appropriate, Inspecteur DeFarge,' replied Rémy smoothly, unbuttoning his penis from his old-fashioned police-issue pants. His cock lay hot and throbbing in his hand. 'Can you think of a way for them to redeem themselves from the filth of their corruption?'

DeFarge's answer was to seize Kasim by his mop of curly hair and pull him up onto his knees.

'Suck my cock,' he commanded, his voice at once menacing and urgent.

'Inspecteur . . . I cannot . . .'

'Unfasten my fly-buttons with your teeth. You have good, strong teeth. Bite my buttons off.'

DeFarge almost came into his underpants as the Arab set about doing just that, his sharp white incisors slicing neatly through the thread which held the buttons on the trousers. *And still he suspects nothing*, laughed the Master. *What fools these mortals are.*

He turned away from the door to watch one of Winterbourne's sluts coming up the stairs from the conservatory. Dark and petite in a very French sort of way, Françoise had brought to Winterbourne all the skills and elegance of a high-class whorehouse in Grenoble. Such a pity Messieurs Rémy and DeFarge did not like women. Françoise was a connoisseur's delight.

She stopped at the top of the stairs, her body naked save for the crystal collar which covered the two tiny scars of her initiation. Sweat trickled down between her breasts, a testimony to this too-hot, oppressive June weather.

'Master.'

He thought of the sleek bullwhip lying in a sinuous coil on his library table and licked his lips. He snapped his fingers.

'Come, slut. I have work for you to do.'

Mistress Sedet was savouring the sensual, orgasmic pleasures of bathing alone.

She stretched out luxuriously in the sunken bath, floating on her back with her dark hair drifting out behind her like a fan and her nipples breaking the surface of the gently lapping, rose-scented water.

Yes, there was a great deal of enjoyment to be had alone. And since the Master had seen fit to neglect her so shamefully, these past few months, Sedet had had plenty of time to learn of solitary pleasures. At first she had felt hurt, disregarded; then angry; and now, simply vengeful. He must not be allowed to imagine that he could disregard her power and not have to face the consequences.

She rolled onto her front and began swimming lazily through the water. The sunken pool in the Great Hall was one of her favourite places. It had seen so many initiations, so many glorious orgies, that it had become imbued with an aura of purest sex. Sedet found it totally invigorating and adored the way it awakened every sensual impulse within her until her whole body was crying out for release.

Luxury.

Twisting and turning, she rejoiced as the warm, pink-tinged waters caressed her between her parted thighs, each ripple stimulating her swollen clitoris and sending pulses of hot hunger through her body. Perhaps she would send out one of the sluts to find her a nice, fresh, innocent lad to satisfy the gnawing appetite within her.

'Mistress Sedet?'

Momentarily irritated by the interruption, Sedet turned on the newcomer, her eyes flashing a frosty fire.

'How dare you disturb me!'

'Please forgive me, Mistress.' Heimdal knew how to be subservient when he had to be and now seemed like a good time. He got down on his knees at the side of the sunken bath. 'You sent for me . . .'

'Ah yes.' Sedet remembered now. She had indeed sent for Heimdal but that had been hours ago. Her expression softened slightly but did not defrost. 'Why have you tarried so long?'

'The Master summoned me to the African Room, Mistress. There were . . . certain items requiring urgent disposal.'

Sedet let out a low hiss of exasperation. As if it were not bad enough being ignored by the Master, he was now trying to deprive her of Heimdal.

'Well, you are here now,' she conceded. 'And you may bathe with me.'

'I am honoured, Mistress.'

'The experience will be for my convenience and pleasure, not for yours, slave.'

'Yes, Mistress. Of course, Mistress.'

She threw him a cake of scented pink soap and, undressing quickly, he slid into the warm waters beside her.

'Soap me. And do it properly. I wish to be brought to orgasm several times.'

'Yes, Mistress.'

As Heimdal set to work with the soap, beginning by

massaging her breasts, Sedet allowed herself to unbend a little.

'How are our plans progressing?'

He lathered up the soap and smoothed it in firm, circular movements over Sedet's full and heavy breasts. He was gratified to feel her nipples swelling at his touch, testifying to her growing satisfaction.

'I have done all that you commanded, Mistress.'

If he had expected praise, he ought to have known better.

'I expect no less than total obedience, Heimdal. If you will not devote yourself utterly to my needs, there are others – equally gifted – who will fill your place.'

Whether or not Sedet's words were true, they made Heimdal slightly nervous. Such was his Mistress's capricious nature that even he found it difficult to predict what she would say or do next. He moved the bar of soap down over Sedet's belly and slipped it between her thighs, rubbing it quite hard over the hard pink pearl of her clitoris. This, at least, pleased her and she began to reciprocate, running her sharp-nailed fingers over his body.

'My wish is only to serve you,' said Heimdal, on safer ground now that he had made her, however fleetingly, a slave to her own pleasure. Her desire was in his hands – and its fulfilment also.

'Good.' Sedet's expression scarcely altered as she rode the wild, white, foam-flecked wave of orgasm. But Heimdal sensed it rippling through her and felt the slipperiness of her sex juice pouring out of her and mingling with the rose-scented water. 'Then when my plans come to fruition you shall perhaps be worthy to share my power.'

'You honour me, Mistress,' began Heimdal, unsure of what to say. 'But . . .'

'What now?' snapped Sedet. 'Frig me again, you have increased rather than diminished my hunger.'

'Yes, Mistress.' Heimdal started rubbing Sedet's clitoris again, and felt her body begin to grow less tense in his embrace. 'Your plans may indeed bring you power, but . . .'

'But what?'

'But there will be danger too.'

Sedet's eyes narrowed and in that instant, Heimdal knew he had done precisely the wrong thing in trying to warn her of the dangers of overconfidence.

'Danger!' Her violet eyes flashed and she tore away from Heimdal's embrace, pushing herself free of him as if he were something distasteful and unworthy. 'What do I seek if it is not danger, worm?'

Pendorran's Gothic mansion was more like a fortress than a house. Perched atop high cliffs that met the full force of the Atlantic gales, its high grey walls and towers belonged to a very different age.

Mara felt its aura of power the moment the tall iron gates swung open to admit them into a large cobbled courtyard, surrounded by small leaded windows. It was not simply a powerful place, it was a *pagan* place, and the excitement of that discovery made Mara's heart race. It felt as though the Mother-Goddess was all around, watching, waiting, judging.

Pendorran himself was as distinctive as his home. Tall, rangy, lithe, he wore his jet-black hair shoulder-length and his sharp, hawkish features were dominated by a pair of eyes the same sea-grey as the ocean thundering against the rocks, two hundred feet below. He wore a loose white shirt, waistcoat and black leather trousers, cut tight and closely moulded to the generous swell at his crotch.

As they walked up to the main door of the house, it opened and an elderly man in a grey suit greeted the trio.

'Good evening, Mr Pendorran.' He gave a small and respectful bow. 'Sir, Madam.'

'Ah, Joseph.' Pendorran pulled off his black leather gloves and threw them at his manservant, who caught them and placed them neatly on a side-table. 'We have guests this evening. They will be staying the night.'

'The suite in the East Wing is already prepared, Mr Pendorran,' replied Joseph. 'I had anticipated their arrival.'

'Good. Then you may take our guests to their room.' Pendorran glanced at Andreas and Mara, his eyes lingering on Mara's svelte and tempting form. She felt the power from those sea-grey eyes and it excited her, despite her doubts about this place. 'Dinner is at eight.'

Pendorran turned on his heel and disappeared along the narrow stone passageway into an unseen room, closing the door firmly behind him.

'I hope you will forgive my master,' Joseph commented apologetically. 'He has little time for the pleasantries of good manners, he considers them trivial, but his intentions are always of the very best.'

Andreas was unimpressed. He had had the heeby-jeebies about this place ever since they'd walked out of the forest and into the middle of a Cornish moor. And then this New-Age goth had appeared from nowhere and just expected them to do exactly what he told them. That annoyed Andreas. He'd never been much of a yes-man, and it was bad enough kowtowing to the Master's every whim without Anthony bleeding Pendorran telling them what to do as well.

He followed Mara and Joseph up the ancient staircase, initially reluctantly but then with a growing interest in his surroundings. This Pendorran was surely one wild and wacky guy, to judge from his taste in art. There were Persian erotic paintings, Indian statuettes of men with three dicks and women who seemed to like them that way, and some old pagan stuff which was a lot weirder than anything Mara had ever had in her grimoire. And then there was the way Pendorran was eyeing up Mara. Andreas began to feel a mixture of interest and apprehension.

'Here are your rooms, sir, madam.' Joseph opened the door onto a sitting room decorated like something out of a pre-Raphaelite painting – all rich brocades and stained glass. 'The bedroom is through there and you will find

I have laid out clothes for you.'

'Clothes?' Andreas and Mara exchanged blank looks.

'For dinner this evening. I anticipated that you would not be arriving with any luggage and took the liberty of looking out suitable attire for you. I hope this is in order.'

'How . . .?' began Andreas. But Joseph was already on his way back down the corridor.

'You will hear the bell ringing for dinner at eight,' was his parting shot as he disappeared down the staircase.

Mara followed Andreas into the sitting room and closed the door.

'It's beautiful,' she sighed, running her fingers over the exquisitely moulded frame of an old bronze mirror.

'Beautiful and odd,' retorted Andreas, crossing the room to the bedroom door and pushing it open. 'What was all that stuff about "anticipating our arrival"?'

Mara shrugged. She at least had learned not to question. Sometimes you just had to believe.

'He wasn't kidding,' called Andreas.

'Kidding? About what?'

'About the clothes. Come and look.'

She went into the bedroom and found Andreas staring down at the bed, on which a dinner suit and an evening gown had been laid out, side by side.

'There's even a pair of socks, for goodness' sake!'

Andreas held the trousers up against his waist.

'Your size?' asked Mara.

'Spot on. How did he know?'

'The same way Pendorran knew where to find us. There are forces at work here that we can't hope to understand, Andreas. We just have to go along with what happens.' She sat down on the bed beside him and stroked his cheek. Heck but he was good-looking. And so, for that matter, was Anthony Pendorran . . .

She felt in the pocket of her shorts and took out the glass sun she had taken from the mausoleum.

'You've got the other bit?'

Andreas fetched the small glass pyramid out of his shirt pocket.

'Here you are.'

'Let's see if they fit together.'

She tried pushing one side of the glass pyramid against the edge of the sun but without success.

'Let me have a go.' Andreas took the two pieces and tried matching flat edge to flat edge. 'No dice. Something's missing.'

'There were five paths of light leading out of the circle at Stonehenge,' remarked Mara. 'Five.'

'So you think . . .?'

'That's right. We've got another three pieces to find before we have the Eye of Baloch.'

10: Pendorran

'"EXTINCT" VOLCANO ERUPTS IN SIBERIA: YAKUTSK THREATENED'
(Reuter, 25 June)

The Great Hall at Polmadoc was full of shadows.

The rough stone walls of the vast dining hall were lined with wrought-iron candelabra, in which burned long-stemmed candles dripping hot wax onto the stone-flagged floor. This room was perhaps the most ancient part of a very ancient house, Mara thought to herself, letting the dancing shadows play on her bare arms, feeling the power of the eternal battle between darkness and light.

On one side of the hall were stone-mullioned windows, thickly glazed against the Atlantic gales. Even on this summer evening, the panes were spotted here and there with salt spray. For this was a wild and elemental place, close to the wild heart of nature.

Anthony Pendorran stood by the open window, his black hair blown back from his face and his profile eagle-like against the evening sky.

'There will be storms later,' he observed as Mara and Andreas entered the hall, ushered in by Pendorran's manservant Joseph. 'Storms of great violence. There is evil in the air tonight.'

Andreas had already marked Pendorran down as either hopelessly pretentious or a complete fruitcake, but it had to be admitted that the man had a certain style – and

Andreas couldn't fault his taste in women. Pendorran's lady-friend, her admirable body draped in a purple velvet gown and her elegant elbow resting on an ornate wooden mantelpiece, was almost worth coming all the way to North Cornwall to see.

Maria Treharne was tall, handsome, a little aloof, but with a playful glint in her soft brown eyes. A long drift of tousled chestnut hair had been swept up into a loose knot, secured by an ornate pin of polished pewter. Andreas knew her sort: five 'A' levels and no knickers. Yes, he rather approved of Maria Treharne.

'It's just as well you came to us tonight,' Maria smiled and extended her hand to Mara and Andreas in greeting. 'You would have been soaked to the skin out there. The storms around here can be quite spectacular, you know, and very sudden.'

Pendorran spun round to look at his guests, his eyes bright, for all the world like some mad bird of prey.

'Storms, floods, fires . . . there are strange powers at work in the world.' He paused, his eyes travelling from Andreas to Mara and back again. 'And there is much that is not quite as it seems.'

'Dinner is served,' announced Pendorran's manservant, just in time to avoid an awkward silence.

Joseph held out Mara's chair as she sat down at the dining table, opposite Pendorran. To the right sat Andreas, to the left Pendorran's lover, Maria, who was gazing at Andreas with a kindling sexual interest. And Mara could feel Pendorran's eyes lingering on her, the white heat of his gaze stirring an answering heat in her belly.

Pendorran lifted his glass to his lips and took a sip of red wine. He looked deep into Mara's eyes.

'You, for example, Miss *Dubois*. You are not quite what you seem.' His gaze snapped round to Andreas and seemed to search deep into his soul. 'Or you, for that matter, Mr *Weatherall*.'

'I really don't know what you're talking about, Mr

Pendorran,' Mara replied, returning his gaze as steadily and as unblinkingly as she could, though her pulse was racing. There was something about this man, something so compelling, something that ripped and burned at her resistance, almost compelling her to submit to the force of his will.

'No,' smiled Pendorran. 'Of course you don't.'

He held his wine glass up to the light, and in the deep red heart of it Mara thought she saw dancing figures, their bodies entwined, consumed by the heat of their own passion.

A little piqued by her lover's obvious interest in Mara, Maria Treharne turned her attentions to Andreas. Not that Andreas minded. For one thing, she wasn't asking awkward questions about whether he was everything that he seemed. And for another, that medieval-style velvet gown was cut so low at the front that it barely skimmed the crests of her nipples. When she leant forward, listening intently to what he was saying, he could hardly help but find himself gazing into the dark valley of her cleavage.

'Do you know Cornwall, Mr Weatherall?'

'Er . . . no, not really. A weekend in Tresco when I was six, you know the sort of thing.'

'You really should let me show you some of the sights.'

As she leant forward, raising her glass in a toast, he wondered if he hadn't already glimpsed two of the more impressive sights of Polmadoc.

'I think I'd like that,' he smiled.

After dinner, Pendorran continued his conversation with Mara.

'It serves no useful purpose, you know.'

'I don't . . .'

'Yes, yes, I know. You don't understand. But I do, *Mara Fleming*.'

Startled, she caught the steely glint in his sea-grey eyes.

'Did you really think you could hide your true self from me, Mara?' Pendorran gently stroked her throat and, taking hold of her chin, forced her to look at him. Reflected in the window behind him, Mara caught sight of Andreas in a steamy clinch with Maria Treharne, his hand cupping the generous curve of her backside.

Mara freed herself from Pendorran's touch, firmly and insistently.

'My name is Anastasia Dubois.'

'Here, there can be no disguise, Mara. Here, all must reveal their true selves.' He raised his voice a fraction. 'Is that not so, Mr Andreas Hunt?'

'What . . .'

Andreas wheeled round at the sound of his name, cursing himself as a slave to habit.

'Calm yourself, Andreas. You play your part well, but there are those who are not so easily deceived. Why have you come here, to Polmadoc?'

'Why should I tell you that?'

Pendorran laughed.

'If you don't, how can I help you?'

Andreas could feel his temper fraying at the edges. He was getting fed up with being patronised by Mr Anthony smart-arse Pendorran.

'What makes you think that we want your help? And in any case, why should you give a toss about helping us? Tell me that, Mr Pendorran.'

'Really, Andreas, there is no need to be quite so defensive. It is almost as if you are afraid of me.'

Andreas was. But he was buggered if he was going to admit it.

Mara intervened.

'I think we should tell him, Andreas. He knows so much already. He probably knows about . . .'

'About the Eye of Baloch?' Pendorran put his wine glass down, very carefully, upon the window ledge. Outside the elements were warring in the darkening sky, streaks of yellow and sickly green mingling with the more familiar terracotta shades of a Cornish sunset. 'Yes, I know that is what you are seeking. I knew that you would come.'

Andreas's jaw dropped.

'You've got the rest of the Eye of Baloch?'

'Not the rest, no. A single piece, that is all.'

'And you are willing to let us have it?'

For a moment, Andreas thought Pendorran was going to laugh in his face. But he just kept on staring out into the night sky, his grey eyes reflecting the turbulence of the coming storm.

'Perhaps. I'm not sure.'

Andreas opened his mouth to say something sarcastic but Mara silenced him with a glare. Andreas Hunt might be sharp-witted and sharp-tongued but in any war of words he could never be a match for Anthony Pendorran.

She walked towards the window.

'I am a pagan like you, Pendorran. I worship and honour the Mother-Goddess.'

Pendorran shivered almost imperceptibly at the lightness of her touch on his strong hand.

'Your devotion does you credit. But there must be more. The Eye of Baloch embodies a terrible power. I must be certain that your quest is a worthy one.'

'It is the quest to destroy evil.'

'You tempt me to softness of heart, I confess it. But I cannot help you unless you can prove yourself worthy, Mara Fleming. Worthy of the gift of power.'

All the candles had been extinguished and the Great Hall lay bathed in the light from a baleful moon.

The storm had passed, a great firework-display of cosmic anger, a storm such as mad gods might make for the torment of helpless mankind. Torrential rain, lightning and thunderous waves had given way to crisp, clear air, velvety darkness pierced by starlight and an ocean so glassily calm that it was positively eerie.

The Hall had been cleared and in the centre of the huge, vaulted chamber stood four figures, marking four of the points in a five-pointed star. At the fifth point stood a charcoal brazier, on which burned a shallow brass dish filled with sweet herbs.

Pendorran raised his hands as though in prayer.

'I must see into your hearts. I must see into your souls.'

Andreas looked across at Maria Treharne. Was she a part of all this? Did she, like Mara and Pendorran – and perhaps even Andreas himself – believe that some sexual rite would put Pendorran in touch with the truth?

Maria gazed coolly back at him, only the slight pout of her full lips and the starlit glint of her dark eyes betraying the sensuality within her. Andreas could feel her desire. It was as though she were made of crystal-clear glass and he was looking into the heart of her, the swirling crimson heart of her lust.

The coiling tendrils of smoke from the smouldering brazier seemed to spin a web of mystical expectation about the four still, silent figures. Andreas felt swimmy, not quite in control of his thoughts and feelings, a warm glow of sexual need creeping over him like a blanket of swan's-down.

To his right stood Mara, her nakedness marble-smooth and perfect in the cool, white moonlight. A silver painted star criss-crossed her belly, her nipples marking two of its upper points and the nethermost disappearing into the mouth of her eager pussy. When she moved, the shadows shifted and the light picked out the large silvery buttons of her nipples, emphasising the delicious fullness of her breasts. Andreas had a fancy to slip his dick between those full, firm breasts, but he had a feeling that that was not part of Pendorran's agenda, not tonight.

He watched as Pendorran stood with arms stretched out horizontally and eyes very wide, lips moving in the words of some silent incantation. The more Andreas looked at him, the more he concluded that he seemed hardly like a man at all, this Pendorran. More like some erotic demon, all black hair and dark, hypnotic eyes that drew you in, daring you to look away.

Of the four of them, only Pendorran was still partially clothed. He was barefoot and wearing only that favourite pair of very tight black leather trousers, which emphasised the substantial size of the erect cock which lay beneath, a slanting baton of flesh across his lower belly. Pendorran's right nipple was pierced and in it he wore a heavy silver star, which distended the hardened flesh.

'Spirits of earth and sea and sky, answer our supplication,' he intoned, casting a pinch of white, grainy powder into the heart of the flames. They flared up with a red and blue light, accentuating the faintly demonic lines of his hawkish face. His gaze fell on each of the other three in turn. 'The spirits are with us this night. Do you feel their presence?'

It was Mara who broke the silence.

'The spirits are within me,' she whispered. And when Andreas turned his head to look at her, he saw a strange new light in her eyes of emerald green.

But it was not to Mara that Pendorran turned – it was to his lover, Maria Treharne.

'You may begin. The vital essences must be prepared.'

With a small nod of her head, Maria walked towards Andreas, taking the greatest care to follow the chalked line of the star. Andreas knew why (he'd read Dennis Wheatley). Step outside the pentacle and whatever was lurking in the shadows had *carte blanche* to come and grab you. What's more, he'd known Mara long enough to suspect that it might not be a load of superstitious rubbish.

Maria was holding a shallow brass dish, similar to the one on which the sweet herbs and oils were burning. She stooped and placed it on the floor at Andreas's feet.

'I must take your vital essence from you,' she told him, her voice soft as a caress from a velvet glove. And she got down on her knees before Andreas, her dark and lustrous eyes never leaving his face.

On this occasion, Andreas discovered that reality

exceeded hope. He had hoped he might get to fuck Pendorran's lady but hadn't been holding his breath. And how here she was, kneeling in front of him, her breasts bobbing as her lips closed about the tip of his penis.

Her cool fingers slipped between his legs and started caressing the tops of his thighs, her fingernails just brushing the wiry curls that adorned his heavy seed-purse. He wanted her to stroke and squeeze and scratch and knead his balls, but she just went on teasing him, almost but not quite touching the juicy globes. She was a skilful pleasure-mistress, entirely in control of his every sensation, building up the feelings slowly and gradually, not letting him give in to the urge just to thrust harder into her soft mouth and spurt his come down her throat.

Not that he was complaining. The sensations were exquisite and the girl had one of the wickedest tongues he had encountered outside Winterbourne. The way she flicked it across the tip of his glans drove him half-crazy with excitement, and as quickly as she had licked away the ooze of his pleasure, more and still more lubricant welled up and trickled down over the domed head of his prick.

She was good at sucking him, too, very good. Her mouth was large and sensual, but when it closed about his shaft it felt like the tightest, the wettest, the wickedest cunt in the whole world. She took every inch of him in without the slightest difficulty, sliding him in until his cock-tip was pressing against the back of her throat and her lips were kissing the sex-root at the base of his belly.

Sliding him out a little way, Maria let her teeth graze his flesh, very, very gently. It felt like heaven. A little harder, and the discomfort would spoil the pleasure, a little more lightly and there would be none of the delicious stimulation which set Andreas's heart racing and the blood pumping through his body, swelling his cock to even-greater hardness.

Almost there, so very nearly there! He could feel the telltale pressure in his loins, the fountain-head of spunk building up, just waiting for the right moment to come bursting out in a white glory of surging, pumping ecstasy.

And then she stopped. He could have wept for disappointment as she slid him all the way out from between her lips.

'Patience,' she smiled.

Patience! It was hard enough not to throw her down on the floor right this minute and thrust between her thighs, without being asked to be patient . . .

When she took his right testicle into the hot, dark cavern of her mouth he forgave her everything. Running his fingers through her thick hair, he savoured the feeling of warm saliva and a wet tongue exciting him whilst light and nimble fingers wanked his shaft lightly and expertly.

This was worth being patient for. How did she manage to be so gentle and yet so wickedly effective? A microsecond before he reached the point of no return, she picked up the brass dish; and suddenly he was coming, his whole body reeling with ecstasy and his cock spurting great thick gobbets of semen onto the polished surface of the dish.

Maria got to her feet without a word and walked across the star to her lover Pendorran, laying the dish on the floor before him. He nodded his approval but his eyes were on Mara Fleming.

Mara knew that Pendorran had the power to see into her heart and search out her deepest, darkest thoughts, and that frightened her. But it also excited her, for Pendorran's power was a supremely erotic force, an irresistible magnetism which transformed all thoughts of resistance into sensual surrender.

'You are the one, Mara Fleming.' Pendorran beckoned her and she found herself crossing the pentacle to stand before him. 'You are the source and host of power.'

'I have certain psychic gifts. I am the seventh daughter of a seventh daughter.'

Pendorran nodded.

'This I had guessed. But there are other things which

cannot be divined except through ritual. Our vital essences, and that of your lover Andreas, must be mingled. Through their joining I shall, if the Goddess wills it, be given the power to judge the honesty of your quest.'

Mara tossed back her long mane of auburn hair and the silver star on her painted bosoms glinted in the moonlight.

'I am not afraid.'

'Get on your hands and knees at the centre of the pentacle. The power is greatest there.'

Mara obeyed, the full white moons of her buttocks thrust back as she crouched on the bare flagstones of the Hall floor. Andreas thought of the secrets of that wine-dark valley between her arse cheeks and longed to be in Pendorran's place, savouring the unparalleled sweetness of fucking Mara Fleming.

Pendorran unzipped his trousers but did not take them off, preferring simply to reach through his gaping flies and pull out the stiff rod of his cock. He cradled it in his hand for a few moments, as though rediscovering the smooth stiffness of it, then knelt down behind Mara, his cock-spike nudging eagerly at the deep crevice.

He ran the tip of his finger down the dark crease, sliding it down to the sopping-wet haven of Mara's cunt and scooping up a little of its juices. These, he smeared liberally over the tightly puckered mouth of Mara's anus, then wriggled his finger inside her, to such good effect that Mara began moaning and shifting from side to side, rotating her hips the better to feel this welcome invader penetrating her backside.

Feeling once again for the heart of her sex, Pendorran pressed his cock-tip against its entrance.

'Come, Goddess,' he murmured and slid his dick into Mara's cunt, burying it up to the hilt in her soft, wet flesh.

Unbearably aroused, Mara pushed herself back onto the twin spikes of Pendorran's dick and his wriggling, twisting finger. Impaled by these instruments of torment and ecstasy, she abandoned herself to Pendorran's inexorable will. For a few moments at least, Anthony Pendorran had become the sole master of her pleasure.

Pendorran fucked her slowly, his self-control maddening her, making her moan and writhe in a delirium of sexual need.

'Please, please . . .'

He did not answer, except with more long, slow thrusts that sent the clear sweet nectar trickling out of her to anoint the stone-hard shaft of his prick.

'Give it to me, now,' pleaded Mara. 'Make me come, fuck me, fuck me *hard*.'

But whatever Pendorran felt, he betrayed no sign of emotion. His expression was impassive, almost trance-like as he buried himself, ball-deep, in Mara's silken cunt.

When at last he came he did so with a silent shudder, his whole body tensing and shaking for a few moments and then visibly relaxing as the spunk gushed and fizzed in Mara's waiting cunt. In contrast, Mara came with a cry of agony which seemed to tear the very soul from the ancient stones of Polmadoc Hall, her body writhing and twisting in a frenzy of excitement, like the body of a woman possessed by demons.

At last she fell back, her whole body covered in sweat as she slumped to the ground, almost insensible with pleasure.

Pendorran got to his feet, zipped his still-rigid cock back into his trousers and picked up the brass dish in which Maria had collected Andreas's tribute. Placing it on the ground between Mara's thighs, he watched the steady trickle of mingled semen and cunt juice enter the dish, meeting and mixing with Andreas's sperm.

Satisfied, he held the dish aloft.

'Behold, my Goddess. Behold the essences of life, the essences of the soul.'

Holding the dish over the burning brazier, he tilted it slightly so that the thick, creamy liquid spilled over the edge and fell in a long stream onto the burning coals. As it fell, clouds of swirling white smoke rose from the brazier, shrouding Pendorran like some spectral cloak.

'Now,' he whispered, and for some reason Andreas suddenly felt very cold. 'Now I shall know the truth.'

The Duchess was not behaving herself today, noted Liz Exley with a mixture of disapproval and excitement. She snapped her fingers.

'Slave!'

'Yes, Mistress?' The elfin-faced woman with the short dark hair and slender figure of a boy looked up from her work.

'Have you not finished yet?'

'I am sorry, Mistress, but you said I was to oil and polish the paddles thoroughly.'

'How dare you show me such insolence!'

With a grand dramatic gesture, Liz knocked the Duchess – and the wooden paddle – flying. The paddle clattered to the floor.

'You are a disobedient slave and a slovenly slave to boot. Take off your panties.'

'But Mistress!'

'Take them off.'

The Duchess of Ellesmere stood up and began wriggling out of her panties. It was no easy task – they were made of ultra-tight black latex which clung to the body in an unforgiving embrace. Why, you needed to powder your body liberally with talc just to get them on, and on a hot day like this they stuck to the skin and had to be peeled off, very, very slowly.

The Duchess was one of Liz's new pupils. Mistress Sedet had instructed Liz to find and train a regular supply of promising slaves and Liz's discreet advertisements in a society magazine had produced a stream of willing recruits. The English aristocracy, it seemed, were as enthusiastic as ever for the darker pleasures of the flesh.

'Bend over that chair.'

Liz inspected the Duchess's backside intently – or

pretended to. Her mind was not entirely on her work today. It was on Harry Baptiste.

Harry Baptiste, damn him.

That night outside the theatre, she'd been convinced that she had finally made a breakthrough, that Baptiste would now fall under her spell and she would bring him back in triumph to Winterbourne. Unfortunately, it hadn't worked out quite like that.

Oh, he had taken her back to his modest Mayfair apartment right enough (plain-speaking Harry Baptiste felt uneasy with the opulence of 10 Downing Street or Chequers). And what had they done when they got there? They had drunk coffee together, that's what! They'd shared coffee and an intelligent conversation about Liz's journalistic career. Definitely not what Liz had planned.

'Mistress?'

The Duchess's voice drew Liz back to the task in hand.

'What is it, slave?'

'May I move now? This is getting rather uncomfortable.'

Liz's eyes narrowed.

'Don't you dare move! You will not move until you are given permission to move, do I make myself quite clear?'

'Yes, Mistress.'

Liz picked up the wooden paddle from the floor.

'This is chipped. You're a wicked and clumsy slave.'

'I know I am, Mistress.' Liz thought she detected just the faintest note of satisfaction in the Duchess's apparent contrition.

She drew back the paddle, its weight satisfyingly balanced in her hand. Baptiste. Harry Baptiste, how she hated that man for spurning her. And how come he had known so much about her? The questions kept tumbling around in her brain.

Assailed by a surge of irritation, Liz brought the paddle down on the Duchess's backside with a satisfying thwack. The Duchess really enjoyed her punishment and Liz was in the mood to be darkly, deliciously cruel. At least there were some pleasures which squeaky-clean Harry Baptiste couldn't spoil.

'Enter.'

Mara pushed open the door of Pendorran's study.

'You wished to see us?'

Pendorran was facing away from them, gazing out of the upstairs window at the angry grey sea.

'Please sit.'

Andreas felt uncomfortably as if he were back in the Headmaster's study at Ashdown Road School, trying to wriggle out of the blame for his latest escapade. Only Anthony Pendorran didn't look like the kind of bloke who'd let you wriggle out of anything.

Mara sat.

'I'd rather stand,' said Andreas.

'As you wish.'

Pendorran turned slowly round to face Mara.

'If you fail . . .' he began.

'We won't fail,' replied Mara firmly. 'We can't afford to fail.'

'If you fail,' Pendorran repeated, ignoring her protestations, 'I can do nothing for you, either of you. And should the Master come here seeking you . . .'. His eyes travelled from Mara to Andreas and back again. There was a cold, clear, unbearably bright light in his eyes. 'I shall be merciless. Do you understand?'

'I understand.'

Andreas cut in.

'Does this mean you've decided to help us after all?'

Pendorran sighed.

'I will set you on the next stage of your quest, no more.' He carried on talking as he gazed back out of the window. Heavy grey storm-clouds were rolling in over the sea and the air felt thick and oppressive. 'Mara, there is a pendant around your neck.'

She glanced down at the chain she was wearing. On the

end hung a tiny glass ornament – a little trinket she had picked up from the jewellery box in her room.

'You have chosen well,' Pendorran continued. 'Touch it.'

Mara did so, and at her touch the glass ornament began to swell and grow, until at last it had formed itself into a four-sided crystal pyramid.

'Now you have what you came for, you must leave.' To Andreas, Pendorran's voice sounded strangely distant and the air in the room seemed to be growing darker and more unbreathable by the second. 'May the Goddess speed you . . .'

'You must leave. Must leave. Must leave . . .' The words seemed to echo in Mara's brain and she felt suddenly dizzy. Was it her, or was the room really getting smaller – shrinking until it was so small that there was scarcely any space to breathe? It was all happening so fast that there wasn't even any time to be afraid.

Pendorran watched impassively. When he was once again alone he sat down at his desk, drumming his fingers on the blotter.

'Was I right? Was I right to help them?' He gazed into space as if seeking inspiration. 'Such power . . . have I placed it in the right hands?'

Suddenly he swung to the left, staring into empty space as though some unseen, unheard presence had just spoken to him. And, startled from his impassivity, he began to question it.

'What did you say, Max? Tell me again.'

Snow lay deep on the mountains, even on the lower slopes which, at this time of year, ought to have been lush with sweet green grass. Strange things had happened to the climate in these last few months, blizzards in July, hot and blistering winds in the depths of winter.

On the snow-bound mountainside two figures were coupling: two naked figures, their bare bodies marble-white against the snow and the girl blue-lipped with cold. Her black hair spread out about her head like a tangled halo, a single stray tendril snaking across her face and the mouth that was open in a plea for mercy.

The man cared nothing for the girl's humiliation and pain. No, that was not true. He exulted in them. The pleasure he derived from fucking her, grinding her pale and helpless body into the snow, was quite indescribable. As his dick drove into her, his mind filled with pictures that made him laugh for the sheer, vengeful joy of his coming victory.

Fuck. Fuck. Fuck. His cock pounded into her like a piston, roughly, mechanically.

Pleasure. Now. White light exploded inside his head as he came into her, filling up her violated hole with the white-hot, seething tribute of his loins.

At the moment of climax, the girl gave a thin, high wail of unwilling ecstasy and a ring of fire burst out of the snowy ground, forming an incandescent, roaring wall of flame. Its orange, red and yellow tongues reached many feet into the air, licking malevolently at the pinkish-blue sky above, encircling man and woman within an impenetrable barrier.

He laughed like a madman now, dropping the girl's limp body onto the ground and stepping straight through the fiery wall, bathing in the flames as though they had been no hotter than the tongues of fawning pet dogs.

When he reached the other side he began his journey back down the mountain-side, his feet leaving scorched and steaming footprints in the snow.

'The plan,' he whispered to himself gleefully. 'It *all* goes according to plan.'

11: Toys

**'TWENTY-SEVEN-FOOT HADDOCK ATTACKS
CROSS-CHANNEL SWIMMER'**
(*Brighton Evening Courant*, 30 June)

The Master thoroughly enjoyed the taste of corruption.

He had never understood how anyone could enjoy
being pure. Without evil, life would lack everything – even
the will to go on. For almost fifty years he had been caged
in a sarcophagus of granite and crystal, in the cellars below
Winterbourne Hall, but he had never lost the memory of,
nor the hunger for, evil. For sublime evil was the very
essence of the Master. And no matter how many others
might seek to dethrone him, the Master was and always
would be the rightful king of all the world.

The wonderful thing about evil was that it was all around
you, even in the unlikeliest places. Who would have thought,
for instance, that a respectable town like Stratford-upon-
Avon would contain a thriving witches' coven?

It had all begun with an official visit to the town for the
opening of a Women's Institute Conference. Not something
the Master would normally go for, but when one stood for
family values and good, clean government, it couldn't hurt
to be spotted eating rock cakes with a bunch of blue-rinsed
old biddies from time to time. Especially when one Harry
Laurent Baptiste kept resisting all attempts to destroy him
and continued his dazzling success as the housewives'
choice.

It worried the Master, this opposing power that he could not see or touch or understand, only *feel*. And in his moments of doubt he was certain he *could* feel it, like an iron hand tightening about his throat, or a lake of blood lapping at his ankles as it slowly rose up his body, a dark tide threatening to engulf him. It seemed to know his every move before he made it, always keeping one step ahead of him, always thwarting him just when the prize was almost in his grasp.

Once Weatherall and the Dubois slut had brought him the Eye, all would be clear. All traitors would be exposed, all deceptions unveiled. All enemies destroyed.

But he was certainly not going to allow his anxieties to spoil his enjoyment of this evening's festivities. He was, after all, guest of honour. The High Priestess of the Coven was an initiate, and had arranged a special little *al fresco* ceremony in his honour. It was to be a select gathering: just the Master, the High Priestess, and the nubile daughter of the chairman of the local Nationalist constituency party. Apparently the girl was pretty, nicely brought-up and had recently alarmed her parents by expressing an interest in witchcraft.

Today it was her sixteenth birthday.

The Master intended to give her a birthday present she would never forget.

'Shh – someone might hear.' Mara listened intently.

'Have they gone?' whispered Andreas.

'Yes, I think so. I can't hear anything.'

Mara and Andreas were in a tight corner. A very tight corner – in fact so tight that there was scarcely any room to breathe. Mara was still trying to come to terms with what had happened to them. One minute they had been talking to Anthony Pendorran in his study at Polmadoc, the next, the room started spinning and shrinking around them.

Until, what seemed like mere seconds later, they found themselves squashed, in an untidy jumble of arms and legs, inside something very small and very box-like. And as if that wasn't bad enough there had been people outside, so they'd had to wait inside for what seemed like hours until the coast was clear.

'Ouch!'

'That's my hand you're standing on.'

'Can I help it if there's nowhere else to put my foot?'

'Let's try and find a way out of here. My bum's going to sleep.'

With groans and curses they eased and wriggled their aching bodies out into the daylight. Turning round to look where they had come from, Andreas gave a chuckle of disbelief.

'It's a Wendy house! My sister's friend had one of those when we were kids. We used to . . .'

Mara silenced him with a glare.

'I don't think I want to know about your sexual exploits in the Wendy house,' she scolded him. 'At least, not until we're well away from here.'

She took a good look round the room. There wasn't much doubt where they were – it was one of those old-fashioned toy shops, with the fancy Dickensian windows and lots of wooden rocking horses. One wall was completely filled by shelves of teddy bears: tiny ones, immense ones, ones with green wellies and fluffy pink ones with ribbons round their necks. Andreas picked up one of the traditional fawn-coloured bears and it gave not so much a growl as a mournful wheeze.

'They don't make these like they used to,' he commented. 'Mine sounded like the QEII leaving Southampton.'

Mara ran her fingers over the silky mane of a large and very splendid rocking horse: a magnificent creation of carved wood, with a real leather saddle and bridle and eyes that seemed to follow you round the room.

'Such a beautiful thing. It's almost alive.'

'It had better not be.' Andreas shuddered. 'Toy shops give me the creeps. I feel as if every cuddly toy in the place has got its beady eyes on me.'

'Speaking of eyes . . .' Mara scanned the toy shop a second time, hoping for inspiration, but the astral vibrations were too confused to read. 'We really should get out of here and start looking for the next piece of the Eye of Baloch.'

Andreas opted for the obvious and tried the front door, but it was treble-locked with no sign of a key.

'We could break a window?'

'And get arrested?'

'No, you're right. There must be some other way out of here. I mean, look.' Andreas rattled the front door. 'These bolts were fastened from the inside. But I don't *see* any other door.' How could there be another door? The walls were lined from floor to ceiling with cupboards and shelves, stacked high with toys.

'Let me concentrate for a moment.'

Mara put her hands to her temples, trying to summon up the force within her. Her psychic strength had been severely drained by the search for the Eye, but the power was still there, faint but distinct. Andreas watched her, entranced by the clean lines of her body, a body whose curves were full yet firm, athletic yet voluptuous.

'Do we have to get out of here just yet?' He slid his hand over her backside and gave it a good grope. 'If we don't, I can think of one or two ways of keeping ourselves amused.'

'Please, Andreas – I'm trying to concentrate.'

She did not tell him, but she could feel it too – the sheer sexuality of this place. It had been the same at Pendeilo, at Whitby, Polmadoc, and now here – wherever here was. All you found yourself wanting to do was fuck, fuck, fuck. And this wasn't like the hunger of the vampire-creatures, a simple appetite to be satisfied a dozen times a day. This was an atmosphere of pure sex as thick and sensual as double cream. Give in to it and you might find yourself lost in pleasure for ever.

'There!'

The inspiration came to her as, for a few brief seconds, her mind cleared itself of the fog of weakness. The right-hand wall looked ordinary enough, a clutter of board-games and train sets on groaning shelves, but Mara had learned that not everything was always as it seemed.

She cleared a space in the jumble. There it was. A tiny gap in the matchboarding, something you wouldn't normally give a second look. But at the lightest of touches that section of the wall began to swing away from her hand, opening onto a sepulchral blackness beyond.

He must be good. *Must* be good. He really must.

Harry Baptiste was experiencing a novel dilemma. He had never had to bother with choices before, and certainly not awkward moral choices between good and evil. It had quite simply never occurred to him that evil was an option. He had always done what came naturally to him – and being a good boy came naturally to Harry Baptiste.

But now he had begun to understand and he *had* to be good, really, really good.

The crystal ring on his finger glowed with a secret inner fire. It felt warm against his flesh and he glanced down at it. As if pleased by his attention it sparkled and throbbed, pulses of seductive energy entering him, burning away at his once-serene resolve.

No, no, he was good by nature and he must stay that way. But why must he be so tempted? Why now?

'It's OK, I think I've found a light switch.'

Andreas felt along the inner wall and clicked down the switch. Sudden light flooded the room and Andreas drew in breath.

'Well, well, well. What have we *here*?'

A slow smile spread across his face. Several years as an investigative reporter on a tacky tabloid came flooding back. That 'Sun, Sea and Sex' story he had written about priapic pensioners in Bournemouth and that exposé of

S/M frolics in a convent school in Stoke Newington. Oh, the games people played . . .

The soft, rose-coloured light flooding the room came from four ingeniously designed lamps placed at its four corners. They were in the form of naked couples copulating in four athletic postures and were moulded from pink frosted glass. On the candy-striped walls hung brightly coloured prints. At first glance they looked like ordinary pictures of characters from children's books – until you looked a bit closer and saw that Big Ears was sucking Noddy's dick.

And then there was the huge rocking-horse. Hell, but it was an unusual creation. It had all the usual gubbins kids enjoyed – saddle and bridle and bit and stirrups to put your feet in. But this particular rocking horse catered for a more adult taste.

Sticking right up out of the saddle were two spikes . . . and it wasn't difficult to guess what they were for. If a woman sat on the saddle, the front spike – hard and dildo sized – would slide up into her cunt while the other – a flexible probe of knobbly black rubber – would insinuate itself into the secret kingdom of her arse. Now that was what Andreas called a good ride.

Not for the first time, Andreas wished he was back on the *Comet*. The punters would love this. It was a playroom, filled to the brim with toys and games and dressing-up clothes . . . but all the toys were for grown-ups. It would make a great front-page exposé. Well, they did say everything was bigger in your caring, sharing *Comet*.

If the atmosphere in the toy shop had been sensual, the atmosphere in the playroom positively reeked of sex. Even the air was lightly scented with the intoxicating spice of cunt juice. How many naked threesomes had romped on the four-poster, with its carved pillars in the form of huge phalluses? How many willing victims had had their oversized school uniform pants pulled down and received six of the best on their quivering buttocks?

Mara felt hot. It wasn't just the sultry, overheated air in the playroom, it was the whole ambience of the place. She felt hot for sex. Hot for Andreas Hunt.

On impulse, she lay down on the bed. At first the mattress seemed to have all the softness of swan's-down, but there was a firm inner springiness too. Bliss.

'Why don't you join me?' she purred.

Andreas kicked off his shoes and stretched out his eager body next to Mara's.

'Mmm, great bed,' he growled. His hand snaked over Mara's thigh. 'Perfect for fucking on. Perfect for fucking *you*.'

Mara giggled. Maybe it was the decor of the place, the jumble of toys that weren't quite toys, but she felt girlish and excitable, like a silly oversexed kid out on her first date.

'Look up there. At the canopy.'

Andreas looked. The four-poster bed had a canopy of painted wood, depicting a woodland scene in which scantily clad wood-nymphs and fairies were enjoying all manner of sexual misbehaviour with massively over-endowed satyrs and centaurs. There was something extremely erotic about this delicious corruption of childhood images, this mixture of the innocent and the lascivious.

'So . . . you'd like me to do that to you, would you?' he chuckled, pushing up Mara's tight black T-shirt and sliding his hand underneath.

'I want you to do *everything* to me.'

'Then come here and let me undress you, you wicked little witch.'

She wriggled like an eel as he started pulling her T-shirt off, and they rolled over and over on the soft bed like randy teenagers. Boy, but she had a great bum. He gave it a hearty thwack as she rolled on her belly and her skirt flew up, revealing her knickers. She let out a squeal, half of indignation, half of delight.

'Beast!'

Her cries were muffled by the patchwork bedcover as he

took a second and a third swipe at her lovely rounded arse. Funny, he wasn't normally into all this spanking stuff. But maybe he'd spent too long in the House of Commons and was now developing a taste for it. He pulled down her panties and got a really good eyeful of Mara's creamy backside. It was just starting to tinge a delicate rosy pink where he had slapped it, and he felt a tremendous urge to smack and smack and smack until it turned crimson under his eager onslaught.

Slap. Slap. Slap. Mara's cries quietened, becoming less shrill as she gave herself up to the pleasure of Andreas's punishing hand. Not that it hurt a great deal – he was no sadist, and Mara had been well and truly trained by Mistress Sedet to accept even the most extreme discomfort as a source of pleasure.

No, this was no C/P frenzy, it was a play-fantasy, a romp in which the two participants were remarkably evenly matched. For just as Andreas was contemplating a bigger, harder slap that would make Mara's rump dance and quiver, she rolled over sideways, throwing him off her and leaping on top of him. There was laughter in her eyes as she pinned him to the bed and started undressing him.

'Time for a taste of your own medicine, tiger.'

'Sounds good to me.'

'You're not supposed to *enjoy* it,' Mara pouted.

Andreas grinned. 'You did. You're all wet and I can see your nipples through your T-shirt.'

'Nice boys wouldn't look.'

'Nice boys wouldn't suck your tits.' His mouth rooted like a baby's for the pendulous fruit of Mara's breast and fastened on the nipple, biting it through the thin cotton.

'Oh!' Mara's startled gasp of pleasure turned into a delicious shiver which shook her whole body and made her tits wobble so alluringly that Andreas's cock swelled to a painful degree of hardness inside his pants. He went on sucking and biting Mara's nipple, and she arranged herself so that she was kneeling astride his right thigh, moving back and forth with a rhythmic motion, rubbing her bare wet triangle against his leg.

'You bad girl,' murmured Andreas, releasing her from her torment for a moment. 'You're bringing yourself off. I can feel your cunt juice soaking through onto my leg. Bad girl . . .'

'You can't stop me,' retorted Mara playfully. And Andreas responded by pressing his thigh harder between her legs, forcing the pleasure out of her with a brutal suddenness. 'Oh, oh, Andreas! Please . . . I'm coming.'

She soaked his trouser leg as she climaxed, an abundant flood of pleasure-juice cascading out of her as her sex muscles clenched and relaxed in that first, delicious orgasm.

'Nice?' Andreas inquired innocently.

'Bad *boy*.'

'You could make me a badder boy,' Andreas replied hopefully. 'You could take of your T-shirt and let me play with your tits.'

To his immense pleasure she did exactly that, stretching her arms above her head as she pulled off the tight black top which hugged the curves of her breasts so assiduously.

The minute he saw her bra-less tits, he went wild with desire. He couldn't remember being this excited by any woman – including Mara – for a long time. It was exactly like being a teenage boy again. Strewth, he could remember it as if it were yesterday, that first terrifying, ecstatic glimpse of a woman's bare tits.

In the bus shelter, it was. He was just sixteen and she was – oh, twenty, maybe even twenty-five, it was hard to say but she'd been around. Sandra, she was called. Sixteen was pretty old to get your first shag in a place like Liverpool, why, there were boys of twelve at his school who reckoned they'd done it with girls. Andreas had kept it a bit quiet about still being a virgin, but Sandra had known. Sandra was like the Social Services – always on call when you needed her.

There wasn't much to do of a Saturday night, so when Sandra said 'Let's go for a walk,' he said yes straight away. He hadn't realised then (boy, was he naive) that she was intending to seduce him!

It was just after ten-thirty when they reached the bus shelter. Sandra came over all tired.

'Let's sit down. Have a bit of a rest.'

'Well . . . yeah, OK.'

She looked across at him in the dusk. The chip shop round the corner was doing lively business but Andreas's thoughts were not on chips. His mouth was dry, his palms wet with perspiration. Sandra cocked her head on one side and undid the groaning top button of her blouse.

'You're not bad-looking, d'you know that?'

'Yeah?' He'd been utterly stunned by that. Good-looking? Him? On the other hand, maybe she was right.

'Yeah. Bit young, but I like 'em young. You can train 'em, see, they don't have any funny ideas.'

To his astonishment she had unfastened all three of her remaining buttons. Underneath, she was wearing one of those white lacy push-up bras, a size or two too small as he recalled – great handfuls of tit-flesh were spilling out over the top of it. He was mesmerised.

'Sandra! What if someone sees?'

Sandra made a funny chuckling noise at the back of her throat.

'Then they'll have to wait their turn, won't they?'

He remembered swallowing hard as – bold as brass and twice as shameless – she slipped off her blouse. He stole a quick glance at his watch. Ten thirty-seven. The next bus wasn't due for forty-five minutes, but even so you never knew when someone might come along. He thanked his lucky stars that it was one of those old wooden bus shelters that you couldn't really see into from the outside.

'Sandra, you can't do that!'

'You can take my bra off you like.'

Now what sort of a proposition was that to make to an

oversexed schoolboy with a copy of *Health and Efficiency* stuffed under his mattress?

'I couldn't.'

'Oh, well, if you don't want to.' She picked up her discarded blouse, as though to put it back on.

He could see opportunity slipping away fast and grabbed at its retreating back.

'Of course I want to!'

'So you're scared?' Sandra looked him up and down, not entirely unsympathetically. 'Well, there's nowhere else to do it. If you want it we'll have to do it here.'

His mind was reeling. Did he want it? You bet he did. Was he scared? Oh come on, what was the point of being scared? At this rate he might die without ever getting his end away. Go for it.

He'd never felt so clumsy in his life. His fingers, fumbling at her bra-catch, felt as huge and useless as sausages. Even his dick felt clumsy and inept. What if it came to it and he couldn't do it? He felt hot and cold and randier than he'd ever have believed possible.

Suddenly he got something right and the catch yielded, the two halves of the elasticated back-strap shooting apart like a catapult. Sandra's huge and heavy breasts flopped out of the padded cups into his astonished hands.

Breasts. He was holding, stroking, fondling a woman's breasts. For a few minutes he couldn't believe it. But Sandra was sighing and murmuring and he knew he must have been doing something she liked, because her nipples stopped being flat pink circles and stiffened into long-nosed, rosy cones that begged to be bitten.

That night was incredibly vivid in his mind. Why was he remembering it now? He hadn't thought about Sandra for years and now here he was in a kinky playroom behind an old-fashioned toy shop, reliving his first sexual encounter in all its Technicolour glory.

Glory? Well perhaps not glory. He was that skinny adolescent boy again and he could feel his cheeks turning crimson as Sandra wriggled out of her knickers. He'd never seen a real woman without her knickers on before.

'You want a shag then, or what?'

Not, perhaps, the most romantic opening gambit, but then romance was something your mum read while your dad watched *Top of the Pops* and had horny thoughts about Pan's People. Let's face it, mouthy she might be but Sandra was a damn fine-looking girl, with long, smooth, miniskirted legs which she uncrossed to reveal a dark and mysterious triangle between her outspread thighs.

Oh yes, he wanted a shag all right. And that night he got one, there in the bus shelter with the Number 38 thundering past and the fear of discovery lending additional spice to his excitement. In fact he'd done it to her twice – once to get the hang of the mechanics and once to get it right. The second time had been brilliant, lying on top of Sandra on the wooden bench with his dick right up her and two massive handfuls of pillow-soft tit. He'd had no idea it would be so much more fun than wanking.

Mara's breasts were soft, too. Soft and firm with long-stalked nipples. She responded eagerly to his frenzied caresses, to the kisses that turned into little bits of passion.

'I want you, Mara. I want you like crazy.'

She unfastened his trousers, helped him out of them, cradled his stiff penis in her expert hand.

'I want you too. I want you to fuck me.'

So lost were they in the urgency of their need that the voice filtered into their consciousness like something in a dream.

'I'm so glad to see you enjoying yourselves – Mr Hunt, Ms Fleming.'

For a second, everything seemed to freeze – time, expressions, breath, even Postman Pat's bright-pink dick on the bedside alarm clock.

Slowly, very slowly, Mara and Andreas turned to look at the stranger. They had not seen him enter the room – had not even noticed the door behind the painted wooden screen.

Mara was first to overcome her shock.

'Who are you? And how do you know our names?'

The stranger was a man of perhaps forty, quite well-built with sandy hair and a strong physique. Andreas noticed that when his mouth smiled his eyes did not join in.

'I am the owner of the toy shop – and this . . . recreation room is mine also. As for knowing who you are, that is of no consequence.' He paused. 'You realise that you are trespassing?'

Andreas swung his legs over the side of the bed and reached out for his trousers.

'I'm sorry we've bothered you. We came here by mistake. If you could just show us how to get out of here . . .'

The stranger gave a dry laugh.

'Nice try, Mr Hunt. But I'm afraid you'll have to do better than that if I'm not to report you both to the police. Let's see – breaking and entering, gross indecency, theft . . .'

'You can't do this!' protested Mara.

'Ah, but I already am doing it.'

Andreas had the man sussed-out.

'OK. What do you want to let us go?'

'That's more like it,' beamed the stranger, sitting down on a carved chair decorated with copulating elves. Mara couldn't help thinking that he was rather good-looking in a rough sort of way. 'I'm so glad you've decided to be reasonable about this. I'm sure we can strike an amicable bargain.' His grey eyes travelled over Mara's upturned nipples. 'All I want is for you to perform for me.'

'Perform!' Andreas's eyes widened. 'If you think . . .'

The stranger raised his hand to call for silence.

'Please, Mr Hunt, hear me out.' He turned to the small painted toy cupboard beside him and opened the doors. Inside was a top-of-the-range camcorder, whirring away quietly to itself. 'As you can see, cinematography is a favourite hobby of mine.'

'You've been . . .?'

'You probably did not notice, but yes, I have been filming your . . . games from the moment you entered this place. Do you see the small hole in the cupboard through which the lens was aimed? It is very discreet, don't you think?'

Andreas and Mara stared back at the stranger in mute horror. Seeing their shock, he continued.

'And so you see, I already have some very interesting footage of you – footage which might cause some considerable embarrassment to a man in your position, am I not right, Mr Hunt? Or should that be Nicholas Weatherall, MP?'

Andreas and Mara exchanged looks.

'All I ask is that you continue your charming diversions – under my expert direction, of course – so that I may film them for my own amusement.'

'You want us to have sex . . . for the camera?'

'Think of yourself as a film star, Ms Fleming.' The grey eyes took in every curve of the full yet slender body. 'You most certainly have all the physical attributes.' He licked his lips and Mara felt the force of his covetous lust. 'You will oblige me?'

Mara hesitated. But her excitement was already taking over from her apprehension. She had been crazy for sex a few moments ago and she was still crazy for it now. Nothing had changed – other than the addition of a possible extra playmate.

'We'll do it.'

'Good. Good.' The stranger adjusted the camera and started unbuttoning his shirt. 'Now, to begin with, I have a fancy to see the beautiful Mara astride my favourite rocking-horse . . .'

12: Market of Souls

'RISING SEAS "MAY OBLITERATE FALKLAND ISLANDS" AS POLAR ICE-CAPS MELT'
(*South Georgia News*, 4 July)

The door of the toy shop closed behind them with a clatter, followed by the sliding home of the two heavy bolts.

Andreas let out a long sigh of relief.

'I'm glad to be out of there,' he declared. 'Aren't you?'

'Oh, I don't know . . .' Mara hugged the erotic memories to her and could not quite regret what they had just done. It had to be faced – she'd enjoyed it, and so had Andreas, whatever else he might claim. 'I thought it was rather fun, doing it for the camera. And he did have a rather nice cock.'

'Nicer than mine?'

Mara pressed her lips against his and slid her hand down the crotch of his trousers.

'Don't be silly.'

They walked down the narrow, cobbled alleyway towards the distant sound of music and voices.

'Where do you suppose we are?' Andreas wondered. All they could see was sky, and bits of sky look pretty much the same, no matter where you are.

'Somewhere . . . somewhere northern. At least, that's how it feels, don't ask me why.'

'Northern – as in Oslo?'

'Not that far north, silly. Carlisle maybe, somewhere old anyhow – look at these old stone walls and cobbles.'

At last the alleyway began to broaden out and they found themselves walking towards a thoroughfare. Not the bland, formulaic shopping centre of a large town, but an old-fashioned high street, with lots of old buildings in greyish stone and a higgledy-piggledy arrangement of market stalls.

Music and bustle filled the air, the sound of brass instruments competing with the high-pitched wail of a folk-singer and a town-crier, shouting above the regular thump, thump, thump of a brass drum.

'What time is it?'

Mara glanced at her watch.

'Almost seven o'clock.'

'In the evening?'

'Yes, why?'

'What's going on?'

'I don't know – it looks like some sort of street festival.'

They walked into the main street and joined the swirling, seething crowd which had gathered around the many stalls. They were not quite like ordinary market stalls, Mara decided. It was more like a New Age gathering, ordinary people mingling with curious characters in outlandish clothes.

There were stalls offering Tarot readings or crystal therapy, others selling second-hand occult books; even a self-styled ranter priest in full seventeenth-century garb, standing on a soapbox and proclaiming the Apocalypse.

'Armageddon's really in fashion these days,' remarked Andreas. 'Just what *is* going on?'

'We won't know that until we find the rest of the Eye,' Mara pointed out. 'Maybe nothing is going on. Maybe it's simply that the new millennium's just around the corner – it makes people jumpy.'

They squeezed and squashed their way between the stalls.

'Look,' said Mara, jogging Andreas's arm. 'That's where we are.'

He followed her gaze to the hoarding above an Edwardian shop-front. It read: 'LANCASTER FISHERIES. EST. 1842.'

A man in a long black cloak pushed past, jolting Mara so hard that she fell against Andreas and he had to catch her to prevent her from falling over.

'Watch where you're going, mate,' grunted Andreas.

The man turned towards him and Andreas saw that he was wearing a grotesque mask; the mask of a devil, black-faced and leering with small red horns. And then, seconds later, the silent figure was gone, lost once more in the crowd.

'Market of Souls, come to the Market of Souls.'

The town-crier emerged from the teeming throng, leading a raggle-taggle procession down the middle of the crowded street. The crier was tall, bearded and rather magnificent in a long robe of heavy gold brocade. Behind him came a young boy in a jester's costume, beating a bass drum almost as big as himself, and a host of masked figures dressed in a jumble of quasi-medieval costumes, processing in silence behind the drum. At the rear of the procession came four masked trumpeters, dressed as medieval heralds.

They made a pretty weird sight and normally Andreas would have passed some sarcastic comment . . . only he couldn't think of anything to say. If he was really honest with himself, all this stuff worried him. 'Market of Souls'? What the hell was a Market of Souls anyway? It sounded like something the Devil might dream up. First Brother Julius and his 'sexual worship', and now this sinister festival. His mouth was dry and his hands were sweaty and trembling.

'Let's get out of here.'

'We can't. We have to find the Eye. It must be here somewhere, that's why we've been brought here.'

'Yeah. I suppose.' All the tiny hairs on the back of

Andreas's neck were standing on end, but no doubt he was just over-reacting again. After all, it was Mara who was the psychic.

'I rather like it,' Mara announced. 'It has a sort of raw energy.' She gave Andreas a sidelong look. 'It makes me feel sexy.'

She slipped her arms around his waist and stood on tiptoe to kiss him, pressing her mouth wetly against his and crushing the fleshy pillows of her breasts against his chest. People pushed past but Andreas hardly noticed them, or the stallholders crying their wares.

'We could find a hotel or a pub or something,' suggested Andreas. 'We'll need somewhere to stay.' Hotels meant beds and beds meant he could get Mara's clothes off again. And this time it would be just the two of them, him and Mara, forget the pervert with the camcorder.

'You think we should?'

'Oh, definitely.' He meant it, too. 'Though they're bound to be booked up, with all this lot in town.'

'OK then.'

Mara set off into the heart of the crowd, her red hair streaming out behind her like a banner. Andreas was right behind. At least, she thought he was. It wasn't until a few moments later that she turned round and realised that he wasn't behind her after all.

'Andreas?'

'Lost someone, little lady?' A leering orange mask in the shape of a pumpkin loomed into her face and a man's hand gripped her bare arm. She prised the fingers free.

'I'm fine, thank you.'

'You don't want to be alone, not in this crowd. You never know what might happen to you.'

'I told you, I'm all right. Please go away. Oh, there he is. Andreas!'

But the dark-haired man who turned round in answer to her call was not Andreas. Andreas Hunt was nowhere to be seen.

214

* * *

Wisps of mist hovered and danced over the deserted plain. The ruined, burnt-out manor house stood jagged and black against the bleached-out sky, an angry shout against its bland English whiteness.

A distant rumbling sound was followed by a tremor which undulated and rippled the passive earth like a great brown piece of carpet. But the watcher showed no sign of emotion.

The solitary figure stood, watched, waited. He had done a great deal of waiting lately, but now he knew that it was going to happen soon, alarmingly soon. He could feel the inevitability in the air, building up to a crescendo of suffocating intensity.

Perhaps it was already too late.

The golden snake slithered about his shoulders, its shimmering coils wrapping themselves about him as it reared its head and began to whisper to him.

Too, too late.

Mara was alone too. She didn't have much choice, seeing as Andreas had wandered off and got himself lost. Still, at least being on her own gave her a chance to explore.

Towards the end of the street the stalls began to thin out a little, and a few yards further on the street opened out into a small market-square. Here, the most remarkable entertainments were in progress. It was more like a scene from a Brueghel painting than an English city at the turn of the twenty-first century.

In the centre of the square, a troupe of dwarves were performing an acrobatic tableau of leaping and tumbling, whilst in amongst their legs careered a wildly barking, black and white mongrel dog with a ruff around its neck and ribbons in its tail. It was chaos. A half-naked strongman was playing the executioner at a guillotine erected on a high wooden dais. One by one, laughing volunteers were led up to the scaffold to bare their necks and show their 'bravery' as the trick blade fell.

Other sideshows, still more bizarre, lined the edges of the square. A woman fire-eater, naked save for an iron collar, bracelets and ankle cuffs, was lying on a bench whilst her assistant played a burning blowtorch over her bare and glistening skin. Two masked 'angels' were having sex up against a wall, watched by a naked man with a pierced and tattooed dick, and a bound and blindfolded woman was licking whipped cream from between another woman's thighs.

Mara walked in a daze through the midst of this freak show, dazzled by the noise and colour and the sheer grotesqueness of the scene. If she had not known otherwise, she would have believed she had wandered into somebody else's nightmare. All restraint gone, all modesty forgotten, the only law that remained was the law of pleasure. A perverse and corrupt pleasure which both revolted and fascinated her.

Aroused her, too. She could not deny the familiar, warm feeling flooding between her thighs, making her gaze linger on the smooth pink dick sliding so effortlessly in and out of that young man's mouth.

Lust made her pulse race, her mouth go dry as dust. She would get something to drink, rest, collect her thoughts, that's what she'd do. Turning out of the square, away from the laughter and light and music, she found a quiet, narrow lane where the evening sunlight cast long fingers of shadow.

The sign read: 'Heaven's Gate Hotel'. A painted wooden sign, swinging gently in the evening breeze. 'Tea, coffee, light refreshments, accommodation.' The building wasn't like any other in the street – not dove-grey stone, but half-timbered and lopsided, in that endearingly organic way that medieval houses have.

It was perfect. She would get a room there, get something to drink, then go out and find Andreas. She walked quickly up to the door and raised her hand to ring the bell.

Before she had even touched it the door swung open. In

the doorway stood a familiar but unexpected figure.

'I . . .'

'Good evening, Ms Dubois.'

The toy shop owner returned her astonished gaze with a steady smile.

'How delighted I am to see you again so soon. Won't you come in? I have prepared the Honeymoon Suite.'

As Mara followed the man up the stairs to the first floor, she asked herself again and again what she was doing here. Why didn't she just turn round and walk away?

Why? Because she wanted to be here, that's why. Because this time, she wanted to know how it would feel to have that eager cock not only on her tongue but in her cunt, in the secret fastness of her arse. The hunger had returned, this time more savage than ever, making her yearn for sexual release.

He turned as they reached the top of the stairs.

'It was rude of me not to introduce myself, Anastasia. My name is Peterson. Charles Peterson.'

Peterson took a bunch of keys from his pocket and unlocked a door.

'Please.' He gestured for her to enter.

He was behind her now, but she could feel his eyes boring into her back, memory and desire mentally stripping her again, returning her to the playroom where she and Andreas had acted out his fantasies. His hand brushed her backside and she felt a surge of guilty pleasure. Why did she find this rather ordinary man so irresistibly attractive?

The room was sumptuously decorated, not at all as she had expected it to be. This was not homely, olde-worlde charm but sensual elegance. In the centre of the room stood a heart-shaped bed, draped with a red satin bedspread edged with black lace. On top of it clothes had been laid out: a black stretch teddy, an ivory satin basque with suspenders and matching stockings, a yellow kimono-style robe embroidered with butterflies and flowers, a diaphanous baby-doll nightdress in flouncy pink nylon. Clothes tailor-made for grown-up games . . .

'Is it to your liking?'

Mara caught the double-meaning in Peterson's question. He wasn't asking her about the room. She let her eyes linger on the erotic jumble of clothes.

'Oh yes, Mr Peterson. It is all quite satisfactory.'

She stooped to examine the clothes more closely, stroking her hand over the folds of the baby-doll nightie. It was a perfectly ridiculous garment and she adored it.

'Why don't you put it on?' asked Peterson, softly closing the door and turning the key.

Why not, indeed? Mara's heart beat a little faster. There truly was something about this place, something in the air that made you feel like all you would ever need was sex – beautiful, frenzied sex.

'Why don't you put it on me?'

She knew she had said the right thing as she watched Peterson's dick swell in his pants. He pulled her to him and reached behind her for the zipper of her dress. It was fiddly and it took time for him to get the hang of it, but that was OK. She wanted it to take time. She wanted his dick to throb as powerfully and as painfully as her clitoris.

The zipper gave a whispering sigh as it yielded to Peterson's insistent efforts and slid down to the base of her spine. She was glad now that, just for a change, she had decided to wear underwear. It would slow things down, prolong the experience and intensify its erotic power. But would her lover like the red half-cup bra and matching panties?

His answering growl reassured her. As he peeled down the front of her dress, a warm night breeze entered the room through the open window and rippled across her skin in the lightest of caresses. Peterson's caresses were not quite so subtle. Once he had stripped Mara of her dress, he began stroking and biting her bare shoulders and back, leaving little marks that turned first white then red on her creamy skin.

'Darling bitch,' he murmured, hooking his finger under the back strap of her brassière. 'You dress to drive men mad with lust for you.' He released the bra-catch and she bent forward, shaking her breasts free of the half-cups and letting the garment fall into Peterson's hands.

Next were the panties, the infinitesimal scrap of stretchy red lace that barely covered her pubis and left the deep cleft of her backside clearly exposed. Peterson pulled them down with a feverish eagerness which left Mara in no doubt, then bent to torment the creamy flesh with dozens of little bites.

Peterson picked up the baby-doll nightdress from the bed. It really was a ludicrous creation: five or six layers of see-through pink nylon edged with a flouncy frill which might just, but only just, cover a girl's modesty. Ludicrous but, oh, so sexy. Mara felt all the excitement of a teenage nymphette as she submitted to Peterson's insistence, raising her arms so that he could slide the nightdress down over her shoulders.

'Beautiful,' murmured Peterson. 'Just right. Why don't you look at yourself in the mirror?'

She glanced towards the wardrobe but Peterson laughed.

'Not *that* mirror.'

She followed his gaze upwards and for the first time noticed the mirrored ceiling – dozens of square glass tiles reflecting the heart-shaped bed beneath. As she looked up she saw how small and vulnerable she looked in the pink nightdress, almost childlike but with a woman's body.

'Put these on.'

Peterson handed her two pony-tail rings, almost exactly like ones Mara had had when she was a little girl. They consisted of two stretchy hoops of elastic, to which were attached little fuzzy pink elephants.

'Do it, Mara. It would please me.'

Dividing her auburn hair into two bunches, she put on

the pony-tail rings. Now she looked exactly like the child-woman that Peterson so desired.

Peterson smoothed his hand over Mara's thighs, lifting the skirt of her nightdress just high enough to show that she was naked underneath.

'You've been a bad girl, haven't you, child?'

Mara's emerald eyes widened in a look of perfect innocence.

'Have I?'

'Oh yes, a very bad girl. You forgot to wear your knickers again. Teacher will have to punish you for that.'

'Yes, please,' Mara breathed. She could hardly believe how excited she was.

'Bend over that chair.'

Mara leant forward over the chairback, holding on to the uprights and waiting for the resounding slap as Peterson's hand came smacking down on her backside. But that wasn't quite the punishment that Peterson had in mind.

She felt him pulling up the many skirts of her baby-doll nightie and smoothing the flat of his hand over and over the full curve of her buttocks.

'A bare bottom. What a shameless girl you are.'

She did not answer him but waited in excited anticipation, her hips gently swaying and her bare feet shuffling on the softly carpeted floor. When she felt Peterson prising apart her arse cheeks, she guessed what was coming next.

Even so, his cock-tip penetrated her arse so suddenly that she gave a cry half of discomfort, half of delight. It felt good, better even than she had expected, to have this man's dick enter the inner sanctum of her most secret pleasure. Here, now, dressed not like Mara Fleming but like some teenage slut, she felt a new and delicious sensation of guilt. Oh yes, she really was a very bad girl – and she richly deserved her punishment.

'If you are a good girl and take your punishment well,' Peterson told her as he plunged his dick into her, right up to the balls, 'perhaps I shall lick my cream out of your backside. Would you like that, my darling little Anastasia?'

'Oh yes, teacher,' she sighed, thrusting out her backside to take more of this wonderful punishment. 'Oh *yes.*'

It was the following morning when Mara emerged from the Heaven's Gate Hotel, bathed, fucked and thoroughly refreshed by the previous night's events.

If she felt a nagging guilt at abandoning Andreas to indulge in Peterson's games, she did not let it spoil the beauty of a sunny July morning. In any case, it was Andreas who had wandered off. He would be all right. A pang of anxiety halted her momentarily in her tracks. He *would* be all right, wouldn't he?

She walked slowly down the street towards the square. Last night's stalls and sideshows were gone, the place almost deserted now except for early-morning shoppers and a solitary red and yellow striped tent.

How very odd, clearing the rest of the fair away and leaving just one tent. As she got a little nearer, she could make out a painted wooden sign: 'MADAME SOSOSTRIS, FORTUNE TELLER.'

Sudden unease gripped her. A fortune-telling booth – it had been a booth not so very different from this one where she had first met Andreas Hunt. Back then, the Master had been playing with them both, a deadly game of cat and mouse, manipulating their minds and bodies for his own twisted pleasure.

Was someone playing games with them now?

More cautious now, she approached the doorway. The tent flap was gaping open, but the interior of the tent was too dark to make out in any detail.

'Enter freely and have no fear, Anastasia Dubois.'

The sonorous voice made her start. Should she turn back, refuse the lure? Or should she let curiosity get the better of her and rush in where angels (and more sensible people) might fear to tread?

Curiosity triumphed. She stepped inside the tent.

It took a few minutes for her eyes to become sufficiently accustomed to the half-light to make out the figure sitting stooped over a small, round table. Behind an oil lamp glowed, giving out a feeble light.

The figure looked up.

'I thought you'd never get here.'

'Andreas! What on earth . . .?'

Andreas grinned and threw off the headscarf. It didn't suit him anyway.

'Sorry, Mara, I saw this empty tent and I couldn't resist it. I figured you'd be bound to come in if you saw it.'

'What did you have to go wandering off like that for?' protested Mara, secretly delighted to see Andreas.

'*Me*? If anybody wandered off it was you. I just got talking to this girl . . .'

'Big tits?'

'Well . . .'

'Thought as much.'

'What about you then, little Miss Prim? Bet you didn't spend the night in the local convent.'

'Er no, actually I found us a room. A whole suite of rooms. Remember that guy at the toy shop? Peterson, his name is.'

'The pervert? Oh Mara, you didn't.'

'I'll explain later. Right now, what we need to do is find the next piece of the Eye. We've wasted enough time.'

'Speak for yourself,' retorted Andreas, fishing in his pocket and taking something out. Unwrapping it from his handkerchief, he chucked it across at Mara. 'Here, catch!'

Mara stared down incredulously at the hard, sparkly thing in her cupped hands.

'This . . . this is the piece we've been looking for.'

'Cor-rect.'

'So how . . .?'

'It was in the toy shop. I had this hunch, see. While you were keeping our jolly toyshop-owner entertained, I sneaked back to the shop and broke in.'

'You did what!'

'Don't worry, I was careful. I mean, I can just imagine the headlines, can't you – "NATIONALIST MP NICKED BURGLING TOY SHOP"? Anyway, I had a good nose round and I found what we were looking for – it was in the bridle of one of the hobby-horses.'

Mara gave Andreas a bone-crushing hug. He didn't struggle. He liked it.

'Andreas, you're a genius!'

'Ah, but am I an irresistible sex-god?'

'You are.'

'Say it.'

'Andreas Hunt, you're an irresistible sex-god.'

'Can you prove you mean it?'

'What – here?'

'Why not?' Andreas pinched Mara's nipple lightly between his finger and thumb, rolling the flesh into a hard, rubbery cone.

'People keep walking past. They might come in.'

'Admit it, Mara, you're an exhibitionist at heart. You *love* an audience. And besides, I'm irresistible.'

He sat back down on his chair and unzipped his flies, taking out his cock. Its domed purple head was as succulent as a plum, its oozing juices making it glisten in the lamplight.

'No reason why we can't be discreet,' he pointed out. 'Feeling tired? Why don't you come and have a nice sit down?'

Lifting up her skirts, Mara sat slowly down on Andreas's lap, his cock sliding neatly and cleanly into the hot wet haven of her cunt. Andreas put his hands on her hips and eased her gently up and down, using her tight wetness to wank his shaft.

'Now, tell me what you did with that guy Peterson,' Andreas whispered in her ear, 'and I swear I'll do it to you a thousand times better.'

13: Masque of Flesh

'GEOLOGISTS CLAIM BEN NEVIS GROWING BY
SIX FEET A MONTH'
(*Geographical Monthly*, July issue)

'Cheviot has arrived, Master.'

Ibrahim stood at the entrance to the Great Hall, his
oiled body glossy and magnificent in the light from a
thousand candles. All two dozen chandeliers had all been
lit tonight, at the Master's command, for later on the
Master would be entertaining some of his fellow Privy
Councillors and he fully intended to do it in style.

'Send him in.'

'At once, Master.'

The Master watched Ibrahim's retreating back
thoughtfully for a few moments and then snapped his
fingers.

'Slave.'

Ibrahim turned back.

'Yes, Master?'

'Take Cheviot to the Hall of Darkness. I will meet you
there.'

Ordinarily, the Hall of Darkness was Mistress Sedet's
preserve, for the Queen had a unique talent for devising
punishments of exquisite cruelty, a she-cat's instinct for
the precise infliction of pain.

But this evening the Master had a mind to appropriate
the Hall for his own ends. Cheviot had returned from his

trip to his Whitby constituency and the Master was eager for results. Sometimes a short, sharp shock could teach a dilatory slave a salutary lesson. He would not tolerate any less than absolutely devotion and complete efficiency from his underlings, even if they were senior back-bench MPs.

He strode down the stone staircase which led down into the cellars of Winterbourne Hall, scarcely giving a thought to that portion of the cellars which remained blocked off by a brick wall. The portion in which his old body lay, still encased within the block of crystal like a fly suspended in amber. So very generous of Mr Hunt to offer his body for the greater good of the cause. And it was really quite a nice body. Certainly it would suffice for a century or so, until he got bored with it and wanted something a touch superior.

The stairs descended from the relative brightness of the corridor into a half-lit, subterranean world where every shadow held the face of a leering demon. This was the Hall of Darkness, a purgatorial realm where sinners could expiate their shortcomings and develop a connoisseur's taste for pain.

Burning torches hanging in iron brackets illuminated the Hall, throwing into relief Sedet's punishment table and the black japanned cabinet in which she kept her collection of manacles and whips. A wooden X-frame stood near to the wall, with dangling leather straps that could be used to restrain the penitent most effectively. On the punishment table lay a selection of spring-jawed metal clips, dildos and gags, designed to reduce the penitent's resistance still further and teach the blissful transformation from pain into ecstasy.

The Master passed through the great gateway into the Hall of Darkness. Cheviot was waiting for him, with Ibrahim by his side, silent and obedient as ever.

'I came as soon as I received your summons, Master,' Cheviot began, almost before the Master had got to the bottom of the steps.

'If you had not,' replied the Master acidly, 'I would have

had you flayed and thrown to the guards for their pleasure.'

Cheviot shuddered. He had seen what happened to initiates who fell foul of their Master's volatile temper.

'Yes, Master.'

The Master opened the prettily inlaid door of the punishment cupboard, selected a half-inch-thick malacca cane and tested its suppleness between finger and thumb.

'You will now give me your report on your visit to Whitby.'

Cheviot's heart sank several storeys. He knew what he was about to say was not going to be what the Master wanted to hear, but it was no use lying. The Master would only read his pathetically transparent thoughts.

'I have made useful contacts and support for our cause remains firm,' he began. 'I have brought back three very talented sex-sluts for Madame LeCoeur to train.'

The Master let out an exasperated gasp and flicked the cane against the palm of his hand.

'Do not bother me with such trivia,' he snapped. 'What of the man who calls himself Brother Julius?'

'He is a petty rabble-rouser, no more.'

'I have heard he is a man of powerful personality, Cheviot, a man of great persuasive abilities. A man who could be useful to my cause.'

'N-no, Master. He is nothing, I swear.'

'So. You failed to initiate the man and now you make pathetic excuses.'

'No, Master. It was not my fault. It was Weatherall and the Dubois slut, they suddenly arrived in Whitby and started asking questions about Brother Julius. They interfered, it was unforgivable . . .'

The Master gave a scornful growl.

'I *sent* Weatherall and Dubois to Whitby, slave.'

'Oh.'

'I sent them there on . . . other business of considerable importance. That is all you need know. If you impeded them in any way . . .'

'No, Master, I did not. I swear I did not.'

The Master laid the cane back on its shelf and closed the door of the punishment cupboard. He fully intended teaching Cheviot a lesson but a simple beating would hardly fit the bill. It was precisely because Cheviot enjoyed that sort of thing so much that it had been so easy for the vampiress Viviane to ensnare him. No, he needed to think of something else – something that would really make Cheviot suffer.

'Ibrahim, strip Cheviot and tie him to the X-frame. There is a little something I would like him to see.'

Ibrahim glided out of the shadows and, undressing Cheviot, attached his wrists and ankles to the massive wooden laths of the X-frame. Cheviot made no attempt to resist. The Master had not expected that he would.

'It is done, Master.'

'Bring in that whore Heimdal brought back from Bangkok.'

The Master watched Cheviot's eyes narrow with the first glimmerings of understanding. He knew how much Cheviot lusted after slim-hipped Thai girls, with their sloe eyes and their flawless, boyish bodies. He also knew how it would torture Cheviot to watch just such a girl being whipped and buggered in front of him when all Cheviot wanted was for those same things to be done to him . . .

The girl was brought in, her face a picture of animal terror. The Master had been undecided about her fate since Heimdal brought her back from Thailand. He sometimes found Heimdal's taste a little suspect – not like Delgado's. Delgado had really known how to pick the perfect whore. Well, tonight was the ideal opportunity for this new girl to choose her own fate. Perform well for her Master, and her prize would be initiation into the immortal realm of the undead. Fail to please, and her prize would be death.

Cheviot's eyes followed the girl greedily as she was forced to get on hands and knees on the punishment table, with her wrists secured by straps. Her blue-black, glossy hair fell forward in a curtain as she hung her head in submission. The Master smiled grimly. He knew he had devised the perfect sexual torture for Cheviot. He could watch but he could not touch; he could only yearn to *be* that pretty Thai whore, the privileged victim of the Master's cruel lust.

The Master took a leather gag and stuffed it into the girl's mouth. She had been at Winterbourne long enough to know how unwise it was to cry out, but he found it stimulating to think of her screaming silently into the gag as the pain became her whole world.

He glanced across at Cheviot as he made his selection from the wide range of instruments on offer. The poor fool was writhing in his bonds, his fingers clenching and unclenching in their yearning to break free and bring relief to his uncomfortably swollen prick.

The tit-clamps were shaped like the heads of Nile crocodiles, their jaws sharp-toothed and eager to close on their prey. They seemed to smile as the Master snapped them shut on the Thai girl's nipples. For a few seconds her whole body went rigid, and sweat poured out of her, coursing over her bare, olive-coloured skin in rivulets. Then she began to move, her hips tilting forward very slightly, as the Master projected lustful thoughts into her pretty young head.

'Oh, Master . . .' groaned Cheviot, overcome by his own lust.

'Will you keep silent!' snapped the Master, savouring Cheviot's discomfiture. 'Or must I gag you like the whore?'

Cheviot fell silent after that but his eyes were round and watchful, following every movement, every cruel caress. When the fat ebony dildo pushed its way into the girl's small and tender backside, he imagined himself as both the victim and the torturer. What bliss it would be both to wield the whip and to feel its cut on his bare and willing skin.

The Master was enjoying himself. The girl was somewhat

more responsive than he had expected and her disobediently wriggling backside gave him ample reason to make her punishment more severe. Her mind was utterly transparent to him, like a glass bowl in which swam exotic fishes of many bright colours, the lurid fantasies which populated this simple girl's brain.

He tasted her memories of life in the Bangkok brothel, sucking cocks and saving a few dollars here, a few more there. Enough, in time, to set up her own whorehouse where no pleasure would be forbidden. A whorehouse where every dream, no matter how dark or how lascivious, could come true.

The Master threw back his head and laughed at the novel way in which the girl's own dream had come true. She had wanted to own the best whorehouse in Bangkok and now she was a sex-slut in the best whorehouse in the entire history of the world. Whatever else it might be, Winterbourne remained the supreme palace of pleasure. And no-one ever refused an invitation to Winterbourne.

No-one, that is, except Harry Baptiste.

Suddenly angry, he pushed the dildo a little harder and its entire length disappeared inside the girl. Even through the thickness of the leather gag, he could hear her moans of protest. Good. He wanted to make her suffer. He wanted them all to suffer for their imperfections. The Master alone was perfect.

Curling his fingers into a fist, he pulled apart the girl's dusky-pink love lips and ground his way into her, ignoring her writhing body, forcing the pleasure from her. Despite the hundreds of men she had fucked, the girl was tight, but her sex was slippery-wet and there was no way for her to conceal her pleasure at what was happening to her.

Cheviot, too, was experiencing pleasure. Unbeknown to him, the Master was manipulating his mind with consummate skill, playing tricks with his desire, forcing him to disobey when he was trying so hard to do what the Master commanded.

It was almost unbearable, watching the Master fist-fucking the whore as she knelt on the punishment table like a she-wolf on heat, taking it, wanting it, demanding it. Her small breasts, distended by the weight of the solid silver tit-clamps, hung down in pointed cones that reminded Cheviot of a beast's dugs. How he would love to lie beneath the she-wolf's belly and be her cub, suckling from her, playing with her pendulous teats, smelling the animal scent of her desire.

And now the Thai girl was coming, damn her. Look at her, wriggling and moaning in her bonds, her arsehole puckering in the tightest of kisses and the juice dripping from her crack as the Master withdrew his glistening fist. Jealousy! Oh how he burned with a jealous lust for the Master's touch.

Too much, it was too much. The pictures in his head would not go away, and they made the watching so much worse. A silent voice seemed to whisper somewhere in the darkness of his thoughts: 'She wants you, Cheviot. She wants to beat you and then suck your dick.'

With a suddenness which made him cry out, Cheviot came, his spunk spurting out in a series of powerful, creamy jets which spattered the dark stone floor with opalescent wetness.

The Master turned his stony gaze on Cheviot.

'Disobedient cur. Have you no self-control?'

'Master . . .' gasped Cheviot. 'Master, forgive me.'

The Master gave a malicious smile.

'Forgive you! Cheviot, surely you know me better than that.'

Cheviot's perverse heart leapt for joy. Perhaps, at last, his beloved Master would take pity on him and punish him in the cruel, sweet, sensual ways that only he knew.

'You are too lenient with your slaves, my lord.'

The Master swung round. Mistress Sedet was standing at the entrance to the Hall of Darkness, her violet eyes flashing fire. She looked more striking than ever tonight,

her jet-black hair piled on top of her head in glossy coils
and her body encased in a black rubber catsuit which
gaped open at breast and crotch.

'My lady.' The Master betrayed no emotion. 'I had not
expected to see you until our guests arrive.'

Sedet came into the Hall, her body hard with muscle
beneath the clinging catsuit, her freshly shaven pussy-lips
protruding through the slashed black rubber in a provocative
pout.

'You should leave matters of discipline to me, my lord,'
she told him, throwing a disdainful glance at the pathetic
figure of Sir Anthony Cheviot, still firmly bound to the
X-frame. 'The Hall of Darkness is my creation.'

'I will discipline my slaves as I see fit.'

Sedet's red lips forced themselves into a cool smile.

'Indeed. As you see fit, my lord. Since you deem it
prudent to keep your own counsel on this, as on so many
matters . . .'

'I have no secrets from you.'

'Indeed?'

His eyes searched her defiant face.

'No more than you have from me, my lady.'

The Master snapped his fingers and Ibrahim surged out
of the shadows.

'Yes, Master?'

'Cut Cheviot down and send him away, he irritates me.
And tell my publicist to wait for me in the library.'

'At once, Master.'

Sedet's black-gloved fingers walked up the Master's
arm and smoothed over his lips, caressing very lightly and
seductively. She pouted her resentment.

'Will you leave me so soon, my lord? Will you not stay
here with me awhile and let me . . . divert you?'

The Master caught her fingers between his teeth, biting
just hard enough to make Sedet gasp.

'My lord – I . . .'

He pulled her closer to him and pushed his hand

between her thighs, slicing brutally upwards so that the side of his hand parted her cunt lips and pressed hard against the exposed head of her clitoris.

'My immortal queen,' he murmured, and rubbed the flat of his thumb across her swelling pleasure. Her eyes half-closed in submission to his desire and he tired to explore her mind, join his thoughts to hers. But, as so often of late, he found an area of her mind barred to him, as though a wall of psychic energy had been built to hide something that she did not want him to see.

'My lord,' she purred, biting and licking his earlobe. And she smiled to herself.

In this game of cat and mouse, they were both cats.

The following night, Andreas and Mara walked out again into the thronged streets of Lancaster.

'Apparently the Market of Souls is supposed to go on for seven nights,' Mara explained. 'It was first held in the tenth century, but the Puritans banned it.'

'For once, I'm with the Puritans,' replied Andreas, idly glancing at a couple in fancy dress, screwing enthusiastically in a shop doorway. There was something macabre in the way the normally staid citizens of Lancaster had suddenly cast off all their inhibitions. Almost like someone had slipped something into the water.

And then there was this terrible apocalyptic weather – the air thick and stinking of sulphur, and so furnace-hot and stifling it was hardly bearable. Early this morning, when the yellow-grey clouds had finally yielded their rain, it had vapourised even before it hit the ground. And that, to Andreas Hunt, was bloody odd.

'Each night there are more stalls and events,' Mara went on, 'and as tonight's the last night there's a sort of mystery play, with angels and devils and the mayor dressed up as God.'

They strolled together towards the main square.

'Now we've got the piece of the Eye, surely we don't

need to stick around here any more,' Andreas pointed out hopefully.

'No, but we don't know where to go next, do we?'

'How do we find out?'

'We wait for another sign. Sooner or later, something's bound to happen.'

'That's what I'm afraid of.'

The town square was teeming with life again – and very peculiar life it was, too. Under an evening sky streaked mustard-yellow and sickly orange, a grotesque pageant was being acted out. Wisps of off-white mist crept along the cobbled ground, licking around the ankles of the revellers, poking at bare flesh with prurient fingers. A man screamed with hysterical laughter as he was strapped to a huge wheel, and naked women danced and shrieked and fought and fucked in a row of rusty metal cages.

'What *is* this?' murmured Andreas.

It was like some medieval painting of Hell. There were even stocks and pillories, imprisoning pretty naked girls who offered up their soft sweet flesh to a masked man with a cat-o'-nine-tails. And masks – masks everywhere. Not simple cardboard masks with holes for their eyes, but elaborate creations of papier mâché, leather and beaten metal; the faces of demons, with eyes that moved and sharp-toothed jaws that creaked and grated into a mechanical smile.

A rat ran over Andreas's foot and he aimed a kick at it. It reared on its hind legs and bared its teeth at him – teeth that were long and yellow and flecked with something sticky and red. Oh my God, he thought as sickening realisation hit him, there were dozens of the buggers, running about all over the place, great fat, sleek rats with pink and hairless tails, totally unafraid of the human life around them.

In that moment, it occurred to Andreas that maybe, just maybe, the world really was going to end.

Someone struck a gong, and a shimmering, echoing sound filled the square, compelling sudden and complete silence. Everything stopped. The laughter, the screams, the fucking, everything. Everyone watched, waited.

'Masque of Flesh,' a voice intoned out of the eerie quietness. 'Behold the Masque of Flesh.'

The gong sounded again and the crowd began to move, the sea of bodies shuffling backwards to form a space in the centre of the square. Through the crowd processed the actors, all masked with the faces of angels or demons, all clad in long and flowing robes except for twin girls who were led into the square in long shifts of white silk, barefoot and blindfold.

'Let the Masque begin.'

The sound of ancient instruments filled the square – crumhorns, lutes, serpents, and the whining, grating drone of a hurdy-gurdy. And then tepid rain began to fall out of the sickly yellow sky, forming clouds of steam as the drops bounced and sizzled on the hot cobblestones.

One of the girls was being stripped by a man in an angel's mask, the other by the 'demon' Andreas had encountered in the crowd the previous night. The girls seemed dazed, perhaps hypnotised or drugged, for they neither struggled nor responded as their clothes were stripped from them and they were forced to submit to the most indecent of caresses.

Snatches of verse floated across the square as the narrator began the masque:

> Hair of silk and skin of snow,
> One maid for Heaven, one for below . . .

Greedily hands smoothed over white skin, exposing and exploring, punishing and caressing.

> Saint or sinner, which shall it be?
> The world shall burn, and so shall ye.

And then a great, shuddering cry which seemed to fill the air:

Kiss the demon, kiss the demon . . .

Mara clutched Andreas's arm.
'Over there.'
'What?'
'Over there, that horse. That black horse.'
'What about it?'
'Look at its eyes.'
The black stallion was tethered to a post beside one of the sideshows. It was a magnificent beast, jet-black with a long mane and eyes that glittered an unnatural ruby-red.
'Don't go near it, Mara.'
But Mara was already walking towards it and – like a fool – so was Andreas. He knew better than to argue with her when she had made up her mind about something. But that horse looked downright evil to him.
Mara stretched out her hand and patted its nose. It seemed to like it. She whispered in its ear and it whinnied, almost as if it knew her and recognised her voice.
'This is it,' she said. 'The sign, I'm sure of it. We have to get on the horse and it will take us to the next piece.' She untied the stallion's rope halter and put her foot in the stirrup, easing herself lightly onto the horse's broad back.
'I've never ridden a horse before.'
'You'll get the hang of it. Come *on*.'
She stretched out her hand to him and he clambered up awkwardly, catching the stallion's ruby eyes as he did so. He could have sworn it was laughing at him.
Almost as soon as he had climbed up behind Mara, the stallion set off – not just gently trotting but stretching out its long legs into a gallop, launching itself into the crowd with such a lunging leap that Andreas was certain he would be shaken off.
It picked up even more speed, its hooves striking sparks

off the cobbles as they flashed by, galloping across the square, galloping, galloping like crazy.

Right smack-bang into a solid brick wall.

The deck of the *Sally-Anne* pitched gently in a light, salty breeze that made the sails on the topmast flutter and dance. And the girls with the tousled hair and the off-the-shoulder blouses just kept on scrubbing that deck with their delightful plump arses in the air. Back and forth, back and forth, pressing down on the scrubbing brush and making the soap-suds bubble up like frothy cream.

Ah yes, the Pirate Room was one of Heimdal's finest creations. Half virtual-reality, half-theatrical props, the Pirate Room had been created in a large outbuilding on the Winterbourne Estate. During the last war – shortly before the Master's unfortunate incarceration in fact – the Hall had been requisitioned by SOE and the outbuilding had been used as a hanger for light training aircraft. Heimdal had spotted its potential instantly, and had employed a team of Takimoto's technicians to add a high-tech dimension to this latest fantasy play-room.

Heimdal loved theatricality. He had always run his own life like a West-End production with himself as the star. And here, in the Pirate Room, he was lord of all he surveyed. Perhaps, before very much longer, he would have a larger scope for his obvious talents.

The headset, gloves and harness created a perfect world of sound and vision, taste and texture and smell. As he switched on the power pack he scanned the scene before him – the tilting deck, the beautiful captives with their low-cut blouses and fat tits, the blue sea stretching away to meet an even bluer sky – and congratulated himself on this latest success.

He was the pirate captain, and he could make those women do anything – absolutely anything – he wanted them to do. With Takimoto's state-of-the-art technology, all he had to do was think about what he wanted and it would happen. He tried sending out a particularly horny thought and one of the girls – a brunette with dimples and shiny pink lips – got up from her hands and knees and unlaced the front of her blouse.

My but she had bit tits, enormous they were. And if he wanted he could think a bit harder and they'd get bigger, just for him. Another thought now, a little fancy that had just crept into his head. Oh yes, he liked that. She had her hands on her hips and she was bending forward from the waist, just as if she were a schoolgirl doing old-fashioned gym exercises. And her tits were swinging free, huge as melons and twice as juicy.

Go on, he told her in the smug silence of his lust. *Go on, do it. Just for me.* And she did. She took hold of her right breast and put it into the petite blonde girl's mouth. *Suck on it, darling, go on, suck on it, oh yes.*

Another figure walked into his field of vision, only this time it wasn't some digital bimbo conjured up by his subconscious, because this woman was real: tall and aristocratic-looking with short brown hair and high cheekbones. She looked good in that seventeenth-century gear, did Candice Dorigo, and with those heavy manacles on her hands she looked so endearingly vulnerable.

Since her initiation she had taken great strides in his estimation. She wasn't just good for information, she'd turned out to be good at a lot of other things, too. Especially pleasing Joachim Heimdal, Lord of Winterbourne.

He took off the electronic harness which he was wearing over his prick and balls. He didn't need that to stimulate him, not now he'd got Candice to do the job.

'Come here,' he commanded and she started walking towards him. 'No, on your knees.'

She dropped to her knees on the deck and he liked that, liked to have a woman literally at his feet. As she got near he put out his booted foot and laid it across her bare cleavage.

'You're nothing,' he told her. 'What are you?'

'I'm nothing.' How she enjoyed being nothing. Lord Heimdal had liberated her from the need to be anything at all, other than the instrument of his pleasure. And he had initiated her into the sensual realm of the immortals. How could she ever thank him enough for that? But she would try to think of a way . . .

'Good. I like a woman who knows her place. And your place is on the end of my dick,' he leered, seizing her by the hair and pulling her towards him so that her face was almost touching his genitals. 'Suck me. And you'd better be good.'

'Oh I will, Lord Heimdal,' she breathed in that oh-so-refined voice of hers, opening her well-bred lips to take him in. 'Please believe me, I will.'

'Shit!'

Andreas clung to Mara's waist and she clung to the stallion's mane as it burst right through the brick wall and out the other side – oddly enough, through a set of burnt-out French windows.

And suddenly, there wasn't a horse any more, only a wispy cloud of black smoke and they were lying in a jumble on the ground, amid the remains of what might once have been a parquet floor.

Mara sat up, breathless, brushing the hair out of her eyes.

'No, it can't be.'

Andreas got to his feet. He knew it was. It had to be, even this ruined, blackened shell of a building was instantly recognisable. No-one else had a house quite like it.

'It's Felsham Manor,' he said, a knot of sadness and guilt suddenly tightening in his belly. 'It's Max's old house.' He could hardly bear even to glance round at the devastation of what had once been a fine old mansion. Oh Max, you pathetic fucker, he thought, what did you have to go and get yourself fried for?

With only a charred lattice of timbers where the ceilings

and roof had been, Felsham Manor was no more than the skeleton of a house. After the initial fire, the elements had taken their toll on what remained – although, strangely enough, nature seemed to have left the place well and truly alone. No weeds, no flowers, no nothing. Just bleak devastation.

'I can't stay here,' said Andreas abruptly. 'I . . . I just can't.' Oh God, why did he feel so bad? 'I don't care if there are a million bits of the Eye of Baloch here, I just have to get out.'

He started trudging over the dusty rubble and Mara caught up with him, putting her hand on his shoulder.

'I know. But I don't think the Eye is here anyway, at least not in the house.' As they walked through the ruins she had to close her mind to the tumult of impressions. 'Let's make for the village, maybe we can get a room for the night.'

At the entrance to the driveway, its ornate stone pillars still intact, Andreas suddenly turned to look back at the Hall. Great, now he was hearing things.

He could have sworn he'd heard a voice calling to him. Max Trevidian's voice.

Mara lay back in the lavender-scented bathwater, scooped up a ball of soap-suds and blew them thoughtfully into a thousand individual bubbles.

'I'm glad to be away from there,' she said. 'But I still don't understand how we ended up at Felsham Manor. I'm certain there's nothing there for us to find.'

'Right now I'd rather not think about Felsham Manor,' said Andreas, pouring Mara a glass of white wine and taking a few sips before standing it on the edge of the bath.

'No. No, you're right.'

Mara picked up the wine glass and turned it round thoughtfully in her fingers, watching the play of light and shade through the frosted glass. Light and dark, good and evil. If only she could make sense of everything. Right now, the only thing she could be certain of was her desire.

Andreas stroked the wet hair back from her forehead.

'What are you thinking?'

'I'm thinking that I want you. Now.'

'Well, well. Good thoughts.' Andreas slipped his hand into the foamy water and under the soft, floating globe of Mara's breast. 'I thoroughly approve.'

He played with her nipple and she lay back in the warm water, sipping the cool wine, letting her tension and anxiety melt away. Her lover's touch held its own magic and she so needed the reassurance of his lust.

'Mmm,' she murmured luxuriously. 'You make me feel *so* randy. Why don't you play with me?'

'Why don't you play with yourself? I just love to watch you wanking.'

There was something utterly irresistible about the sight of Mara playing with her clitty. It never failed to drive Andreas crazy with jealous desire, watching her giving herself pleasure, playing her own body like some ethereal instrument.

Mara did not reply, but slid a little lower down in the water, drawing up her knees so that they were wide apart and her cunt lips gaped. The warm bathwater lavished greedy kisses on the coral-pink flesh of her inner labia. No place, however secret or intimate, was safe from its lewd caresses.

Andreas's hand skimmed the surface of the water, brushing away some of the thick, scented foam which veiled her belly and her sex. The only scent he wanted to smell now was the musky aroma of her desire, the only sight he wanted to see the utterly arousing spectacle of her fingers disappearing between her fleshy outer love lips.

He kneaded her breast and Mara wriggled, eel-like, in the tropically warm bathwater.

'Nice. Really nice. Don't stop.'

He had no intention of stopping. It turned him on more than he could say just to stroke his lover's breast while he watched her masturbating, just for him. She was putting on his own private sex-show, turning herself on by knowing how much she was arousing him.

Mara's fingers slid down her taut belly and into the wet tendrils of her pubic curls, twisting and winding them about scarlet-nailed fingertips before plunging on. With her left hand she spread her sex lips wider, and as she did so the warm water touched the exposed head of her clitoris for the first time. She shivered with total pleasure.

'That's it, my darling. Wank yourself.' Andreas took the bar of soap and started massaging Mara's tits with it. 'I want to see you bring yourself off.'

Mara slid the index finger of her left hand into the long, tight tunnel of her vagina. At its entrance the wetness of warm, soapy water gave way to the far more sensual wetness of slippery sex juice, a clear, sweet tide which flowed out of her and into the fragrant foam.

With the middle finger of her right hand, she began to frig herself. There were moments when she felt that no-one could pleasure her as perfectly as she could pleasure herself; for she knew her body with a shameless intimacy, understood every secret place and the thousand different ways in which it could be stimulated into vibrant lust.

Andreas soaped Mara's breasts with an assiduous pleasure, taking the greatest care not to neglect the hard pink crowns of her nipples, which he pinched lightly between soapy finger and thumb. He was in an ecstasy of frustration, a deliciously maddening state in which the anticipation of pleasure was so wonderful that he just kept on wanting it to go on and on and never stop. Lustful fantasies flew in and out of his thoughts, and he pictured himself wanking onto Mara's soapy breasts, or putting his dick between them and squeezing them tight around his shaft until at last he would spurt his cream all over her neck and face.

He watched her pleasuring herself – eyes half-closed, breath quickening, belly and thigh-muscles tense with expectation. Mara's sensual scent was mingled with the lavender perfume of the bath-oil now, creating a musky cocktail which made his head spin and his dick strain for the consummation of his need.

He followed her fingers, moving slowly between her cunt lips, making lazy waves in the scented water. She was close to orgasm, he knew that. When she wanked herself, she always began slowly, gradually increasing the speed of her strokes as her excitement began to overtake her; and then, when the dazzling goal was almost in sight, slowing again to make it last, building up towards a shattering climax.

It was too much to bear, simply to sit back and watch her giving herself the pleasure he wanted to give her. Stripping off his shirt and pants, Andreas threw them across the bathroom, kicking off his shoes and not even bothering about his socks.

'I'm going to have you, Mara Fleming, you sexy little vixen.'

Her eyes widened, their brightness a little hazy from the power of her lust, her smile sexy and welcoming.

'Then you'll have to come and get me.'

What the hell? Why shouldn't they have sex in the bath? Who cared if they slopped water all over the floor and annoyed the people in the room downstairs?

All he cared about, right now, was getting inside Mara Fleming's deliciously perfumed cunt.

'What will it be, sir, madam?'

The relief manager at the Causeway Inn stood behind the bar polishing glasses, glad of customers to pounce upon.

'Er, pint of Speckled Hen and . . .' Andreas raised a quizzical eyebrow in Mara's direction.

'White-wine spritzer please.' Mara perched herself on a barstool next to Andreas.

'Nice to have you staying here, if you don't mind my

saying so.' The barman set the drinks on the bar and took the money. 'To be honest, we can do with the business.'

'I thought you got lots of tourists around here in the summer,' said Mara, sipping her drink.

'Ah yes, well, we used to. But since the big house burned down last year . . .'

'Felsham Manor?'

'That's the place – know it, do you?'

'Only slightly – through an acquaintance.'

The manager nodded thoughtfully.

'Rum business that was, the Fire Brigade never did find out what caused it. I'm new here myself but the locals say it put people off coming, and then there were the floods.'

'Nasty,' observed Andreas.

'Very, sir. Washed half of Ely away.' The manager leaned over the bar counter, glancing conspiratorially to left and right like a double-agent in a spy film. 'And then there's the Wanderer, of course.'

'The Wanderer?'

'Yes, sir. There's some very odd tales about our local ghost. Not met him have you?'

'Not as I recall.'

'There's some folk round here reckon it's the restless spirit of the owner of Felsham Hall.'

Andreas looked up from his drink.

'What – Max?'

'I dunno sir, a Mr Trevidian I think his name was. Anyhow, I reckon it's a load of old nonsense myself – ghosts indeed!'

'Yeah,' said Andreas uneasily. 'Nonsense. I'm sure you're right.'

At the far end of the bar, hunched over a half-empty glass, sat a solitary figure in a long, dark coat. He smiled to himself as he listened to the barman pontificating. A wide-brimmed fedora shielded his face and tousled brown hair, but from time to time he darted covert glances, always at the same two people. Andreas Hunt and Mara Fleming.

'You here on holiday then, sir?'

'Sort of. We've a little . . . business to transact.' Andreas looked at Mara. 'Quite urgent business.'

Mara took a sip of her cold drink. The air was sweaty and oppressive, building up towards thunder. She could feel it in the pricking of her palms, the hairs standing up on the back of her neck. And there was something here . . . a presence . . .

'Tomorrow,' she said, laying her hand on Andreas's. 'It'll wait till tomorrow.'

As dusk deepened into night, Andreas and Mara sat drinking in the bar. Up in their hotel room, the assembled fragments of the Eye of Baloch lay in a jumble inside the bedside cabinet.

Silent. Unseen. Incomplete and quite incapable of harm.

But at the very heart of the crystal fragments something strange was happening. A snowstorm, a swirling mist of flakes, dancing with a secret, silent joy.

14: The Spirit of Bannockburn

"TWENTY MORE CASES OF NYMPHOMANIA IN
DUTCH CONVENT: PSYCHIATRISTS BAFFLED"
(*The Scalpel*, July issue)

It was a hot day, blisteringly hot. An unforgiving sun
burned down out of a sky as deadly as white fire, parching
the crops in the fields and distorting the horizon in a
shimmering heat-haze.

Andreas and Mara were out walking in the countryside
near the fenland village where they were staying. The fields
here were flat as steppes, dotted only sparsely with small
strands of trees or strips of ancient hawthorn hedge. But
on a small rise at the edge of a farmer's land stood a
tumulus – a prehistoric burial mound which had been
excavated in the late nineteenth century.

Mara sat down on the grass beside the entrance to the
burial mound – a square doorway with a stone lintel, piled
over with grassy earth.

'If we're going to find that last piece of the Eye we have
to do *something*,' remarked Andreas, sitting down beside
her. 'I mean we can't just stay here forever, kicking our
heels.' He took a deep breath. 'We could go back to Max's
house.'

Mara shook her head.

'No, not Felsham Manor. I'm virtually certain that's not
the right place for us to look.'

'Then how did we end up there?'

Mara shrugged.

'It was probably just the pull of old memories and presences that drew us there, and distorted the astral pathways. There's a great power in memory and past emotion.'

'So we might be in completely the wrong place?'

'Well . . . no, I don't think so. I don't think the last piece is far away. Sometimes I think I can almost see it, I can feel it's energy but I just can't quite reach out and touch it.'

'And is there a way to find out where it is?'

'I think so – I hope so. We need to divine its location using white magic. We can use the power of Tantra to put us in touch with the energy fields.' She laid her hand on the sun-warmed, grassy mound of the barrow. 'Can't you feel the spiritual energies in this place? It's perfect for a ritual. Come with me.'

Taking Andreas by the hand, she led him through the doorway into the low-roofed interior of the ancient barrow. Darkness wrapped itself around them like a thick cloak, the air at once very cool, very still, as though time had suddenly halted in its tracks.

The dragon's crystal eye on Andreas's talismanic bracelet glowed and glittered in the darkness, as though it recognised the power of this ancient and sacred place.

Mara reached out and ran her fingers over the age-smoothed stones which formed the walls of the ancient burial chamber. There was no hostility in this place, only the silent greeting of pagan spirits to their sister. There was no fear, only a sense of welcome.

'Spirits,' intoned Mara. 'Spirits of the ancient earth, assist our quest.' Her voice echoed around the low-vaulted chamber, weaving a net of sound.

She pulled Andreas towards her and they kissed. But this was no ordinary kiss, for as their lips met Andreas felt a jolt of energy pass between them, and for a brief moment he thought he glimpsed faces in the darkness – brown-skinned faces with bright eyes, watching, waiting, lusting.

'Lie down,' whispered Mara, breathless from their kiss.

He did so, and Mara knelt astride him, her thighs and sex bare under her floaty skirt. She felt behind her and unzipped Andreas's flies. The roughness of her caresses surprised him but filled him with a curious excitement. He liked, from time to time, to have her dominate him and insist on having her wicked way. Here, in the impenetrable darkness of the barrow, abandoning himself to her will felt delightfully wicked and depraved.

He reached out in the darkness and touched her thighs. Obliged to explore her entirely by touch, he made new and arousing discoveries about her body, like the way the firm flesh of her thighs quivered at his touch, and the different textures of her skin at calf and knee and the very tops of her thighs.

But there was little time simply to explore and to enjoy the sensuality of blind touch. For Mara had seized hold of his prick and, half-whispering, half-chanting some incantation he could not even begin to understand, she raised herself on her knees, positioning the very tip of his cock between her love-lips.

She bore down with the gentlest of pressure and, almost imperceptibly, the domed head of his cock slipped a half-inch or so into the secret tunnel of Mara's sex. A half-inch and then no more. He thought he was going to die of frustration, longing only for her to pump down hard on his dick and ride him to a spurting, jerking climax.

'Self-control, Andreas,' she gasped as he clawed at her thighs and tried to get her to ride him. 'Please, Andreas, if the ritual of divination is to work, we must have self-control . . .'

Self-control was the last thing Andreas wanted to think about right now. He was lying in the darkness, on the cool earth, with his swollen dick poised to slide up to the hilt in his lover's cunt; and here Mara was, as cool and still as a statue.

Her white marble thighs pressed hard against his hips

and her hot, wet labia released trickles of juice which ran from the dome of his glans right down over his foreskin and down the length of his shaft to its root, making his scrotum sticky with the secretions of her desire.

'Just a little further,' he pleaded. 'Let me slide just a little further inside you.'

'No,' she gasped, her head thrown back and her body tense with the effort of not moving. 'The magic . . . we mustn't break the power of the magic. Can't you feel it, building up inside us?'

Andreas had lost track of what he felt. His emotions, his sensations, his thoughts, all were jumbled up inside him, and he was on a rollercoaster ride in which he hardly knew what was real and what was a creation of his own frustrated desire. Pictures swam in and out of focus in his head, but he couldn't understand any of them, and as soon as one had gone another took its place, more baffling than the last. All he could remember was the desire to fuck, fuck, fuck.

Mara too longed to have her lover completely inside her. The desire was almost too powerful for her, but she knew she must not fail. Only by controlling her desire could she channel its power into the quest for enlightenment.

And, little by little, pictures were taking shape. Pictures of such vivid clarity that she no longer knew what was in the present and what was in the distant past.

She was no longer Mara Fleming – Mara Fleming the traveller and white witch. She glanced down and saw that she was wearing animal skins, roughly stitched into a short tunic which left one shoulder and one breast completely bare. Her hair still tumbled down her back but it was a wild tangle.

She was in a cave with painted walls. Somewhere nearby, in the flickering light from a bonfire, a man was using a flint knife to carve up the carcass of an antelope, and Mara could hear the screams and squeals of children playing rough-and-tumble games on the filthy, bone-strewn floor.

Looking down, she saw that the man between her thighs was not Andreas Hunt. He was dark and bearded, his mouth open in an animal growl as she ground down on his penis and his hips reared up, forcing his dick harder into the heart of her cunt. The wild beast in his eyes drove her to ride him harder, faster, tightening her thighs about his hips, raking her long fingernails over and over his bare chest.

It was more like fighting than fucking, their bodies suddenly rolling over and over in the dirt, his cock in her cunt, her thighs wrapped tightly about his hips. They spat and scratched, communicating not with words but with the violence of their passion.

And then she was on her back and her caveman lover was on top of her, his powerful thighs glistening with sweat as he pumped those final hard strokes into her, bruising her with the power of his hunger as he forced the glittering prize of pleasure from her loins.

Pleasure that was more agonising and more unbearable than the most terrible pain. Pleasure that dissolved consciousness, turning reason to delirium and sight to hallucination.

When she opened her eyes and looked up, it was not her lover that she saw but a black stallion towering over her. A black stallion with red eyes.

And slowly and deliberately, it winked at her.

'The Spirit of Bannockburn,' Andreas read out as he played the torchbeam over the smooth black stone. 'Are you sure . . .?'

'Sure as I can be.'

'Well you'd better keep a look-out for the local plods, or I'll be down the station trying to explain why I'm clambering all over a statue in the middle of the night.'

The Spirit of Bannockburn was just about the most famous thing ever to have come out of the Cambridgeshire village of Great Girlington. Winner of the Epsom Derby three times, the black stallion had so captured the villagers' imagination that they clubbed together to have a statue erected in his honour.

As Mara held the torch, Andreas ran his hands all over the weathered black marble.

'I can't feel anything but stone. You couldn't be wrong, I don't suppose?'

'Try its eyes, Andreas. Its eyes.'

He had to stretch to reach the stallion's head.

'No, nothing, just carved stone. Hang on a minute, ouch!' He leapt back, shaking his hand.

'What happened?'

'Something burned me!'

'Here, hold the torch, let me try.'

Mara stuck the torch through Andreas's belt and climbed up onto the statue's inscribed plinth. Standing on tiptoe, she just managed to reach the horse's head and ran her fingers up its muzzle towards the eyes.

She touched the left eye.

'You're right, just blank stone.'

'Aren't I always right?' joshed Andreas.

'About once in a blue moon.'

'Cheek! You'll get a smacked bottom if you talk like that, young lady.'

'And we'll both get a night in the cells if you don't pipe down!' retorted Mara in a stage whisper.

Her fingers moved across the horse's head to the right eye. The moment she touched it, an energy surge like a massive electric shock sizzled and cracked through her fingers.

'Oh!'

'Told you – it's wired up to the mains or something.'

Mara did not pull her hand away, but by a massive effort of self-control forced herself to keep her fingers cupped around the carved stone eye.

'Yield to me, yield to me,' she whispered under her

breath. 'I shall never give you up, I cannot.'

All at once the stone beneath her fingers began to change, first becoming as cold as ice and then very hard, angular, shiny-smooth like cut diamond.

'Yes . . .' Mara let out a sigh of relief as the perfect crystal pyramid fell from the stone eye of the statue and into the palm of her hand.

But as the last piece of the Eye of Baloch surrendered itself to Mara's greater power, the stone from which it had come gave out a low, keening wail which sounded as though it came from the very centre of the world.

When Harry Baptiste entered a room, heads turned. Not just because he was the Prime Minister, but because he was a very attractive man – attractive and unattainable, or so it seemed. And there was nothing like unattainability to add to a man's essential attractiveness.

Liz had been surprised to receive a dinner invitation from Baptiste. After all, she had absolutely no success in seducing him on their last meeting, and had found his cool, almost academic, interest in her frankly maddening.

But as soon as she saw him again she burned for him. It wasn't just that she wanted to win him for her Master – though she craved the Master's favour. No, she wanted Baptiste for herself, she found his cool detachment irresistibly erotic. She must, and would, find a way to transform this statue of a man into living, breathing, lusting manhood.

The Ancien Régime was a very discreet restaurant, one of Baptiste's favourites. He detested intrusions into his private life and was uncomfortable with the adulation he often received from his enthusiastic public. Here, at the Ancien Régime, he was always guaranteed a low-key welcome and a table in a secluded alcove.

When he arrived, Liz was already waiting for him, dressed in the most elegant and alluring dress in her well-stocked and highly provocative collection. Well, she couldn't let an opportunity like this pass her by, could she?

The black satin sheath dress clung to her like a lover's embrace, the strapless bodice boned to support and emphasise her small but nicely formed breasts. She wore black gloves to the elbow and a black velvet choker decorated with a heavy diamond and sapphire brooch which added that all-important touch of class.

She got to her feet to greet Baptiste and he was treated not only to a splendid view of her cleavage, but to a smooth, sleek length of stocking-clad thigh as the side-split in her dress slid open, stopping just short of her lacy stocking-top.

Baptiste cleared his throat and tried not to let his eyes linger too long on Liz's very obvious assets.

'Do please take a seat, Ms Exley.'

'Liz. Please, you must call me Liz.'

He smiled uneasily.

'Er . . . Liz. Yes.'

As he sat down and the waiter slid his chair beneath him, Baptiste felt the crystal ring growing hot about his finger. He tried not to look at it, but it coaxed him until his eyes flickered to it, to the white fire at its core.

Go on, a voice seemed to whisper to him from the heart of the ring. *Do it. Take her. She wants it and you know you do too.*

No, no, I don't, he told himself, meticulously smoothing out the creases in the damask napkin as he spread it across his knee. I don't want her, and I won't do it. I can't let myself.

A waiter glided to the table, smiled, nodded.

'You are ready to order sir, madam?'

Baptiste felt something stroke itself up from his ankle to his knee; something that felt suspiciously like a stocking-clad foot. He swallowed down the lump in his throat, but the lump in his trousers wasn't quite so easily dealt with.

He forced himself to look Liz in the eye.

'Are you ready Ms . . . Liz?'

The very tip of her tongue protruded between her parted lips, licking across her glossy scarlet mouth.

'Oh *yes*, Mr Baptiste. I'm ready.'

Baptiste cleared his throat. It was getting hot in here. And the ring on his finger felt so hot it was almost burning his flesh.

Take her, Baptiste. Take her. She wants you to pull down her panties and take her. The voice in his head was horribly clear, as though a devil were sitting on his shoulder, pouring temptations into his too-receptive ears. He wouldn't listen, he wouldn't. Only he couldn't help listening.

'Dressed lobster for me,' Baptiste folded up his menu and handed it to the waiter, 'and a plain grilled sole to follow.'

Liz scanned the menu lazily, not caring about any food except the sexual energy she could feel bubbling and sizzling inside Harry Baptiste.

'Smoked salmon,' she said peremptorily. 'Grilled sole and champagne – the Krug.' Her eyes gazed deep into Baptiste's. 'I love champagne, don't you? It's such a sexual drink. You can't possibly have inhibitions when you've had a few glasses of champagne.'

Baptiste hardly knew what to say in reply, he was transfixed by this woman. If he hadn't been, would he have asked her to meet him a second time? And in a restaurant where anyone might see them together? Not that there was anything wrong in a bachelor meeting an attractive, unmarried woman for dinner. For dinner, nothing else. That wasn't wrong, was it?

So why did it feel so wicked?

Have you ever put your dick up a woman's arse, Baptiste?

The whispered question in his head came as such a shock to Baptiste that he knocked his empty wine-glass over.

'Are you all right?' purred Liz, leaning a little further over the table so that her breasts threatened to spill out of the boned black bodice. 'Only you look a little . . .'

'Fine. I'm fine.' Baptiste wiped his brow with a crisply laundered handkerchief. Everything about him was magnificent, Liz decided, from his wavy black hair and sculptured ebony skin to the cut of his suits and the artless elegance of everything he did. She was going to enjoy teaching this good man to be bad.

You'd enjoy it, said the voice. *All you have to do is make her bend over that chair, then you pull her arse cheeks apart and just* . . .

No. Baptiste scrunched up his table-napkin in his determination not to listen. Somebody was putting bad thoughts into his mind, and it was so hard to fight them when you'd never had a bad thought in your life before.

'I was honoured to receive your dinner invitation,' Liz remarked, lifting her champagne glass and taking a sip of the cold, bubbly fluid. She hadn't lied about her liking for champagne. Now, as a vampire slut, she had no need to eat or drink to survive, but that did not stop her enjoying the sheer decadent pleasure of champagne. She hoped Harry Baptiste liked it, too – if she could get him just a little drunk, his resistance would be all the weaker.

'I am delighted that you could come,' replied Baptiste, eschewing the champagne in favour of a glass of iced mineral water. 'Out of interest, why *did* you come?'

Liz laughed. He realised that he liked it when she laughed. That wide, red mouth opened like a crimson peony and he could see the glistening pink within, the wet pink tongue that promised so many forbidden pleasures. No, not that. He must stop thinking like that.

It's all right, Harry. It's natural. Take it from me, I should know. I was naive like you once. Why don't you just try it?

'I came because I find you fascinating, Mr Baptiste.'

'Fascinating?' Baptiste was genuinely puzzled. He was not a vain or conceited man.

'Fascinating and attractive.' Liz's silver fork speared a morsel of smoked salmon and carried it to her lips. 'Very attractive. To be honest, Mr Baptiste, you intrigue me. No wife, no girlfriend, no mistress – don't you enjoy the company of women?'

'Of course I do,' replied Baptiste. And to his surprise and consternation he heard himself add: 'I enjoy your company, Liz.'

Excellent, thought Liz, toying with the food on her plate. Better and better. I will have you yet, Harry Baptiste. I will have you and I will enslave you for my Master.

'So you asked me here because you find me attractive?'

'I . . . yes, I suppose I did.'

'You desire me? Want to go to bed with me?' She was really going for it now, almost forcing him to take the bait.

'I didn't say that,' Baptiste replied with as much coolness as he could muster.

'Ah, but it's what you were thinking, wasn't it?' Liz cast a perfunctory glance around the restaurant. There was no-one to see them here, in this discreet alcove. And if they did, why that would only serve her purpose all the better. She laid her hand on Baptiste's. 'It's all right, Prime Minister, I understand. Even ministers of the Crown have natural desires, urges they need to satisfy. And I know just how to do it.'

Reaching into the top of her strapless dress, Liz lifted out the hard, juicy apples of her breasts and rested them on the boned bodice, like sweetmeats on a shelf. Baptiste's eyes grew round with fascinated horror and desperate lust.

'Please, Liz – you mustn't!'

'There's no-one to see.'

'No, you mustn't . . .'

'All I want you to do is bite my nipples. Is that such a terrible thing? All I want is to give you pleasure.'

Baptiste could taste the saliva gathering in his mouth, his taste-buds tingling with the anticipation of Liz's long brown nipples, rolling around on his tongue. All he had to do was bend over the table and he could have that new and exciting taste he so craved.

Tit-flesh tastes sweet, Baptiste. But then you wouldn't know that, would you? You'll never know if you don't do it now.

Would he have given in to temptation? Would he have resisted and walked away? Baptiste had no way of knowing, for at that moment the pager on the waistband of his trousers began to bleep.

It was like the sound of the alarm clock, waking him from a seductive but terrifying dream. Perspiring, his heart pounding, Baptiste got to his feet, pushing back his chair.

'I'm sorry, I have to go now.'

'But Harry, you can't leave me . . .'

'I have to go.' His eyes lingered a few seconds longer on Liz's bare tits and then he tore his gaze away. 'Believe me, I really do.'

As he left the restaurant, Liz watched him with narrowed eyes, glittering with jealousy.

You may have escaped me this time, Baptiste, she told herself. But next time, you won't be so lucky.

Mara rolled onto her back but Andreas was merciless, coming after her with kisses that darted between her thighs with a relentless accuracy.

'Oh, oh, no, I can't . . .'

'Oh yes you can,' murmured Andreas, rasping his tongue hard over Mara's clitoris.

Mara writhed and moaned, the bed beneath them creaking at the sweet savagery of Andreas's onslaught. It had been quite a night. Far from depressing Andreas, finding the last part of the Eye of Baloch seemed to have elated him – and when Andreas was elated, he liked to show it with his fingers and his tongue and his cock.

It was just like meeting him again for the first time, all the excitement and the delicious terror, the newness of a first-time lover's body under your fingertips, and the feel of his cock finding its way into your waiting haven, dripping with anticipation.

They hadn't slept, but who needed to sleep? Mara's

whole body ached from the violence of their lovemaking, but it sang with the deep satisfaction of a perfect fucking.

Her clitoris was tender and swollen for Andreas had brought her to a dozen orgasms, maybe more. She had lost count of the clenching spasms of ecstasy that had racked her naked body.

'I just can't get enough of you.' Andreas licked and nibbled at Mara's inner labia and she wondered how much more pleasure she could bear. 'You make my cock hard like a steel bar.'

'Andreas, please . . . it's too much.'

Andreas took no notice of Mara's feeble protests, fastening his lips and teeth more tightly about the turgid stalk of her clitty.

'I'm going to make you come again.'

'I can't . . . I can't, it hurts . . .'

'Come. I want you to come.'

She hardly recognised this forceful, almost brutal Andreas who had made a plaything of her tired, but willing, body. His fingers were in her cunt and arse, stretching and thrusting and teasing; his teeth nipping and his tongue lapping at the exposed head of her clitoris.

Through the open window a hot wind blew – a gusting wind too hot and dry for a summer dawn. It blew across Mara's nipples, raising them into hard crests of longing, licking the sweat from her sticky body.

'Ah. Aaah.' The pleasure was too intense, overloading Mara's ability to control it. Every nerve in her body was jangling, the overheating circuitry of her passion sending her into spasms of unbearable anticipation.

Here it was now, coming, coming, coming.

'Aaah!'

As the spasms of her orgasm died away, receding like waves on a distant sea-shore, Mara allowed herself to relax, sinking back onto the sweat-soaked pillows. A half-smile played about her lips.

'Andreas, what *has* got into you?'

Andreas flopped down beside her, planting kisses that led in a trail from her auburn maiden-curls up over her belly to her breasts and throat.

'Didn't you like it?'

'Like it? I adored it.'

Andreas stretched out his arm and slid open the drawer of the bedside cabinet. Inside lay a jumble of crystal pieces and the painted sun they had found at Whitby.

'Why don't we try and put it together?' he suggested, taking out the pieces one by one and laying them on the mattress.

Mara sat up and watched him laying out the pieces.

'They hardly look as if they would fit together,' she remarked.

'They must do.' Andreas picked up the first two pieces, staring at them as if willing them to fit together. 'They must.'

He pushed the pieces together in turn, trying to find exactly the right combination, but it was like one of those desperately frustrating 3-D jigsaw puzzles – a good deal harder than it looked.

'Here, let me.' Mara took the pieces from Andreas and laid them back on the mattress. 'It's no good trying so hard,' she explained. 'What you have to do is let the pieces find each other.'

'How?'

'By feeling their natural magnetism.'

Mara closed her eyes and held her outspread palms an inch or so above the crystal pieces, feeling their vibrations, matching like to like, guiding them towards each other along the pathways that each had chosen.

'There.'

She held it up to the light, a rough-cut sphere of crystal, slightly cracked in places, with the painted sun as the pupil and the main part of the eye a dark and clouded green.

She got off the bed and walked towards the window, holding the Eye before her, lifting it so that the sunlight played through the crystal and made it glow a mysterious and lustrous emerald.

Looking into the depths of the crystal sphere, she saw Andreas's face reflected in it. She smiled.

'We've found it! The Eye of Baloch.'

Andreas's reflection grinned back at her.

'Yes,' he said. And his voice changed suddenly, to a dark and menacing growl. 'But *I* have it.'

Terror gripped at Mara's heart as she saw Andreas's reflection begin to change, the familiar face distorting, melting . . .

'No!'

Clutching the Eye to her she wheeled round, convinced that what she had seen must be an illusion, some trick of the light.

But as she turned to confront her fear she let out a gasp of horror and disbelief, darkness overwhelming her as the unfamiliar face grinned at her and terror stole her consciousness away.

Leaving only mocking laughter, echoing through the room.

15: Captives

"NIGERIAN MAN PECKED TO DEATH BY PENGUINS"

(*West African Wildlife Review*, 15 July)

Mistress Sedet stalked into the boardroom, chic and sophisticated in her pale grey suit and seamed nylons. Her glossy black hair was twisted up into a high chignon, her face immaculately made-up to emphasise her large and lustrous violet eyes.

'To heel,' she snapped, and jerked on the leash. At its end, on hands and knees, crawled Liz Exley.

'By Jove, what have we here?'

Emmanuel St Hilaire, chairman of the oldest merchant bank in the whole of the City of London, sat with folded arms at the head of the boardroom table, staring down its empty length at the two figures entering the room. He had been promised a 'private entertainment' for his birthday, but he hadn't expected it to be quite this good. How on earth had that fellow Heimdal known about his rarefied tastes in women?

Liz slunk along on the end of the leash, the chain-link collar tightening whenever she hung back or resisted her Mistress's instructions. Liz did not feel particularly well-disposed towards her Mistress today – for Sedet had forced her to wear this ridiculous cat costume.

Black it was; a shiny black PVC bondage suit with zips that offered admittance to the most intimate pleasure-grounds of her body. A swishing black tail slithered behind her, and she wore a PVC cat-mask, complete with pointed ears and whiskers.

'Kitty. Oh, Kitty,' sighed St Hilaire, completely ignoring the sexy but imperious Sedet and letting his eyes roam all over Liz. 'Would Kitty like a drink of cream?'

Sedet jerked the leash and Liz let out a hiss of displeasure.

'She is a very badly behaved kitten,' Sedet sniffed disdainfully. 'I think you should beat her first. Teach her better manners. But the nature and degree of her punishment are entirely up to you.'

Emmanuel St Hilaire was in seventh heaven. Not only did he have this delectable cat-woman to be his sex-slave, he was also allowed to do whatever he liked to her. He thought back to his schooldays at Gordonstoun and how even the thought of the cane on his backside had given him an erection.

Most of the other boys had stuffed paper down their pants to lessen the pain but not St Hilaire. He had begged to have all twelve strokes of the cane on his bare flesh. So he knew how much this wayward kitten would enjoy the experience, if only she had him to show her how.

He walked across to the heavy Victorian sideboard which had been used as a drinks cabinet for the directors since his great-grandfather's time. In the drawers at its base he kept some of his toys – the things he liked to play with in moments of stress. There, he still kept the leather strap his father had beaten him with when he was a small boy and the pair of soiled lace panties his mother had sometimes gagged him with when he had been naughty. To this very day, he could not resist the scent of a woman's soiled knickers.

In amongst the many treasures of Emmanuel St Hilaire's sensual odyssey lay the very metal ruler his prep school headmaster had used to such stinging effect. Wielded with skill, it could be the cruellest and the most sensual of punishments. He felt confident that Liz would enjoy it as much as he did.

'Poor, poor Kitty,' he murmured, stroking Liz's masked face. Sedet jerked the chain again and Liz spat and hissed. 'Oh, naughty Kitty, bad Kitty. Kitty needs to be taught some manners.' He smoothed his hand over the curve of Liz's rump then slid down two of the zips, revealing two juicy segments of bum-flesh.

'She will probably cry out,' observed Sedet casually. 'She is a very undisciplined animal.'

'Good, good. Then I shall beat some discipline into her. I have always felt that discipline was something not so much to be endured but enjoyed.'

Liz whined and groaned as St Hilaire set to work on her backside, slicing the metal ruler through the air with such energy that it whistled before hitting her buttocks with a loud smack. In truth it was a very small punishment for one of Mistress Sedet's pupils to bear.

Far more difficult to withstand was the humiliation. As St Hilaire beat her, Liz gazed up at Mistress Sedet, who stifled a yawn as she watched her slave beaten as though it were the most tedious thing in the world.

'Good Kitty. Good, good Kitty.' Liz winced slightly as St Hilaire's fingers explored the reddened flesh of her rump. He was a stricter disciplinarian than she had anticipated and in spite of herself she could feel herself getting excited. 'Does Kitty want some cream now?'

'Answer him!' Sedet struck Liz on the side of the face with the end of the leash.

'Yes, please.'

Slap. Mistress Sedet glared her disapproval and Liz hastily corrected herself.

'Yes please, sir.'

Emmanuel St Hilaire unbuttoned his old-fashioned suit trousers and took out a penis which was surprisingly vigorous for a man in his early fifties.

'Drink it down, Kitty. Drink it down, every drop.'

He pushed between Liz's lips and she sucked on him, grateful for the taste of his desire on her tongue. Sex was her sustenance now, not food, and when St Hilaire came in her mouth, the flood-tide of his spunk would bring with it an injection of pure, reviving energy.

But that did not stop her resenting Mistress Sedet with her imperious ways and her love of humiliation. Liz knew that she had only been brought here to keep her in her place.

Well, Sedet, you'd better watch out, thought Liz silently. Things are going to change around here when I deliver Harry Baptiste to the Master.

It was dark when Andreas woke up – so dark and airless that for a few seconds he thought he was back in the crystal, his spirit a captive in the Master's old body.

It wasn't until he heard the clink of the chains around his ankles that he realised his captivity was of a more prosaic kind. Tiny wafers of light filtered in from a small, high window; just enough to pick out a patch of rough stone, damp and mossy, and the metallic glint of heavy chains attached to rings in the wall.

Was this the Master's doing? Had he finally worked out that Andreas Hunt and Mara Fleming were not as dead as he'd thought they were? In a moment of panic, Andreas felt for the protective bracelet and was relieved to find it still fast about his wrist, the dragon's talismanic eye still glowing red. Maybe not the Master then . . .

'Andreas . . .?'

He started. He had thought he was alone.

'Mara?'

A chain scraped across the floor and he felt fingers stretching out, straining at the limit of the chain to touch his. They locked.

'It is you, isn't it, Andreas?'

'Of course it is. Who else would it be?'

'It . . . it wasn't Andreas Hunt I saw back there in the

hotel bedroom. Whoever it is, he has the Eye.'

Andreas groaned. Had they really been through all that for nothing?

'What happened? My head feels like somebody stepped on it.'

'I don't know. One minute I was in the hotel room with you, putting the pieces of the Eye together . . .'

'Hang on a mo. I don't remember being in the hotel room – only getting the last piece of the Eye from that statue of a horse. Then there was a funny noise and that's the last thing I remember.'

'It wasn't you . . . at the hotel? But we were together all night . . .'

'What did you get up to – or shouldn't I ask?'

'Let's just say we didn't play Scrabble.'

'And you really thought it was me?'

'Andreas, he *was* you. Only . . .' she paused. 'Only he couldn't have been you, could he?'

They sat in silence for a while, fingers still linked, listening to the sound of water dripping down the walls. The air was chill and damp and foetid, like the air in a tomb.

'What's going on, Andreas?'

'I . . .' Andreas peered into the darkness and almost thought he could see it closing in on them. 'I haven't a clue. But whatever bastard it was who brought us here, he's got the Eye of Baloch now.'

The heavy door of the cell grated open, the ancient wood scraping across the rough stone floor. Slowly, a ribbon of light appeared, widening to a yellowish-orange glare which flooded the chamber.

In the doorway stood a man without a face. Clad in a long black robe, his massive body showed muscular and well-formed beneath the heavy fabric. On his head he wore a black hood with holes for eyes, nose and mouth, and he carried a burning torch in his right hand. A bunch of keys hung from his belt. Was this their abductor?

'You will come with me,' he said, his voice quietly menacing. He turned to someone behind him and unhooked a key from his belt. 'Release them.'

A girl stepped forward, also masked; but she was naked, her fair skin decorated with tattoos on the breasts, buttocks and shaven pubis. On her hands she wore thick leather gauntlets, the fingers of which were decorated with curved silver claws.

Andreas watched her walk towards him and contemplated his chances of escape. She was little more than a slip of a girl, slender, practically defenceless. All he and Mara had to do was wait until they were unlocked from their chains and then try to give the gorilla the slip.

The girl crouched beside him, slipping the key into the broad steel band which locked tight around his wrist. Andreas feasted his eyes on the way the girl's small breasts quivered as she did her work. First the left then the right cuff clicked open.

'You may stand.'

He got slowly to his feet. To his right, the girl was unlocking Mara from her manacles. Wait a second, a second longer, bide your time, Hunt, you impatient sod, or you'll blow it.

Now.

He lunged at the girl, anticipating some slight resistance but not the steel-muscled power which sent him reeling across the cell, to fetch up with a sickening crunch against the far wall. He looked down, shocked, at his right arm and saw a line of four parallel claw-marks beneath the torn fabric of his shirt sleeve. A little blood seeped from the gouged flesh.

'Andreas – are you all right?' gasped Mara.

'I . . . think so,' replied Andreas, gaping at the slender masked girl who was handing the key back to the man in the long black robe. How come a girl who looked like a waif could pack a punch like a bucking mule?

'I would advise you to treat Katje with respect,' said the masked man, a note of amusement in his voice. 'Or you will find it is the worse for you. Now, if you would follow me.'

'Why the hell should we do anything you tell us?' demanded Andreas, seriously irritated now. 'You trick us, you kidnap us, you chain us up . . . And who are you, anyway?'

The blank, masked face stared back at them impassively. The reply, when it came, was delivered without a trace of emotion.

'I am the gaoler. Will you come with me, or would you prefer to die now?'

Stunned into silence, Mara and Andreas followed the masked gaoler and the girl along a narrow passageway, so low-roofed that Andreas had to stoop to avoid striking his head. The girl walked directly in front of him, her tattooed body phantasmagorical in the dancing light of a double row of burning torches.

Despite his misgivings at the masked man's words, Andreas could not help appreciating the girl's physique with a connoisseur's eye. Such a spare and slender frame, almost too thin to be attractive and yet powerfully, yes *powerfully* sensual. Just look at the way those slim hips swayed, perfectly balancing the lithe torso and the firm buttocks, decorated with brightly coloured tattoos in abstract patterns. And as she turned right through an archway, Andreas caught tantalising glimpses of those tattooed breasts, bright with spirals of colour.

They passed through the archway and into a high-vaulted chamber lit by dozens of tall, red candles. The candlesticks were made of black wrought iron, twisted into phantasmagorical shapes.

Around the edge of the room stood shadowy figures – men and women dressed exactly like the two who had brought Mara and Andreas to this place, the women naked and hooded, and the men masked and dressed in long robes.

'Welcome.'

The single word, uttered in a low whisper, echoed around the vaulted chamber. Andreas drew Mara closer to him, not quite sure if he was protecting her or she him.

'Undress the male,' said the man who had brought them here. Naked girls emerged from the shadows and began stripping off Andreas's clothes. It wasn't that he objected to being stripped by beautiful naked girls, but their expressionless, hooded faces turned his blood cold with fear. 'Bring the female to me.'

Strong hands seized Mara and brought her to the masked man.

'The female, as you commanded.'

The masked man contemplated Mara with a covetous gleam in his eye.

'She is as yet untouched?'

'As you instructed, Lothar.'

'Excellent.' Lothar licked his lips in anticipation of pleasures to come. Dry-mouthed and resentful, Andreas struggled in the grasp of the three deliciously naked young women who were holding him back.

'Lay one finger on her . . .'

Lothar turned his gaze, rather wearily, on Andreas.

'I have my master's orders and my master's authority. I shall do as I please – to her and to you.' He snapped his fingers. 'Strap him into the harness.'

Beauties with steel-hard muscles took hold of Andreas and laid him, face-down and struggling, on the rush-strewn floor. He heard a clanking of chains and pulleys, and then suddenly his legs and arms were wrenched backwards. Metal cuffs fastened about his wrists and ankles and then there was a tremendous jerk which made him feel as though his arms and legs were being pulled out of their sockets.

The harness consisted of four chains and cuffs, attached to a central mechanism which could be raised and lowered by means of a hand-cranked pulley. One moment Andreas was lying face-down in evil-smelling rushes, the next he was being hoisted up by his wrists and ankles, watching the floor recede.

About five feet off the ground, Andreas found himself suspended in mid-air, going nowhere, just hanging there. The discomfort in his shoulders and back was quite extreme, and he cursed under his breath.

'Silence. The prisoners must be silent at all times.'

Andreas was beginning to hate this Lothar character.

'I've told you, I don't have to do anything . . .'

His words were cut short by a sudden, searing pain which shot right through his body. What the . . .?

'A small electric shock. Triflingly small. Stronger and more painful punishments can be applied if they are deemed necessary. I do hope they will not be.' Lothar sounded as if he was lying.

'Please, why have you brought us here?' asked Mara. 'Why . . .?'

'Be silent, wench.' Lothar gestured to two of the female attendants and they came forward.

'What is your will, Lothar?'

'Give our troublesome young Englishman a taste of the pleasure and pain which await him.'

Andreas was determined to resist the sensual onslaught, but he was only human, and the girls possessed an inhuman skill. His body was their helpless plaything, his arms and legs restrained and his cock hanging down, entirely at their mercy.

'His dick is passably well-formed,' observed one of the girls, her soft Germanic accent sending thrills of guilty excitement through Andreas's body. Her gloved fingers smoothed down the length of his semi-erect shaft with a tantalising, gossamer lightness which stirred an ocean-deep tide of sensations in his belly.

'He has good, heavy balls,' reported the other girl. Andreas felt her leather-gloved palm tightening around his scrotum as she weighed and caressed his love-eggs with a knowing skill.

'Proceed,' said Lothar, his hands drawing Mara towards him and straying over the juicy hummocks of her backside.

Andreas no longer knew if he was in heaven or in hell. There were lips as soft as a spider's web around his cock-tip and claws as sharp as a tigress's digging and gouging at the hypersensitive globes of his balls. There were teeth biting his nipples and a feather-soft tongue lapping delicately at the secret world of desire between his arse cheeks.

He was a puppet in chains, a doll at the mercy of these faceless, merciless women with their tattooed breasts and their relentless claws. It was useless trying to struggle. No matter how he twisted and turned, their hunger pursued him, greedy lips and tongues devouring his flesh, claws raking, mouths sucking at the fount of his desire.

His cock felt as though it were on fire, his balls aching and tingling with the exhilaration of mingled pleasure and pain. He wanted to fight the feeling, but he seemed to have lost all will. All he could think about was making it last.

Lothar watched with apparent satisfaction for a few moments before turning his attentions to Mara.

'I trust you will be more co-operative,' he said, curling his fingers about the neckline of Mara's blouse. 'Or it may not go well with your lover.'

Mara returned the unblinking, unnerving gaze with a confidence she did not feel.

'I will do whatever you wish.'

'Obedience is the greatest beauty a woman can possess.'

Lothar's hand tightened about the thin fabric of Mara's blouse and tore it open in a single, swift movement that exposed the bare breast beneath. His leather gauntlet felt cold and hard on her white and delicate skin, and she shivered at this first, ungentle caress.

Andreas felt her spirit calling to him above the tumult of her thoughts and desires:

Go along with it, do anything he says, save yourself . . .

He tried to telepath his reassurance to her but pain and pleasure had set up a barrier around him, disrupting his thoughts, making him aware only of the gnawing excitement rising up his prick and the unwilling desire flowing out of Mara like a flood-tide.

Fuck, fuck, got to fuck, got to have him inside me . . .

Lothar's robes parted to reveal an erect cock sheathed in studded black leather. The studded sheath covered not only his prick but his balls and when he took Mara's hand and placed it on his genitals the contact felt curiously unreal, like caressing a statue.

At a click of Lothar's fingers, two masked men stepped forward, removing their long black robes to reveal muscular, oiled bodies.

'Bend over,' Lothar instructed Mara.

She did so and one of the men supported her arms, whilst the other knelt on the floor and began toying with the pendulous fruits of her bare breasts.

She felt Lothar pressing up against her, pulling up her soiled and tattered skirt and discovering the delights of the naked backside beneath.

'Obedient *and* shameless,' he murmured. 'How very agreeable.'

He drew back his hand and gave Mara's rump a hefty slap which made her buttocks quiver. She let out a little gasp of protest.

'Be silent!'

Slap. Slap. Slap. Lothar's hand knew exactly the right way to inflict a punishment which both chastised and titillated. Mara could feel her juices flowing, betraying the lust she felt towards this faceless stranger. Already she was anticipating the agony of pleasure as he pushed his studded dick into her cunt, possessing her with the force of his own desire.

Even so, when it came, the knife-thrust of Lothar's prick took her by surprise, slicing into her cunt with an impetuous arrogance that thrilled her to the core. She could not suppress a song of sheer delight.

'Yes, oh, oh, yes.'

This time Lothar did not rebuke her but answered her desire with harder and deeper thrusts that took him so far into her cunt that the studded leather pouch of his balls was rubbing against her vulva.

Lost in the web of her own and Lothar's lust, Mara did not see the dark figure watching from the doorway of the chamber. But she felt the strangest sensation, as though someone were watching her intently, lasciviously – and the feeling excited her still more.

Pleasure came to Andreas in a savage torrent that drained all the energy from him, leaving him hanging drained and hollow as a dead fly in a spider's web. His mind reeled, his body ached from the excess of his pleasure. Scarlet claw-marks raked his flesh and his cock was throbbing. He could take no more.

But for him and for Mara, the torment had only just begun.

Once more in the darkness of their cell, Andreas and Mara watched another distant dawn rise through the tiny window.

'You didn't have to enjoy yourself *quite* so much,' remarked Andreas.

'You heard what Lothar said. I had to obey him or something terrible would happen to you. Do you suppose I would risk that?'

Andreas supposed not. Under the circumstances it was pretty bloody silly, being jealous of Mara. As far as the Master was concerned, Mara was a vampire sex-slut. It was hardly reasonable to expect her to behave like a Sunday School teacher. All the same, it had driven Andreas crazy with frustration, watching her get it from that arrogant bastard, Lothar. Who did he think he was – the Master?

'I just wish I knew why he was doing this to us,' sighed Mara. 'All this talk about "fulfilling the commands of his lord and master" gives me the creeps.'

'Listen.' Andreas silenced Mara and they listened together.

'Footsteps. Someone's coming.' Mara's heart was pounding. Would it be Lothar again, come to subject them to yet another session of sexual torture?

The door of the cell opened and the room was flooded with light. A man walked in, tall, arrogant, self-assured. But it was not Lothar.

'Good morning,' smiled the newcomer, his voice heavy with irony. 'I trust you spent an agreeable night. I do so like my guests to feel that *all* their needs are catered for.'

Mara took a step back, blinking in astonishment and fear.

'No, it can't be . . .'

At the sight of her confusion, the tall man with the shock of wavy blond hair threw back his head and laughed.

'Ah, my dear Mara, I see that you recognise me. Do you not find me irresistibly handsome? Did you not enjoy our night of passion in that hotel bedroom?'

Mara had turned ashen-pale. All her fear came back, memories of that morning when she had looked into the Eye of Baloch and seen Andreas's reflection change into the face of this man.

The man turned to the masked guards behind him.

'Lock us in the cell, Lothar. I wish to talk to our guests alone.'

The heavy door swung shut and a key grated in the lock.

Mara backed away, sensing the stranger's dark spirit filling the cell, feeling his overwhelming dominance demanding ultimate submission. She knew now that this man was the architect of their captivity – and the thief who had stolen the Eye of Baloch.

'My name is Zacchaeus Brabant,' said the blond stranger. 'You will not have heard of me.'

'Why have you brought us here?' asked Mara.

'Yes, what the hell do you think you're playing at?' demanded Andreas. 'How come a total stranger gets to throw us in a cell and do anything he damn well likes with us? Or is it just what turns you on? I think you owe us an

275

explanation, Mr Brabant – if that's your real name.'

Brabant's upper lip curled into a contemptuous sneer.

'I owe you nothing, *Mr Andreas Hunt.*'

Andreas felt dizzy with panic. *Oh shit, oh shit, oh shit.* Of course, the Eye of Baloch – if this guy had it he'd know everything, every damn thing, wouldn't he?

It was Mara who broke the horror-stricken silence.

'Are you an enemy of the Master?'

Brabant's grey eyes twinkled with malevolent amusement.

'The Master? Now what would I know of anyone calling himself the Master?'

'The Eye of Baloch,' cut in Andreas, now more infuriated than terrified by Zacchaeus Brabant's teasing responses.

'What of it?'

'You've got it, haven't you?'

Brabant studied Andreas's agitation with amusement for some moments, then reached into the pocket of his robe.

'Ah, you mean this?'

The Eye of Baloch lay in the palm of his hand, many-faceted, cold and radiant. Even Andreas could feel the power emanating from it, like a wall of icy fire that prevented anyone from touching it except its possessor. He reached out his hand towards it but was thrown back by a force that burned and seared.

'I would not advise repeating that exercise, Mr Hunt,' remarked Brabant coolly. 'Unless, of course, you are stimulated by the prospect of infinite and unceasing pain.'

Mara stared at the Eye, transfixed, shaking with the current of energy passing between it and her body. Images seemed to be tumbling and spinning in her brain. Pictures from a thousand different locations.

Pictures of destruction.

'What can you see, Mara?' demanded Brabant, his voice syrupy and seductive.

A tidal wave swamping a Caribbean beach, a whole

village crushed and obliterated in the impenetrable wall of sky-blue water. Riots in the streets of Edinburgh. A carnival in Oslo, turning suddenly from an innocent celebration into a savage sexual frenzy. A long-extinct volcano, tongues of crimson and orange fire licking their way down its flanks towards the peaceful French town in the valley below.

'I . . . I can see terrible things, disasters, wars . . .'

'Excellent, Mara. Truly excellent.'

Faces, too. Brother Julius . . . Pendorran . . . lovers from her former life, faces of world leaders, others she scarcely recognised . . . and another – one glimpsed only fleetingly – the face of Max Trevidian.

'No, no, I don't want to see any more.' With a supreme effort of will she tore herself away from the power source which drew her in.

Brabant held the Eye aloft, turning it round and round in the torchlight, admiring it from each and every angle.

'The Eye of Baloch,' he declaimed. 'The Eye of Power. Do you know how long I have been looking for this?' He glanced from Andreas to Mara and back again. 'And now you have been kind enough to deliver it to me. So kind.'

He raised his right hand, clasping the Eye in his palm, letting its inner light radiate out, forcing Andreas and Mara to feel the extent of its power.

'The Eye of Baloch! Destroyer of gods, all-seeing, all-knowing, the power from which no secret can be hidden!'

Brabant's eyes gleamed. He hesitated for a moment, holding the Eye aloft in his right hand, glorifying in his possession of its power.

And then he tightened his fingers about the crystal sphere, squeezing, crushing, destroying the Eye as though it were made of nothing more resilient than spun sugar.

'The Eye of Baloch,' he whispered. 'Dust!'

With a shower of sparks it crumbled into tiny, powdery fragments; and in the sudden darkness of the dungeon, Zacchaeus Brabant's laughter echoed like the knell of universal destruction.

16: Seductions

"T.C.C.B. STUMPED AS BLACK RAIN HALTS
SECOND TEST"
(*Cricket Today*, July issue)

It has been too long since Winterbourne staged one of its magnificent orgies, thought the Master to himself.

He relaxed on his golden throne in the Great Hall, the raised dais affording him an unrivalled view of the bodies coupling in and around the rose-scented, sunken pool.

Brandon Fortescue, the West End theatre designer, had worked wonders on the Kama Sutra set, building arches and secluded pergolas underneath the vaulted ceiling of the Great Hall. Sumptuous drifts of brocade, chiffon and muslin adorned the pillars and hung in curtains between the arches, forming cosy corners where guests could recline in comfort on softly upholstered couches.

The Master was enjoying himself. He would reward Heimdal well for his initiative – an orgy was just what he needed to revive his flagging energies and restore a more even temper. Ever since Baptiste had come to power and things had started going wrong, the Master's savage resentment had made its presence felt all too painfully among the sluts and slaves of Winterbourne. Tonight, the Master could sit back and enjoy his sluts taking revenge on his unwary guests.

Soft, sensual music filtered into the Hall as the musicians played and sang an ancient Hindu song of seduction.

Concealed in the perfumed clouds of incense wafting from a thousand joss-burners, was a more subtle scent – a cocktail of powerful pheromones and psycho-active drugs created in Takimoto's Kyoto laboratories. Add to this Madame LeCoeur's armoury of aphrodisiac cordials and unguents, and the atmosphere was perfect for sensual surrender.

Mistress Sedet knelt between her Master's parted thighs, sucking on his cock and thinking rebellious thoughts. If all went as she hoped, if she could somehow find and obtain the mighty Eye of Baloch, there might yet be a new regime at Winterbourne and she – its Queen – would be all-powerful, Mistress of all the Empire of Lust. The Master would pay for his neglect and disregard of her. But, for now, she must bide her time, veil her thoughts from him, lull him with her butterfly-soft caresses until the time was right to strike.

The Master gave a contented sigh as Sedet worked her skilful mouth up and down his shaft. She certainly knew how to prolong the pleasure, building it up and keeping it there, on a plateau of semi-orgasm, until at last the climax came, in a rush of ecstasy so powerful that he was instantly ready to begin all over again.

He relaxed and enjoyed the spectacle which Heimdal had arranged for his delectation. Tonight fifty guests had been invited, each one's personal tastes thoroughly investigated for any little peccadillos which might be pandered to – and exploited.

Take Cassandra Millefiore, for example. Ex-supermodel turned serious actress, now an Italian MEP, she kept very quiet about her fondness for sixteen-year-old boys. But Heimdal knew – he had made it his business to find out – and now Cassandra was enjoying the company of two of the most adorable Indian boys Heimdal had ever had the pleasure of initiating.

One of them – nineteen if he was a day – was so slightly built and downy-cheeked, his caramel-coloured skin so smooth that he could have passed for thirteen or fourteen. His dick was long but pencil slim, his balls small and hairless. He looked for all the world like an innocent schoolboy, though Othalie LeCoeur had discovered him in one of the most sordid bordellos in the whole of Calcutta. The Master watched in amused pleasure as Cassandra Millefiore crouched on hands and knees like a she-dog, lapping at one boy's cock whilst the other boy – a strapping lad of sixteen summers with a fuzz of black hair on his upper lip – knelt behind her and licked at her cunt.

Oh yes, this was excellent entertainment. The Master glanced away from the pretty tableau to feast his eyes on Ibrahim, who was playing the unfeasible part of harem eunuch with surprising aplomb.

This particular playlet had been worked out in advance for the delectation of one Julian DeGracy, a television mogul who had been giving Takimoto's Empire TV a hard time in the ratings war and who, therefore, had to be swiftly and effectively persuaded to change his mind. DeGracy was playing the part of the intrepid Englishman who strays unwarily into the Maharajah's harem.

At this precise moment, DeGracy was thoroughly enjoying the role he had been allotted. Positively swamped by gorgeous harem-girls in see-through blouses and wide-legged chiffon pants, he was spoilt for choice when it came to the fucking – should he have the brown-haired girl with the ruby in her navel, or the icy blonde who was parting her thighs to show the white-gold muff-hair curling out of her split-crotch pants?

But then it didn't really matter, did it? With Madame LeCoeur's aphrodisiac wine to spur him on, he could take every single one of them and still go on fucking until dawn.

DeGracy lay down on the costly handmade carpet and submitted to a pair of small, knowing hands smearing scented oil all over his body.

'Mmm, yes, that feels absolutely bloody marvellous, darling, just a bit lower if you could . . . oh *yes*.'

The Master smiled to himself. There were, of course, certain substances contained in the perfumed massage oil – substances which might cause a man to lose his reason and cast away his every inhibition. When Ibrahim entered the 'harem', ferociously resplendent in his eunuch's costume, DeGracy would respond lasciviously to Ibrahim's feigned anger, loving the whip, craving the pain, simply begging Ibrahim to do to him what no man had ever done before.

For Heimdal had done his research very thoroughly indeed: he knew all about Julian DeGracy's secret desires. DeGracy would probably not even notice the sudden, sharp pain, or the spurt of blood as teeth punctured his throat.

The Master felt the spunk rising in his balls as he observed two women – a mother and daughter – enjoying a beating from the hand of Lord Heimdal himself. It was good to see Heimdal enjoying his work – his cock was like tempered steel beneath his skintight pants. He was manipulating the bullwhip with great skill, so that it flicked across both women's backs in a single stroke. Soon, very soon, he would get out that beautiful cock of his and teach the two women a consummate lesson in lust.

And then, all at once, a very peculiar feeling began to spread over the Master. He felt suddenly immensely cold, with just the faintest hint of fear. He shook himself. It was quite absurd. The Master never, ever, felt fear.

A dull yet intense light from some unseen source was flooding the Great Hall, seeping into it like water through cracked porcelain. Everything seemed muffled, the Indian music fading away until it was so faint that the Master could not hear it any more. And something else was happening, too. As the light flowed into the room, every thing and every body it touched froze in time and motion.

Still. Silent. Unmoving.

The Master grew pale beneath his deep golden tan. Something that he had not instigated – something that was not in his power to control – was happening before his eyes. He stared in disbelief from face to face; from Joanna Königsberg to Heimdal; from Julian DeGracy to the black slave Ibrahim, and it was like looking into a horribly distorted mirror.

Each of them wore the Master's own face.

He looked down at Sedet, still crouching at his feet, and once again his own face gazing back at him, grotesquely smiling. No, no, this couldn't be happening. This was some trick.

He got slowly to his feet, and as he did so, a hundred Masters opened their mouths and began to chant as one:

'That which you seek is gone. That which you seek is gone.'

Over and over again the words mocked him, a sing-song chant that reverberated around the Great Hall. A hundred pairs of eyes, staring, unblinkingly, into his own.

It rose up from the centre of the sunken pool, a huge crystal eye; its greenish sphere transparent and at its glowing heart a familiar figure.

'No. This is not happening.'

The Master drew in breath at the sight of his old, destroyed, imprisoned body, resurrected to torment him in this ghastly apparition. It seemed to float on air, as though swimming in the greenish light which filled the centre of the great crystal eye.

It turned its empty eyes on him and mouthed a single word:

'Gone.'

And, a micro-second later, the Eye of Baloch exploded in a shower of icy fragments.

The water clock almost filled the whole of one wall, its drip, drip, drip marking the passage of the seconds. The seconds that remained until eternity.

On the other side of the room, huge windows opened out onto a red and raging sky. Zacchaeus Brabant stood with his hands on the window sill, peering out onto the artificial sunset.

'What . . . What is it?' Afraid, yet driven by a strange fascination, Mara crossed the room and stood beside him.

Brabant answered without looking at her.

'Geneva.'

'But . . .'

'Soon it will burn.'

'Please.' Mara laid her hand on Brabant's. It felt hot, almost feverish to the coolness of her touch. 'Why am I here? Why have you brought Andreas and me to Geneva?'

'I never intended bringing Hunt here,' replied Brabant. 'It was you alone that I sought, Mara Fleming. And it is you that I intend to take with me.'

A cold fascination clutched at Mara's heart.

'Please explain. I don't understand what you're saying. Where are you taking me . . . why?'

'I have never met a psychic like you, Mara Fleming.' This time Brabant turned to look at her, his eyes bright as an eagle's in his cruel yet handsome face. 'I have never met a *woman* like you.'

The intensity of his gaze made her tremble. Even without the Eye of Baloch he could see into her soul, she knew that. It was no use trying to veil her thoughts and emotions from him. He *knew* that she desired him, just as much as he desired her.

'Of course,' Brabant continued, smoothing his hand down over Mara's glossy curtain of auburn hair. 'Your friend Andreas Hunt will have to die.'

'No!'

'He is a complication and I do not tolerate complications, Mara Fleming.'

Brabant returned to his contemplation of the angry sky. The sunlight burned such deep shades of crimson and scarlet that Mara was sure she could make out little tongues of flame licking at the edges of the storm clouds hanging over the city.

'Is there no way . . .?' she whispered, sliding to her knees before Brabant. 'Is there no way that I could persuade you to spare Andreas?'

She parted the folds of Brabant's robe and bent to kiss his feet, running her tongue over the bare and sensitive skin, climbing higher, little by little, planting the most delicate of kisses on ankles and knees and thighs.

'I would serve you well,' she whispered, sliding her hands up Brabant's thighs until her fingertips were a tantalising millimetre from his pubic curls.

'Then show me how well you would serve me. Empty words mean nothing to me.'

Mara met Brabant's challenge with spirit. Slowly she peeled off the silk robe she had been given to wear by Katje, one of Brabant's favourite serving-girls. Underneath she was naked, with no adornment save the seductive power of her own beauty.

'Feel my devotion,' she breathed, taking hold of Brabant's hands and placing them on her breasts. 'Feel how I desire you, how I seek only to give you pleasure.'

His roughened fingers played with her heavy breasts, pinching and squeezing.

'Such power in you, my little vixen. Such great power . . .'

Her lips traced a featherlight tracery of saliva up the front and inner surface of his thighs, pausing again and again just short of Brabant's balls. She felt his frustration, knew how he longed to have the touch of her mouth on his prick. His breathing was hoarse and laboured, the tip of his dick wet with need.

'Pleasure me, vixen.'

Suddenly, overcome by the force of his desire, Brabant seized Mara by the hair and forced her face up against his throbbing penis.

'Pleasure me, or watch your lover die.'

Heart thumping wildly in her chest, Mara opened her mouth to receive the stiff rod of Brabant's prick. It tasted salty and strong, and she began sucking and licking at it with genuine enthusiasm. Even if she had not been trying to save Andreas's life, she would willingly have given Zacchaeus Brabant anything he demanded of her.

She heard Brabant's breath escaping in a low hiss of satisfaction and realised with a start how much it excited her to know that she was giving him pleasure. But who was he, this Zacchaeus Brabant? And how could he both terrify her and fill her with wild and wanton desire?

Slowly and delicately, resisting Brabant's rough thrusts, Mara let her tongue play along the turgid shaft of his prick. Her hands crept up his inner thighs, and cupped the twin fruits that hung there, their hairy purse tense with expectation and heavy with seed. She squeezed them gently and Brabant gave an appreciative shudder, twisting long tendrils of her hair about his strong fingers.

'Slut-hearted witch,' he breathed.

And he forced her to take his dick much further into her mouth, thrusting so hard that its tip nudged against the back of her throat, almost making her retch. But she accepted his sex with greedy lust, sucking and biting at his shaft, tightening her lips about its root.

It was not just his sex which was seeking to possess her; as he thrust in and out of her willing mouth, she felt the strength of his dark spirit invading her heart, her mind, testing her will to resist. What power on earth could resist the velvet caress of the seductive images filling her thoughts? Closing her eyes, she saw herself lying on a magnificent four-poster bed covered with white lilies, her skin translucent as alabaster, her lips a glossy crimson, inviting kisses.

She was bound to the bed by ribbons of vermilion silk, so fragile that she could easily have freed herself if she had wanted to, the symbols of a spiritual and sensual captivity to which she had consented, body and soul. Wrists and ankles tied to the uprights of the bed, she lay like a white star on a white cloud, her body entirely offered up to the vagaries of Zacchaeus Brabant's desire.

Mara could feel fingers and tongues running all over her body, tasting and testing, soothing and arousing, awakening a raging torrent of desire which could not be stilled. And then he was on top of her, and she had neither the strength nor the will to resist him. Her hips rose up to meet the sabre-thrust of his penis and it felt as though molten fire were entering her body, setting her soul aflame . . .

Brabant forced Mara to swallow every drop of his semen as he spurted into her throat, filling her up with the creamy-white elixir of his pleasure. He held his cock inside her for long, luxurious moments, enjoying the sensation of her tongue licking the last drops from his shaft. Then he withdrew and contemplated his prize.

'Have I pleased you?' Mara looked up at him, her eyes moist with supplication.

Brabant pushed his index finger between her lips and she sucked on it like a babe at the breast.

'Shall we just say that if you continue to give me pleasure, I may perhaps consider allowing your friend Mr Hunt to live.'

Andreas was taking his punishment like a man.

In less different circumstances, he probably wouldn't have minded being strapped to a punishment table and given a good seeing-to. After all, Inge was a most attractive young woman, with her statuesque physique and her waist-length plait of flaxen hair. It felt good, good to have her straddling him like this, taking his dick between her hard and muscular thighs, having her wicked way with him.

And, oh, what it did to him to be fucked by a woman who was entirely naked except for a pair of shiny black knee-boots with the highest, spikiest heels he had ever seen. It was like finding yourself in the middle of the centre spread in a girlie magazine.

There was, however, a drawback to all this erotic stimulation. This was, after all, the same Inge who had told him that in order to appreciate ultimate pain, he must first experience ultimate pleasure. He had to admit, though, that at the moment she seemed exceptionally interested in ultimate pleasure . . .

All six feet six of Inge's remarkable frame towered over him, her knees and thighs tight about his hips and the small buds of her breasts scarcely quivering on her hard-muscled torso. Andreas had been with a fair few women in his time but none of them were remotely like Inge. Inge had all the strength and aggression of a Siegfried mixed with the potent sexual allure of ten Bardots and a dozen Marilyn Monroes.

Her cunt was so tight that it was almost painful to be fucked by her. Not that she wasn't well-lubricated: seldom had Andreas known a woman produce so much sex juice before her climax. It fairly dripped out of her, running down Andreas's shaft and out through Inge's fat sex lips onto his balls.

He had seen women with shaven pussy-lips, women with pierced and tattooed pussy-lips, and women with abundant pussy curls; but never a woman who had cropped her pubic hair to a quarter-inch in length, forming a bristly covering which both stimulated and tormented as it ground against the root of his dick. It was a good kind of torment, though; the sort you wanted to go on for a long time.

Inge's long blonde plait fell forward over her breasts and swished over his bare belly like a cat's tail. He wished his hands were free so that he could catch it and tug it hard, forcing her to bend lower over him and kiss him with those plump pink lips of hers. But he was entirely helpless, hers to command, hers to pleasure or torment as she might choose.

His dick felt unnaturally swollen, huge like an arm and a fist, ramming up into Inge's virgin-tight hole. With each downward thrust of Inge's hips his foreskin was pushed back, exposing the hypersensitive head of his phallus to her cunt's unrelenting caresses.

He wanted to hold back, resist the warm tides of pleasure lapping at the edges of his will. If he could resist the pleasure, then perhaps there would be no pain.

It was a crude sort of logic, but it was all he had to hold onto. Don't let her do it to you, he kept telling himself over and over again. Don't let her get into your brain, fight the pleasure. He could feel Inge's cunt twitching, climaxing, trying to force him to give in to the enjoyment of the here and now. If Mara were here he would surely be able to fight, she would give him the strength, show him what he ought to do. Only Mara wasn't here. That prick Zacchaeus Brabant had taken her away and Andreas hadn't a clue where they were.

He was coming. There was no fighting it any longer. He dug his fingernails into the palms of his hands until he drew blood but it was not enough to derail the thundering express-train of his climax.

Now, now, now. *Now.* He cried out with the suddenness and the violence of his orgasm, unable to control the convulsive jerking of his body as his cock spluttered its surrender into her tight, wet vulva.

He fell back, exhausted, onto the punishment table, his head spinning and his pulse racing. Waiting for it to happen. Waiting for the pain.

She unfastened the leather straps holding him to the table and he sat up.

'I am going to blindfold you. You will make no attempt to resist.'

Too right I won't, thought Andreas. He had already tried that one. Inge had muscles where no self-respecting young lady ought to have muscles, and she was quite capable of decking him with one hand tied behind her back.

He submitted to the blindfold, a silk scarf bound tightly across his eyes.

'Stand up.'

He stood and, to his chagrin, the mere touch of Inge's

hand on his arm made his cock stand up too. That was the trouble with his libido, it had no shame.

'Bend forward over the table. Hold on to the sides to brace yourself. I am going to begin your punishment with a little obedience training . . .'

Knock.

Inge let out an exasperated sigh.

'Who's there?'

There was no answer, only a repeated knocking at the door of the cell.

'Wait, wretch. Do not move, or your punishment will be all the more severe.'

Andreas heard Inge's footsteps receding into the distance as she left him and walked away towards the door. He heard the bolts slide back and then the door scraping across the stone-flagged floor as it opened.

'I . . . aah . . .!'

Inge's voice rose to a high shriek and then there was silence, relieved only by the sound of something heavy falling to the ground and then a clinking noise, as though something metallic had been thrown onto the floor.

Andreas stayed where he was for a long time. He couldn't be sure that Inge wasn't playing a trick on him, just waiting for him to disobey him so that she could pounce on him and think up some vicious punishment.

'Inge?'

Silence.

He waited a few moments more, then tentatively fumbled with the silk scarf which covered his eyes. It fell away and he turned to face the door.

There, lying half in and half out of the cell, was Inge's prone body. He crossed the cell and nudged her with his foot. She was out cold. And on the floor beside her lay a key-ring with a single key.

He picked it up and saw the initial on the key-fob. A letter M.

M – for Mara?

* * *

In the Master's Westminster office, the Nationalist Party Whips were experiencing a taste of their own medicine.

Although Harry Baptiste's vitriolic attacks on the Nationalists had been a fraction less vehement of late, the Master believed in maintaining absolute Party loyalty through stern discipline.

Liz Exley was the natural choice when there was discipline to be meted out. Of late, Liz had been displaying exceptional loyalty and enthusiasm. She had learned a great deal from her Mistress Sedet's sublime lessons in cruelty.

The Master watched from his armchair as Liz put the Whips through their paces. She did, undoubtedly, wield the cat with a high degree of skill which would normally have excited the Master's sexual appetite to fever pitch. But today, the sight of the Chief Whip's backside reddening under her bare-breasted fury only aroused a vague and rather distant interest.

He was trying not to think about the vision he had had in the Great Hall at Winterbourne. No-one else had experienced it, it was almost as though it had never happened. But the Master knew it had happened and the black tide of fear lapped inexorably at the corners of his brain.

As she wielded the cat-o'-nine-tails, Liz stole glances at her beloved Master. He seemed preoccupied – almost withdrawn. And that made her angry – angry that Sedet should enjoy the position of supreme power at the Master's side whilst doing nothing to advance his cause.

Well, things would change for ever when Harry Baptiste was in the Master's thrall and Liz Exley became his new Queen.

17: Encounters

"GREENPEACE VOICES RADIATION FEARS AS GREAT PYRAMID GLOWS IN DARK"
(*Cairo Daily Press*, 25 July)

Caves.

Andreas had been stumbling through dark, dank, foetid-smelling caves for what seemed like hours. Or was it only minutes? Or even days? He had completely lost track of time. Whatever game it was that Mara was playing, he wished she would stop it right now.

Finding the right door had been easy. It was as though the key had led him to it and practically unlocked it all by itself. Then came the difficult bit – descending a flight of uneven steps into pitch darkness, relieved only by the tiniest of lights that danced and winked like some distant firefly, beckoning him on into the darkness but never getting any closer.

This had been going on for so long now that he was beginning to think it was a trick. Maybe it was some elaborate punishment dreamed up by Inge – or worse, Zacchaeus Brabant – and at the end of it they would be waiting for him, grinning, with a pair of red-hot pincers.

A slithery wet thing brushed his face and he almost threw up. What *was* that smell? Most probably it would be better if he didn't know, but it reminded him uncomfortably of a decomposing rat he'd once found in the air-conditioning.

He stumbled on, cursing the light under his breath as he followed it through twisting, sepulchral passageways. Too late to go back now. If only he knew where he was headed. Was the passageway sloping down, or up? It was impossible to tell, the darkness played such tricks with your mind.

But at least that horrible smell had gone now and the cave walls felt drier under his palms. Wasn't the light getting closer, too? He was sure it was. At first little more than a pin-prick, it was enlarging even as he looked at it, getting brighter and steadier too, so that it dazzled him so much that he had to shield his eyes with his hand.

Good God, that was bright – it was all or nothing down here, and now he couldn't see a thing because it was as if someone was shining a torch straight into his eyes. Blindly he fumbled on, feeling along the walls as he went, shuffling his feet along the cave floor. It felt smoother, not so stony any more.

And then there was no cave wall any more.

Andreas stumbled out onto the grass, rubbing his eyes. He was seeing things, he was definitely seeing things.

He found himself in a moist, warm, wooded valley with gently sloping sides and a silver river winding through its heart. Brightly coloured birds flitted from tree to tree and enormous butterflies drank from the pink and yellow cups of immense flowers. At his approach, a huge golden snake slithered down out of a tree and inched its way off into the undergrowth, its metallic scales sparkling in the soft, buttercup-yellow sunshine.

In the middle of this curious idyll stood a man with tousled brown hair, baggy cords and a shabby check shirt. Hands thrust deep in his pockets, he was gazing thoughtfully into the middle distance. At Andreas's approach he turned and gave a sheepish smile.

'Hello, Andreas.'

Andreas ran the conundrum through his mind, rejected it, did a double-take.

'Max?'

Max Trevidian took a couple of steps towards him across the soft, springy grass. Andreas felt quite faint. His brain already had quite enough to cope with, without this.

'I'm sorry about all this,' said Max apologetically. 'I really didn't intend . . .'

Andreas swallowed.

'Hang on a minute. *You're* sorry? Hell, Max – you're supposed to be dead.'

'Yes, I know.'

'So what's been going on? Where have you been all this time?'

Max paused, scuffing the ground with the toe of his shoe.

'I am dead.'

'What!'

'I'm not sure what happened, or why it happened, but I'm dead. I'm a spirit, a ghost, call it what you like. One of those things I used to say I didn't believe in.'

'Is it . . . permanent?'

Max laughed.

'How many people do you know who are temporarily dead?'

'But I'm *talking* to you!'

'My Aunt Aurelia used to talk to Julius Caesar but he was dead too. Sorry, Andreas, but physiologically speaking I'm a stiff.'

Andreas sank down onto a fallen log, pushing a hank of hair back off his face.

'I'm not sure I can handle this.'

'You want to try being dead.'

'What's it like?'

'Difficult.'

A horrible thought struck Andreas.

'Max . . .?'

'What?'

'Am *I* dead?'

Max shrugged.

'Not yet.'

'What's that supposed to mean?'

'It means there's a distinct possibility that you might be, if things don't work out.'

'Things? What things?'

Max sighed.

'Honestly, Hunt, you can't possibly be as dim as you make out. Armageddon, that's what. The end of the world. Somehow, I'm supposed to stop it happening.'

Zacchaeus Brabant's private jet soared high over the Swiss border. But not quite high enough for the clouds to conceal the long lines of flame and smoke running along the banks of the Rhine.

Mara looked down out of the plane window, her blood chilling at the sight below. She felt so confused, so uncertain about Brabant, sensing a dark power within him yet desiring him so much that she could refuse him nothing.

She felt a hand on her shoulder. Brabant was stroking her cheek as though she were some favourite pet animal.

'You are not drinking your champagne,' he observed, luxuriating in the deep cushions of the richly upholstered couch.

'That . . . down there. Is it your doing?'

Brabant toyed with the stem of his glass.

'Perhaps.'

'And what about all the other disasters – the floods and the earthquakes and the riots? Are you responsible for them, too?'

'Partly. I am merely the spark, the magnet.'

Mara tore her gaze away from the window and met Brabant's gaze.

'But why?'

Brabant drew her to him, deftly unbuttoning her blouse and putting his hand inside, cradling her breast.

'You spoke of the Master. You asked me if I knew of him.' Brabant's eyes narrowed to glittering grey slits. 'Yes,

Mara, I know him. He is my bitterest enemy. I have pursued him for more than six hundred and fifty years.'

Mara drew back for a moment, troubled and confused. 'But surely . . .'

'How old did you think I was, Mara – thirty-five, forty?' Brabant was looking at her but his eyes seemed to see right through her. 'Once I was a young man, but that was more than half a millennium ago. Before I met the Master.

'One dark night in the summer of 1348, when plague raged across Europe, the Master cursed me for all eternity. I was an alchemist and magician then, a scholar in search of ancient truths.

'That night, I performed a ritual of spirit-raising. I sought enlightenment from the spirit of the great magician Albertus Magnus but I was a young fool – young and ambitious and careless. Instead of Albertus Magnus, I conjured the demon-spirit of the Master.'

Mara felt Brabant's fingers tighten about her breast, forming clawlike talons which raked across the soft flesh and made her gasp with discomfort.

'Even in those far-off days the Master's was an ancient and ruthless spirit. I was no match for him. He crushed me like an insect, cursed me for my effrontery by damning me to eternal life. He laughed as he spoke my curse: "You will live for ever, Brabant," he told me, "but you will age as other men, and my eternal youth and strength will mock you for your insolence."

'One hundred years I endured the ravages of age, my body ageing and crumbling before my eyes, and yet my spirit burning young and strong within me. And then at last I discovered the elixir which restored my youth and strength to me.'

Brabant turned his grey eyes on Mara. They glittered with a fierce, compelling intensity.

'The Master may have forgotten me but I have not forgotten him. Five hundred years I have sought revenge and I will not rest until I have it.'

He drew Mara to him and crushed his lips against hers, his tongue darting into her mouth, possessing her, hungry and vibrant as the life and hatred surging within him.

'I must and will defeat the Master,' he told her, tearing off her clothes, baring the hard pink crests of her nipples. 'And I need you, Mara. I need you at my side. Join your power to mine. Together we shall be the Master's nemesis.'

'Y-yes.' Mara's breath escaped in a sigh of assent. She could refuse Brabant nothing. She was under his spell, ensnared by the power of his glittering eyes, his overwhelming will. 'We will destroy the Master . . .'

'Show me, Mara. Show me the strength of your devotion to me.' Brabant clawed at her flesh, his eyes wild, his cock a menacing spike beneath his loose-cut black pants.

Mara felt her soul tremble, some deep fear within her rebelling for a moment before her body's urges took over and all she could think about was the desire, the thirst for more and wilder sex.

She tore off the remainder of her clothes – the cotton skirt, the white lace panties – and revealed her unashamed nakedness in all its glory. The smell of her sex was strong, a musky odour of desire wafting from the glossy auburn triangle at the base of her belly.

'Possess me,' she whispered and crouched, belly down, on the softly upholstered couch, her bum cheeks parted to reveal a puckered kiss of welcome.

Liz Exley was on the prowl and this time she had no intention of letting her prey escape.

At last she had done it. She had persuaded Harry Baptiste to invite her to his country house for the weekend – not to Chequers, where there would be an inconvenient number of servants and hangers-on to take an interest in a certain Ms Exley – but the Tudor cottage he had bought in Hampshire as a retreat from the cares of office.

No-one would disturb them here. The two bodyguards were otherwise engaged (one reading *Penthouse* in his car

and the other fast asleep after the best fucking of his life)
and it was just the two of them, Liz and Baptiste, sitting in
his kitchen enjoying a light and intimate supper.

This time she was playing it cool – no heavy stuff, at
least not to start with. She was wearing white denim jeans
(tight but not too tight) and a soft chambray shirt which
showed off her athletic figure without making her look
tarty or threatening. Now that she was beginning to
understand how to play it with Harry Baptiste, his fate was
well and truly sealed.

'You cook well, Ms Exley,' Baptiste observed, spearing
a steamed mushroom with his fork.

'Liz, please. Surely there's no need for formality now.'

'No, no, of course not . . . Liz. It's just that in public life
one becomes so accustomed to keeping one's distance.
There are always things – and people – one needs to be
wary of . . .'

'But not of me, I hope?'

'No.' For a moment, Harry's voice held a note of doubt.
But it resolved itself almost instantaneously. 'No, of course
not.'

Liz put the pan in the sink and sat down opposite
Baptiste. My, but he was gorgeous, he really was. Even if
she wasn't doing this for the Master she'd want to play
around with Harry Baptiste. Tall, ebony-black and elegant
without being aloof, Baptiste was every girl's idea of the
perfect consort. His cock was undoubtedly enormous and
Liz looked forward immensely to making its acquaintance.

With complete casualness she undid the top button of
her shirt.

'My, but it's getting warm in here,' she observed. 'These
summer nights can be so oppressive.'

'We could eat outside on the verandah,' suggested
Baptiste.

'No, let's stay in here,' replied Liz hastily. 'It's so much
cosier, don't you think? More wine?' Without waiting for
Baptiste's reply she topped up his glass, making absolutely

sure to slip in the powder Madame LeCoeur had given her.

Baptiste looked at Liz across the table and felt something he hadn't often felt before: naked lust. Why had he done it? Why had he invited this woman here, when he knew she would drive him crazy with those pouting lips and those slim, snaky hips?

Why? Because he couldn't resist her, that's why. He'd tried to get Liz out of his mind but she found her way into his dreams, wearing that black satin sheath dress she'd had on in the restaurant, unzipping her bodice and letting her breasts tumble out into his hands. It was torture and in the end it had been too much for him.

He watched her carry a forkful of food to her mouth, the tip of her tongue protruding from those full red lips, taking a little lick before her mouth opened and she took the food into her mouth, engulfing it with eyes half-closed, as though she were tasting the tip of a man's swollen penis.

A sip of wine would take the dryness from his mouth. Ah yes, that was good. A nice, crisp white with a fruity bouquet and a certain background muskiness which he couldn't quite put his finger on. But it tasted good and – my! – but it made him feel good too. More excited, yes, but more . . . well . . . relaxed, too.

That's better, Baptiste, purred the voice in his head. *You're feeling better now, aren't you? Why don't you have another drink?*

His hand hovered over the glass, then moved away. No sense in overdoing things. Baptiste was a man who enjoyed all pleasures, but in moderation.

'It was good of you to come here and cook for me, Liz.'

'I adore cooking,' Liz replied, fixing him with her cornflower-blue eyes. 'There's something so sensual about it, don't you think?'

'I . . . well, yes, I suppose you're right. Sensual and creative.'

'I always think if you can cook a perfect gourmet meal, you can achieve perfect sex. It's all about understanding your passions, you see, and knowing what satisfies your lover's appetites.'

Unclean thoughts were flitting through his mind, not for the first time. Thoughts of Liz's well-honed body, naked and glistening with melted butter. She was bending over the kitchen table, her buttocks parted and the golden butter trickling down her back into the deep crease between her arse cheeks. And she was smiling, just for him.

Baptiste reached under the tablecloth and discreetly readjusted his burgeoning prick. There was no restraining it when Liz Exley was around.

You like touching yourself, don't you, Baptiste? Feels good, doesn't it? But it would feel so much better if they were Liz's fingers on your dick. Why don't you ask her? Why don't you ask her to jerk you off?

He couldn't understand the whispering voice in his head. It was driving him crazy, whipping up his lust into a kind of whirling dust-storm that clouded his reason and dulled his will.

Another sip of wine. It tasted even better than the first: crisp, mellow, seductive. Its coolness was the coolness of Liz Exley's blue eyes, the touch of her slim white hands.

Liz got up from the table to fetch the dessert from the fridge. Baptiste's eyes followed her across the kitchen, devouring her every movement. Look how those firm buttocks moved inside those white denims, as if they had a life of their own! Look how the centre seam pressed hard into her crotch, so that when she turned round to face him he could see not only the line of her panties, but the way her vulval lips were held apart.

He thought how fragrant her panties must be, after being pushed right up into the wet haven of her cunt; and his erection throbbed painfully at the mental image of himself, his face pressed up against a pair of Liz's soiled panties, breathing deeply as he inhaled the essence of her sex.

'Cream, Harry?'

Liz's voice was itself as smooth as double cream lapped from a silver spoon. Cream. Baptiste thought of the cream that he longed to spurt into her and lick from her cunt, her arse, from the valley between her perfect breasts.

Cream.

'Y-yes, please.'

She leant over to pour the cream onto Baptiste's plate and he saw that the top two buttons of her shirt seemed to have come open. He couldn't resist looking. Underneath she had on one of those totally indecent peep-hole bras you saw strippers wearing on stage. Not that Harry Laurent Baptiste was in the habit of frequenting strip-joints, far from it, but you couldn't serve as Chairman of the All-Party Obscene Publications Committee for three years without having your eyes well and truly opened.

Mmm. Red it was, that really tarty pillar-box red nylon that cheap underwear is always made of. And this wasn't the sort of bra a girl would normally wear under her clothes – it was the sort she'd wear to bed. She seemed to take absolutely ages pouring the cream and Baptiste could see her right nipple clearly, a hard pink cone poking through the peek-a-boo bra-cup like a strawberry on top of a luscious ice-cream sundae.

Liz sat down opposite him and picked up her spoon. There was cream all over the bowl of it and she started licking at it, putting out her long pink tongue and running it over the silver. Baptiste was in an agony of frustration, shifting on his seat in a vain attempt to escape the burning hunger in his dick.

Cream, Harry. Thick, glutinous double cream. How would it be if you poured some of that cream over her tits and licked it off? Do you think it would taste good?

Damn this voice inside his brain, caressing and exciting him. Was it some hitherto-unsuspected aspect of his personality, some latent reservoir of lust now threatening to burst its banks? He could feel himself losing control, pushed nearer and nearer to the edge. If he fell, if he gave in and did all these things he so wanted to do, there could be no going back.

Once he had tasted pleasure like that, his thirst would never be satisfied.

Liz bit into a strawberry, letting just the tiniest trickle of mingled juice and cream run down over her lip onto her chin.

'I'm so careless,' she giggled and put out her tongue, lapping up the sweet pink ooze. I could do that, thought Baptiste to himself. I could lick the pink juice from your flesh, Liz Exley. I *want* to.

That's right, Harry, relax. Stop fighting it. There, just put your hand on your dick. Good, isn't it? But it can't be comfortable, wearing those tight trousers when you've got a hard-on like that. Tell you what, Harry, why don't you unzip your fly and take out your cock . . .?

His mind was woozy from the wine – he supposed because he didn't often indulge – and a creeping warmth was stealing over him. Liz was an understanding girl, she wouldn't think badly of him. He was only doing it so he'd be more comfortable.

Reaching under the table, he slid down the zipper of his pants. Underneath, the abundance of lubricating fluid dripping from his glans had soaked through his white silk boxers, making them translucent. The wet fabric was clinging like a second skin to his dick, masking nothing of his desire. And it was so very easy simply to slide his hand through the vent and ease out the fleshy rod, stroking his overheated shaft with a palm still cool from the chilled glass of wine.

He was so bound up in the pleasurable release that his eyes half-closed and his thoughts began to swim, forming a fascinating kaleidoscope of erotic images, all of them centred on Liz Exley.

When he found the strength to open his eyes, she was standing over him, with her shirt open right down the front and her tits shamelessly provocative in their red peephole cups.

'I wouldn't do this for anyone but you, Harry,' purred Liz, slipping her shirt off and reaching behind for the bra-clasp. 'Really I wouldn't. But you're special.'

He caught his breath in an ecstatic gasp as she released the bra-catch and pulled the red lace cups away from her tits.

'Do you like them, Harry?' She trailed the red nylon bra playfully over his shoulder, then down over his belly and onto the hypersensitive purplish head of his prick. He couldn't understand why he wasn't feeling shame or embarrassment, only excitement. 'Your beautiful prick says you do.'

She took his hand from his shaft and, dazed and unresisting, he watched as though he were a spectator in someone else's dream. Were those really his fingers, unbuckling Liz's belt and unfastening the top button of her jeans? Was he really sliding his hand underneath her panties and feeling the smoothness of a freshly shaven pussy?

Oh yes, Harry. That's much better. The voice in his head was exultant, urging him on. *More, Harry. Strip her off and do whatever you want with her.*

Baptiste heard his own voice whispering, hoarse and very far away.

'It's wrong.'

No, Harry, it's not wrong. It's natural. It's natural to want to get your dick inside a beautiful woman. It's right to want to fill her with your come.

'I couldn't. Could I . . .?'

Do it, Harry.

Baptiste felt as though he were looking at Liz through a gauzy veil, a soft-focus lens which made her seem unreal yet incredibly alluring, like an actress in an arty porn film. Oh, he wanted her. He wanted her with every nerve and fibre in his body. His manhood swelled and strained for her, his balls aching with the need to pay her the explosive tribute of their desire.

On his finger, the crystal ring glowed and burned, and in its depths a dark mist swirled, dangerous and seductive.

Do it now. Look, she's pulling off her panties, she's holding her pussy lips apart so you can see how hard her clitty is for you. She wants you, she wants you. DO IT NOW.

Yes, do it now. Do it now and feel the pleasure. He looked at Liz, lying back over the kitchen table with her legs apart and nothing on but stockings and red suspenders. Why not? It would be so easy . . .

'No!'

With a strength of will he did not know he possessed, Harry Baptiste took hold of the ring and wrenched it from his finger. It seemed to contract about his flesh as he pulled and clawed at it, but he tore it off and cast it, spinning, across the room.

Unseen and unheard in its clouded depths, the figure of a dark, bearded man screamed his fury to a mocking universe.

Paris. Mara knew it well. One of her earliest sexual adventures had been with a Parisian poet called Raoul and his nymphomaniac sister Marie-Claude. For six blissful weeks they had lived together on Raoul's houseboat, sharing everything – especially each other's beds. In those days, Mara had been barely more than a child, inexperienced and hungry to learn about the world of sexual pleasure. Marie-Claude had been an inspirational teacher.

But that had been light years ago and now she had returned to Paris in very different circumstances. She wasn't staying in a humble houseboat but in the finest five-star hotel in the whole of the city. And the man in her bed was neither Raoul nor Andreas Hunt: it was Zacchaeus Brabant.

If only she knew that what she was doing was right. If only she could be sure whether Brabant was her ally or her foe. But Mara's psychic powers were clouded and dulled, and she could not even join her spirit to Andreas's, to know if he was safe, let alone read Brabant's thoughts. All she knew was that Zacchaeus Brabant had declared himself the Master's deadly enemy and that, in order to save Andreas, she must do exactly as he commanded her.

She did not trust Brabant and yet there was a certain guilty pleasure in obedience to another's will. And, in submitting to the commands of Zacchaeus Brabant, Mara found herself tempted by the freedom of sensual submission.

'This is my own personal suite of rooms,' Brabant told her as they got out of the lift at the tenth floor. 'No-one else may use them. I live here whenever I am in Paris.' He slid the key-card into the lock and punched in a combination. The door swung inward.

'You must be fabulously wealthy,' observed Mara as she followed him into the spartan elegance of a hallway lined from floor to ceiling with cool white marble.

'In six hundred years, one has ample time to accumulate money and possessions,' replied Brabant icily. 'It is not wealth that I seek.'

'You seek only revenge?'

'I seek what is mine by right.'

Brabant took off his jacket and threw it onto the bed: a huge, soft mattress covered by a black silk throwover. He looked casually bohemian in his dark trousers and loose black shirt, with his blond hair falling in corn-gold waves to his collar.

'Go into the bathroom and take off your clothes, Mara.'

Mara knew better than to disobey. She might not be able to read his thoughts, but there was always a possibility that he could read hers. Not that she had the ability to think rationally any more. The power emanating from Brabant was so tangible that it made her dizzy and disorientated. When he was close – and he rarely allowed her to stray from his side – it was as though the force of his will enclosed and ensnared her, its sensual power caressing away her resistance and her suspicion.

And, try as she might, Mara could not escape the force of her own desire for Brabant.

She pushed open the door of the en-suite bathroom and walked in. Its walls and floor were of the same plain white marble, edged with black, but the room was dominated by a huge sunken bath in the shape of a five-pointed star.

It was a hot and steamy summer's day in Paris, threatening thunder, but here in Zacchaeus's apartments the air was as cool as a tomb. Hot water lapped the edges of the pentagram bath, wavy columns of steam rising into the cool air from its surface. A scent of wild violets wafted on the air, fresh and sweet.

Mara pulled her T-shirt off and unbuttoned her shorts, wriggling them down over her hips. She was wearing neither bra nor panties, and her nipples were already semi-stiff from rubbing up and down on the inside of her T-shirt. Her clitoris tingled from the constant abrading of her shorts, the centre seam of which had worked its way insidiously between her pussy lips. It would be so nice just to relax in the hot water and let her fingers slide onto her clitoris, rubbing and stimulating and bringing herself off . . .

'Get into the bath.'

Brabant was standing in the doorway, his bathrobe open at the front and his cock standing proud.

'Get into the bath,' he repeated. 'I wish to see you masturbate.'

His words made Mara start. Had he read her mind? Had he guessed at the greedy hunger within her?

She sat down on the edge of the bath and let herself glide into the water. Much hotter than blood heat, its embrace felt tropical and luxurious.

'Good. Now pleasure yourself.'

Almost independent of her own volition, Mara's fingers crept towards the luxuriant haven of her pussy, its lips already parting in a smile of welcome. Her left hand moved to her breast, her fingers kneading and pinching her nipple; and waves of sensation rippled through her like the lapping waves of bathwater, kissing and stroking her naked body.

She knew Brabant had power over her, knew that power was growing with every second she remained within his clutches. His eyes glittered with a hypnotic intensity, daring her to disobey him, defying her not to want every kiss, every caress.

But little by little, her will was ebbing away. And very soon, unless she fought him, all that remained of her spirit would be the desire.

Max Trevidian was standing alone in Harry Baptiste's kitchen. It was the middle of the night and Baptiste was asleep, but that didn't matter because Max wasn't here to pay a social call.

The crystal ring still lay on the floor where Baptiste had thrown it – a small, innocuous, harmless-looking trinket. Max bent down and picked it up, and as it lay in his palm it began to glow.

'You're a damned nuisance, Delgado,' Max remarked, slipping the ring into his shirt pocket, 'and wily with it. I put you in the keeping of the purest-hearted man alive and still you almost escape.

'But never mind, it was time we met again. You see, Delgado, I have a use for you now . . .'

18: Deceptions

In the greenish light of a Parisian dawn, a tatty houseboat
bobbed at its moorings, occasionally nudging against the
riverbank as one of the *bâteaux mouches* returned to the city
with its cargo of all-night partygoers.

Inside, on a bunk bed, Andreas was deepening his
acquaintance with Marie-Claude Pénichet and her poet
lover, Raoul Descartes. Most especially with Marie-Claude,
for in addition to being not at all bad-looking, Raoul's
girlfriend had the advantage of being a complete nympho.

Andreas hadn't hitched since he was a kid and he
certainly didn't remember it being this much fun. He
didn't even mind Raoul taking 'artistic' pictures of him
fucking Marie-Claude to illustrate his next volume of
poetry. Hell, no. Just as long as he got to Paris in time to
save Mara – and just as long as he got to screw Marie-
Claude in a couple of dozen different positions on the way
there.

Marie-Claude was handsome in a very French sort of
way – small, dark, petite and yet voluptuous. Her eyes were
dark as polished jet and she wore her black hair in a short,
glossy bob which showed off her long and slender neck.
One of the things which particularly excited Andreas was

that her body was tanned all over – breasts, backside, every inch of her an even, golden brown.

'You like my body, *oui*?' She sprawled on the bunk bed, belly down and thighs indiscreetly parted, craning her neck to pout at him coquettishly.

'I like it. *Oui*.'

'I want you . . . how you say, *frapper*? I want you to beat me.'

'Oh yes?' Andreas contemplated the pert backside and gave it a light, playful slap with the flat of his hand.

'*Non*! Not like that!' she scolded him. 'Harder. I want you to beat me like I am the most *méchante enfant* you have ever beaten.'

Raoul put down his Polaroid camera on the table and opened one of the cupboards which lined the interior of the houseboat. He took out something which looked a little like a misshapen table-tennis bat, and handed it to Andreas.

'It is her favourite,' he explained. 'Made of three layers of very stiff cow-hide, hand-sewn and polished.'

Andreas tested the paddle between his fingers. It was almost as hard as wood, but with a certain lethal springiness which he was sure Mistress Sedet would enjoy.

'You're sure you want me to . . .?'

Marie-Claude repeated her oh-so-sexy pout.

'*Chéri*,' she rebuked him. 'You are English and the whole world knows how the English love to be beaten. No-one understands the pleasures of punishment like *les Anglais*.'

She wriggled her little bottom so invitingly that he could hardly deprive her of what she asked. A few strokes across the bare backside, that was all she wanted. Well, what English gentleman could resist an invitation so prettily made?

He swung the paddle back and brought it down on her bum cheeks, surprising himself at the loud explosion made as leather struck flesh. How alluringly her buttock flesh jumped and quivered at the blow. As he lifted the paddle for a second stroke, he saw the paddle's blanched white imprint on her backside, turning a deep shade of coral pink.

Thwack. Thwack. The paddle came crashing down on Marie-Claude's backside, but she showed no signs of flagging. Click. Click. Raoul recorded the scene for posterity, calling out the odd word of encouragement as Andreas gained in confidence and enthusiasm.

It felt surprisingly good to be so in control of this woman's passion. Andreas felt his cock swelling to renewed hardness at the sight of Marie-Claude's reddening backside, quivering under the force of his blows. Her thighs were apart and with each new blow he stole another glance at the ripe split fig of her pussy, glistening with its own secret juices.

'*Chéri*, you may fuck me now,' Marie-Claude announced, turning her head to look at him. 'You give a very good beating, though not quite as severe as *cher* Raoul. Sometimes, I cannot sit down for days when Raoul has beaten me.'

Not quite sure whether to be flattered or insulted by Marie-Claude's assessment, Andreas threw down the paddle and feasted his eyes upon the treasure trove between the Frenchwoman's thighs. She had large, fleshy outer labia, and her inner lips were deep pink and quite protuberant, so that they emerged from between the outer lips like the tips of eager pink tongues.

'Marie-Claude adores to be fisted,' remarked Raoul. 'But she will do anything you ask of her, isn't that true, *chérie*?'

Marie-Claude rolled onto her back on the narrow bunk bed, her dark eyes sparkling.

'Anything, *chérie*.' She ran her fingers up her flanks and over the brown points of her breasts. 'I hunger for your touch.' She pulled apart her fat pussy-lips and Andreas took in the full glory of her treasury, the succulent pink pearl in its fur-trimmed casket.

Suddenly he was overwhelmed by a desire to taste her and pressed his face between her thighs, drinking in the intoxicating scents of their last coupling.

He put out his tongue and lapped at the milky lake welling up from the heart of her sex. The sweetness of her come, mingled with the salty-sharp taste of his semen, only served to intensify his thirst; and he pressed his face much harder into her cunny, darting his tongue into her tight love-tunnel.

Making Marie-Claude climax was almost too easy. Hardly had he got his tongue inside her when he felt her sex-muscles spasm in wave after wave of pleasure and a second tide of honeydew flooded his tongue.

'Such a talented tongue you have, *Monsieur Anglais*,' giggled Marie-Claude, pulling him on top of her and crushing her lips against his. 'I simply cannot control myself when I feel him kissing my clitty.' She raked her fingers over his bare back. 'Ah, but how can I make amends for my lack of self-control . . .?'

She answered her own question by wrapping her thighs around his back and deftly engulfing his prick in her warm, wet cunt-flesh.

'Feels good, *chéri*?'

'Mmm, feels *very* good.' Andreas hardly had to do any work at all. Marie-Claude was pumping away beneath him, her hips powerful and her cunt tight as a gloved hand around his penis. Oh yes, this was good all right. If he wasn't so worried about Mara he wouldn't mind spending a couple of decades like this.

In and out, in and out, smooth like the motion of the boat on the water. Feeling the excitement building up a head of steam, just that right sort of tension, making your heart pound, and then . . .

'Oh, oh yes,' groaned Andreas, grabbing hold of Marie-Claude's hips and thrusting that last crucial millimetre into her as his spunk boiled and bubbled into her cunt. 'Oh,

Marie-Claude, wherever did you learn to fuck like that?'

If he had expected Marie-Claude to make some sort of flippant reply to his question, Andreas certainly hadn't expected her to scream.

'Ah, *mon Dieu*, Andreas! *Qui est-ce?* Who is this?'

Feeling Marie-Claude suddenly freeze underneath him, Andreas rolled off and turned round. Both she and Raoul were staring fixedly at a man in corduroy trousers and a check shirt, who was standing at the end of the bed. Raoul was holding a Polaroid photo.

'I took a picture. I took a picture of him – why is he not in my picture?'

'Who is that?' repeated Marie-Claude, belatedly clutching the bedcovers to cover her nakedness. 'And how did he get in here?'

Andreas sighed.

'Hello, Max,' he said. 'I see your sense of timing's perfect, as usual.'

'Get a move on, Andreas,' replied Max. 'We've got work to do, remember?'

Zacchaeus Brabant and Mara were walking along the Champs-Elysées.

'I was born here,' he told her. 'Many, many years ago when all of this was still fields.'

'You are not Swiss, then?'

Brabant gave a humourless chuckle.

'Switzerland is a good place for a man to go if he wishes to lose himself. It is such a supremely dull place that no-one thinks to ask questions about a man who does not age, a man who has remained exactly the same for century after century.'

'Then why return to Paris?'

'Because, my dear Mara, this was where the Master cursed me.'

Mara felt electricity crackling in the too-hot, too-still air. It was like breathing in the heat from an oven. Gazing around her, it seemed to her that every passer-by, every car, every tree, every building, all were listening and watching and waiting.

'Paris was the place where the Master sought to destroy me and, now that the Eye of Baloch no longer exists to impede me, this is where you and I together will destroy the Master.'

'Listen, Andreas, for fuck's sake.'

'I *am* listening. You're just not making any sense.'

Andreas was drinking in a Paris bar with a dead man. A dead man with no dress sense, who kept harping on about the end of the world.

Max thought of the time ticking away and forced himself to be patient. You'd think being dead would teach you patience, but it hadn't worked like that with Max.

'You and Mara found the Eye of Baloch, yes?'

'Yes.'

'And then this bloke Zacchaeus took it off you?'

'With you so far. But . . .'

'I told you, Andreas, shut up and listen. What did the Master tell you about the Eye?'

'He said he wanted it because it would enable him to see through all deceptions and find out who it was that was trying to interfere with his power.'

Max nodded.

'That's true enough . . . as far as it goes. But the Eye of Baloch has – or should I say had – a very dodgy reputation. Legend had it that the Eye embodied immense destructive powers.'

'And did it?'

'No. Quite the reverse. You see, what the Eye of Baloch did was *prevent* things from getting out of control. Whilst it was in existence, it prevented the end of the world from ever happening.'

Andreas flicked a peanut into his mouth and munched thoughtfully.

'Hang on. You mean that now Brabant has destroyed it . . .?'

Max put up his hand.

'Shush. There are certain spells and rituals which can be performed to bring about the end of the world – spells to cause raging fires or floods, spells to make the moon crumble or turn all living creatures to stone. But none of them could work whilst the Eye of Baloch was in existence.

'That is why, long ago, the pieces were split up and hidden in five different places. As long as just one piece of the Eye existed, the Apocalypse was never more than the plot for a horror film. But now Brabant has got his hands on all the pieces and destroyed them, all he needs to do is conjure up sufficient belief in the end of the world to make it happen. And that is why he needs Mara – without her powers, he would not be able to capture sufficient psychic energy to empower the spell of universal destruction.'

'Max.'

'Hmm?'

'You're still not making sense. I mean, why on earth would a good-looking bastard like Brabant, with money and mistresses coming out of his ears, want to bring about the end of the world?'

Max stared into his drink. He wished he had a reflection to stare back at him.

'Because, Andreas, Brabant wants to die.'

'So why doesn't he just stick his head in a gas oven or something?'

'Six hundred years ago the Master cursed him to eternal life. He's done everything, seen everything, grown to hate and despise everything. Destroying the world and everything in it is the only way he can die . . . and achieve the ultimate revenge.'

'Oh.'

'Now do you see what I'm getting at?'

'Kind of. Let Brabant stuff the Master and the whole world gets stuffed. What are we going to do?'

315

Max patted his shirt pocket.

'We're going to play the ace up our sleeve.'

Mara lay on her back on the couch, eyes closed, letting the masseuse run her hands all over her body.

The girl was one of Brabant's 'handmaidens', girls he had seduced into his service to fulfil his every need. And now he had instructed them to attend to the needs of Mara Fleming.

A trickle of warm oil ran between her breasts and down her belly, gathering in the little well of her navel like nectar in the cup of some precious flower. Despite her resistance she could feel her fears, her anxieties, her doubts, ebbing away.

The girl was young, small and almost childlike, with skin as soft and sweet as the flesh of a ripe peach. How old was she – sixteen, twenty-five, a thousand? Her full lips had the pout of a sulky child and her breasts were tiny buds, barely formed on her pubescent chest; yet those brown doe-eyes held all the knowledge of the centuries. Her hands were small and dainty, yet those slender, white-skinned fingers were as strong and unforgiving as tempered steel.

'Do I please you, my lady Mara?'

Mara looked up at the girl through a haze of pleasure. Silken caresses were smoothing the warm oil all over her belly and up into the secret creases beneath her full breasts. The girl's long, brown hair hung in two swishing plaits which accentuated the impression of extreme youth, but her lips were moist from the constant flicking of a greedy, tongue-tip, moistening the plump and tender flesh.

'It is . . . it is most agreeable.'

'You honour and gratify me, my lady.'

'Why . . . why are you . . .?'

'To pleasure you is my only duty and my only care. Does this please you, my lady?' The girl's fingers began working at the flesh of Mara's lower belly, her caresses never quite reaching the margin of her pubic hair but awakening the most lewd and lascivious thoughts in Mara's swooning brain.

'Oh. Oh yes. *Oh* but that feels so good.' Mara's back arched slightly, lifting her torso a fraction off the bed as she offered herself up to the mystery of these ecstatically-pleasurable caresses.

'That is as it should be. Please, my lady, lie back and allow me to continue.'

'What is your name?' asked Mara through a sun-glow of seductive warmth that began at her poor, neglected clitoris and spread out to take over her entire body.

'That is not important.'

'Please. I should like to know.'

Somehow – although nothing else seemed to matter much any more – it seemed desperately important that Mara should know the identity of this child-woman, this seductress with the body of a schoolgirl and the mind and skills of a whore.

'My name is Lucretia.'

'Lucretia,' murmured Mara, half-drunk with ecstasy. 'My sweet Lucretia . . .'

Mara realised, with a vague twinge of alarm, that her limbs felt heavy and she could barely speak for the huge, warm waves of delicious pleasure washing over her body. She felt helpless, an increasingly willing victim of this so-innocent and so-knowing handmaiden's relentless skill.

What was in that massage oil? Lavender, yes, she was sure she could smell the sharp, spicy tang of fresh lavender, but there were other scents, more arcane, less easily identified. Doubtless Zacchaeus Brabant had instructed his handmaidens in the art of aphrodisiac massage, mixing essential oils, alchemical tinctures and rare spices to create the delicate perfumerie of lust.

She could fight it if she wanted. Surely she could . . . Vague thoughts of rebellion passed through Mara's head, but the will to fight was not there. Her psychic powers seemed dulled too, as though some other, darker force were feeding upon them and controlling them through the subtle magic of desire.

'You will permit me to caress you more intimately, my lady?'

Although the girl's words were framed as a question, they were a statement of fact. Mara had not the slightest intention of refusing Lucretia's caresses.

'Caress . . . mmm, yes . . . touch me . . .'

Fingertips brushed lightly over the crests of her nipples, already painfully erect. A gloss of oil slicked over the plump ovals of her breasts, circular movements massaging it into the skin, making it ache and tingle for joyous release.

In her mind's eye, Mara was no longer in this hotel bedroom, but back in Brabant's mountain retreat, strapped to his punishment couch whilst Brabant himself towered over her, his cock stiff and menacing as it hung above her parted thighs.

'Yield to me,' he seemed to be whispering in her head. 'Yield to me and together we shall destroy the Master. Yield to me utterly, mind and soul, and I will show you pleasure greater than you have ever dreamed of. Yield to me, Mara Fleming, trust and be guided by me . . .'

Lucretia's fingers slipped lightly down over Mara's belly, building up the pleasure until it hovered just short of a crescendo.

'Part your thighs for me, my lady Mara.'

Mara obeyed the hypnotic voice as though she were in a dream, drawing up her knees and letting her thighs slide apart. Her love lips pouted open and a trickle of clear honeydew ran out from between her gaping labia onto the soft bedspread beneath her.

'You have a beautiful cunt.' Mara felt Lucretia's sharp-nailed fingertip trace the long line from pubis to arse, just briefly grazing the hood of her clitoris and making her moan.

'So sensitive . . . please don't hurt me, please don't . . .'

'Beautiful and juicy, like a ripe peach.' The fingernail dug a little more deeply into the soft, hypersensitive flesh, and this time Mara gave a long, low whine of fearful pleasure.

'Oh, oh. No . . .'

'Yes, my lady. Lucretia understands what it is that you really want, what gives you the greatest pleasure. Relax and let me give you that pleasure, my lady Mara.'

Incapable of any resistance – and beyond the point at which she could readily distinguish between pleasure and pain – Mara submitted utterly to Lucretia's ruthless caresses. And every word that Lucretia had spoken was true, for the feelings building up in Mara's loins were of the purest ecstasy, a fire of hunger so hot and all-consuming that nothing could extinguish it save the inexorable march towards orgasm.

Lucretia picked up the vial of massage oil and emptied it over Mara's pubis. It was warm, almost hot, from the spirit lamp, and made Mara shiver with pleasure that verged on discomfort. Trickles of the oil ran in all directions, all over her lower belly, down into the forest of her pubic hair and then down further still, into the long, wet crease between her shameless outer labia.

A long, hot finger of scented oil ran right over the exposed head of Mara's clitoris, and she twisted and turned under the merciless heat. But there was no escape from this most cruel caress, no escape from the hunger which was building up inside her, making her long for release.

'Shall I touch you, my lady? Shall I touch you . . . there?'

Lucretia's finger brushed over Mara's clitty so lightly that it was scarcely a touch at all, more a breath of air, or the beating of a butterfly's wing. But the result was electric.

'Touch me. Yes, touch me, touch me now.'

When at last Lucretia's finger pressed down hard on Mara's clitoris, and began manipulating it with broad, slow, circular strokes, Mara felt as though her whole body was being masturbated, her entire being forced to open itself to the onrush of ecstasy.

Her cunt muscles twitched once, twice, held in a breathless spasm, waiting, waiting, waiting.

Lucretia's fist entered Mara's cunt with a sudden and unforgiving violence which brooked no resistance. Not that Mara would have resisted, even if she could. Her mind and body were utterly at the mercy of this child-woman with the cruelly knowing hands.

'Come, my lady. Come.'

As though summoned by Lucretia's sensually whispering voice, Mara felt her body tense for an instant and then fling itself into glittering ecstasy, like a diver casting himself naked and unafraid from the top of a high cliff, into the swirling ocean below.

As Mara lay panting on the bed, she heard Lucretia's voice somewhere in the darkness of her ebbing desire.

'Your pleasure is my pleasure, my lady.'

From his hiding-place in the wardrobe, Andreas watched Mara undergoing the cruellest torment of her life.

What had happened to Mara? How could she have been taken in so completely by Zacchaeus Brabant? He longed to do something, anything, to help her, but he knew that he must wait his moment.

It seemed like hours had passed when at last Lucretia and the other handmaidens filed out of the room, leaving Mara sprawled naked across the bed.

'Sleep now, my lady. Tomorrow, the Lord Zacchaeus has much work for you to do.'

The door closed and Mara was at last alone. Was she asleep, or merely drugged? With some trepidation, Andreas pushed open the door of the wardrobe and stepped into the room.

'Mara.'

The naked figure on the bed did not move.

'Mara, it's me. Andreas.'

Mara stirred just a fraction, like a sleeper stirring in a dream. Andreas sat down on the bed beside her and pushed matted tendrils of auburn hair off her face. On impulse, he bent to kiss her, and suddenly she responded, drawing him to her and parting her lips to let him dart his tongue into her mouth. At last she sat up.

'Mara, are you all right?'

Mara's eyes flicked open and she blinked, rubbing the back of her hand across her face.

'Andreas? But . . . you're in Switzerland. I had to leave. Brabant said he would kill you . . .'

'I'm here now. Max helped me.'

Mara sat up with difficulty. Even here, in the middle of the biggest fuck-up Andreas had ever got mixed up with (and there had been a few), he couldn't help noticing how eminently suckable those nipples were – long and hard and juicy. Maybe there would just be time . . .

'Max?' Mara stared at Andreas as though he were quite mad.

'Max,' Andreas confirmed. 'And before you say it . . .'

'But Max is dead. Isn't he?'

'Er, yes. Sort of. Dead but still kicking, if you know what I mean. Look, I'll explain it some other time. What matters right now is that we have to do something about Brabant. Something to stop him.'

'Zacchaeus is going to destroy the Master. Why should we want to stop him?'

Andreas felt for the crystal ring in his pocket. He was more used to Mara being the one doing the explaining. He took a deep breath.

'Why? Because he doesn't just want to destroy the Master. He wants to destroy the whole fucking world.'

19: Unmasked

"PANIC IN JAPAN AS SUN FAILS TO RISE"
(Tokyo Daily, 1 August)

Morning sunlight filtered through the curtains of Mara's private hotel suite. But it was no ordinary sunlight. It seemed tinged with a purplish greenish darkness which made the sun itself look sick and turned the sky a bilious mauve.

But then again, this was no ordinary morning. Today, the world was going to end.

Andreas awoke from an uneasy slumber, one arm about Mara's shoulders and the other hand resting on her belly. The sheets beneath them were rumpled and sticky, testifying to a long night's dedication to passion.

'Are you awake?' Andreas kissed Mara's throat and she stirred, growling with pleasure as his kisses skipped lower to the crests of her nipples.

'I am now,' she smiled and rolled Andreas onto his back. Her strong thighs held him in a vice-like grip but he liked it. Boy, did he like it. Only Andreas Hunt could react to imminent world destruction by getting a hard-on.

She wiggled her adorable backside, taunting him with her parted pussy lips and her jiggling breasts. Andreas retaliated by reaching up and grabbing both breasts, squeezing the pillow-soft flesh as though it was modelling clay and he was a particularly precocious child.

'I should go,' Andreas observed, stealing a glance at the

323

bedside clock. Almost six o'clock. 'Brabant might be here
any minute, and I daren't risk letting him see me.'

Mara shook her head.

'He won't be here just yet. He told me . . . he has
preparations to make for tonight.'

Andreas shivered. Tonight. It sounded like last-minute
arrangements for a party, not the end of everything. The
Big Bang to end all Big Bangs.

'All the same . . .' he hazarded. 'We shouldn't take any
more chances than we have to. But you feel so good . . .'

'You still want me?' Mara asked him, tightening her grip
on his thighs but kneeling up so that her cunt was tantalising
inches from his stiffened and aching dick.

'You *know* I do.'

'Again?'

'I always want you, Mara Fleming.'

'Then you'd better come and get me . . .'

Before she had an opportunity to escape his grasp, he
was upon her like a hungry wolf, devouring her thighs with
kisses and holding her so tightly that she could scarcely
wriggle.

'And what happens now?' demanded Mara.

'You get to sit on my cock,' replied Andreas, gazing into
Mara's eyes. And slowly, deliciously slowly, he took her by
the hips and slid her down so that his cock nuzzled its way
into her waiting quim and he thought he might die of
pleasure. Well, there were worse ways to go, and if
everything went wrong and Brabant really did fuck the
whole, wide world, Andreas thought he might quite like to
go with his cock up Mara Fleming's pussy hole.

'Don't just lie there,' purred Mara. 'Fuck me.'

Andreas responded with hard, bucking thrusts of his
pelvis which forced his dick right up against the neck of her
womb. Mara threw back her head and her auburn mane
fell in rich, red waves down her bare back. Little trickles of
sweat coursed between her breasts and Andreas fantasised
about lapping up the salty stream, licking her whole, ripe

body and existing for ever and ever, just on the taste of her sex.

'Good, good. That feels so good,' murmured Mara.

Thighs clenched tight about Andreas's hips, she bent forward so that her tits swung ripe and juicy above his mouth. He craned his neck to taste her breast, like a child bobbing for apples, and succeeded in catching her right nipple between his teeth.

Mara responded to eager nips of his teeth by pushing down harder on his dick, rubbing herself off against the root of his penis, so that her pussy lips gaped wide and her juices trickled down over his balls.

'Oh Mara, Mara, do it to me, please do it to me,' gasped Andreas, holding her tightly as he rose to meet her thrusts. 'Do it to me hard.'

They felt it simultaneously, that tell-tale warmth which sets the whole body tingling and makes the entire world contract until all that exists is the fire between your thighs, warming, burning, consuming.

'Aah. Ah yes, yes.' Mara's breath came in stuttering gasps as pleasure overwhelmed her and she fell forward onto Andreas's chest, both their bodies bathed in sweat.

Andreas's cock jerked inside her cunt, an angry serpent spitting venom into the pit of her belly. At that moment, he forgot everything but the sensations filling his consciousness. Max, the end of the world, Brabant and his band of psychotic nymphos . . . everything paled into insignificance beside the sheer, unadulterated joy of spurting his come into the silky-smoothy sheath of Mara Fleming's cunt.

Reality closed in almost immediately, like a black-gloved hand about its helpless victim's throat. Andreas pulled Mara towards him, slid his hands down over her backside, trying to fill his mind with every aspect of her – her scent, her touch, her taste, the feel of her nipples grinding into the flesh of his chest. He wanted to remember every smooth curve of her silken body.

'I have to go now.'

'Yes, I know, but . . .'

'I have to. Brabant will be here soon.'

Mara did not reply. What was there to say? What could she say? In a few hours' time, if everything went according to Zacchaeus Brabant's hideous scheme, eternal darkness would rain down upon an unsuspecting world.

Andreas kissed her. She could feel his heart beating, the steady thump, thump, thump echoing the sound of the ticking clock on the bedside table. Never had time seemed so precious, or so fragile.

He got up and put on his clothes, half afraid to hang around in case Brabant turned up, half inclined to stick around and punch his head in. But he could hear Max's exasperated voice at the back of his mind: 'Get your pants on, Hunt, and pull yourself together. This way, at least there's a *chance*.'

'Goodbye,' he said, hardly daring to look Mara in the eye. He squeezed her hand, the gesture seeming absurdly fraternal. 'It'll be all right, you'll see.'

'I . . . yes, of course it will.'

'So long then.'

'So long, Andreas.'

The door closed and suddenly time seemed to race by much faster, like a runaway train with no driver, speeding down the track towards certain destruction.

So long . . .

She opened her fingers and looked at the ring lying in the palm of her hand. A simple ring of engraved crystal, cloudy at its heart as though filled with a swirling and malevolent inner life. The evil soul of Delgado.

Would it work? Did Max's crazy plan have a chance – even a *ghost* of a chance? She had no way of knowing.

But she had to try.

Queen Sedet twisted a lock of Heimdal's hair between her gold-tipped fingers and watched him wince. Kneeling at her feet, he gazed up at her with a puppy-dog devotion which was not entirely feigned. Sedet had a powerful ability to seduce men's minds and bodies to her service. Even now, his cock was twitching its appreciative response.

Yes, powerful, thought the Master to himself as he watched grimly through the half-open door.

'The Eye of Baloch is gone, my pretty slave,' hissed Sedet, wrenching back Heimdal's head by his mop of golden hair. 'Gone, destroyed! And by whom . . .?'

'Mistress,' gasped Heimdal, his cock uncoiling into instant rigidity. 'Mistress, I swear it was not I . . .'

Sedet gave a humourless laugh and pushed him away.

'You are pathetic, do you know that, my *Lord* Heimdal? You make me laugh. You flaunt your so-called psychic gifts, yet you have done nothing to serve me. Nothing!'

Heimdal's blue eyes glittered with resentment but he maintained a respectful silence, head bowed, offering his body to his mistress's service. Not for the first time, he wondered how he had allowed himself to be lured into this dangerous game.

'Get out of my sight.'

Heimdal raised his head, surprised.

'Mistress?'

'I said, get out of my sight this minute, wretch!' Sedet's face was a mask of cold fury, and Heimdal knew better than to antagonise her further. The Queen could be very, very unpleasant when she was provoked.

He backed out of Sedet's chamber, closing the door behind him with an audible sigh of relief.

'You are a miserable worm, Heimdal,' observed the Master drily.

'Yes, Master.'

'However, you have served me adequately in this matter and if you continue to serve me with *complete* devotion you shall perhaps not be severely punished.'

Heimdal knew when not to argue.

'Thank you, Master. You are most gracious.'

'Quite. Now leave me and attend to your duties. You

may remove the Italian slut's body from my chamber, I have finished with her now.'

'As you wish, Master.'

The Master paid no further attention to Heimdal. He was of little consequence and easily controlled. Of more concern was Queen Sedet . . .

In the beginning, he had feared that it was Sedet's dark power which had cast up barriers around him, clouding his psychic sight, frustrating all his plans. Now, through Heimdal's talent for treachery, he had learned of the foolish power-game which Sedet had been trying to play against him.

Admittedly he felt a sneaking admiration for her, for she was his immortal queen, his dark consort, his worthy partner in eternal lust. And he had perhaps engineered her resentment of him through his neglect of her sensual needs.

But through her childish plotting she had endangered him, threatened his supremacy. Worse, she had distracted him from his quest for the true author of all his ills, that dark and sinister unknown force which was seeping through the entire fabric of the universe.

She would have to be taught a lesson.

He pushed the door of Sedet's chamber and it swung open on silent hinges. Inside, the Queen was sitting at a small ebony table, inlaid with mother-of-pearl. On the table sat a crystal pyramid, over which Sedet was passing her hands, eyes closed, lips moving in some soundless incantation.

Her mind was filled with pain and fury as she tried to read the future, to understand what was happening. It was all so cloudy, the images meaningless and distorted . . .

'My Queen.'

Sedet froze, her violet eyes snapping open. Slowly, very slowly, she turned to face the Master. A fraction of a second later, a smile appeared on her scarlet lips, hiding her fear.

'My Lord, I was just . . .'

The Master smiled too, a thin-lipped smile that was almost a sneer.

'Yes, Sedet. I know exactly what you were doing. In fact, my dear Queen, I have always known.'

She watched him in stunned silence, her mind blocking him out and her body rigid, aggressive in her alarm. He closed the door and walked towards her, quite slowly, making the suspense last, making her suffer for her foolish betrayal.

His fingers stroked her hair and she shivered.

'Not receptive to my touch, Sedet? No longer hungry for my caresses?' he taunted her.

Eyes flashing anger, she tried to push his fingers away but there was a sudden, invincible strength within him, a strength which seemed to drain every ounce of energy from her own body. Claw-like, his fingers dragged down the side of her face and neck, leaving white welts which in seconds had turned a rich crimson. And then his fingers fastened on the black velvet of her robe.

'Unhand me!' she spat, trying to wriggle out of his grasp. But the Master had no intention of doing anything of the kind. He was actually rather enjoying himself. It reminded him of the days of his youth, back in Egypt, when she had been merely a temple slut and he had been the great High Priest, her lord and master and source of eternal power.

'You are mine, Sedet. *Mine*. You were mine when I raised you from the dust and you are mine now, forever, for all eternity.'

Sweeping the crystal pyramid onto the floor in a shower of bright fragments, he tore at the fabric of her dress. She was powerless to resist him.

And more than that. She was excited. Hungry, Her cunt dripping honeydew as it had not done for four thousand years. Once again her Master was taking possession of her, marking her with his mark, taking her for his own.

'Understand this,' the Master cried as he stripped her and forced her to her knees. 'That you can never be other than my Queen, for you are the chosen one, the vessel of my sacred power.'

Her breasts were golden in the lamplight, sweat trickling down into the valley between them, like the mighty river of her desire. He could smell the wanting in her, and his cock exulted in her beauty, her fear, her dark mystery.

'Master,' whispered Sedet in an ecstasy of lust, parting her crimson lips to beg for the taste of his cock. 'Master, I am yours for all time. Yours to command. Yours to destroy. Yours to fuck . . .'

And the Master laughed as he possessed her and tasted the sweet elixir of her submission.

Darkness. He bloody hated it.

Never had a Parisian night seemed so impenetrable. A power cut had plunged most of the city into moonless blackness and no-one at the power company seemed able either to find the cause or to put it right.

Inspector Gérard Maillot, of the Sûreté, sat in his office and scowled. *Merde*. Another power failure – the fourteenth in as many weeks – and this time, almost the whole of Paris was affected. The cacophony of wailing burglar alarms filled the night air outside, where an inadequate and demotivated police force was trying to keep the lid on a troubled city.

Hot August nights, ruffled tempers, and now this. Hysteria, looting, arson, religious mania, where would it all end? Perhaps that fruitcake of a TV astrologer was right and the world really was about to fall off its axis and get sucked into the sun.

'Another spot of bother in Pigalle,' announced Lieutenant Peluche, sticking his head through the door and plonking a report on Maillot's desk.

'What is it this time?'

'Bit of an orgy, Inspector. Seems the floor show at the

330

Perroquet Rose ended up in a free-for-all and then there's the trouble down at the Seminary. Naked nuns all over the damn place . . .'

Maillot sighed and mopped his perspiring face with his handkerchief.

'Anything else?'

'Nope, not for now. Well, I did hear there was some nutter at the Eiffel Tower saying the world was going to end tonight, but you can't keep tabs on every crackpot in Paris, can you? From what I've heard, he seems harmless enough.'

Mara had never been more scared in her entire life. More scared or more excited.

She stood with Brabant beneath the vast base of the Eiffel Tower, its four iron legs forming a canopy above them. The blackness of the night sky seemed to surround them like an opaque blanket, dotted here and there with the feeble yellow glimmer of an emergency lighting system.

Zacchaeus Brabant was magnificent in his exultation. Placing the lantern on the grass, he turned to look at Mara. The orange light, shining up at him from below, cast pools of brightness and shadow on his face, making him look not so much like a human being, more a demon.

'Undress,' he commanded her.

Mara met his gaze, but she longed to look away. When she looked into Brabant's eyes, she could feel the full hypnotic force of his stare, the power that drew her in, destroying her will, making her want to obey him.

'Quickly, Mara. The time will soon be upon us, the stars are correctly aligned – can you not feel the power in the darkness all around you?'

His eyes caressed her, sapping her will, draining her of the energy she so desperately needed if she was to fight him. Only the memory of Andreas's kiss, the lingering taste of his come in her mouth, reminded her that she must be strong. Somewhere beyond the feeble circle of orange-yellow light cast by the lantern, a car alarm sounded and a woman screeched with unearthly, hysterical laughter:

'*Prenez-moi, prenez-moi, je suis à vous. Je suis à tout le monde pour toujours . . .!*'

Mara undressed slowly, automatically, feeling the darkness taking over her body as each new inch of skin was bared to the hot, sultry, unpleasantly sticky night air. Where was the blessed coolness of night that she remembered so well? The balmy stillness of that first summer evening when she had fucked Andreas on the beach at Whitby, and then tiptoed away into the darkness, believing that they would never meet again.

Would she ever see Andreas again?

'You are more beautiful than I remembered, Mara Fleming.'

Brabant's husky, sex-filled voice seemed to banish every other sound, creating a cocoon of stillness about the two figures standing beneath the Eiffel Tower. His fingers traced the plump fullness of her breast and she saw how his dick swelled in his pants, an arrow of menacing lust that would not miss its target.

Mara caught his hand and took it to her lips, her eyes never leaving his face as she opened her mouth and began sucking and licking his fingers. Brabant's lips twitched into a dark and lustful smile.

'Such sensual power. If I did not know you for a white witch, Mara, I would say that you were the wickedest slut in the whole world. A worthy consort indeed for the most powerful man who has ever lived . . .'

He laughed, but his voice was oddly devoid of humour. Withdrawing his fingers from between her lips, Mara watched him throw off his clothes, tearing at the buttons, flinging the discarded garments onto the parched and dusty grass.

Despite all she now knew of Brabant's madness and vengeful deceit, she still could not deny the man's physical beauty. His wavy, corn-blond hair framed a high-cheekboned face dominated by piercing grey eyes which commanded not only attention, but obedience.

His torso was smooth and well-toned, the rippling golden skin hinting at the steel-hard muscles beneath. Slim hips and a taut belly led down to strong thighs which framed the golden globes of his balls. The thick pipe of his uncircumcised cock lay cradled in the palm of his hand as he began slowly wanking, bringing himself to the very brink of pleasure but no further, preparing himself for his last and most potent ritual.

Mara trembled inwardly but she knew she must not let Brabant see her fear. Fear might allow him to penetrate the barrier of her thoughts, see into the secrets of her heart, overcome here and use her power, as he had planned, for her own – and the world's – destruction.

'You are certain that this ritual will destroy the Master?' she enquired with seeming innocence.

The trace of a sneer crossed Brabant's handsome face.

'That worm has lost all power to resist me. Tonight, my dear Mara, he will die.'

'And what of us, Lord Zacchaeus – you, and I, and Andreas . . .?'

'Have no fear, sweet child. All your torment, and mine, will be at an end for ever.'

The heart that had once been Anastasia Dubois's thumped in Mara's chest as she listened to Brabant's words, now understanding their full, sinister meaning.

She watched him helplessly as first he drew a magic circle about them, then traced a pentagram with fine, crystalline powder. She could do nothing to stop him, only wait; wait for that moment when she would have her one and only and final chance. On her finger, the crystal ring shimmered with a cloudy brilliance, an inner life swirling and twisting as whispered words filled Mara's head:

Destroy. Destroy everything. Fuck and destroy, destroy, destroy.

Brabant turned with a smile of satisfaction. How could he look so calm? How could a man who was about to destroy the world face eternity with a smile on his face?

'All is prepared, Mara. It is time to join your power to mine.'

'What would you have me do?'

'Lie on the ground and spread your thighs. I must fuck you within the magic circle as I speak the incantation. At the moment when our eternal essences are joined, the spell will be empowered . . .'

He must die, Mara. Obey, obey. He must die . . .

She tried to shake the words out of her head, but it was as though someone half-remembered were standing behind her shoulder, whispering into her ear in a familiar voice that made her flesh creep.

Brabant knelt between her thighs, his eyes half closed and his lips moving in the words of a murmured incantation. She caught snatches of Latin, mingled with meaningless jumbles of sound and syllable. A horrible, creeping darkness, darker by far than the night sky, seemed to be wrapping itself around them, cutting them off from the light, squeezing all the oxygen out of the air so that she could scarcely catch her breath.

And all the time this terrible, burning lust in her belly, stronger than her hatred and her fear, making her long for the feel of Zacchaeus Brabant's cock thrusting deep in her belly.

Do it, Mara, yes, do it. Destroy, destroy, destroy . . .

Stab.

Brabant's cock speared her with a single, brutal thrust that sent shock-waves through her body and her soul. Suddenly they were fucking, his hands on her hips and her thighs wrapped around his waist. Fucking like mad creatures, the sweat pouring off them and their bodies moving in a jerky yet synchronised rhythm.

A low electrical whine filled the air, punctuated by loud crackles and flashes of light as brilliantly coloured forks of lightning slashed the thick black blanket of the sky. The whole world held its breath.

And Mara knew what she must do.

The Rt Hon Anthony LeMaître MP, leader of Her Majesty's Opposition, was attending an all-night sitting in the House when the storm broke over London.

The Master had been cruelly robbed of his psychic sight these last weeks and months, his energies gradually draining from him like water from a leaking tap. And consequently there had been no warning of the coming tempest, nothing to presage the sudden cacophony in the heavens as thunder ripped through the night sky and boiling torrents of rain began to fall onto the steaming grass.

Across the floor of the House, Prime Minister Harry Baptiste paused momentarily in his faultless delivery, glanced up at the ceiling and then resumed his speech on trade tariffs. The Master felt bile rising in his throat. Baptiste was a cool customer, there was no doubt of that. And yet . . . and yet, was he mistaken in detecting a new seed of darkness in the man's unblemished soul? He would have him yet. And when he did, no power on earth would prevent him from destroying Baptiste like the insect he was.

Suddenly lightning illuminated the House more clearly than sunlight on a summer's afternoon. And in that split second everything became clear. A flash of psychic insight cut through the months-old fog that had befuddled the Master's brain and at last he understood. Somehow, he was receiving an astral message of awesome clarity and power. A message from the vampire slut Anastasia Dubois.

Pictures entered his brain and chilled his blood. He saw the Eiffel Tower standing against the night sky, forked lightning and flames crackling out of its summit like electrical waves from a radio mast.

Paris. A city in turmoil. A city incited to an orgy of sin, a celebration of its own unwitting destruction. Cities all over the world, poised on the brink of oblivion.

Who? Why? His mind focused on the Dubois slut, her body taut and shuddering beneath the thrusting form of a naked man. A man whose features reminded him curiously of someone he had once known . . . known and destroyed . . .

The man turned his face and the Master found himself looking straight into the mocking eyes of Zacchaeus Brabant, the man he had punished and destroyed over six hundred years ago. Or *thought* he had destroyed.

Sudden realisation entered the Master's soul like a sword-blade of razor-sharp ice. *Now* he understood. Understood everything that had happened these past months, the disasters and the frustrations and the sense of a dark and opposing power.

Oh yes, he understood all right. And he knew this thing had to be sorted out pretty damn quickly.

If there was still time.

'Sin, my children! Rejoice and sin as you burn . . .'

Zacchaeus Brabant's voice sounded over the whole of Paris, the whole of the world. It came out of every television set, every radio, every VCR, every cinema screen. Pick up the telephone and Brabant was speaking to you. Lock your door and try not to listen, and he was there in your head, whispering to you and you alone. There was no escape.

Brabant fucked Mara with a joyous abandon, pinning her helpless body to the ground, grinding pubic bone against pubic bone, revelling in the youth and strength within Mara's soul.

'Die!' snarled Brabant with an insane laugh. 'You who call yourself the Master, helpless worm, die for what you did to me.' His cock pumped hard into Mara, bringing her nearer the climax she fought but could not resist for much longer. 'Die, world. Delight in your sin and burn with me in eternity!'

Lightning sparked across the Paris sky, across the skies

of London and Delhi and New York and Mombasa. Rivers of boiling lava threatened Tokyo and Oslo and Berlin. Oceans rose up in immense tidal waves and cracks appeared in the earth's crust, menacing towns and cities and villages across the globe. And everywhere men and women fucked like beasts, seemingly unaware of the danger as they answered the call to lust.

A hot wind blew across Paris, carrying tiny grains of sand that stung and abraded. Mara felt the treacherous warmth of orgasm spreading through her belly, destroying her will, forcing her to answer Brabant's final thrusts as he took the last, slow strokes towards his climax.

As his cock twitched, Mara fought through the mist of her own pleasure to seize hold of Brabant's hand. Lost in the exultation of his triumph, he hardly seemed to notice as she slipped the crystal ring on to the third finger of his right hand.

For a split second, a remembered face stared back at her out of Zacchaeus Brabant's eyes. The face not of Brabant, but of Delgado, whoremaster and one-time Lord of Winterbourne. Delgado, whose love for the Master had turned to such a potent desire for destruction.

Delgado . . .?

A moment later, the forces of chaos turned the night sky into a maelstrom, and the iron girders of the Eiffel Tower began to crack and distort in the heat of an all-consuming inferno.

20: Lords of Winterbourne

"EIFFEL TOWER SPOTTED ON THE MOON"
(Sunday Stun, 3 August)

The man with the tousled brown hair and the check shirt strolled down the Champs-Elysées, surveying the mess that had been central Paris. It was going to take a lot of clearing up. But then again, nobody was perfect, and all in all he didn't think he'd done too bad a job on his first assignment – though Andreas would probably think differently.

'Max Trevidian, Psychic Investigator,' he murmured to himself with a smile. 'Worlds saved, Apocalypses averted. No job too big.'

So what do I investigate next? he wondered. Only time would tell. After all, he hadn't been a ghost that long. He still had a lot to learn about being dead. Like where to go for a bank loan to buy a 1956 Morris Traveller.

Now that *was* something worth investigating.

Mistress Sedet purred like a tigress as the Master applied tit-clamps of purest gold to her painted nipples.

'You honour me, my Lord.'

'You are my Queen. What other woman is deserving of such an honour?'

The Master felt a glow of smug self-satisfaction flood his loins. His Queen was once more loyal and subservient. Brabant was dead and would no longer be inconveniencing him, and already the Master was regaining the power of astral sight which would prove so useful to him in acquiring ultimate supremacy.

Sedet pouted in mock jealousy as the Master pushed the love-balls up high in her vagina.

'You do not prefer the Exley slut, my Lord?'

The Master laughed.

'I will share her with you. She has skills – and energies – which are pleasing to us both.'

'Or the Dubois slut?'

The Master ran his fingernails over Sedet's upraised rump.

'The Dubois slut is talented and useful, but you are my Queen.'

Sedet savoured the feeling of her Master's caresses on her tightly puckered arsehole. She had not enjoyed so much attention from him in months and she was in a better mood than she had been for a long time.

'Perhaps I misjudged her,' she conceded. 'Her and your slave Weatherall. They served us well in the matter of Zacchaeus Brabant.'

'Indeed.' The Master knelt behind her and nudged the tip of his swollen prick against Sedet's puckered hole. It yielded eagerly, almost hungrily, swallowing him right up to the balls. 'I look forward to receiving their full report when they return to Winterbourne. But for now . . .' He shoved into her a little harder. 'For now, my Queen, let us refresh our sexual energies through our coupling.'

Kneeling submissively at the foot of the bed, her hands chained behind her back and a studded dog-collar about her neck, Liz Exley looked on and burned with jealous anger. He should have been mine, she seethed. Mine, mine, for ever.

But Heimdal laughed inwardly as he watched. Winterbourne was back to normal, all was as it should be again. He felt not a trace of resentment. It had been good sport and, after all, he did have the whole of eternity in which to win the power he so richly deserved.

Andreas was having difficulty believing it but he and Mara were definitely still alive. Just.

That had been a bloody near thing and, let's face it, Paris would never be quite the same again – especially not the Eiffel Tower. As he and Mara snuggled up in their hotel room, he thought of the enormous crater where the Arc de Triomphe had stood, the blackened shell of the Louvre and the top half of the Montparnasse Tower, now lying upside down in the middle of the Paris ring-road. Quite some party.

'Andreas . . .' Mara wriggled closer, rubbing her gorgeous backside against the ever-eager swelling of his prick.

'Mmm.' He reciprocated by sliding his arm round and taking a juicy handful of tit-flesh. The nipple was hard as a brazil nut.

'Did you think . . . did you think everything would work out OK?'

Andreas hesitated for a split second before lying.

'Yes, of course I did. Max was sure it would.'

'You didn't think Brabant might win?'

Andreas nibbled Mara's shoulder affectionately.

'Don't be daft. No man stands a chance when you're around.'

'Even you?'

'Especially me.'

A knock on the door interrupted Andreas's lustful train of thought, and reluctantly he rolled off the bed and put on a robe. He padded over to the door with bad grace.

'Yes?'

'Télégramme pour Madame.'

Andreas paid the boy and took the envelope, handing it to Mara. She opened it and read it out aloud:

"GRATIFIED TO HEAR OF YOUR SUCCESS STOP OUR TRUST IN YOU APPARENTLY JUSTIFIED STOP PENDORRAN STOP"

'*Apparently* justified? The arrogant sod!' snorted Andreas.

'I thought Pendorran was rather sexy . . .' teased Mara. 'Sort of . . . distinguished.'

'Oh, you did, did you?' Laughing, Andreas threw Mara back down on the bed and straddled her. 'And what about me? Am I sexy enough for you?'

Mara pouted her glossy red lips at him and suddenly he was as hard as iron for her, all over again.

'Darling,' breathed Mara, pulling him down and crushing her lips passionately against his. 'Darling, there's no-one in the whole world quite like you.'

The morning after the great storm, the Eiffel Tower was little more than a flat and twisted jumble of melted iron girders, in some places still red and shimmering with heat. Nothing could have survived the inferno that had destroyed Paris's most distinctive landmark.

A lone figure stood amid the rubble, looking out over the wounded city. A crystal ring sparkled on the third finger of his right hand.

They don't understand, he thought to himself. None of them understand.

I *cannot* die. Not unless the world dies with me.

LUST AND LADY SAXON

Lesley Asquith

Pretty Diana Saxon is devoted to her student husband, Harry, and she'd do anything to make their impoverished life in Oxford a little easier. Her sumptuously curved figure and shameless nature make her an ideal nude model for the local camera club – where she soon learns there's more than one way to make a bit on the side . . .

Elegant Lady Saxon is the most sought-after diplomat's wife in Rome and Bangkok. Success has followed Harry since his student days – not least because of the very special support lent by his wife. And now the glamorous Diana is a prized guest at the wealthiest tables – and in the most bedrooms afterwards . . .

From poverty to nobility, sex siren Diana Saxon never fails to make the most of her abundant talent for sensual pleasure!

0 7472 4762 5

HEADLINE
Delta

BONJOUR AMOUR

Erotic dreams of Paris in the 1950s

Marie-Claire Villefranche

Odette Charron is twenty-three years old with enchanting green eyes, few inhibitions and a determination to make it as a big-time fashion model. At present she is distinctly small-time. So a meeting with important fashion-illustrator Laurent Breville represents an opportunity not to be missed.

Unfortunately, Laurent has a fiancée to whom he is tediously faithful. But Odette has the kind of face and figure which can chase such mundane commitments from his mind. For her, Laurent is the first step on the ladder of success and she intends to walk all over him. What's more, he's going to love it . . .

0 7472 4803 6

HEADLINE
Delta

Now you can buy any of these other
Delta books from your bookshop or
direct from the publisher.

FREE P&P AND UK DELIVERY
(Overseas and Ireland £3.50 per book)

Passion Beach	Carol Anderson	£5.99
Cremorne Gardens	Anonymous	£5.99
Amorous Appetites	Anonymous	£5.99
Saucy Habits	Anonymous	£5.99
Room Service	Felice Ash	£5.99
The Wife-Watcher Letters	Lesley Asquith	£5.99
The Delta Sex-Life Letters	Lesley Asquith	£5.99
More Sex-Life Letters	Lesley Asquith	£5.99
Sin and Mrs Saxon	Lesley Asquith	£5.99
Naked Ambition	Becky Bell	£5.99
Empire of Lust	Valentina Cilescu	£5.99
Playing the Field	Elizabeth Coldwell	£5.99
Dangerous Desires	JJ Duke	£5.99
The Depravities of Marisa Bond	Kitt Gerrard	£5.99

TO ORDER SIMPLY CALL THIS NUMBER

01235 400 414

or e-mail <u>orders@bookpoint.co.uk</u>

Prices and availability subject to change without notice.